Praise for Mark Kimmel's writing...

Mark Kimmel's emphasis on the spiritual implications of extraterrestrial contact adds an important dimension to the discussion of this, the most important event in human history.
— Dr. Steven Greer, The Disclosure Project

Fiction is perhaps the most palatable way to break the ice on the whole subject of our place in the cosmos.
— Brian O'Leary, Former Astronaut

Mark Kimmel has not only crafted an exciting story, but courageously takes us into possibilities that each of us should ponder.
— Dennis Weaver, actor, author, environmentalist

Trillion is a captivating story that will inspire readers to create a sustainable future for themselves, and for this planet.
— Robert S. Ivker, D.O., President
— American Board of Holistic Medicine

What an inspiring amazing hybrid human he is! His books should be made into phenomenal visionary films! He has such inner grace and majesty and an inner knowing and compassion about the alien agendas.

— Naomi Semeniuk, New York

Trillion reminds me a lot of the Celestine Prophecy, but with a cosmic point of view.

— MK, Book Distributor, Green Bay

From successful conservative businessman to fiction writer, Mark has not only succeeded in transitioning himself, but has written a wonderful story about the larger purpose to our lives.

— Debra Benton, Author - *How To Think Like a CEO*

I couldn't put it down, a real page-turner. It was like reading about the past four years of my own life.

— Commercial Airline Pilot, Denver

This is a story that carries you along on an exciting adventure that will keep you involved.

— Gerald L. Evans, Boulder, Colorado

Trillion includes vitally important truth, woven into the framework of a fascinating fiction story.

— Jill Hull Strunk, Minnetonka, Minnesota

Trillion

Once you know, you can never go back to merely believing.

Mark Kimmel

PARADIGM BOOKS

BOULDER, COLORADO

Trillion

Mark Kimmel

Book I of the Paradigm Trilogy

Printed in the United States of America.

www.cosmicparadigm.com

Kimmel, Mark
Trillion / Mark Kimmel
p. cm

ISBN NUMBER 0–9720151–2–4

1. Metaphysical — Fiction 2. Paranormal — Fiction

I. Title

First Paperback Printing
September 2004

PARADIGM BOOKS
BOULDER, CO

For Heidi who encourages me to be myself,
for Amber who insists on daily hikes,
and for my celestial allies.

This planet is an imperative in the friendly, organized universe.
It is time for its people to grow up and take
their rightful place in the cosmos.

Most people simply cope with what life hands them, and do not act as if there is more to the universe than their existence on this sphere.

— PETER JONES

ONE

"You idiot!" Ryan Drake shouted to the wind. "You could've killed us both." He pounded the steering wheel and fought the temptation to pursue the driver of the van. "Jerk." After swerving to avoid the oncoming vehicle, his dusty Jeep rested in sagebrush beside the narrow dirt road.

The emblem on the van's side marked it as a United States Government vehicle. In his rearview mirror, Ryan watched it retreat in a cloud of dust. After a hundred yards, it turned and headed for the main highway.

Ryan set his jaw and tasted grit. He pulled his white Jeep Grand Cherokee back onto the road and proceeded toward the sign, HARMONY CENTER. He was not about to allow some minor incident to interfere with his visit. He was much more interested in the strange facility in this remote corner of the Navajo Reservation.

Most of the other vehicles in the parking area were pickups with Arizona license plates. His Jeep's plates were the green and white of Colorado. Ryan pulled in next to a light green sedan at the far end of the row. The lettering on the side of this vehicle, beneath a United States Government Seal, read Immigration and Naturalization Service.

While he was expected, out in the desert it was polite to give people a little notice before banging on their door. He stretched his arms and flexed his hands. After working for ten days in the hard ground at Ben Tsotsie's archeological excavation, he was a different person. Back home, he would already have rung the doorbell a second time.

Harmony Center appeared to consist of two traditional looking Navajo hogans and a huge glass and aluminum geodesic dome — a glistening white blister on the desert's ruddy skin. The dome had to be over a hundred and fifty feet at its base. The larger hogan was a clay-red hemisphere about thirty feet across with a door facing the parking area. The other hogan was the same height and color but much smaller in diameter. It reminded him of an inverted ice cream cone. It had a chimney at its peak, but no visible door.

Ryan had wondered about these unusual structures as he had driven past them on his way to Ben's dig, a mile or two farther down the road. They seemed somehow out of place. Ben had told him they sat atop an extensive underground facility.

Except for the windblown dust that covered everything in this part of Arizona, the grounds were immaculate — none of the clutter typical of Navajo settlements. A small beat-up trailer was parked near the dome.

To the east, Fortress Mesa towered 2,000 feet above. Its cap rock, a sheer three hundred feet of weathered sandstone, was silhouetted against a cloudless sky. It dwarfed the two terra-cotta beehives and the sparkling dome. He studied the imposing façade and wondered if a climbing route existed and what he might find on the mesa's summit.

To Ryan Drake's right, the sun reflected off a silver water tank and a ten-foot satellite dish. Farther right, photovoltaic arrays baked in the sun. Harmony was two miles from the nearest paved road, twenty miles from the nearest town, Kayenta. There was little telephone or electrical service on the Reservation, none here. These high tech utilities seemed out of place in the undeveloped landscape.

Through dark lenses, he surveyed his worn jeans and hiking boots. His cleanest shirt covered a freshly showered body. Officesoftened hands showed the results of digging for artifacts in the dry ground of the high desert — scrapes and blisters had replaced his neat manicure.

The outside temperature was probably in the mid-seventies. Thank God he was here in October. This place could be an inferno in July.

Ryan tilted his head left and scratched his salt and pepper stubble. It was testimony to the fact that he enjoyed getting grubby, part of his relaxation process. Only ten days old, it appeared to have grown for three weeks. His beard had appeared early in his teen years, dark and full. His senior year of college he had sported a luxuriant full growth. He would remove it when he returned for work — a successful CEO could get away with a lot, but not being unshaven.

He glanced at the Avocet strapped to his wrist: 12:05 PM 05410 Ft. The electronic watch/altimeter was a prized possession that he had kept functioning for over ten years. He pushed a button on its side: OCT 14.

He was about to get out of his Jeep when the door of the largest hogan banged open and two people emerged, a dark complexioned man and a slim blonde woman who towered over him. In his black outfit, the man reminded him of a caballero. She was more like a marathon runner, thin but healthy. And she was young, at least ten years younger than himself.

Ryan could barely hear Sarah Smith's words as she asked, "What else can I —"

"Where are they?"

"There are no others."

"You're gonna be so sorry, you bitch," the man shouted and slammed on his black western hat.

"But you have seen all."

Ryan was tempted to go to Sarah's aid, but hesitated. He did not know the lithe woman that well and had never seen the man before.

The man grabbed her arm. "I know you're lying —"

With no apparent action on Sarah's part, the swarthy man stopped in mid-sentence. His hand fell to his side.

He turned and walked to the light green sedan, did not look

around, and paid no attention to Ryan. As it sped from the parking lot, the sedan spewed gravel against the rear of Ryan's Jeep.

Since the terrorist attacks on U.S. soil, the INS had shifted its priorities toward defending the country's borders, insuring that no new terrorists entered. What did an INS agent want here in the middle of the Navajo Reservation, hundreds of miles from the Mexican border?

Ryan stepped out of his Jeep, grabbed his hat as the breeze lifted it from his head, and walked toward Sarah.

Bright sun highlighted the blonde hair cascading onto her slim shoulders. She reminded him of a gold crowned princess from a fairy tale. At their two previous meetings, she had hidden this splendor under a western hat.

He clasped her cool outstretched hand. "Are you all right?" he asked.

"I sorry you see." So unlike dark haired Navajo women, yet Sarah Smith spoke as if she had learned English here on the Reservation.

He wanted to inquire more, but decided he would learn about it when she was ready.

As they strolled toward the larger hogan, Sarah's stride matched his. She moved like a cougar drifting across an open space. Her large mirrored lenses reflected the landscape.

Ryan had first met her last Friday when she wandered into their camp. "Out for morning hike," she explained. She sipped coffee with them and told Ryan about Harmony Center, "One and half mile that way." She pointed northwest. "You pass it on way to excavation." The exchange had been friendly, unaffected.

When they went to work, the slender woman climbed down into the trench to look at the layer that the team was working. Ryan explained pre-Columbian culture, the significance of Ben Tsotsie's archaeological dig, how they had unearthed a stratum that Ben believed predated the Anasazi. The attractive woman's tactful manner and genuine curiosity impressed him. In his experience, most beautiful women were aloof, self-involved.

Sarah had shown up again on Monday in an ankle-length flowered dress that reminded Ryan of an old John Wayne movie. The garment did not hang quite right on her slim frame. As before, she kept her dark glasses and hat on during her entire visit.

From a large cardboard box, she had supplied fried chicken, bean salad, tortillas, and cold drinks. Tasty, but the caraway seeds on the chicken and in the bean salad were a bit much.

As they ate, she had asked Ryan about his work. He explained about environmental monitoring equipment and small company organizations. She seemed to grasp his comments about business, but appeared dismayed at his discourse on electronics. She asked him if he was happy and gave him a stack of papers. She said they described Harmony's vision. He glanced at the strange words, but did not probe further. He was interested in her, not printed material. She had a gentle way about her that he had seldom encountered.

Before she departed, she invited him to lunch. "To see facility and meet rest of my people." He had watched as she walked to her pickup and drove down the dirt road to Harmony Center. That was two days ago.

Sarah held the door to the larger hogan and Ryan stepped inside. He removed his dark glasses and placed them in his shirt pocket. As his eyes adjusted to the dim interior, he was surprised to see that the hogan was unfurnished. There was only a spotless floor of southwestern tile. The interior sides were stuccoed but not decorated. Two small windows provided light.

They walked ten feet toward the back and down green-carpeted steps. Each stair, wide enough for three people, was lit from the side. The long staircase descended to a landing dominated by massive oak doors.

"I come to Harmony year ago." She wore a western shirt with pearl snaps, a silver belt buckle, no turquoise. Her clothes, clean and pressed, showed no signs of wear. But her boots were dusty — like everything else in this desert.

He was about to inquire where she had lived before coming to Harmony, but he stumbled on the bottom stair and caught himself. Damn, he got nervous around beautiful women, especially Nordic blondes. He noted that she wore no wedding ring.

She ignored his embarrassment and continued, "Our facility below ground — to avoid hot summer."

Ryan hurried to open the tall, heavy door. As he held it for her, he glimpsed a spacious room with a high ceiling and polished tile. At its center was a long table with a dozen southwestern chairs, heavy wood and leather. At one end, bright orange napkins, plates, silverware and glasses were arranged for a meal. The smell of cooking greeted him. He removed his dusty hat and smoothed his hair.

In contrast to the desert above, the room was almost cold. The spacious dining area with its high ceiling resembled that of an elegant hotel. Green landscapes and winter scenes decorated the walls. The recessed lighting was subdued.

He noted two men at a low table in the far left corner. As they rose, Sarah motioned toward the white-haired one. "That is Dr. Victor Adamson, founder of Harmony Center. He work with Navajos to construct buildings."

A bear of a man in his mid-sixties strode toward them. Erect posture, broad shoulders, like a soldier in review but without the stiffness. He wore blue jeans and a plaid shirt. The other man followed behind.

"Hello, Ryan," Dr. Adamson greeted him like an old friend. His full head of white hair, receding from a high forehead, accented his blue eyes. Dr. Adamson did not offer the customary handshake, but put a husky arm around Ryan's shoulder.

"Welcome." The word resonated as if echoing from a canyon. Cheeks furrowed at the ends of his broad smile, neat rows of white teeth. His friendliness did not disturb Ryan. He had the distinct feeling he had met the white-haired man before.

"This is Peter Jones." Sarah smiled and indicated the second man who had joined the group.

Peter was six inches shorter than Ryan, had narrow shoulders, and his western outfit hung from his frame as if it were a size too large. Except for bushy black eyebrows that capped squinting eyes, his head displayed no trace of hair. He looked older than Sarah, about fifty, about Ryan's age. In his left hand, he held a maroon book.

Peter mumbled, "H-H-Hello," and bobbed his head when Ryan grasped his hand.

His thin smile and rigid demeanor reminded Ryan of a college professor. Something about Peter's stiffness made Ryan think that the bald man struggled to merely stand. His eyes had a cloudy look about them.

"I understand you're staying with Ben Tsotsie. I know him through his cousin, Cody," Dr. Adamson said. "Several members of that family have been most helpful." His words were like those of a Midwestern native, but each had a deep resonance. "It required five years of discussion just to convince the Navajos that our facility would not disturb its neighbors," his chuckle reverberated. "They leased this piece of land to us for forty-nine years."

"Th-Th-There are no neighbors," Peter Jones said.

"This is a bit off the beaten path," Ryan said. "Guess that's why I like it out here."

"Tell us about yourself." Peter rattled off the words as if he were happy to finish with them. His face contorted as he spoke, as if it was expelling the words from a blowhole.

"All right," Ryan said. "I live near Boulder, in Colorado. I run a company there. We manufacture instrumentation that measures air and water pollutants. We also operate a system that collects data from locations around the world and we supply the results to government agencies and others."

"Do-Do-Do you have a family?" Peter Jones asked.

"I have two grown children," Ryan replied.

"And you are divorced," Dr. Adamson said in a forthright and deliberate tone. His words were not hurried as Peter's had been.

Ryan glanced at the white-haired man. "Why yes. How did you know?" His instincts told him that this man knew a lot about him, a lot more than he was letting on. Where *had* he met him?

Dr. Adamson smiled and said, "Please, before you talk more, sit down to some food." His rumble commanded attention and they moved toward the table. Sarah took the seat at the end of the table and motioned Ryan to the place on her right. Peter sat down directly across from him.

"I have something to which I must attend," Dr. Adamson said to Ryan. "Enjoy your lunch."

Ryan glanced at Sarah. When he looked back, Dr. Adamson had disappeared leaving the three of them alone in the room. Ryan had not heard any retreating footsteps or the closing of a door.

In a few moments, Navajos came through a side door with

heaping plates of salad, mixed greens with tomato and cucumber slices. They passed around corn tortillas, broiled chicken, two kinds of salad dressing, sliced melon and orange quarters. Pitchers of iced tea and water were already on the table.

Ryan reached for the dish of salsa and spooned a little onto his plate. As a student at Arizona State University, one of the first things he had learned to enjoy was the food of the Southwest.

When Sarah picked up her fork, Ryan turned to her and politely inquired, "Where did you live before coming here?"

She froze, glanced at Ryan, and turned to Peter.

As if he were an actor given his cue, Peter blurted out, "You-You-Your world is in danger." He looked at Ryan as if he expected a response.

Ryan leaned back and gauged the stuttering man. "I guess I can agree with that," he said at length. "This world can be a dangerous place. There're some back alleys I wouldn't go in at night."

"Your world is dying."

"Oh, now I get it, you're referring to the environment."

"The environment is one. There are others."

"Such as?"

"Men from this country scheme to subjugate this planet." Peter Jones's words came at Ryan like the firing of a machine gun. The bald man's right hand pressed his jaw as if urging his mouth to cooperate with his brain.

"I doubt that. The United States has never been know as an aggressor," Ryan said. "This country is the greatest democracy in the world."

"Much is good about this country."

"Hey, we found something to agree about. America is a great country."

Ryan took a bite of the chicken and grimaced. Caraway again. He spotted the small black seeds. What was caraway doing in southwest chicken? The flavor clashed with the spicy salsa he had spooned onto it.

"Most people simply cope with what life hands them, and do not act as if there is more to the universe—" Peter paused to catch his breath. "—than their existence on this sphere." It was apparent that he was reciting words he had memorized.

16

Ryan started to say something but returned to his plate instead. This stuttering invalid did not understand how the real world worked, but how could he, bottled up on a remote Indian Reservation. Peter talked like a revolutionary from some third world country. Was that why the INS was interested in Harmony?

Then Ryan thought again. All Peter had tried to do was express a few different ideas. Wasn't that why he'd come to the desert? He realized that he had not really listened to what Peter had said. Normally he was able to appreciate the other party's point of view. Usually he relished playing it back to them and forcing them to see both sides. Somehow Peter was different.

After the exchange the conversation wandered pleasantly. He told Sarah how he'd scaled the Eiger, at nineteen, and about hiking in Nepal and New Zealand.

Although Sarah admitted to some athletic success in her youth, she emphasized that she was just learning about the desert. When she was not eating, Sarah played with a delicate medallion, three concentric circles honed from gold and blue stone, on a thin gold chain. Ryan was acutely aware of her physical presence.

Peter said nothing more, although he seemed to listen with great interest. The bald man traced notes on a small pad that he kept positioned on top of his book. His eating was slow and awkward.

As they munched on the melon and oranges, Sarah asked, "Have you heard of woman they found yesterday?"

"One of Ben's crew spotted her — stumbling alongside the highway. He took her to the clinic in Kayenta. Is there any news?"

"She died this morning," Sarah said. Misty gray eyes held his attention, an adult version of a big-eyed doll. "They say it was from exposure, and from a beating. How terrible — wandering in this desert, hurt, all alone. She was not Navajo." With her right hand, Sarah brushed strands of hair behind her ear.

"The Immigration and Naturalization Service thinks she was from Mexico and that she was in the country illegally. That man, who left as you arrived, is Raul Viejo. He is with the INS. He interview me again and again."

"What about the guy in the van?" Ryan had not forgotten how the larger vehicle had raced down the center of the narrow road, its driver oblivious to his white Jeep.

"He is Luis Litchfield from the Bureau of Indian Affairs."

"What do they want with you?"

"They believe we were harboring the woman from Mexico." Sarah spoke with a mildness that reminded him of Mrs. Martin who had taught him fourth grade. In the world of business, one did not encounter many gentle ladies. Ryan was sure he would hear more about the dead woman — news traveled fast in this barren region.

"Would you like to see our facility?" Sarah asked when they finished eating.

Ryan nodded and she pointed him to a side door.

They walked down a short hall, white walls and ceiling, light linoleum. The tall ceiling and broad hallway give no indication they were underground. An unusual scent replaced the smells of lunch, almost medicinal, not altogether unpleasant.

"We are at the hub," Sarah announced after a dozen steps. Hallways angled off in several directions. "Directly under the dome. Our five buildings can be entered from here, like the spokes of a wheel."

"You hide the size of your facility well." He calculated the expense involved in building such a place in this remote niche of the Four Corners. Everything was spotless, everything looked new.

"Three years in construction."

"Pretty fancy for missionaries."

Sarah smiled. "We are revealators. We unveil truth. Missionaries try to convince people what they believe."

Down a short hall, she opened double doors into a large room with thousands of books. "This is the library." Her voice fell to a whisper as they stood in the doorway. A young Navajo woman sat at a desk lost in her reading. "It is open to all."

Ryan approached the floor-to-ceiling shelves. The books were filed by author: THE WORLD AS I SEE IT by Einstein, THE ROAD LESS TRAVELED by Peck, Plato's REPUBLIC, RE-AUTHORING LIVES by White. Racks of current magazines and newspapers lined one entire wall: THE ECONOMIST, NEWSWEEK, SCIENTIFIC AMERICAN, NEW YORK TIMES.

Seats were arranged for viewing the television. Three racks of videos. He noted a few of the titles: CASABLANCA, THE GRADU-

ATE, NATIONAL GEOGRAPHIC, THE STORY OF ENGLISH. With this much print and video around, why didn't Sarah speak like an American?

He glanced at a rack of electronics. A VCR sat on top of a highly polished metal cube with unusual pentagonal knobs and rounded sides and corners. Lots of equipment for just receiving television signals. If Brauk, the technical genius from his company, were here, he could probably explain it.

They returned to the hub and went down a different hall. They passed a glass door, LABORATORY. PLEASE KEEP CLOSED. He peered into the lighted room. Microscopes and glassware covered a long white workbench. "We work on environmental contaminants."

Ryan saw his reflection in the glass of the door. He noted the incline of his head and centered it.

His habit of tilting his head to one side or the other, examining both sides of every issue, had started young. His Irish mother had insisted on his name, Ryan, to balance out the English surname contributed by his father. "To remind you of your glorious Gaelic heritage," she often said and told him stories of her family and their immigration from Ireland to America in 1916. Like the inhabitants of their respective ancestral islands, his parents had disagreed about many things. Arguments about child rearing, politics and racial matters never ceased. Both parents had sought his support. Now he bifurcated everything.

Without further comment, Sarah ushered Ryan back to the hub and down another hall with more light linoleum. She opened large, fireproof doors. Ryan surveyed electrical distribution equipment, a bank of batteries, and a large furnace and fans for moving air about the underground complex. "Air filtration system," she said.

He nodded his understanding. Why was she intent on showing him every room in this complex? And what was Peter trying to prove with that debate at lunch? From their discussions at Ben's dig, Sarah knew he was a businessman, knew he was committed to making things happen within his country's economic system. Maybe she just didn't get it. Maybe she was some kind of a radical nut. Sure she was attractive, but was it even possible to have a personal conversation with her?

A staircase, white tile, white walls. "These lead to rear door and high temperature incinerator," Sarah said. "It is small hogan. Would you like to see?"

Ryan declined.

They returned to the hub and Sarah led him down a broad hall with light blue carpeting. They passed several open doors, lights on. Ryan paused long enough to see that each of the suites contained a desk, queen bed, and bathroom. Two looked occupied. Nice accommodations for the Reservation, an underground Holiday Inn, adequate but not showy.

At the end of the hall, Sarah opened a door into a room lit only with a shaded lamp. Peter sat next to the bed on which a gray-skinned woman lay. She appeared to sleep. The unusual smell was particularly strong in the room.

"That is Amelia," Sarah said as she gently shut the door. "We do not expect her to be with us long."

"I am sorry —"

Sarah held up her hand and said, "We will rejoice when she begins the next stage of her journey." As they strolled back to the hub, Sarah's right hand rested on her medallion.

In silence they climbed tiled stairs.

The image of Amelia stayed with him. There was something strange about her. He had visited sick people, been in hospitals, but he had never seen that peculiar skin coloring.

At the top, they emerged into the bright light of the geodesic dome and a botanical garden. At its center, tall ponderosa and piñon pines nestled among juniper and sagebrush. A small stream meandered about the display creating a moat next to the gravel path. Cottonwood trees and willows grew next to the running water. It was as if someone had brought together all the plants native to the southwest and created a controlled environment for them.

Sarah put on dark glasses; Ryan donned his weathered hat. "We study plants and teach Navajo agricultural techniques."

"What kind of tree is that?" he asked. He pointed to a clump of squat trees that seemed out of place.

Sarah gestured to a Navajo whom she introduced as George Tomichi, the man who lived in the trailer near the dome.

"An Australian tea tree," he said, "leptospermum." He pulled off a leaf and handed it to Ryan.

"We make lotion from it," Sarah said. "It is the only non-native species in this dome." The leaf's medicinal odor was that which permeated the lower rooms.

They strolled around the periphery of the dome. Raised wooden beds contained a variety of plants. A black-haired woman worked at planting sprouts in sandy desert soil; two Navajo men and three women looked on.

They exited at the far edge of the dome, a multiple door entry.

Sarah extended her hand. "Perhaps we will talk more." Something about the way she spoke and moved made Ryan eager to continue their conversation.

As he drove back to Ben Tsotsie's dig, Ryan thought about the visit he'd just had. That underground facility with its many rooms was unique, but he had seen nothing that would lead the INS to believe the Mexican woman had lived there.

Sarah Smith was the most interesting woman he had met in years, maybe ever. He knew their lunch was somehow important to his future, but he couldn't say why. He just felt it. He'd had these premonitions before and in each case they had proven unimaginably accurate in retrospect.

He'd like to know her better, a lot better. But Peter Jones and she seemed wound up in their own little retreat, far from his world. He resigned himself to going home to Boulder in a few days and, in all likelihood, forgetting about her.

The white man views land for its money value. We Indians have a spiritual tie with the earth, a reverence for it that whites don't share and can hardly understand.

— HARRIETT PIERCE

TWO

Ben Tsotsie wore Navajo working garb: black jeans, a plaid western shirt, and a black, broad-brimmed hat with a silver band. His braid spoke of his attachment to the traditional ways of his people. The notebook and pen in his shirt pocket pointed to his training as an archaeologist.

Ryan Drake and the Navajo had become friends as undergrads at Arizona State University. They had stayed in touch and seen each other several times over the intervening thirty years.

A month ago, Ben had called Ryan, told him about his new excavation, and insisted he come visit. At the time, Ryan thought it unusual, out of character for Ben to issue such an impulsive invitation. Still, the more he thought about it, the better the chance to spend time in the desert sounded. He told Ben he would come as soon as his divorce proceedings were final. He then set about to make a hole in his business schedule.

This morning they had been reminiscing about their perpetual struggle to get out of bed and get to Anthropology 209 at 8:05 AM with Dr. Whittaker. The feisty young professor was famous for springing pop quizzes. It seemed like every time there was a late-night protest meeting, the next morning Whittaker sprang a quiz. It was funny now.

"So, Ry. When did you lose it?" the Navajo asked.

"Lose what?" Ryan Drake went to the espresso machine at the end of the folding camp table.

"Damn," he shouted at the open back of the machine. Looking up, he said to Ben, "When they sold me this thing, they didn't tell me about all the adjustments."

Each morning the battery and propane powered coffee maker had provided them with exquisite latte — one of Ryan's fetishes. But the machine never complied with his desires without adjustment. Fiddling with mechanical devices was his least favorite thing to do. It always irritated him. He had installed an automated espresso machine at the office — there he had people to service it. He closed the back and said, "What did you ask me?"

"Your passion for the land. When did you lose it?" Ben asked. "The Ry Drake I remember from college wanted to save the world. I remember some demonstrations and a jail cell."

"Yeah, I remember." Ryan paused to pour milk into a cup of Kona and started it steaming. "Two companies ago," he said, "after I made a million bucks."

"You have strayed from the lessons of my family's hogan."

"Oh?"

"They're still there."

"What?" Ryan asked.

"Opportunities to speak out."

"Yeah, but I don't do that anymore."

"Why?" Ben asked as Ryan handed him a steaming cup.

"Too busy."

"But you always seemed to know about the future, how the planet was in danger. Have you lost that too?"

"Now I just focus on business."

"The Harmony people talk about the bigger picture."

"Yeah, but they're unrealistic." Ryan pointed to the papers on the table. He had arisen early and read a few of the pages. "Hey, I'm doing my part. Sanitas is building instrumentation to measure pollutants in parts-per-trillion. We've got contracts with state, federal and international agencies. Our Global Watch system gives us a worldwide presence. That's what it's all about — small steps to make things better."

"Navajo honor their teachings." Ben sipped his latte. His dark eyes observed his old friend. Ben and Ryan had talked about the people down the road after Sarah had visited that first time. Ben said that he had used their library and gotten to know them fairly well. "That Sarah has a way about her," Ben said.

"She is very pretty." Ryan thought of yesterday's lunch and the sun on Sarah's hair.

"Too skinny."

"Not for me."

"A white man's woman." The Navajo laughed and reached across to poke Ryan's shoulder.

Ryan had been at Ben Tsotsie's dig eleven days. Ben's Navajo crew had worked it since April. The old dirt road to the archeological excavation, two ruts in some places, wound its way southeast from Arizona Highway 59, past Harmony Center, and ended at an abandoned mine, a mile beyond their camp. Ben had parked his green and white trailer on flat ground not far off the road. The other necessities of the camp, including a blue portable toilet, rested in a slight depression. A nearby tent housed the implements of the dig and the boxes of unearthed artifacts. The actual excavation site was on a knoll, fifty yards away.

Ryan stood and looked west. Across the valley, Black Mesa dominated the western horizon. Its dark rim was 3,500 feet higher than the paved road that ran south from Kayenta. The Mesa derived its name from the piñon trees on its higher slopes. Their dark green stood in sharp contrast to the encircling pale desert. Behind this tranquil facade, the gigantic Peabody Mine, a major source of revenue for the Navajo Nation, extracted coal from the top of Black Mesa. The road to that extensive complex was forty miles to the northwest, off US 160.

When the Navajo crew arrived, Ryan and Ben walked to the excavation with them. Ben's crew had made a deep trench with steps to reach the stratum of interest. Twine and labels marked important aspects of the excavation. Another archeologist had explored this site seventy years before, but Ben had convinced ASU and the Navajo authorities to allow him to undertake a second dig. In February he had received a grant and, two months ago, uncovered the unexplored zone.

Ryan used a trowel to remove a piece of bone. After he dusted it, he labeled it and placed it in a box for later study. He returned with a brush and swept away another layer of dust. Working desert soil that had been compacted over the last thousand years was strenuous and tedious, unusual work for the CEO of a technology company. Ryan could not think of any of his contemporaries who would be interested. They were more at home on a golf course or behind the tiller of a sailboat.

For the first time in many years, Ryan Drake was not using his special talent to predict where things, personal or business, were headed. Ordinarily he would be thinking about some project or meeting, having planned his schedule months in advance. This time, before he'd left for the desert, he'd been careful to set only a few appointments: his quarterly Board meeting of the Colorado Conservation Commission, his own Board meeting for Sanitas, the publicity event which Sam Wellborn had insisted upon, and his meeting with Nick and Nick's father. Not much compared to his normally hectic routine. Now, rather than working to project and synthesize, he saw his future as a blank sheet of paper on which he was preparing to draw a fresh picture.

As the sun slid behind Black Mesa, the temperature dropped fifteen degrees. They sat at the camp table and ate T-bone steak, barbecued beans, and green salad with ranch dressing. "This is living," Ryan said. "Thanks for getting me away from that damn office."

After eleven days without instant communications and the incessant chatter of the media, he had retired his supply of antacid to the back of his Jeep. Ryan Drake, CEO of Sanitas Technologies, was ready to examine some basics.

He knew that he was reaching the end of his time at Sanitas. They had built it from nothing to a success. He had recently spoken to his friend Aza O'Sullivan about his increasing reluctance to put up with the demands of investors who understood little or nothing about Sanitas's business. He took a sip of his second bourbon and water and remembered his last day in the office.

"This is unacceptable." Nick spit out the words as soon as he and Ryan were connected. "Everybody else will be here — as they promised."

Ryan sighed as he pictured his youthful caller in his downtown Chicago office, close cropped hair, suit and tie.

"I need you here," the youngster said.

Nick had consummated his investment in Ryan's company twenty-four months ago. In the ensuing period, he had demonstrated his inexperience with investing in early-stage companies by voting against several budget items. They had subsequently proven to be worthwhile expenditures that had increased both revenues and profits.

"I want the others to see what a really great job you've done."

Ryan interrupted the young man. "My company's ahead of plan, right? Revenues double last year. Profitable."

"Correct," Nick conceded.

"On track for next year?"

"Yes, but —"

"— Yes, but nothing. We are or we aren't. Which is it?" Exasperated, Ryan reached into his pocket, retrieved a slim cylinder, and removed the top tablet. He slid it into his mouth and crunched the antacid.

"All right. I agree, things are going well," Nick said.

"Thank you."

"The best —"

"— of anything in your portfolio," the CEO finished the young man's sentence for him.

"But I need you in Chicago — next Tuesday." The voice on the line struggled for control. Nick was accustomed to getting his way with company presidents.

"My vacation begins tomorrow, period," Ryan said. Except for Nick, everyone had agreed to modify his or her schedule.

"Coming to talk about Sanitas can wait until I get back," he said.

"My father doesn't wait for anybody."

"I'll be back in two weeks. How about Wednesday, the thirtieth?"

"I'll check with my father."

"Let me know."

"Where are you going? What if I need to talk to you?"

"There are no phones. I'll call when I get back." Ryan pushed the button that disconnected the call. He reached into his pocket, plopped another antacid tablet into his mouth, and thought how unnecessary the argument had been. All he wanted to do was take a little time away from the office. It would be different if things were not going well.

Ryan walked next door to the threesome seated in the conference room, but did not sit. "I hope these are the final changes," he said to no one in particular. His tone was raw from the confrontation with Nick and the beating he had taken in divorce court earlier that day. He flashed his copy of the legal document the group was reviewing. Last night, after a full day in court with Judge Rita Sanders, he had given them his comments on it.

"Anything else?" The document was the latest iteration of a revised agreement with TTT Instrumentation Corporation, their major foreign distributor. TTT accounted for thirty percent of their sales and provided service coverage internationally. Without such an arrangement, a company the size of Sanitas could not afford to sell outside the United States. The worldwide market for their products was five times the domestic. If they could not agree on new terms, Sanitas was facing a major setback.

None of the CEO's key people offered anything further.

"Well, OK. Let's hope this does it. I'll set up the closing for right after I get back." Recovering from his telephone altercation, he smiled and added, "I appreciate all your hard work." He turned and walked to his office.

Everything now hinged on that damn agreement. If TTT didn't sign it, Sanitas would have to retrench, lay off people, and he'd probably be looking for a new job. Plus he'd lose the half million bucks he'd invested — the half million that his ex-wife's attorney had convinced Judge Sanders was now worth ten million. If that happened, he would really be in bad shape.

Now, in the gathering darkness of the desert, Ryan Drake gazed at the unspoiled panorama of his surroundings, the wooded mesa to the west, the broad intervening valley. He inhaled the scent of sage and felt his body relax another notch. The problems of Sanitas could wait until he returned.

Leaning back in his camp chair and looking up, he watched as the first stars appeared: sparkling diamonds scattered across charcoal velvet — hard to imagine they were so far away. Scientists measured their distances in light-years. Earth's nearest neighbor, Proxima Centauri, was four light-years distant, trillions of miles away.

As Ryan basked in the night sky, Ben built a campfire.

"Each of those is another sun." Ryan pointed upward. It was one of those conversations that one had around a fire, wandering here and there, no real thread of continuity. Discussions such as this required down time. "I'm sure one of them must have intelligent life. Have you ever seen a UFO? That kind of stuff?"

"My people have seen lights in the sky," Ben said. "We do not talk about them."

Ryan knew he was treading on his friendship with Ben when he asked, "Why not?"

Ben took a long time to respond. Ryan could tell he was carefully weighing his answer. At last he said, "When the lights arrived in 1947, we reported them. White men came and said that my people were drunk and that the lights were only lightening and meteors. One of my cousins complained to the Navajo Police and showed them a photo. He disappeared. Others have also disappeared for what they have seen, for what they know to be true."

Ryan studied Ben's face in the flickering light from the campfire.

The Navajo looked back at him and said, "Do you see that bright object?" He pointed overhead.

Ryan looked up. A round light, much brighter than any star, scooted across the night sky. He could not tell how high it was. The object moved from northwest to southeast. On other occasions, Ryan had seen satellites, reflecting light from the recently set sun. This one appeared to be brighter than others he recalled.

"Sure, it's a satellite."

"Watch closely." Ben closed his eyes.

Almost as if it was responding to Ben's words, the bright object blinked once.

Ryan could not take his eyes off it. He sensed it was something different, something not normally seen in the night sky.

Without slowing, the bright object took a turn to the west. Again, without slowing, it turned north. In a few moments it halted. As Ryan watched, it slowly faded from sight.

"What was that?"

"My people tell of visitors from beyond this world, long before the white man came to our land," Ben said and smiled. "They taught my people many things."

Ryan nodded that he had heard. He and Ben had debated the source of many of the Navajo's legends. The possibility of beings from an off-world civilization visiting his planet did not conflict with Ryan's view of this world, nor did it frighten him.

The night air cooled. Ryan slipped on his jacket and warmed his hands over the flames. He looked over at Ben. The Navajo's eyes were closed, but Ryan could tell he was not sleeping because his head rested squarely on his shoulders. Ryan returned to studying the night sky.

It was great to have time to think about things. He was glad he had accepted Ben's unexpected invitation. Although the blank sheet puzzled him, he did not feel at all insecure about it. He hoped that before he left the desert he would be able to sketch something of his future on his white tablet.

"Hello the campfire." The words, from beyond the fire's light, were clear but not loud.

Who the hell was that? Startled, Ryan arose and peered in the direction of the voice. "Who's there?" he demanded.

"It's Victor Adamson. May we approach?"

Ryan recognized the rumble of the tall man's voice. "Sure, come ahead," he said to the darkness. He sat his drink down next to his chair.

Dr. Victor Adamson, Sarah Smith, and Peter Jones edged into the campfire's circle of light. The fourth person was a Navajo whom Ben acknowledged with a nod. All were dressed in dark western garb and wide-brimmed hats. Each carried a backpack. Hiking boots had replaced their western boots. They could have passed as a group of tourists with a native guide.

"Good evening," Dr. Adamson approached Ryan and Ben. "We have hurried up the road and are a bit exhausted. May we trouble you for some water? This is Cody Tsotsie, Ben's cousin." He indicated the Navajo, an older man dressed in black.

"Would you like to sit?" Ryan indicated his camp chair and large rocks near the fire.

Each of the people from Harmony carried a water bottle. Why did they need our water? Ben had towed the hundred and fifty gallon tank from town.

"We are pleased that we found you awake," Dr. Adamson said.

Sarah helped Peter to Ryan's chair and then seated herself on a nearby rock. Her movements were athletic, confident, but not sensual, more like a black panther settling onto its space.

The older Navajo walked over and grabbed Ben by the arm. The two of them wandered off into the dark.

The faint numbers on Ryan's Avocet read 9:12 PM. He filled Ben's water pitcher from their tank and grabbed some paper cups. He returned to the group around the campfire and asked, "What brings you out at this time of the night?"

"We have had to abandon Harmony," Dr. Adamson said.

"Abandon?"

"In the morning, a contingent from the Immigration and Naturalization Service will invade it. They have already blocked the road to town and have people stationed along the highway. We decided that it was better not to be present when they arrived."

"Ben's crew was questioned," Ryan said. "What's going on?"

"They believe we are harboring Mexican illegals."

"Did they bother to talk to you?"

"The men you saw yesterday. They search everywhere," Sarah said. Her gentle voice was clouded with anxiety. "But they say we are lying."

"Let me give you some history." Dr. Adamson held up his hand. "After Harmony's completion, our first visitors were the Navajo. They came to learn agricultural techniques, use the library, and listen to our vision.

"Although we had submitted the necessary paperwork to them, the Bureau of Indian Affairs ignored our existence. Six months ago, two BIA agents made a brief visit and we showed them around, showed them everything. They made notes, took pictures.

"Three weeks ago, two men showed up, unannounced. Luis

Litchfield, from the Bureau of Indian Affairs, and Raul Viejo from the Immigration and Naturalization Service. They asked questions about our facility and our relations with the Navajos."

Sarah said, "Last week, when I went into Kayenta, I was stopped by INS agent — he ask me for identification and question me."

"This morning, our Navajo gardeners and students were questioned as they turned into our side road," Dr. Adamson said. "This evening, vehicles and men gather at that intersection. We have done nothing wrong, but reason is not likely to prevail in these circumstances.

"We sense that we are being set-up for an incident. I am sure you are aware of the deaths that occurred with government raids in Texas and Idaho. Tomorrow, rather than asking for an additional meeting to discuss things, the BIA and INS are planning to take over our facility."

In the aftermath of the terrorist attacks, federal agencies had been given more latitude to strike suspected locations. Initially Ryan had worried about the possible loss of freedoms, but he had not read of any unreasonable actions because of this new policy. "Hold on," he said. "What makes you think they'll do that?"

Dr. Adamson said, "That is the information we have. We believe our sources are reliable. The INS does not want to create some kind of a standoff that could take weeks to resolve and bring unwanted public attention. The federal agencies consider this land to be under their guardianship and reason that they are freer to act here than if we were on someone's private property."

Ryan shook his head at the vision of armed men tearing through Harmony's spotless complex. "What about Amelia?" he asked.

"She departed last evening," Sarah replied.

Ryan turned to her, "I'm sorry. Everything seems to be happening at once."

"We would have left sooner…" Sarah's words trailed off.

"May I speak to you, alone?" Dr. Adamson motioned Ryan to one side. They walked out of the light of the campfire and toward the road. As they walked, the white-haired man placed his arm around Ryan's shoulder. "Amelia has been sick for several months.

31

She wanted to make her departure from Harmony. Well before this confrontation with the INS and BIA, we had planned to resettle Peter and Sarah in a new location, but we waited."

"Let me help. I have connections." Ryan was convinced they had done nothing wrong. "We can go to the top levels of the INS and BIA." His anger at the situation built. His jaw tightened, fists clenched. He was surprised at his reaction on behalf of people he did not know that well.

"We are headed into the desert." The white-haired man said it with finality.

Ryan ignored Dr. Adamson's tone. "Do you know what you're doing?" He motioned to the surrounding terrain. "This is the roughest part of the Reservation, dry, remote. The Navajos don't go out there without vehicles or horses. Hiking for any distance is near impossible. There's no nearby settlement. You've got to know what you're doing."

From Ben's dig, Kayenta was the nearest town, twenty miles northwest along AZ 59. To the northeast, on the other side of Fortress Mesa and twenty-five miles across a barren wasteland, was Mexican Water, a small trading post. Almost no one lived amid the rugged terrain to the south of the excavation.

"I have lived here for many years." He said it in such a way that Ryan understood that Dr. Adamson had known this wilderness long before Harmony Center was built.

"How far are you going?"

"Peter and Sarah are headed for Shiprock."

"Shiprock? That's a hundred miles. Peter's in no condition —"

"We have a friend with a car, after we cross Fortress Mesa." The Harmony leader motioned east to the formidable plateau.

"You want to climb up there?" The Mesa was silhouetted against the rising gibbous moon. The sandstone of the cliff was bad rock, too loose for technical climbing. During the past week, Ryan had considered scaling the sheer face, but dismissed the idea. One night Ben and he had heard a slab crumble from above.

"Cody knows a route to the top."

"Why? Why?"

"The authorities will have trouble tracking us there."

"Why not go around?"

"It is much longer. Over the top is only a few miles. Besides, once we are on top, there are trees to hide us."

"Come on, let me go with you to the INS." Ryan thought of his father — an attorney wired to many high-ranking Washington types. The last time Ryan had seen him, at his eightieth birthday party, dark-suited men had surrounded him.

"No."

"But there's no water."

"This is the way we will handle it." The words left no room for argument.

"You're going now? Tonight?" Ryan asked.

"Yes."

"How long do you think it'll take?"

"One day to cross the mesa, after we reach the top," Dr. Adamson replied. "Peter walks slowly."

An image flickered across Ryan's mind: a group of novices picking their way across an arid landscape. Except for Peter, they looked fit, but Sarah had admitted she was not an experienced outdoors person.

"Can I help?" Ryan's mind buzzed. He'd read newspaper accounts of overreactions by law enforcement officers. The Los Angeles police and Rodney King. The DEA had killed a man in Denver by going to the wrong house. Sarah had been open with him, shown him every room at Harmony. Whatever Harmony was, he was sure they were not part of some scheme to hide Mexican illegals — their facility was way too fancy. The idea was ridiculous, smugglers did not have libraries or exercise rooms.

Ryan felt his sense of adventure surface. He had seldom used it during the years he had concentrated on acting like a CEO. "How about if I come along? Once we're on top, crossing the Mesa shouldn't be too hard." He had a couple of days before he needed to be back in the office and a good hike would be welcome. Ben wouldn't mind if he left a day early. Maybe this would be part of reconnecting to his lost passion.

"Thank you," the white-haired man said. "I had hoped you might join us. Can you leave now?" They turned back toward the camp and Dr. Adamson removed his arm.

"Let me throw my things together," Ryan said as they re-entered the light from the campfire. "Do you have food?"

"We have plenty of caraway seeds," Sarah said and grinned when he reacted.

He started toward his Jeep, but noticed Ben in heated conversation with Cody. He walked to where they stood.

"Are you serious?" Ben turned to Ryan. "You're going into the desert with them?"

Ryan nodded once.

"You drive Jeep to Shiprock?" Cody asked Ben. It was obvious the two men had been discussing this.

Ben looked at Ryan and said, "All right. I'll take care of your Jeep — but you don't know what you're getting into."

"Hey, I'll let you know how it turns out." He gave his friend a light punch on the arm.

Ryan rolled up his sleeping bag and air mattress and retrieved his pack from his Jeep. He checked to be sure his hiking essentials were still there and stuffed in a few personal items including a flashlight, supply of antacid, and change of clothes. The full pack weighed no more than thirty pounds. He grabbed his hat and an extra water bottle and headed back to the campfire. As an experienced hiker, Ryan always carried a pack in his Jeep. With a little food and water, he could go off into the wilderness for a week or survive a vehicle break down on some back road.

When he returned to the group, Dr. Adamson said, "Ryan, may I suggest that you take the license plates off your vehicle."

The white-haired man turned to Ben and said, "Replace Ryan's license plates with your own. In the confusion of the raid, Ryan's Jeep will be taken for your vehicle and few questions will be asked. When you get his Jeep to Shiprock contact this number." He handed Ben a slip of paper. "The person who answers will tell you where to deliver it."

"What about my truck?"

"You probably should not return here for a few days," Dr. Adamson said. "No one will question a dusty old truck parked in the sagebrush. Be sure to bring your plates back from Shiprock."

Ryan slapped Ben's shoulder. "Thank you my friend, for everything — taking care of my Jeep, my leaving early. I know this seems a bit strange, but I feel like I'm back in the old days when we didn't do everything by the book. Maybe this is part of what I came here for. And don't let the INS hang any of this on you — it's my deal. If they give you trouble, give them my name and address. OK?"

Ben looked as if he wanted to say more, to issue a further caution, but all that came out was, "Ry, are you sure you want to do this?"

"Yeah." Laughing, Ryan added, "Hey, let me know when you do another dig." He tossed Ben the keys to his Jeep and hoisted his pack.

Ben walked over to his cousin and whispered to him. Ryan could not make out the words, but he sensed that Ben was telling his cousin to look out for his friend.

"Take care of my coffee maker," Ryan shouted over his shoulder as they moved out. He noticed that Ben was already carrying an armload of artifacts toward his Jeep.

Ryan and the threesome from Harmony walked to the road and followed Cody southeast toward the old mine. The old Navajo's gray hair showed from beneath his broad-brimmed hat. Ryan could see little of his face except a weathered jaw and full lips that exposed jagged teeth. Two were capped in silver and caught a glint of moonlight when he spoke. He strode like a man who had spent many years in the open. He spoke to Ryan only once cautioning him not to use his flashlight.

No man is worth his salt who is not ready at all times to risk his body, to risk his well-being, to risk his life, in a great cause.

— THEODORE ROOSEVELT

THREE

Night on the high desert was always cool — the dry air allowed a cooling off from the higher temperatures of the day. From a high of seventy-five, it was already down to sixty and would probably drop to fifty by morning.

Dr. Adamson said that the INS was operating on the assumption that the Harmony people had no suspicions about the pending raid. Furthermore, he said he was quite sure the INS had not detected their night escape.

Peter shuffled behind, encouraged along by Sarah and Dr. Adamson. The bald man's progress was a sequence of staggers, each one concluded before he fell to the dirt road by the thrust of his other foot. Yet he refused to take anyone's arm.

The two ruts with sagebrush in the middle wound over a low ridge. The Navajo stopped to allow the stragglers to catch up.

Looking back towards Harmony, Ryan saw the headlights of many vehicles where the gravel road intersected the main highway. With arms around each other, Sarah, Dr. Adamson, and Peter stopped and stared at the gathering army.

Another half mile and they arrived at the old mine, a mere

depression in the ground with a few upright timbers. Cody led them across its rocky tailings. He told them that from here their hike would be in open country, no roads.

The moon provided just enough light to illuminate their passage in shades of gray: light sand, dark bushes, darker shadows. The only sounds that disturbed the silence were the crunching of boots on pebbles and the scraping of pants on an occasional bush. The smells were of sage, the dust raised by Peter who stumbled ahead of him, and an occasional whiff of tea tree. They descended into an arroyo, smooth with blown sand.

This was the rendezvous point for their supplies. Ryan was introduced to Teddy Leupp and three llamas. They already carried the clothing and camping gear of the Harmony people. Ryan watched as Cody added his sleeping bag and pad to the pack of one llama. He judged their bulging packs held sufficient gear and food for several days. Cody handed him the halter of a llama and introduced it to him as Boomer.

Four years ago, in his last break before launching Sanitas, he had hiked with llamas, using them to pack into a remote area in New Zealand. He had found them to be intelligent sure-footed creatures with personalities similar to dogs. During that hike, he'd discovered that they made a twittering sound when startled — a valuable asset one night when a wild boar found their camp. Approaching Boomer, Ryan petted his neck and talked to him. The animal's ears hinged forward and back. His large brown eyes watched the man holding his rope.

Depending on their size, llamas were able to carry forty to sixty pounds of supplies. Each llama was saddled with a frame weighing about twenty pounds to which two saddlebags were hung, one on each side. They would provide no help to Peter Jones whose shuffle slowed the group's escape. Ryan was surprised that neither Cody nor Teddy had provided a horse for Peter.

The group formed into a procession, Cody leading, Teddy Leupp at the rear. For support, Peter leaned against Boomer's pack. Everyone else slowed his or her pace to accommodate Peter's shuffle. After a quarter mile, they found a rock ledge and climbed out of the ravine.

For the next mile they traveled across a treeless, bushless, rolling terrain of exposed rock. Waves of ruddy sandstone glistened in the light of the waning gibbous moon. Tufts of grass clung to life in shallow pockets of dirt. Ryan envisioned an ancient beach with water lapping against the shoreline eon after eon, building soft, gentle folds and domes. In the moon's luminescence he could almost see and hear the waves against the sand of the beach. A few million years ago, the continent had sunk and the sand was molded into rock, the marks of the undulations preserved under the pressure from tons of water. When the continent lifted again, the sandstone had been uncovered by wind and rain.

At the southwestern slope of the mesa, with Harmony well out of sight, they reached a scattering of trees and bushes. Dr. Adamson walked over to Ryan and pointed east. "Go that direction with Peter and Sarah. Teddy and I are going south, to leave a false trail. Cody will rejoin you in a few minutes."

Ryan handed Boomer's rope to Cody. The three men and three llamas headed down the slope. After a short distance Ryan lost track of them in the junipers.

He led Sarah and Peter a hundred yards to hard ground. Cody and two llamas returned by a circuitous route. The Navajo took advantage of the moonlight to obliterate all signs except the tracks leading south. Then Cody led them east through a juniper-dotted, rock-strewn landscape.

As they climbed the steep slope of the mesa, Ryan paused to glance southeast — a sparkling blanket of diamonds from one horizon to the other. The dry air of the desert had allowed thousands of faint points-of-light to emerge. He tilted his head upward and felt swallowed by the expanse of the heavens. His earth-rooted backdrop receded and he stood as if on a pinnacle, prepared to launch himself into the vastness of space.

He took a step sideways. The ground gave way. He fell and sharp spears of a yucca stabbed his leg. He put his hand out to break his fall and it too was impaled on yucca. "Oh shit," he said rolling to his left.

He struggled to his feet and examined his right hand in the dim light. "Pay attention to the hike," he told himself. "Plenty of time later to look around." The yucca had pierced the skin between his thumb and forefinger. He unknotted his kerchief and wrapped it around the wound. Retrieving Boomer's rope with his left hand, he headed after the others. After one step, he reached down and pulled a yucca spear from his leg. It hurt enough to let him know he had gouged it — and to help him concentrate on keeping up.

The route wound through jagged fragments that had cleaved off the rock face. At the head of the group, Cody and Peter struggled upward in a wide ravine that cut into the side of Fortress Mesa.

Cody, Peter, and Sarah tried not to dislodge rocks, but twice Ryan grabbed Boomer and pulled him to one side in response to a shouted warning. In both cases, a sizable stone came tumbling down the steep incline of the gully.

When they neared the top, the procession stopped and Cody asked Ryan to come forward. "Give her llama," the Navajo motioned to Sarah. Ryan looked ahead to see a small cliff with a narrow cleft in its face. "Go up," Cody said. "I hand packs."

Ryan handed Boomer's rope to Sarah and climbed through the narrow gap. He found himself in a piñon and juniper forest. Looking down he saw Cody hoist one of the llama's side packs to him. After ten minutes and three additional packs, Ryan grabbed Sarah's hand as she scrambled up. The Navajo pushed Peter up the rock and Ryan and Sarah pulled him to the top.

He heard Cody encourage Boomer and the scraping of hooves. Llama and Navajo soon appeared and Cody went back for the other pack animal. If the INS tried to use horses to pursue them, they would never be able to get them through the rubble and up here.

"How are you doing?" Ryan asked Sarah.

"I have problem." She was on the ground, examining her left foot.

"What is it?"

"My boot created a blister."

Ryan dug into his pack and handed her a package of moleskin. She eyed it and Ryan's hand wrapped in his kerchief.

"I am not familiar with this," she said, examining the material in the dim light.

"Here, let me show you." Ryan used his pocketknife to cut a square from the sheet of soft flexible material and applied it to her heel. In the dark he could feel that she had a long narrow foot.

When she had retied her boot she said, "Well, let's be going."

With that she arose and lifted her backpack. He smiled at her use of the less formal phrasing.

Ryan reached for his pack and flinched — his hand was swelling. He grabbed Boomer's rope and said, "What do you say, Boomer. Let's be going."

"How are you with Peter's discussion of yesterday?" Sarah asked as they started out.

"I've thought about it." Ryan tilted his head left. He was frustrated. He wanted to know more about her, but she kept diverting their conversation into an intellectual discussion.

"You are trapped in economic slavery." Her gray eyes glistened.

"Economic slavery? Look at all the great things we have. It's the economy that's responsible for our prosperity, we're hardly slaves."

"Your view is myopic."

"My vision's fine."

"There is nothing wrong with prosperity, until it becomes an end in itself. Consuming and accumulating have become the primary goals of people in America. Yet huge numbers of others in this world are occupied with just survival. Americans must recognize this disparity and its consequences."

"OK, I'll admit that we consume more than our fair share, but that's probably not going to change. And, hey, I'm happy with the way things are."

"I am sorry. We do not explain our viewpoint." Sarah shook her head in frustration. "Some in key positions foster economic disparity for their own purposes, you are wrong to defend it."

"I just don't see what it has to do with me." If she weren't so damn pretty and warm hearted, he'd just ignore her.

"Despite your success at cocooning, these things do touch you," she said gravely.

"Cocooning?" he reacted. "What do you mean cocooning?"

"Insulating yourself, failing to recognize the broader reality."

"Hey, I take care of my family and employees. That's as much as I can do. I also work harder than most people."

Sarah said, "Until you eradicate the attitude that legitimizes violence in any form, you will not eliminate it on this planet. Until you correct the degradation of your environment, you will not reverse this world's slide toward cataclysm. Until you unmask the secret centers of power and those who increasingly enslave you, you will continue to be manipulated."

"But America is a beacon of freedom. Everyone here makes their own choices. And we develop technologies that help less developed countries and reverse environmental problems."

"On the surface that appears to be true," Sarah said. "But you must begin to see beyond the programs fostered by an elitist few. If you cannot visualize a society without its primary focus on self-centered values, you will never create one.

"The people of this planet have the opportunity to create a plentiful, peaceful and beautiful world — a world free of violence, free of pollution, free of slavery. But you must embark on this path soon or the forces of money and power will enforce outright autocratic rule in this country, and then the rest of the world."

"We're a democracy. It'll never happen."

"Fearful people give up freedoms to feel safe. Comfortable people fight to preserve the status quo. Each crisis eats away at the clarity with which people see what is right, at their willingness to assert fundamental values. This process gradually allows ruthless men to increase their power."

Ryan dropped behind. He did not want to continue this conversation. A part of him relished returning to the civilization Sarah was criticizing.

He wished he had his cell phone, but he had not bothered to bring it with him. Few homes on the Navajo Reservation even had conventional telephones. The nearest cell phone transmitter was probably in Gallup or Cortez — way out of range. The Navajo Police and other emergency services used high power vehicle radios.

Had the INS detected the absence of Sarah and Peter yet? Was it possible they were running across this desert only to find themselves in the arms of waiting INS agents? What if this whole thing was a false alarm? What if Dr. Adamson was mistaken about the raid?

In a few hundred yards, the fugitives stopped in a dense stand of piñon. In the dim light, Ryan could see that someone had erected a canvas lean-to and a crude table. Cody said this was the camp he used for deer hunting. He pointed out a trickle of water from a small spring. When released, the llamas bolted for it. Ryan pushed the button on the side of his Avocet: 07390 2:17 AM.

Gathering them around, Sarah said, "We will wait here for light. Try to sleep. Cody will care for llamas."

Ryan was about to question her assumption of authority, but let it go. Neither did he question her when she asked to see his hand. She examined it, dabbed ointment on it, and wrapped it in a clean white cloth. Her gray eyes obviously functioned better than his in the dim light.

They pulled out ground covers from the llamas' packs and spread them in places where it was flat enough to sleep. Peter and Sarah selected a space off to one side. Ryan dropped his backpack on a second ground cover and unrolled his bag and mattress.

Ryan Drake awoke with a start. The sky was slowly turning gray, shedding its night blanket. The camp was quiet. He had been awakened from a dream.

Nick was in his office. Leaning back in his chair, Bally loafers resting on the top of Ryan's desk. On his face was a satisfied grin and he spoke to someone seated opposite him, "We did it! That jerk Drake will be so fucking surprised when he gets back from his damn vacation."

Ryan had helped create Sanitas and made a success of it. He had seen the potential of Chad "Brauk" Braukington's prototype instruments, predicted their success, and convinced three venture firms to invest in developing them into a real business. At the time of the initial money, he had negotiated a half million-dollar purchase of shares for himself plus the stock options due a seasoned miracle working CEO.

The National Bureau of Standards had located a facility in Boulder, Colorado in the 1950's. In the 1970's the National Center for Atmospheric Research and the National Atmospheric and Oceanic Administration had located in Boulder. Brauk conceived a way to use the excess computing and communications capabilities of these facilities to construct a worldwide pollution monitoring system based on Sanitas's instruments.

When Sanitas's instrument business had proven itself and they sought investors to fund the Global Watch System, Nick had purchased $5 million of stock, at triple the price the original investors had paid. Having paid that higher price, Nick thought he deserved special treatment.

After a few minutes, he slipped back to sleep.

Ryan Drake knew it was a prison because he could not get out. He was always alone in his cell. The walls of this bizarre jail were transparent. He could watch the people next to him, above, and below. The guards who sat in a central tower could watch all of them and could see through their cells to other cells and other guards.

He went about his daily activities. He got up at home, went to his office, drove his car, and flew on airplanes. Yet he never left the prison. The cells were without sound barriers. As he went about his activities, he could hear others make observations. He reacted to their censure and modified his behavior. In turn, he commented on their activities and took delight in his ability to influence their actions by his judgments. He and his friends in the adjacent cells "helped" each other conform to the ever-present gaze of the guards and the other prisoners. From time to time, the jail walls faded and he was in his office in Boulder. However, the feeling that others were watching and judging did not leave him.

Ryan startled awake and looked around. Had he heard something? No sound from the llamas, just the absolute stillness of the desert at night. His hand throbbed, but he turned over and was back asleep in a few moments.

If I can put one touch of rosy sunset into the life of any man or woman, I shall feel that I have worked with God.

— GEORGE MacDONALD

FOUR

"So, what do ya think of that Harmony bunch?" Raul Viejo, Immigration and Naturalization Service agent from Phoenix, leaned against the hood of his vehicle and puffed on a Macanudo. He felt expansive in the early dawn. Everything was on plan.

"Never did get what that blonde bitch was saying — bunch a missionaries!" Luis Litchfield, the Regional Director of the Bureau of Indian Affairs, took a swig from his thermos. "All I know is they're perfect for this set-up. Those buildings are real weird — lots a underground rooms to hide people — right?"

"That place don't look like no smuggler's hideout, but it will when we're through rummaging around." Viejo gave the side of his vehicle a hard kick. "They'll be explaining their way out of this for weeks."

"Like I said, a perfect set-up."

"Don't be too sure. That Sarah gave me some kind a jolt the other day. I still don't know what happened."

"She's spooky all right. I beat it out a there the other day. Ran some dumb Indian off a the road." Litchfield laughed.

Viejo looked at his co-conspirator. The man was drunk. Oh,

44

well, in a few days he wouldn't need his old buddy. Luis had been easy to recruit once Viejo stumbled on the way in which the BIA agent had been skimming from the Navajos' federal grants. After that it didn't take much of a threat, or a payoff, to insure his cooperation.

After this load made it to Iowa, he'd pay Luis off and forget him. This job was his finale. Once he got paid, he'd have enough to get out of the INS, out of the country. This raid on Harmony was the perfect smokescreen for the largest and most lucrative run of his five-year smuggling sideline.

"Buses oughta be rolling pretty soon." Litchfield slurred his words as he gulped from his thermos.

"Yeah, everybody's here." The INS man surveyed the growing crowd. Two vans of INS men, armed with automatic weapons had just arrived from Nogales, on the Mexican border. They readied themselves for the attack. Jeep Cherokees with Navajo Police were positioned down the road in either direction — their job was to capture the Harmony people and any illegals if they tried to flee along the highway. Nobody would be stupid enough to attempt an escape to the east — desert and an un-scalable mesa. He had them boxed in. Nearby, two FBI agents dozed in a dark sedan. Five INS agents huddled at the turnoff to Harmony.

"What about that flame last evening?" Litchfield asked. "Sure was bright."

"Just burning trash. They don't expect a thing."

"Hope they didn't burn the evidence — ha, ha."

Viejo looked at his drunken partner with disdain and took a long pull on his cigar.

"Well, you did tell Hoehn that you'd bring in evidence, didn't ya?" Litchfield asked.

Viejo did not respond. Yes, he had promised his boss that he would collect evidence. However, the best he had been able to manufacture were the clothes and gun in the duffle bag at his feet. They would have to do. He hoped that the jacket of the woman he had thrown out of the car would provide a definitive link between her and Harmony Center.

Viejo recalled how the woman had struggled when he had pushed her from his car. He'd punched her twice, once in the stomach, once in the back. She'd tried to crawl back in. He'd kicked her several times, peeled off her jacket, and rolled her into the ditch. He had not intended that she die, but it had happened. Probably just as well, she might have talked.

"So how'd you finally convince Hoehn?" Litchfield asked.

"The woman," Viejo replied. "Plus a little hint that they might be terrorists." He watched Litchfield's eyes light up at this most improbable suggestion. "Nothing specific, just a hint. You know how preoccupied he is with that kind a shit."

As the head of the INS office in Phoenix, Oscar Hoehn had responsibility for Arizona, including its border with Mexico. His principal responsibility was securing that border. Raul Viejo was taking advantage of the current paucity of federal agents in the interior of the United States.

"Your friends in Iowa better appreciate this," Litchfield said

"Hey, the people behind this are ultra rich. Believe me, they're paying top dollar." The INS agent took a draw on his cigar.

"We're gonna make a lot a money." The BIA man grinned.

Viejo smiled. He hoped his associate would never find out how much the company in Iowa was indeed paying. He'd told Luis they'd split everything — after expenses. He chuckled at how high his expenses were going to be.

He was pleased the way things were working. After weeks of meetings, discussions with everyone who could possibly be interested, and Litchfield's sworn statement, he had received a green light for the action. Because Mexican illegals were at the center of it, the FBI and Navajo Police had deferred to the INS.

When Viejo saw that every INS agent in northeast Arizona as well as the FBI agents and Navajo Police were accounted for, he picked up his satellite phone and dialed a number. He let the phone ring three times and hung up. He repeated this again, letting it ring twice. This signal would be relayed to his accomplices who waited with the busses. Because the circuit had not connected there was no record of the attempted calls.

Over the past six weeks, Viejo's confederates had rounded up almost a thousand men and women. Some of them were recent arrivals from Mexico, others wanted to leave Arizona, and all had paid money to be transported further away from the border and to new work. The flow of illegals coming into the country had dried to a trickle and unscrupulous employers were paying record premiums for willing workers.

"Why so many guys?" Litchfield pointed to the men armed with automatic weapons.

"Told Hoehn there was thirty a them. Had to make it look good," he laughed. "Get everybody away from the highway."

"Well, I'm ready," Litchfield patted the 44-magnum pistol on his belt.

Viejo checked his own gun, ground the remains of his cigar in the dust, and shouted to the assault team, "Let's go."

Ryan Drake awoke, startled at the bright sun. A few feet away, the others talked excitedly. He glanced at his watch/altimeter: 7:13 AM. What were they doing up?

He reached out with his right hand to pull the sleeping bag up around him but could not grasp the material. Squinting he looked at the white bandage — it was red and bulged like a plum. He unwrapped it and looked unhappily at the red mass that had once been his thumb and forefinger.

When he struggled to the lean-to, bare footed, Sarah asked, "Everything all right?" She was rubbing a yellowish lotion on Peter's back. It smelled like tea tree.

"Sure," he mumbled.

She nodded, but gave a smile to let him know that she suspected otherwise. "Would you like coffee?" She set down the lotion and went over to the camp stove. This morning her hair was tightly wrapped into a chignon.

Ryan watched her graceful movements. Through bleary eyes he glanced at Peter. He too seemed wide-awake, resting his elbow on one of his books. Cody sat watching the others.

Sarah returned with a mug of steaming liquid, tan with milk. He grasped it in his good hand.

"Let me see." She squatted and reached for his injured hand.

Ryan offered it to her. "It should be fine in a day or two," he said.

Sarah's large gray eyes studied his hand and pulled out two small slivers of yucca. She cleaned it with hydrogen peroxide and covered it with a fresh bandage.

The coffee tasted bitter and Sarah had put in too much milk, but he did not complain. How could she look so good after sleeping on the ground last night?

With a stumble, Peter arose to help Sarah prepare food. Their Navajo guide, seated off to one side, said nothing.

Ryan sipped coffee and leaned back in the camp chair. His hand slid into the pocket of his jacket and he fished out an envelope. His secretary had given it to him the day before he left for the desert, but he had not looked at it since then. The enclosed sheet was torn from a spiral notebook, ragged edge. The words were printed:

> Dear Senor Drake,
>
> Thank you very much for your help. My children are safe. I feeling better and will return to work monday.
>
> God Bless You
>
> Theresa

As he had walked through the assembly room, a week before he came to the desert, he had spotted Theresa Alvarez hunched over her work area. The left side of her face was swollen and purple. He suspected a recent beating. He directed her supervisor to call 911 and went to comfort her. While the paramedics attended to her, he summoned the crisis intervention team from Boulder County Safehouse. After an hour-long counseling session they took her to gather up her two small children. Ryan told the Safehouse counselors that she could take the rest of the week off with pay.

He looked up as Sarah and Peter laid the food out on the rough table: melon, tortillas, a bacon and egg and potato scramble. They helped themselves and sat down. Cody took a plateful and planted himself on a nearby stump. Ryan noted caraway seeds in the scramble.

Sarah said, "We have bad news."

"Oh?" Ryan paused his eating.

"INS stormed Harmony at six this morning," she said, "Twenty armed men, led by Raul Viejo. When they did not find us, they tore the place apart. They believed there were thirty of us, that Mexican illegals were hiding there, and that we were dangerous."

"I can imagine your absence was disconcerting," Ryan chuckled.

"More important," Sarah said, her voice grim, "they killed George — our chief gardener. You met him."

"No! Oh, no," Ryan said. His fists tightened until the pain in his right hand made him startle.

"George tried to stop them from destroying the dome," Peter stuttered. "We urged him to leave. He loved the garden and wanted to be sure it got watered."

"Were we harboring illegals?" Sarah stood. She motioned to Peter and herself. Answering her own question, she continued with angry words. "You had a tour. We hid nothing from the INS. We are not armed. We are not trying to overthrow the government. We just want to show what wonderful things can happen when people understand our message."

"Message?"

"The papers I gave you."

"Oh yeah, right. Will you go back now?" Ryan asked.

"The INS is in no mood for negotiations," Sarah responded. Her voice had resumed its gentle tone. Her eyelashes and eyebrows were the same light blonde as her hair. She had a model's high cheekbones. "They are not interested in hearing our message. They want to link us to illegal smuggling. We will proceed." She placed her hands on her hips.

"I could help." Ryan was disturbed. George's death made this more than an adventure.

Ryan's experience at four companies had taught him that the INS was understaffed and focused on capturing illegals with criminal records, disease, or terrorist intent. They regularly interviewed all employees with Spanish and Middle East surnames. On the other hand, Ryan didn't see how even the most inexperienced agent could suspect the Harmony facility was being used for smuggling.

"We must go on to Shiprock," Sarah said.

He had eaten several bites of scramble before the natural question occurred to him. "How'd you learn about all this? Do you have a cell phone? A radio? CB?"

Sarah said, "I remotely viewed the events at Harmony."

"Remotely viewed?" Ryan reacted. This situation was getting

weirder by the moment. He glanced around. Just the three of them and Cody over by the llamas. He tilted his head left and leaned back into the camp chair. He liked these people and trusted his instincts, but this was crazy. How could they possibly have information on something that happened miles away and only a short while ago? There had to be a reasonable explanation. Ryan glanced around, hoping to find an additional Navajo to explain things.

Sarah said, "Ryan, there is a whole stratum of existence that you, and most others, know little about. Some people refer to it as the spirit domain or the spirit level. Others use the more general term, 'the universe.' One of your most popular science fiction movies called it 'the force.' These perceptions are all incorrect. They are explanations from people trying to explain something that they themselves do not fully understand. This world's vague concepts of universe mind and celestial reality are primitive."

"Well, I don't believe anyone can see something happening miles away," Ryan said. He planted his feet on the ground, pulled his jacket about him, and plopped his hands in his lap. "At least not without a video camera. And I sure haven't felt the effects of any celestials."

"Oh, but you have," she responded. "Do you think your being here is a coincidence?"

Now Ryan was really taken back. He stared at Sarah, then at Peter. What was he, the CEO of Sanitas, a pragmatic levelheaded realist, doing here anyway? Was this just an adventure? Wasn't he just helping to get Sarah and Peter across Fortress Mesa?

Reconnecting to the immediate conversation he asked, "So you have some sort of a special ability and you can see distant events?"

"Yes," Sarah said. "We can see distant things with a skill known as remote viewing. May I show you?"

"Sure."

Sarah thought for a moment and then said, "All right. Walk behind the lean-to and hold out any number of fingers. I will call out the number."

After stumbling to his sleeping area and putting on his shoes, Ryan did as he was asked. He held up two fingers, shielded from Sarah's view. He also made sure that neither Peter nor Cody could see them.

"Two," Sarah call out.

He switched and held up four fingers.

"Four."

"Tell me which ones."

"The thumb of your left hand and three fingers on your right."

Ryan walked back to her shaking his head. "Pretty amazing. What did you call that?"

"Remote viewing."

"I just find all of this so hard to believe." Some of the flakier people he had encountered in Boulder claimed that they could contact higher powers, claimed they foresaw events in their dreams. But, as far as he knew, none of them were able to do it on demand, nor did they claim to see actual events as they transpired.

"I learned to communicate with celestials when I was very young. Peter is able to do it also. Both of us are able to remotely view things."

"What you're saying is very strange." Ryan shook his head.

"Celestial-reality is as real as our physical surroundings," Sarah picked up a rock. "You understand the structure of atoms, electrons orbiting a nucleus. Although this physical world appears to be solid, it is predominantly space. Things are not always as they seem." She tossed the rock and hit the trunk of a nearby tree. The noise startled a bird resting on a branch and it fluttered away.

He'd encountered ardent women before, ones dedicated to saving the environment or to animal rights. Could he have a relationship with a woman as intense as Sarah? As he learned more about her, he could see that her beliefs were as important a part of her as her Nordic beauty. Did he even want to have a relationship with someone who believed she talked to spirits?

"Celestials are everywhere. They are intimately involved in your daily life."

Ryan did not reply. He just studied his two companions.

"Do you really believe that something as wonderful as this planet functions by itself?" Sarah asked. "This is the result of billions of years of hard work."

Ryan said, "Now, you're going to try and convince me that celestials control physical things?"

"Yes, celestial beings use both direct intervention and evolution to accomplish physical ends," Sarah said. "They are able to take primal space-energies, put forces in motion for materialization, and then let evolution take over. From time to time they adjust the natural process — it is a symbiotic relationship. That is how the celestials created this beautiful world. It didn't just happen by chance."

"What proof do you have?" Ryan's head tilted right.

"What we have told you is true," Sarah said, "whether you believe it or not." She looked at him with clear, unwavering eyes. It was that look, which never faltered, that convinced him that she might be telling the truth.

"But how do I know that the INS really raided your facility?"

"Last night, you saw the lights of their vehicles near Harmony."

"True."

"You said you would help us cross this Mesa. By the time we reach the other side, you will have your proof."

Cody informed them that they would need to hike about six miles to the only point where they could descend. They discussed it and decided that the thick growth of piñon and juniper would shield them in case the INS used a search plane.

After Ryan rolled up his bag and mattress, he walked a short distance through the trees and found the rim of Fortress Mesa. From the position of the sun, he judged that they had crossed from the south side of the mesa to the north. They were probably on a narrow neck of land connecting two larger parts of the mesa.

Miles away, he saw the sandstone cliffs of another mesa and towering buttes in the distance beyond that. For as far as he could see, there were no roads, buildings, or power lines, only shades of brown and red.

Overhead, a shiny speck winged its way westward – probably the Denver to Los Angeles flight. He had taken it many times, looked down on this bleak landscape, and thought what a desolate place it was. From the air, sparse trees marked higher elevations and shadows traced the occasional deep canyon that wound its way across the desert's otherwise smooth surface. From thirty thousand feet, mesas looked like irregular cookies that some giant baker had plopped on a beige baking tray. Sunshine broiled them into formations of stark beauty.

The white man had willed this worthless land to the Navajos. The largest tribe in America controlled an area the size of West Virginia. Eking out a meager living, many lived without electricity, most without phones or paved roads.

As he soaked up his surroundings, he heard voices. "—today is too soon—" silence "—will follow—" silence "—piction for him—" He listened for more, but as soon as he concentrated the voices died away.

The cliff on which he stood was two thousand feet above the barrenness below. He imagined a giant slab of cap rock crashing onto the slope of the Mesa, splintering into a thousand chunks. To his back was the piñon forest; in front, space. This was his idea of spiritual.

His son, Darren, and daughter, Danielle, loved the outdoors. As a child, Danielle was better than her brother at catching fish, although she refused to touch them. One time she hooked a large trout. When she saw how big it was she insisted that it was a "mommy" and demanded her father put it back. Now, they were both grown up with lives of their own. He wished one of them had come to the desert with him.

A bush behind him rustled. Startled, he turned and saw Sarah approach. She walked to the edge and peered into the distance. "I have learned to love this desert."

"I can see the buttes at Monument Valley." Ryan pointed to the northwest. "There, on the horizon. I think it's one of the most beautiful places on earth."

"We drove through Monument Valley. It is breathtaking."

The two of them stood together for a time drinking in the stark beauty of the panorama. Then they walked back to Cody's camp and cleaned up all traces of their occupancy.

They hiked through the piñon and juniper forest on top of the mesa. With Peter Jones leaning on him, Cody led the way following a twisting game trail through the tangle of trees and brush.

Rocks, visible in daylight, displayed orange, green, and gray lichen, tse'laad — a sure sign of a milder climate than the desert floor. Red wild-flowers, 'azee'haajinii, Indian paintbrush, dotted the landscape. The llamas lowered their heads to graze on the tall grass. While they saw no deer, their scat was everywhere. Animals like these would not survive the hot summers on the desert floor, yet they appeared to thrive at this higher elevation.

After three hours, they paused for lunch. Peter needed to rest. Cody told them the way down the mesa lay at its far edge, another three miles. He was anxious to reach there before dark, but realized he could push Peter only so fast.

After a turkey sandwich, Ryan retrieved his sleeping bag and lay down. It had been a long time since he'd had empty moments and he wanted to take advantage of them before returning to the office. The smell of gadbididze', juniper, permeated the dry air. He inhaled deeply; even his vacations seemed to be busy with schedules and planned events.

Everything at Sanitas had looked good as of the end of June. In July they discovered that TTT Instrumentation had entertained discussions with someone else for comparable products. Sanitas responded to the potential competition by incorporating a patented breakthrough into its instruments that significantly increased their measuring sensitivity.

At their last face-to-face meeting, the president of TTT had agreed to renew the contract with Sanitas, but had demanded changes in delivery terms and payment for technical support in countries outside the European Union. Ryan hoped the proposed contract changes his team had submitted would satisfy TTT. If they lost their international channel of distribution and service, his company would be in serious trouble.

Piñon nuts were scattered on the ground — in the store at home, they cost $14 a pound. He cracked one between his teeth. Its sweet taste flooded his mouth and he searched for another.

A wispy cloud floated by, borne on the breeze that rustled through the trees. He studied the pine needles overhead, dark against the blue sky. Their shadow made an interesting pattern on his clothing and sleeping bag.

He chomped another pine nut. Not too many years ago, people had fed themselves off this land. Such wild areas were fast disappearing, overrun by encroaching civilization. In America, apart from a few designated wilderness tracts, this Reservation was one of the last unspoiled areas.

Somehow, in this wilderness, some of Sarah's ideas didn't seem so far-fetched. He knew that Native Americans attributed everything to one spirit or another and told stories about the ancients. However, in light of scientific discoveries, saying spirits were in charge of everything was too much to swallow.

It was clear that Sarah was special, a passionate woman with unique ideas and skills. He was certain she believed the things Peter and she were saying, that they were not some sort of con artists. Just how did one go about proving that there was something more than that which was detectable with scientific instruments? Using a wind-sculpted rock as a pillow, he fell asleep.

"That's what I said." Raul Viejo shouted into his vehicle's satellite phone. "Attacked me."

"He wasn't a Mexican?"

"No."

"This is trouble, you know," Oscar Hoehn said.

"Hey, he was impeding."

"Did you have to kill him?"

"He was about to shoot me."

"You said there were thirty of them." Oscar Hoehn was talking on his cell phone, just outside his daughter's hospital room. Hoehn had planned to be at the site of the raid, but his daughter's sudden illness had taken precedence.

"That's right," Viejo said. He was relieved that Hoehn had not been present. Litchfield and he had concocted the story that the harmony people were harboring Mexican illegals. Litchfield had initially balked at the lie, but Viejo had persisted. The number of people at Harmony Center had grown along with the need to make the story convincing.

"So where are they?" Hoehn asked.

"Must a left at night. Out in the desert somewhere."

"The desert!"

"Yeah, they're hiding."

"No Mexican illegals?"

"They all left together."

"So what did you find?"

"Clothes with Mexican labels." Viejo turned to watch the assault squad remove their gear and prepare to move out. "The Indian had a Mexican pistol. Looks like this place held a lot of 'em — like I told ya, lots a underground rooms. The FBI took the clothes and gun for examination."

"Any records?"

"Some papers — weird anti-American stuff. They must a burned most of it. The incinerator's still hot."

The written report of the raid would indicate that one of the FBI men had opened the outside door to the smaller hogan. It enclosed a cylinder about six feet in diameter with a cement floor and a chimney. In the center of the floor, an iron grate was supported over a propane burner. The cylinder was still warm and a pile of ashes remained from alleged files that had been destroyed. A stairway led from the smaller hogan to the underground rooms.

"I want to talk to them." After a sleepless night with his sick daughter, the senior INS man was in no mood to be embarrassed by a raid that produced nothing.

Viejo knew the dead Navajo would cause a real stink, but the man had surprised him. After he shot him, he forced the old Mexican pistol into the man's hand and fired off a round.

"Hey you know, Jake Ashton, that FBI guy from Gallup?" Viejo could see a directive coming and tried to divert his boss' new order. "Well, he found some unusual gear. It was with their satellite dish electronics, but he can't figure it out. Thinks maybe they coordinated the whole conduit of illegals from right here. Reported it to Washington."

"Find them," the INS supervisor said.

"Hey, we busted it up. That was the whole idea."

"I want to talk to those people."

"I say forget them. It's a waste a time chasing people around the desert."

"Let me talk to Morgan."

Viejo motioned to Joe Morgan, the head of the invasion squad, and handed him the handset.

"Who shot the Navajo?"

"Viejo, sir. At least I think so. I wasn't there."

"I want a full report on the incident," Hoehn said.

The connection sputtered and Viejo could hear the shouted

words. He began to formulate a backup plan.

"Yes, sir," the big ex-Marine nodded.

"Stay there. Find them."

"Yes, sir. I'll get on it."

"I'll send you an airplane," Hoehn said.

The big man passed the handset back to Viejo. "I'm going to look around," he said.

"Raul," Oscar Hoehn said to his subordinate. "I'll post a twenty-five thousand dollar reward. Tell Litchfield to spread the word. The Indians are always looking for cash."

"All right."

The connection went dead.

Viejo motioned to Litchfield and explained things. His confederate promised to start questioning the locals to find out where the people from Harmony might have gone and who might have helped them.

Just what he wanted, stuck in the desert while Morgan chased a weird bunch of missionaries. Why couldn't Hoehn let it be? Oh well, the important thing was his busses got through while everybody's attention was on the raid. Pretty soon he'd retire in Mexico. He pulled out a Macanudo and clipped its end. For now he had to play along.

Each of Viejo's bus drivers had a different route he would follow after passing out of the Navajo Reservation. The ten busses planned to spread themselves along several less-traveled routes all converging at a facility near Ames, Iowa. Each driver had checked out his route by auto over the past six months. Viejo's trick was using US 160 to get the busloads of illegals from Arizona into the Midwest while staying off the Interstate Highways. The key to his scheme was getting law enforcement personnel occupied with the raid on Harmony while the busses passed through the bottleneck around Kayenta twenty miles to the north.

The buses were a nightmare for the men and women crammed into them. Each bus, an old repainted school bus, normally held fifty or sixty people. By making use of every available inch of floor space, Viejo's confederates had packed a hundred on each bus. Furthermore, once the buses started to roll they did not stop for hours at a time and then only at some out of the way side road. Many of the passengers did not eat for the twenty-two hour trip, some were sick the whole time. Two thousand five hundred per head would be paid to Viejo at the time of successful delivery; he would net over a million and a half dollars after expenses and payments to people like Litchfield.

Now as Viejo scanned the various police frequencies on his radio, he heard no reports of anyone stopping suspicious busses. Viejo walked over and joined Morgan and his men. Half began a systematic search of the immediate area. The other half of them set out on the road to the old mine.

Humanity must step up and take charge of its destiny.

— ROBERT S. MCNAMERA

FIVE

"Can we talk?"

Startled awake, Ryan Drake sat up. He blinked his eyes a couple of times and checked the time — he'd slept an hour and a half. He focused on Peter Jones and said, "Sure. What about?"

"About the universe," he stuttered.

"OK." Ryan motioned him down and shifted to a comfortable position on the hard ground.

He glanced about to be sure they had not been joined by any INS troops. Beyond Peter he saw Cody sleeping next to Boomer — surely the warning twitter of the llamas would have awakened him. Ryan concluded they were alone.

He looked at Peter. Despite his physical handicap, the bald headed man had done his best on this trek. Men of lesser determination would have called long ago. Ryan admired perseverance and decided he was beginning to like Peter.

"That Earth is an isolated world is a mistaken perception." Peter struggled to connect his words. He grasped one of his three maroon books in his hand. It was wrapped in its protective plastic.

Ryan nodded that he had heard. He was beginning to understand Peter's garbled words more easily. It was as if a deeply buried piece of Ryan Drake resonated with Peter's novel concepts. He decided to put aside his skepticism and just listen to what Peter was saying. After all, once they climbed down off the mesa, his job was over. He could afford to be polite for a few more hours.

"Earth is only one of the inhabited planets within the Milky Way. This galaxy is one of seven that contain such worlds. The inhabitants of most of these planets are intelligent humanoids."

"OK, I'll grant you that we probably aren't the only inhabited planet," Ryan said. "But, given the exacting biological conditions for higher life forms, there can't be that many inhabited worlds."

Ryan had followed claims about inhabited planets and extraterrestrial visitors. Some reports touted nearby planets with lots of aliens; others continued to ridicule the whole idea of extraterrestrials. Preoccupied with affairs at Sanitas, his information had been limited to newspaper reports and an occasional television newscast. He knew the official posture of the government was that insufficient proof existed.

Appearing from behind a clump of junipers, Sarah joined the pair. As soon as she sat down she pulled out a bottle of the yellow lotion and began to rub it on her hands and forearms.

Peter continued, "The Milky Way and the other six inhabited galaxies are in an elliptical orbit around the Cosmic Nucleus — the only stationery point in the cosmos. The path of these seven inhabited galaxies is as well known to celestials as the orbits of the planets in this solar system. As with the rest of the cosmos, these seven galaxies are currently in an expansion phase — but not as the result of some Big Bang. Rather, it is the periodic respiration of the cosmos."

Peter set his book down and used his right arm to depict the elliptical orbit of the galaxies about the Cosmic Nucleus, his left hand. Then he showed the Milky Way and the position of the sun on one of its spiral arms. The far side of the Milky Way faced the Cosmic Nucleus.

Sarah said, "Celestial beings began materialization of this region of our Galaxy about a trillion years ago. The oldest planet is about four hundred billion years old."

"Four hundred billion years?" Ryan said. "No astronomer theorizes anything in the universe is that old, let alone a planet. The time of the big bang was a few billion years ago and planets did not form until way after that."

Ryan looked at his two companions. What Sarah had just proposed was a universe hundreds of times older than anything science theorized. Where did she get these outrageous claims? Then he reminded himself to remain open.

"The initiation of the universe happened long before the so-called Big Bang," Peter stuttered. "Your astronomers calculate that explosive beginning based on regression analysis. What they are really observing is the universe's current respiration cycle, not the true onset of the universe of time and space."

"Your scientists' quest for knowledge is only a few hundred years old," Sarah said. "Could not they be mistaken?"

Ryan did not reply. He was still wondering if the universe could possibly be a hundred times older than astronomers calculated.

"Think of it," Sarah said. Her enthusiasm bubbled like a pot ready to cast its contents onto a hot stove. "There are seven galaxies that are ubiquitously inhabited — within their swirling star clusters are trillions of worlds of intelligent material beings."

"Trillions of inhabited planets?" Ryan glanced from Sarah to Peter. Both were intent on his reaction. "That's more than Star Trek," he joked nervously.

Discussions like this troubled him. Although he would never admit it, he always felt uneasy trying to grasp grand concepts and huge numbers. He remembered someone telling him an interesting way to conceptualize a trillion: Given that 86,400 seconds passed in a day, it would take almost 32,000 years to accumulate a trillion seconds. He had accumulated a mere 1.5 billion seconds to his most recent birthday. A trillion was a really big number, but Sarah and Peter were throwing trillions around as if he was supposed to comprehend. Big numbers reminded him of discussions of the United States' budget and all those dollars the government spent.

First Sarah and Peter had told him there were spirits all around them and talked about communicating with them. Then they had insisted that celestials were in charge of physical evolution. Now it was a huge number of planets and dates long ago. Ryan was comfortable with new concepts, dealt with them all the time, but this stuff was really stretching credibility.

"Beyond these seven inhabited galaxies are millions of others that do not yet contain life," Peter said.

Ryan held up his hands and skeptically surveyed his companions, "So, what makes you think you know all about this? Oh, I know, more celestials."

Peter pointed to his book. "In here."

"What is that book anyway?"

"The Cosmic Book."

"That book contains universe truth," Sarah said. "The truth of who you are and why you are. In it are the details of that which we have but touched upon."

"Let's take a look." Ryan motioned for Peter to hand it to him. The bald man hesitated, looked at Sarah, and carefully unwrapped the book. He passed it to Ryan.

Ryan opened the heavy tome and tried to make sense out of its unfamiliar characters. They appeared to be some sort of hieroglyphics. "What language is this?"

Peter and Sarah looked at each other. Then, as though they had taken a collective deep breath, Sarah said, "Ryan, I am going to tell you something that we have divulged to few." Capturing him with her large gray eyes, she continued, "It is most important that you treat this information with respect and not discuss it with anyone until the appropriate time."

Ryan nodded. He did not know Sarah well, but he would not betray her secret.

She glanced at Peter and then back to him, "We are from Phantia."

"Never heard of it."

"It is… another planet."

"Sure. Come on, Sarah. Give it to me straight." He could not resist a small laugh.

"We are from a planet named Phantia. It is a different world, many light-years away."

"Fine. So tell me, where are you really from?" He had trouble getting the words out in a polite tone. This whole thing was degenerating into nonsense and he had little patience with fools.

"Phantia," Sarah said again, pronouncing it like fan-cha. She checked to make sure he heard the word. "Ryan, we are from a different world."

His eyes confirmed that she was the same person he had met a week ago, been with for the past two days — maybe some radical ideas, but otherwise pretty normal. Her words did not compute.

"I knew those crazy ideas had to come from somewhere," he said with a smile. "But, I'm not buying you're from another planet. No way."

"We traveled trillions of miles to get here." Sarah spoke patiently, as if she were a teacher giving him a geography lesson. "We arrived at Harmony less than a year ago and are just now becoming acclimated to your planet."

"You're kidding, right?" His head tilted left. This happened in the movies, in sci-fi books. He couldn't be out here with aliens. His heart raced. "Listen, I've been around, you know. I've traveled all over the world. Met weirder people than you two. I wouldn't have gotten very far if I'd believed stuff like this." He folded his arms across his chest.

In a calm and measured voice, Sarah said, "What I have told you is true. We are not from Earth. We are from Phantia."

As if he was listening to a friend regale him with an implausible story, he folded his hands behind his head, leaned back against a rock, and said, "OK. Where's your spaceship?"

Sarah ignored his question and said: "Earth is undergoing a period of rapid technological evolution, but the normal balance of forces is not present. You possess technology in advance of the proper celestial foundation. This is causing grave imbalances and will lead to a terrible disaster if not corrected.

"Other planets, like Phantia, have been able to navigate through such periods of intense change without self-destructing. That is because we had a cosmic foundation. At home, we found ways to integrate economic abundance and advancing technology with celestial reality, found ways to overcome violence, found ways to advance without destroying our planet or enslaving its people."

Could they indeed be from another planet? If it were true, it would be wonderful. He didn't buy that extraterrestrials were necessarily hostile. Any extraterrestrial able to travel here had to be more advanced than the people on this planet. He thought of the Star Wars movies, the books by Asimov, Bradbury, and Herbert. They'd had friendly extraterrestrials in them. What if his world was on the receiving end of more advanced civilizations' attempts to communicate?

Waiting until she sensed his concentration had returned, Sarah continued, "Sending human teachers to reside on another planet is a most extreme measure. It indicates the precarious situation that has developed here on Earth. It is time for this planet to undergo an awakening and emerge into its rightful place in the cosmos. A wondrous future awaits you, if we are successful. Disaster looms if we are not."

"You're trying to convince me there are humans on other planets, not some sort of reptilian monsters?"

"Most other inhabited planets are home to humans, humanoids if you prefer. For thousands of years, they have visited your planet. Only a few resemble each other as closely as do you and I."

While he heard what Sarah said, what struck him most was that they might be the words of a being from another planet. If what they were saying was true, he was involved in a momentous event — he was having a conversation with someone from another planet.

No one spoke or moved. Ryan could feel their focus on him.

Sarah scooted closer and said, "You have noted the difference in our eyes. Because we have less illumination on Phantia than here on earth, our pupils are larger than yours. Our planet is farther from our sun. Evolution provided us with more sensitive eyes so that we could function there. Other than these small differences, our DNA and genetics are quite similar to yours."

She displayed her right hand. The lotion had been completely absorbed by her smooth delicate skin.

Ryan stared at it.

Sarah said, "Take it."

He hesitated.

"I won't bite you."

Ryan wavered, as if about to play with a friend's pet snake or touch a wild animal. Yet, these five fingers had helped to fix his food, had tended his wounds.

He reached for her hand, took it into his own, and blushed at the foolishness of it. Her skin was like that of a teenage girl, trimmed and natural looking nails, few wrinkles. Fine blonde hair covered the back of her hand.

Her fingers were slightly longer than his, slightly thinner — different, but not the hand of an extraterrestrial from billions of miles away.

Hollywood images flashed across his consciousness, vicious creatures intent on destroying humanity, ghoulish insects feasting on their human captives. He thought about E.T. and Close Encounters and the possibility of friendly extraterrestrials. But those had not looked human, those did not have skin like a teenage girl, and blonde hair.

Still holding Sarah's hand, Ryan asked, "If you're from another planet, how can your DNA and genetics be similar to mine?"

Without attempting to withdraw her hand, she said, "Once you agree that the cosmos is orchestrated and friendly, it is easy to accept that such well designed patterns would be used to produce material beings on many planets. Even humanoids that look different employ the same basic DNA and genetics. Most of them are warm blooded and breath an oxygen and nitrogen mix."

"OK. Your hand's a little different," he said. "Does that prove you're not from Earth?"

"Look at my eyes. Have you ever seen eyes like these in people from this planet?"

"They are a little different." Her large, soft gray eyes had fascinated him from the first. Now, as he scrutinized them, he saw that the irises were larger than any he'd ever seen in a human, large like a deer or cat. They were not unappealing — but they were without question larger than normal. He was amazed that he hadn't studied them until she pointed them out.

"I am from Phantia." Although she spoke in a soft voice, her gaze did not waver.

Ryan remained unconvinced. He looked at her skeptically.

Sarah studied him. He felt that she was reading his doubts.

"Close your eyes." She clasped his hand. "Do not open them until I tell you to." Seeing his reluctance, she said again, "Go ahead. Close your eyes and relax."

At first nothing happened. Just a beautiful woman holding his hand.

Then, in his mind's eye he was at the entrance to Harmony, the two ruddy beehives, the geodesic dome, the impressive facade of Fortress Mesa close behind. Unlike a projected picture this view engaged his peripheral vision and he was able to step within it and glance from side to side. With sudden perceptiveness he understood that he was seeing Harmony through the eyes of another, through Sarah's eyes. Moreover he was able to feel her sense of wonderment at seeing her new home for the first time, wonderment at standing on the surface of a different planet. The realization shocked him, but a sense of calm comforted him. He resolved to follow her lead and squeezed her hand.

The scene changed. He saw Harmony as if he were suspended from a hot air balloon. The scene had a greenish hue as if he were seeing it through night vision goggles like those he had used in Viet Nam. In his mind's eye he glanced about for support, something to hold onto, and tightened his grip on Sarah's hand. He felt her steadiness and relaxed his grasp. He noticed a white-haired man standing before the large hogan, eyes shaded by his raised hand as he looked upward. He felt Sarah's apprehension as she first viewed the bleak desert of her new home.

The scene changed again and he saw the curvature of the planet. He saw it unassisted, as if from an orbiting platform in the full light of day. The continent of North America lay beneath him; the immense globe filled his peripheral vision. Harmony was an indistinct spot somewhere in the beige desert of the Southwest. Thick clouds covered the Midwest; the California coastline touched the radiant blue of the Pacific; the vastness of Canada lay to the north. Like an astronaut seeing his home planet from space, a sense of awe and wonderment filled him. He wished that everyone could have this vision of oneness, land without boundaries, pristine waters, nature untouched by the hand of man.

The globe began to rotate and he viewed the broad expanse of the Pacific, the breadth of Asia, the coastline of Europe, and back to the North American Continent. The planet's beauty startled him. To the casual observer, this celestial gem did not reveal congested cities, or man's steady replacement of the natural with concrete, asphalt, and garbage. Despite his great height and no apparent support, he had no fear of falling. Ryan felt the reassuring grip of Sarah's hand.

A view of Earth as a tiny sphere, blue water, green and brown land, patchy white clouds. A view of the sun surrounded by a starry backdrop. While successive views played across his mind's eye, Ryan felt exhilaration. Earth bound humans could but imagine the view presented to him. Yet here he was, traveling away from Earth as if aboard a spacecraft. His home planet receded into the background and disappeared amongst the fantastic brilliance of the stars.

He saw view after view of star-studded space. Individual stars displayed different intensities and hues, giant red, tiny white. The constellations first appeared as from Earth, then shifted into unrecognized configurations. He had the sensation of motion, but vast distances impeded measurement. Nearby points of light reminded him of cabin lights piercing the darkness of a mountainside. In the distance, the Milky Way, undistorted by atmospheric interference, became a sea of individual suns.

The immensity of the universe struck home, as it had impressed Sarah when first she traversed these vast distances. He could feel her sense of awe and, for the first time, truly appreciate the vast distances between even the nearest stars. Having seen this, he knew he would never again believe that mere chance or blind evolution could create anything so incredible.

His home planet reappeared, blue water, green and brown land, and patchy white clouds. Ryan looked for familiar shapes, but the contours of the oceans and continents were unrecognizable. Then they settled onto the surface of Earth's twin, amid a verdant landscape of rolling emerald hills. In an astonishing flash he understood it all, understood that the things Sarah had been telling him were true.

Eyes moist and hands trembling, Sarah knelt and touched the ground of her beloved home planet for the last time. Then she turned and waved to her children. Ryan felt her emotions as she stood on the rim of her grave — life, as she had known it, was ending as surely as if she were dying. She joined her team in their white robes and entered the craft that would take them to the interstellar transport that waited in orbit.

He glimpsed a sleek craft on an expanse of concrete, obscured by a crowded amphitheater. The companion who held his hand was the center of applause. A young blonde woman in her twenties hugged her with both arms. He felt Sarah's love and understood that this was a daughter she had left behind on Phantia. A small child clung to her leg and cried out in strange words. He felt Sarah's attachment and anguish in his own heart.

Distinguished bald men and blonde haired women addressed his companion and the others in white robes. He recognized Peter Jones standing straight and proud to his right. Others he did not know, but were clearly associates of Sarah's, stood on either side. A shimmering figure appeared and addressed the crowd. Ryan sensed that all the humans in the crowd saw and heard what he knew was a celestial personality. He understood that without Sarah's skill he would not be able to see the celestial, but knew that most people on Phantia possessed her same skill.

He looked up at what appeared to be a slightly smaller sun. It left a chill in the otherwise summery air. In his empathic appreciation, Ryan reveled in the coolness.

Ryan and his companion approached a golf-cart-sized vehicle. With a faint whine, it whisked them to a glass and stone building. Inside women and men scurried about. They acknowledged his companion with strange words. Tables and chairs of unusual materials, tall doors, small windows. The dark-wood trim reminded Ryan of an older office building, something out of the 1930's.

They viewed a zoo-like park filled with all manner of beasts roaming free. Lions, leopards, deer, moose resembled those on Earth. Others were quite different, like the animals of Australia, familiar yet unique. He wanted to stay and understand more of what he was seeing, but the view faded.

They were back on the vehicle. It moved without the noise or smell of an internal combustion engine. Other vehicles, shaped like those that would have been at home on Earth, wound down the busy boulevards of a medium sized town. His sense of smell was more acute than on his home planet. None of the vehicles emitted noxious exhaust.

Views of broad city streets with modest landscaped homes, each a different bright color. Each building was unique, many dis-

the structure of the rock, its atoms and their arrangement. He knew that most of this heavy object was vacuity, but could not understand how space felt so solid against the skin of his hand. This common rock gave new meaning to the phrase, "things are not always as they appear."

He reached out to touch the bark of a nearby juniper and pulled a few berries from its branch and examined them. He looked at his clothes and noticed the tear where the yucca had pierced his leg and the ragged threads around the hole. He touched the bandage on his hand and felt the soreness beneath.

With a new appreciation for things he did not previously understand, he looked back at Sarah and Peter and asked, "How did you get here?"

"In a space craft," Peter replied.

"The pictions I showed you were a replay of my voyage," Sarah said.

Ryan digested the information and asked, "Where is the spaceship now?"

"After we arrived at your world and had a chance to become acclimated, it was returned to its home planet. You see, we came in transportation piloted by another race, a people billions of years older than my people or yours.

"We could not let a spaceship capable of transporting humans so similar to yourselves fall into the wrong hands," Peter said.

"The last thing this planet needs is more technology to pull it away from what is important," Sarah added.

"What is the name of the place," he asked. "The name of the place you're from?"

"The planet is called Phantia. The city you saw is called Ur'Geay."

"Most people imagine that extra —" He looked at his companions and stumbled over the word. "Extraterrestrials are hostile and very different than us."

"When crashed extraterrestrial spacecraft have been recovered, their passengers have been treated as hostile," Sarah said. "Most were killed."

"In times past they might have been revered as gods," Peter said.

Ryan was keenly aware that very human-like extraterrestrials uttered these words about other space travelers.

"That your world has been visited by material beings from other planets makes our situation easier in some ways," Sarah said, "but only if your people are told the whole truth, only if they can be convinced that we are friendly."

"The way in which people have been taught to fear and hate extraterrestrials makes our presence here very difficult," Peter said.

"The pervasiveness of ridicule surrounding UFOs and extra-terrestrials is one of the major accomplishments of the covert community and their affiliates in the media," Sarah added.

He had known from the beginning that Sarah and Peter were presenting him with a new way of seeing things. At first he had resisted, now he felt like an open can of sardines. What he had just experienced was incredible, the most incredible thing that had ever happened to him in his life. Before he had merely believed, now he knew. He also knew it would change him, change him forever. He saw that his blank sheet contained a distinct image — the blue water, green and brown land, and patchy white clouds of a distant planet.

Exhausted he closed his eyes.

Courage is being scared to death and saddling up anyway.

— JOHN WAYNE

SIX

Sarah arose and wandered nearby. It required a while to recover from the emotional strain of reconnecting to her former life. This was the first time she had used her pictioning skill to recall these vivid memories for another.

She had felt Ryan's stress as she pictioned her journey for him, and as he had come to realize that she really was an extraterrestrial. She had also felt his empathy for her and what she had left behind.

Depending on his actions from this point forward, they might become friends. She hoped that Ryan would see the pictioning session for what it was. Too many earth dwellers had misinterpreted contacts with extraterrestrials as abductions, as something distasteful.

She thought back to her arrival at her adopted planet, just over a year ago. In those days she was known as J'Li D'Rona.

'*Where are we?*' She had communicated to the spacecraft's commander. J'Li was quite sure he was at the ship's controls which were located in a separate section of the spaceship. The atmosphere there was slightly different, controlled for his comfort and that of his crew.

'*Near the planet's moon,*' the commander replied in a similar mind-to-mind format. Without this ability the myriad languages of the universe would present a considerable obstacle.

'*Please report our position,*' she communicated. Her message would inform those on her former home planet of her progress. Somehow this frail connection fortified her. If everything worked out, she would soon be on her new world, would begin a second life.

She paused and considered the fact that she had rematerialized. Her brain was working. She turned her head and looked around. Everything seemed as it had before. Yet now she and this ship were light years away from her old home planet. As they left orbit about Phantia, they had dematerialized and transported across trillions of miles. Now she was material again and near her new home. She had been told that interstellar space flight with its dematerialization and rematerilaization was not without its risks, particularly for humanoids of her type.

She flexed the muscles in her body. Each felt weak, useless. Unable to release the restraining mechanism of her couch, she lay back and sniffed the sterile air of the chamber. She could hardly wait for the fragrant bouquet of her new terrestrial life. Would their food be interesting? Would she ever again taste the wondrous flavor of orinfs? Would it be at all like her former home? What about flowers? Would there be romms?

In a few minutes, she tried the restraint again. This time the mechanism yielded. Standing, she stretched, flicked on overhead lighting, and congratulated herself that their interstellar trip had been successful. Her memories of that portion of the trip were like a series of snapshots. She wished she had been able to absorb more of the incredible experience of traversing the trillions of miles from Phantia.

She stripped out of the garment she had worn for the trip and picked up her new garb. The clothes had been fashioned on Phantia. They were meant to resemble those worn by earth dwellers, to last until she could acquire replacements on the planet below.

She reached for the handle of her door with some trepidation. When she opened it, her second-in-command, H'Df, lay crumpled at her feet. Blood covered the front of his robe. Pained eyes looked up to her. She stooped to feel his pulse — it was weak. She pushed the emergency call on his belt, caressed the side of his face, and went to check on the others.

In addition to H'Df, one other member of her team had been fatally injured during rematerialization. They were taken to a special room on the ship where they underwent spontaneous decomposition. The crew and surviving members of her team had stood by and wished them a wondrous Journey.

A third Phantian, now known as Peter Jones, had suffered severe nerve and muscle damage. Although his mind remained sharp, Peter's voluntary muscular functions were far from normal. Forced to dematerialize again as they orbited their new home, he had remained that way for months.

Now, amid the rocks and trees of Earth's desert she looked at her companion from Phantia. Their regimen of exercise and massage, begun as soon as they were fully rematerialized at Harmony, had worked wonders. Peter was eighty percent cured. If she could get him into the hands of an experienced physical therapist, she believed that he would be restored to his former self. In the meantime, they would struggle across this desert and hope that the INS did not catch them.

Any interrogation was sure to reveal their origins. They did not possess the distortion skill of an earth dweller. Then they would be killed or turned over to covert agencies and forced to cooperate in their nefarious work. Peter and she had learned from the experience of other extraterrestrials to fear the consequences of being apprehended. They needed to deliver their message, to make contact with more people like Ryan Drake.

'*We are far from our days at the academy,*' she communicated to Peter without words.

'*Those days seem idyllic,*' Peter responded with a smile.

Since his injury communicating mind-to-mind was the easiest way to express himself. From a complete invalid he had begun to function normally, to walk, and to speak English. She was proud of the conversations he had initiated with Ryan Drake, proud that he was traversing the desert.

As a girl of seven she had gone to the desert with her class from school. It was their first overnight excursion, two hours away from her home in Ur'Geay.

They had all enjoyed climbing the soft sand of the dunes and rolling down their sides. It did not matter that sand got in her shoes and clothing. It was sheer freedom and delight for the twenty children. Even her teacher had joined in the fun.

Then they played a game of conceal and hunt. The teacher volunteered to be the hunter. She told the children to hide in the sand and she would try to find them.

As their day ended, the teacher assembled her class for the trip home. Sarah and the others lined up and the teacher counted: eighteen. Two were missing. The teacher told the children to stay with their chaperones and went off to find the missing two, twin boys — they were always in trouble for something. She returned as darkness began to set in, without the twins.

"Did any of you see where the boys went?" the teacher asked. The teacher went through the group asking when each child had last seen the boys, but no one had hidden near them nor had they seen where they had run to.

When at last she came to J'Li, the youngster said, "I know where they are. I saw them in my head."

The teacher studied her for a time. "You are young to possess the skill, but it is possible. Tell me."

"They are in our vehicle, over there," J'Li said. And she had been right.

Sarah smiled at that old memory. After that incident she had begun the training for remote viewing and pictioning, the youngest to have ever done so. Now as she studied her surroundings, she wished she were back on the safety of Phantia.

She looked at Ryan Drake again. Her celestial-allies had told her that he would become her protector. She could not envision how that might happen, but she would know when that moment came. She blinked to clear her thoughts. First they needed to complete their trek across the mesa.

Sarah closed her eyes and quieted her mental processes. She saw that the INS search party had found their rendezvous place with the llamas near the old mine. They were now spread out searching for the fugitives' tracks.

"INS come." Cody said in a quiet voice.

Ryan opened his eyes to see the Navajo kneeling beside him

Sarah stood nearby and motioned for quiet. To the west, he heard the drone of a small airplane.

Ryan jumped up, rolled up his sleeping bag, and handed it to the Navajo. He grabbed Boomer's rope and they started off through the trees.

He'd been to another world. What he'd seen and felt had been as real as if he'd been there physically. He was positive it had not been a dream. He was in the company of aliens, extraterrestrials. Sarah and Peter had crossed trillions of miles of space to get here. Now what?

He had read about UFO's and purported abductions and had wondered about the hostility attributed to extraterrestrials. Amid all the confusing and contradictory news reports, the sci-fi books, movies and TV, it was impossible to know what was true. Government bureaucrats had admitted to past lies about terrible things that happened during the cold war — nerve gas experiments, radiation tests on orphans, mind control investigations. Now he understood that someone had lied about their knowledge of extraterrestrials, created an enemy where none existed. If they had lied about such an important thing, what else were they capable of?

Ryan tried to picture himself as part of Peter and Sarah's orchestrated and friendly cosmos. As one person on a single planet out of many, could he be significant? The Phantians had traveled trillions of miles to get to Earth — someone regarded this remote planet as important.

Ben Tsotsie had helped to set him up to encounter these extraterrestrial visitors. Why? How much did Ben know?

Late afternoon, they descended a steep trail off the top of the mesa and into a narrow gorge. Someone had strung camouflage netting between the vertical sides of the rocks. It had not been in place too many days, as the ground underneath had tufts of erect grass and bushes with healthy leaves. Exhausted, Peter slumped to the ground.

Cody cautioned them, "Remain under net. Peter rest. Then travel to Lobo's ranch."

"The INS search party followed our tracks up the side of the mesa and they found Cody's hunting camp," Sarah said to Ryan. "They discovered where we had buried our trash and now they're convinced they are on the right trail. If we are intercepted out here and our origins discovered, no one will question our disappearance into some secret government facility. I also thought you should know, they've issued a $25,000 reward for our capture."

Ryan said, "Great, now we'll have everybody looking for us."

"We cannot risk interrogation," Peter stammered. "We need to tell many people about the cosmic paradigm, before the authorities discover who we are."

Ryan looked at the two extraterrestrials. In a contorted sort of way, it was all rather funny. Here he was, in the middle of the desert with two extraterrestrials, one who stumbled and stuttered, fleeing from federal agents. What a great story for the folks back home. Who would believe?

The man in the wheelchair watched the others and waited. They had gathered in Washington, DC for a series of critical meetings. Earlier others had been linked with them by a conference call that included people from six countries.

Tall windows in the conference room faced onto K Street, but revealed only the brick and glass of the building across the street. The windows were a special triple pane that effectively shut out all noise as well as any external listening devices.

The other walls of the room were decorated with paintings commissioned by the men who used this room. They depicted various activities — a movie shoot, an aircraft manufacturing plant, the floor of the New York Stock Exchange, a military battlefield, a boy on a bicycle delivering newspapers, a modern hospital operating room, and an offshore drilling platform.

In one corner of the room, Jonathan Olson spoke into a cell phone. The investment-banking arm of his multi-national financial empire was brokering the merger between a major United States bank and one in Japan. Ten years ago he had served as Treasury Secretary.

Dark-suited men in their sixties and seventies sat around the long conference table. He had known most of them for twenty years, some longer. He knew them well enough to know that they all considered themselves elitists, a cut above "commoners."

They were discussing the printed page that had been distributed in anticipation of the afternoon sessions. The title at the top of the page read, CONGRESS.

Ernest Steiger glanced at the eight names on the sheet.

Directly across from him was Oliver Vanderbush. The sun-tanned sailor from Beverly Hills headed America's largest conglomerate producing recorded music, films, and television programs. Seated next to him, Seymour Naughton, at eighty-seven the oldest man in the room, was honored by Madison Avenue as its preeminent image-maker. Down the table was Warren Ophir, from the Defense Intelligence Agency. He was in deep conversation with James R. W. Smith, a key man at Britain's largest newspaper and publishing conglomerate, but not its owner. To practice media management one did not need to own newspapers, one needed only to control their sources of information, to control what got printed and when, and in some cases to control editorial policy.

Ernest Steiger eyes came to rest on a young man in his late thirties, John deBeque. He sat between two men and answered their queries. Although he was young, the older men treated him with respect. The wheel-chaired man liked deBeque. He could say that about few people. Unlike his own inept children, this young man was ruthless as well as smart, comfortable around men of immense influence, willing to carry out their orders without question. Ordinary people were like cattle, willing to be led. John deBeque was far from ordinary.

His eldest son, Richard, had brought deBeque home from Harvard one Thanksgiving — his own family had been unable to fund a trip back to California. After that weekend, he had taken a particular interest in the lad. When deBeque's parents died in an automobile accident, he provided the young man funds and paved the way to graduate school. When he graduated, Steiger arranged for a series of jobs within his publishing empire. When the top spot in their Washington-based organization became available, Steiger had recommended the young man and introduced him to the others. After a careful screening, they had seconded his suggestion.

"Does anyone have questions?" Olson asked when he disconnected from his call. His presence had been requested because of his friendship with the first man on the list.

"Anyone have an update on Williams's standing?" Steiger asked the group. His Midwest accented words were direct, spoken as if he wished to waste no time with the affairs of lesser men.

"According to our latest poll, he is leading by nineteen percent," Smith volunteered. Although his organization was based in London, it owned several newspapers in the United States.

"Shit," Steiger said. "That's worse than the latest numbers I saw from my people."

"We have seen to it that the polls don't show how well he really is doing," Warren Ophir smiled. His ingenuous smile had deceived many, adversary and friend. Ophir was this group's primary connection to the intelligence community and its labyrinth of affiliates.

Steiger said, "I trust that none of us are actively supporting his candidacy." He noted that two men further down his side of the table looked away in answer to his implied query. He suspected that they had seen the election moving away from their candidate and were busy currying favor in Williams's camp.

"We could always leak some of the interesting things we've collected," Ophir laughed. The others around the table chuckled and nodded. The man from covert operations was famous within the group for digging up dirt, real or fabricated.

When the murmurs died down, Olson said to John deBeque, "Show Mr. Williams in." The group's lobbyist and its only public spokesman rose and went to the room's tall double doors. John deBeque ushered a man of regal bearing into the room. He indicated that their guest should take the seat at the head of the table.

Steiger had studied Leonard Williams's recent statements. Some of his proposed programs conflicted with their agenda and he had a history of catering to certain "marginal factions" in his home state. If he won, he would most certainly require a reminder of today's proceedings. Like most politicians, it was hard to judge how he would behave after assuming a new position.

It would have been so much easier if the incumbent had a chance of being re-elected. However, he had foolishly insisted on pushing his conservative agenda without compromise. The commoners in his home state saw the Senator's programs benefiting his contributors at their expense. Now they had a chance to retaliate and Steiger had no doubt that their angry voices would be heard in a little over two weeks.

"Good evening gentlemen," the candidate addressed the group. "This is a most unexpected pleasure." He acknowledged Jonathan Olson with a surprised look. Williams glanced at each face. From the way he nodded to some, it was obvious that he knew a few of the men around the table, but not all. It was also obvious that he was uncomfortable that he had not been invited to shake hands with everyone. Williams had taken crucial time away from his campaign to make this unscheduled visit. Until this moment, he had believed he was meeting with deBeque to straighten out a minor glitch in his campaign funding.

Steiger enjoyed these biannual meetings. What was this? Oh yes, his seventeenth. The election of candidates from either political party worked out almost as well for the affiliates. The Republicans catered to the wealthy and turned their heads as big businesses merged and prospered, an important element in their game plan. The Democrats kept the masses happy and tended to consolidate power in Washington, another important factor in the scheme. The important thing was to keep things moving in the right direction. Tying up key candidates like Williams was essential.

"Leonard, let me come right to the point," Olson addressed his friend. They knew each other from real estate transactions, before Williams's entry into politics. "As you are aware, the bulk of the funds this group has committed to you are in, shall we say, escrow."

The candidate started to say something, but held his comment. He realized that the men at this table and their network of wealthy individuals and political action committees controlled a major portion of his remaining funds, and probably the funds of his opponent. The campaign was entering its final weeks when spending for television spots was at its peak. Without their funds, his candidacy would have little or no media exposure in these final days. The group had withheld its money until this moment of maximum leverage and Williams knew it.

"We wish to discuss certain actions you will take, if you are elected," Olson said. He chose his words carefully. From deBeque's briefing, the group knew the candidate was a man with a memory for details.

"I thought we'd discussed the conditions of your money. We had a deal." Williams glanced at deBeque. To date the young man had been his only contact with this group. "My god, the election is two weeks away."

"You will undoubtedly be appointed to one of the armed services oversight sub-committees," Olson said. "These committees regularly hold secret hearing. You will make the transcripts from those hearings available to us."

"What do you mean us?"

"To this group." Olson motioned to the others around the table.

"But they're secret."

"This group has received such information since 1950," Olson said. What he did not say was that this group as well as the covert community already had their own people in each federal agency and the information being requested would probably duplicate what they would already know. What no one voiced was the real reason for today's meeting: Compromising a potential political adversary.

Steiger saw the candidate's face register apprehension and comprehension.

"Your opponent, the incumbent, agreed, prior to being elected six years ago." Olson motioned and deBeque placed a two-page document in front of Williams. "This document will memorialize our understanding. You will also note that we will inform you about particular votes we wish cast."

After the candidate carefully scrutinized the pages, he raised his eyes to stare at the men around the table. "You people think this is some kind of a game. Well it's not. Peoples' lives, our country is at stake. You want to sell this information, leak it out. I have the right to vote my conscience. I won't be part of it."

When the candidate offered the pages back to deBeque, Steiger decided that the man simply did not understand who ran the country. Soon after he was elected, he would find out how powerless he really was.

John deBeque did not receive the pages. "We do not wish to

withhold our money, but —" He shrugged his shoulders and offered Williams a pen.

The candidate, still holding the pages, studied the men around the table. They returned his gaze with cold, unswerving eyes. Their faces said nothing, as they awaited the final act of a man already condemned. When Leonard Williams finally accepted the pen offered by deBeque, the wheel-chaired man could not resist a thin smile.

"As far as we are concerned, this meeting never took place," Olson addressed his old friend. "You never met with any of us."

After Williams retreated from the room, a House candidate from New York was invited to the seat at the head of the table.

Sarah found Ryan pacing under the camouflage. She said, "The INS men are coming this direction."

"How's he doing?" Ryan Drake motioned to the dozing Phantian. Peter lay on his air mattress, head propped on his backpack. He had fallen asleep as soon as they stopped to rest.

"Peter is healthier than he appears." Sarah rubbed the yellowish lotion on her bare arms. "His condition is due to the rematerialization process we underwent. He is much improved, compared to when we first arrived here."

"Tell me about him."

"Peter was my mentor at the Principal Academy of Phantia. It is one of the most prestigious places for studies on the planet and Peter was one of its major attractions. He had a staff who researched and helped prepare his lectures."

"What did he lecture about?"

"History. He knew more about the technological and economic history of our planet than anyone. Like your world, our history is shrouded in mystery — particularly as one goes further back."

"But I thought celestials were in charge. Surely they know all about your history. Weren't they there when it happened?"

"Part of the material experience is allowing mortals to discover for themselves. Just as on your planet, we have astronomers, physicists, chemists, and biotechnologists. We also have an economic system. The difference is that Phantia has moved through the era when economics dominated our planet. Economics is now subservient to the well being of all; it is a tool, not an end in itself. Peter had researched how this had all evolved, how we had arrived at a stabilized plateau. You see it was not always so peaceful on Phantia. In olden times we too had wars."

"Tell me more about Peter."

"Like me, Peter's long-time mate is dead. He has a son, an archeologist, who looks like he will follow his father. Peter grew up in the southern hemisphere of our planet in a place call Eth'Pa. As he was growing up, his culture was just being elevated to the planet-wide economic norm. He was among the first to attend a technological institution of any kind.

"I did not meet him until much later, after he was already famous. As the story goes, he was an instant sensation at the Academy. No one expected a child from a backward area to be brilliant. Peter turned out to be a child prodigy. He mastered various areas of technology before he was sixteen. But his real love was history. He was determined to find out the why and how behind technology and its development. Once he dug up the evidence he began to speak out.

"Peter developed the ability to enthrall an audience. He was really quite a performer, kept people mesmerized for hours about economics and its interplay with technology. Can you imagine traveling half way around your planet to listen to an historian? Well Phantians did. Peter was a celebrity."

"How old is he?"

"Peter is seventy-eight of your years?"

"He looks about forty or fifty."

Sarah smiled, "Before you ask, I am sixty-six."

"I don't believe it. You look about thirty six."

"Thank you. I will take that as a compliment."

"So how does this rematerialization stuff work?"

"I don't fully understand it. It is not a technology that Phantians possess. As I said, we came in the spaceship of another planet, the Albians. They have been doing it for millions of years. I came through it fine. Two of our companions died."

"I'd like to know more about it."

"Ryan, there is something more important than how we got here." Sarah's large gray eyes held him. "In case the INS captures us, I want you to know about it — so you will understand *why* we sacrificed so much to be here."

"I have been wondering about that."

Ryan was nervous as he envisioned their pursuers racing across the mesa toward them. They had not spoken of it, but the INS search team was surely getting closer.

Sarah said, "You need to know about the organization of the cosmos, about the complex hierarchy of celestial beings. The mortals of your world have trouble perceiving this vast organization because it operates at a higher level. However, as illusive as it may seem, it is very real."

"And extraterrestrials are a part of it?"

"I know it's confusing," Sarah said. "Extraterrestrials — anyone not born on this planet — may be either mortal or celestial.

"The mortal extraterrestrials who visit this planet come from civilizations much more advanced than Phantia's or yours. Although they are not celestials, they have the ability to dematerialize their spaceships — that makes them invisible to you. This has contributed to the mystery surrounding their scattered appearances."

Ryan nodded that he had heard, not that he necessarily understood what she had said.

"Celestials are found throughout the cosmos. They create and supervise galaxies as well as assist us."

"Hold on. You telling me some kind of invisible beings go out and create galaxies?"

"Yes, celestial beings with unique personalities and fantastic powers command the forces of creation and evolution," Sarah replied. "There are others who rule this vast creation. After your trip to Phantia, do you still believe that the delicate balance of planets and stars is maintained without periodic adjustments, without intelligent controls?" She saw the question on his face and said, "There is a gravity controller, a celestial-being, who manages the gravity forces of the sun and its surrounding planets, including Earth's. A corps of celestial beings has been on Earth since its beginning."

Ryan focused on her stunning gray eyes. They were surrounded by tiny wrinkles in her tawny skin as she concentrated on forming the unfamiliar English words.

"The functioning of the universe of time and space requires the integral working of an almost infinite number of celestial beings," Sarah said. "Without them there would be chaos.

"The celestial beings on this sphere report to the sovereign of this local group of inhabited planets who in turn reports to the galactic rulers, and so on to the Central Nucleus of the cosmos."

"So the universe isn't democratic?"

"No. Nor is it a republic or a federation. The same celestials control the universe today who have been in charge for billions of years. In many cases they were created for this sole function. No mere mortal would ever be allowed to administer something so precious."

"Okay, so the universe is organized by celestials," Ryan said. "I think I can buy that. And I accept that you and Peter are good guys, good mortals, but there must be some bad ones. Everything I've read and heard about aliens —"

"Your people are extrapolating from their own violent history. The universe is organized under a system of lawfully administered celestial control," Sarah said. "Other planets function in harmony with this celestial scheme."

"The people I saw on Phantia?"

"Everyone on Phantia knows about the administration of the universe by celestials. The celestial you saw on Phantia is the ruler of my former world. The peace and tranquility of that planet is due to his wise guidance. The darkness and confusion of Earth is the exception.

"Maybe this will help you understand the celestial organization. Consider the number and type of organizations you have in this country — government, commercial, educational, social." She waited until Ryan nodded, acknowledging her statement. "Think of the millions of people involved in these tasks in your country alone. Now expand that to the organizations involved worldwide. Then multiply that by a cosmos filled with inhabited worlds. Celestial beings control every one of these spheres and attend the individuals on them. It is indeed vast. The celestial hierarchy in charge of our galaxy is centered at the heart of the Milky Way."

"In a black hole? Don't they exist on clouds?"

"No clouds. No black hole. Celestial beings are domiciled on material spheres."

"If celestials control everything, why don't they swoop in and take charge?"

"No celestial-being can challenge your free choice," Sarah said. "It is a cosmic edict. You must care for yourself, and your world. How you do it, is up to you."

"Why are extraterrestrials interested in Earth?"

"Mortals from other planets are interested in the welfare of a sister planet. We worry that this world will destroy itself by misusing powerful technologies such as nuclear or those reverse-engineered from crashed extraterrestrial spaceships. The universe is interconnected. What happens on this planet affects all."

Ryan reached for his water bottle and took a long drink. "So, you risked your life to bring this information to Earth?"

Frustration showing, Sarah said, "I am sorry that you do not grasp the importance of the cosmic paradigm, the changes it will cause, the promise it holds."

"I see esoteric ideas. I don't see their practical application."

"Let me try this another way. Can you agree that your astronomers don't have an explanation for how your planet came to be?" Sarah asked.

"They have theories."

"But that's all they are, theories. Does the Big Bang theory explain everything, or are even your own scientists beginning to challenge it? How much of the total mass of the universe do these theories account for? Does random evolution or chaos theory explain how DNA was created from basic chemicals?"

"They're theories. They're not perfect."

"For a moment open yourself to the possibility that there are celestials controlling the Milky Way Galaxy, beings that keep things stable, beings that bring life to planets. Open yourself to the possibility that this planet is part of a orchestrated and friendly universe teaming with similarly controlled planets, all supervised by higher, wiser powers."

"After that trip yesterday, I'm pretty open, but I still don't see the practical side of it —"

The buzzing of an airplane interrupted his words. They watched as it flew into the narrow canyon, circled where the gorge widened, and returned toward the west. Had it zeroed in on their hiding spot?

Sarah went to check on Peter.

Ryan popped an antacid tablet into his mouth and wandered off toward the rock lip overlooking the canyon. His mind drifted, inspecting the rock face for a possible escape route, thinking about what Sarah had said, worrying about Peter and the INS pursuers.

Ordinarily Ryan would have enjoyed a drink. He was convinced it calmed him in situations like this, besides he liked the taste of bourbon and water. But he found he had no desire for alcohol.

He glanced at his Avocet. He was surprised to see the elevation reading at: 06720. The Mesa's top had slanted down as they came east plus they had descended from its top and into the protection of a ravine at the head of a gorge. He peered at the valley's narrow floor, a thousand feet below, but saw no trail. The upper walls of the canyon were smooth and unbroken. To get down, they would have to negotiate three hundred feet of sheer rock face.

To the east, where the gorge widened, a small stream appeared out of the shadows before disappearing into the desert beyond the mouth of the canyon. Sunlight, reflecting off its surface, created a silver serpent. Within the valley, patches of green grass and cottonwoods contrasted with the surrounding desert soil. Although the sun was still high, the southern cliffs and the canyon's floor lay in shadows — dim enough that a satellite photo might not disclose a hiking party. Close observation by an airplane was another matter.

A hawk circled below him, riding the gorge's thermals, hunting breakfast. In ever decreasing circles the graceful bird closed in on its prey until it swooped. A few moments later, it climbed over Ryan's head, a fuzzy gray ball in its talons. This sparked an old memory.

Many years ago, before his father sent him away to boarding school, Sam Wellborn and he had trudged through snow in an open field near St. Louis; each had a 22. A fuzzy gray streak leapt from cover. His friend spun and got off a shot before the rabbit disappeared over the hill. They ran up the slope, laughing and shouting, feet churning the white powder. When they popped over the top, the gray streak took off again. Ryan took two shots before it departed over another rise. "Lucky we aren't hunting dinner," Sam had snickered. They had laughed and enjoyed the sunny winter day.

His boyhood friend was now the campaign manager for the leading Presidential contender. At Sam's request, Ryan had agreed to allow Sanitas to be used as the site for a campaign stop. When he returned to work, one of the first things he needed to do was be sure everything was prepared for Carlton Boyle's visit.

There is one great and universal wish of mankind expressed in all religions, in all art and philosophy, and in all human life: the wish to pass beyond himself as he now is.

— BEATRICE HINKLE

SEVEN

It was almost dusk by the time they slipped to the edge of the cliff. Cody showed Ryan the piton he had hammered into the rock to the left of the water that trickled into the gorge. The Navajo had fed a long rope through a carabiner attached to the piton.

Sarah and Ryan carried full packs along with water and snacks. Peter carried a small pack with his personal items. Cody had the Phantians' other things. They left the two llamas tethered under the camouflage. The camping gear and emergency supplies remained with them.

Sarah told them quietly that the INS search team was getting close, but the airplane had not spotted them. Their pursuers had fanned out to find possible descents from the top of the mesa. Two men were following the tracks south, but had not caught up with Teddy and his llama.

Cody told them that the first part of the hike would be the most difficult. It was too steep to see below as the Navajo disappeared over the side. Ryan kept the rope taut enough to ensure that he could arrest a fall before any serious damage occurred.

Sarah stepped over and helped Ryan feed the rope. "How is your hand?"

"This isn't going to be fun, but I can do it." He flexed his injured hand.

Sarah went next. They attached the upper end of the rope to her belt. Cody controlled her descent from below while Ryan rested his hand. Sarah's cat-like athletic ability showed. She descended as fast as the Navajo fed her rope.

Cody raised a knotted end of the rope back to the carabiner and Ryan made a harness for Peter. Ryan helped the bald extraterrestrial scoot to the edge of the cliff. Then he jerked twice on the dangling rope and eased Peter over the edge. Sarah and Cody lowered him.

Ryan waited impatiently. He expected the INS at any moment. Lowering Peter took almost a half-hour.

Finally Cody raised the rope and Ryan started his descent. Each grasp of the rock with his right hand was painful. Cody and Sarah fed him rope and he searched for handholds.

Ryan heard the llamas twitter. He grabbed at a protruding rock, lost his grip, and sailed into space. He groped for another hold but the face of the cliff had angled away. Unable to cry out, he tried swinging himself, but only banged his sore hand onto rock that was closer than he thought. While the llamas twittered anew, he dangled from a rope attached to a single piton in a rock seventy-five feet above.

He had scrutinized the gorge and noted the smooth face of the cap rock. He suspected that it had been worn smooth by an occasional cloudburst that dumped water over the side of the Mesa at this low spot. He had also noted a frightening lack of ledges or cracks, a necessary component of rock climbing. Now, as he was experiencing it up close, he wondered why Cody had chosen to descend in this particular place, and what narrow shelf the others rested on.

Cody and Sarah lowered him a few feet. He found a protrusion and grabbed on. Like the experienced mountain climber he was, he used the smallest crack or outcropping to secure a hold for a foot or hand. In a few minutes he joined the others and found himself standing beneath a substantial overhang. Wind and water had sculpted a large cave in the face of the Mesa. The Anasazi had built dwellings here. Now they were reduced to crumbling adobe bricks.

The Navajo undid the knot from one end of the rope and quietly pulled the dangling length upward. After it passed through the carabiner, it fell to their level with a whoosh and a thud.

Darkness enveloped them as they descended the narrow trail, Peter in front with Cody. Ryan used his right hand for balance and clutched the cliff with the other. Sarah crept ahead, but the rock face often obscured his view of her. Since the trail was hidden by the rock overhang, Cody whispered that they could use their flashlights.

This would have been so much easier in broad daylight. On the other hand, their timing had probably saved them from discovery by the INS's airplane. Now the shadows hid them.

The trail's surface, worn smooth by the wind, was only two feet wide. In places it appeared to have been hand-chiseled from the sandstone. The ancient inhabitants had used it to bring food and water to their cave dwelling. Ryan imagined the dropoff, inches from his right foot. This was as tough as any of Colorado's fourteeners — he had not attempted any of those at night.

Sarah eased forward. The pale braid looped over her pack was her most visible feature. She had fastened her hat to her belt. He lost sight of her as she scooted around the next bulge in the cliff.

Suddenly he heard sliding and scraping. Then, "Help! Help!" He heard something smash onto the rocks below.

He rushed forward, edging around the corner of the cliff, but could see no sign of Sarah or her flashlight — the trail had taken an abrupt drop.

He spotted her white braid dangling off the edge of the cliff.

"Hurry. I'm slipping," she screamed.

Ryan stepped forward, lost his footing on the slippery gravel, and landed on his backpack. Scraping along the rock face, his left hand clawed for a hold. A jagged rock tore into his left thigh and almost bounced him off the ledge. He found a crack, stabbed his fingers into it, and held on. His skidding stopped, not far from Sarah. He braced himself, left foot against the cliff.

With his right hand he grabbed her left arm. "Gotcha!" He yelled, "Grab my leg." He felt taunt muscles straining beneath the skin of her slim arm. An excruciating burn caused his right hand to tremble.

Her hand groped for his leg and grabbed on. "Got it," she said and exhaled. He squeezed her arm as tight as his damaged hand would allow.

"I'll scoot back."

Ryan extended his leg. But his boot slipped and he slid forward on loose sand. Without warning, he was on his back. The entire lower half of his body dangled into empty space. Only his left hand's grip on the rock knob prevented the two of them from falling hundreds of feet into the gorge.

Sarah screamed. His clutch on her arm and her grasp on his leg were all that stood between her and a terminal fall.

"Oh shit!" he muttered. "Hold tight." Adrenaline pumping, he flexed his arm and inched his body back up the narrow trail. He almost passed out from the pain in the hand that held Sarah's arm.

Swinging his left leg back onto the trail, he wedged his foot into a narrow crack in the rock face and pushed backward until he felt relatively secure.

"That's as far as I can go." Sweat drenched his shirt. "You'll have to pull yourself up." Breathing hard, he thanked God for those workouts at the health club.

Sarah inched her body up over the edge and with a small cry rolled over his leg and onto the trail. He sensed her whole body heaving and knew she was crying with relief. Her pack had fallen into the canyon.

He relaxed his clasp on her arm and moved to hold her hand. She grasped it, felt the bandage, and relaxed her grip. He lay back, his foot planted, both hands throbbing.

"What happened?" Cody's voice floated up to them. He was a hundred yards down the trail and did not need to shout. His voice echoed in the quiet of the narrow canyon.

"Sarah fell over the side," Ryan said in a low voice, "but she's okay."

"I come back?"

"No. Stay there."

Sarah held on with both hands. At that moment she did not seem like a wise extraterrestrial messenger, only a frightened woman. Ryan tried to imagine what she must have been feeling:

light-years from home, trekking across the remote desert of a strange planet, dependent on strangers to keep her safe. And now, an almost fatal fall.

When her breathing returned to normal, she relaxed her hold.

With his encouragement, she released his leg and reached for the solid rock of the cliff. She turned and sat up with her back against it, but continued to hold his hand.

"Trail wider here," Cody said.

"Go ahead, we'll be along in a minute." Ryan swung his legs around and sat up. They perched in darkness. Both flashlights and Sarah's backpack were at the bottom of the gorge.

Sarah was about to say something, but Ryan stopped her. Audible over his own heavy breathing, he heard the echo of voices from above. He put his finger to his lips, hoping she would see it and not speak.

She squeezed his hand; he squeezed back. In the dim light, her eyes glistened and he could make out the curve of her mouth. He wanted to kiss her, hold her, and make her feel safe.

Sarah returned his gaze, but then pulled back.

He had the distinct impression that he had heard her say, "Thank you." But he was positive her lips had not moved.

The voices from above became louder. "I heard them," a throaty voice said."

"They went this way," a different man said. "See the piton."

"Call Morgan. Tell him we need climbing gear and rope, lots of rope."

With his free hand, Ryan brushed loose rocks off the trail and over the side — a pebble waterfall echoed down the gorge. He stood on the narrow trail, gave a gentle tug, and pulled Sarah to her feet. They had no time to recover.

After a few deep breaths, she whispered, "I'm okay. Let's go."

She scooted sideways along the ledge. Taking a tentative step, she whispered, "I can walk the rest of the way." She released his hand.

At that moment a loud voice from the top of the cliff yelled, "This is the United States Immigration and Naturalization Service. You are ordered to stop or we'll shoot."

Ryan and Sarah flattened themselves against the rock wall.

Powerful flashlights played off the cliff above and below them.

Remembering that he had not seen the trail when he had looked into the gorge from the top, Ryan turned to Sarah and whispered, "Let me go first." He eased himself around her.

"Give yourselves up or we'll shoot."

Ryan halted, but the lights shown nowhere near him. He moved ahead.

"Last chance. Stop or we'll shoot."

Ryan stopped again. He was now fairly sure the men above had no idea where they were, or even how long ago they had departed the camp.

Bang! Bang! Bang! The sound of pistol fire echoed in the canyon. Ryan heard bullets ricochet off the cliff wall, but they were far from his position. The INS was firing indiscriminately, hoping to scare them into surrendering.

He felt a hand on his shoulder and froze. "Keep moving," Sarah said. "They do not know where we are."

A new voice from above said in a quieter tone, "Hey, Viejo. Cut it out. You have no idea what you're shooting at."

A harsh argument echoed down the gorge behind them. In two hundred yards, they caught up with Cody and Peter and to everyone's relief the trail became easier.

"I hope it takes them a while to get a rope," Ryan said to Cody. The fugitives stumbled forward in the growing dark.

When Ernest Steiger returned to his home in Winnetka, Illinois, it was late that night. He was not ready to sleep so he went to his study and recorded his recollections of the meeting with Leonard Williams and the other candidates. As he wrote in his diary, he recalled his introduction to the media affiliates forty-five years earlier.

"MGM. Universal. Paramount. They're all lined up." The speaker, James Vigilant, was a well-known producer of the silver screen. "No more Ester Williams or Ozzie and Harriet. Instead of breaking hearts we're out to capture genitals."

"We can't shift that fast," another man from Hollywood, Darien Grayson, said. "There are existing contracts, shootings in the pipeline. Plus we're talking new screenplays. It's going to take time."

"Marilyn Monroe is going to be very big," Vigilant said.

As a newcomer and the youngest in the room, Ernest Steiger had watched the assembly of powerful and influential men. At the request of his ailing father, they had allowed him as a substitute. In those days, he was not confined to a wheel chair. Having advanced from his initial job as a reporter, he was the robust and energetic publisher of Cincinnati's major newspaper. His father owned that newspaper and several others as well as one television and three radio stations.

In the early 1950's, someone in the group had named them, the "media affiliates." The name had stuck, although no one used it outside these gatherings.

The next speaker had been Seymour Naughton, head of New York's most prestigious advertising agency. He reported that the advertising association had recently adopted a code of ethics that spoke to truth. He snickered when he pointed out how the revolution in advertising had moved from selling products to selling the big seven: happiness, security, acceptance, success, power, comfort, and sex. It was easy to tell the truth about a product when the ad's image contained the real message.

The final report had come from a man who did not identify himself. Unlike the others around the table, young Steiger did not know his name.

The man spoke to the state of the Cold War. His grim assessment included details of Soviet penetration of the United States' intelligence community. He said that his organization was rooting them out and using disinformation to cloud their effectiveness. He cautioned the group to watch for books, screenplays and articles by Communist sympathizers, and to report them to him. He also gave them a briefing on recent developments within the military and covert communities.

After the man excused himself, the meeting turned to coordinating the media affiliates' message to the public. Seymour Naughton had summed up the meeting by saying, "We've got them. This is turning out to be better than a drug cartel. It's legal and everyone's buying into it — whether they realize it or not."

Remembering these early days, Steiger was disturbed by the aging of the media affiliates. It used to be so straightforward: three television networks and a handful of Hollywood studios. Now there were more television networks and studios than he could keep track of. Yet, their carefully constructed consumptionist Box had survived the hippies of the sixties, the environmentalists of the seventies and eighties, and the excesses of the nineties.

Now they were faced with a new danger, the Internet. Its open access and freedom of discussion threatened to expose the confines of the Box. But with large investments in advertising, they were commercializing it. When the value of their stock tumbled, Steiger and two of the other media affiliates had bought major blocks of the shares of companies that specialized in Internet search engines. It was only a matter of time before they would be able to take control. Then they would direct users to their preferred sites, sites in concert with the Box.

Over the past ten years, he had watched as many of the media affiliates coasted on their earlier success. Steiger made a note to address the situation with two of the others to whom he felt close. If they were to reach their ultimate goal, they needed new blood.

In the wee morning, Jimmy Lobo's ghost light was a beacon for the fugitives. It drew its power from an electrical line running into his property. Like many Navajos, Lobo burned it to ward off evil spirits. His dirty white mobile home stood next to a windmill and water tank. A six-foot TV dish glistened in the moonlight. Lobo's place stood at the mouth of the canyon. An older model Ford was parked near the front door.

Ryan, Sarah, Peter, and Cody hurried toward the transportation for the next leg of their efforts to slip away from the INS.

Out in front, Cody yelled, "Lobo. We're here." As the fugitives trudged to the mobile home, its owner came out onto its rickety stoop. He greeted Cody as an old friend and ushered the four inside. A short muscular man, about forty, Jimmy Lobo wore a western shirt and black jeans. His feet were bare. From a sullen weathered face, dark eyes examined his guests. His shoulder-length hair held no traditional braid.

They used first names in hasty introductions, and then placed everyone's packs in the trunk of Lobo's car. Lobo produced a basket of oranges and a box of donuts. Sarah grabbed for a piece of fruit and whispered to Ryan, "Orinfs are my favorite."

"What did you say?" Lobo asked.

"I said I love oranges." She glanced at Lobo as she peeled the skin from it.

"What about one of these? Ryan reached for a glazed donut.

"No thank you." Sarah scrunched her nose and pulled a granola bar from her pocket.

Recalling Sarah's distrust of Lobo, Ryan remembered to touch as few surfaces as possible and wiped his fingerprints from everything he did. He knew his prints were on file from his stint in the military and from certain government contracts with which he had been involved.

"May I use your telephone?" Ryan asked.

"No phone," Lobo gestured to his trailer.

Ryan slipped into the bathroom to wash up with soap and water. He was examining his hand — it had broken open and was oozing fluid. A knock interrupted him.

"Hurry," Sarah whispered. "The INS got ropes and are coming down the canyon." Ryan turned off the faucet and wiped off his fingerprints.

When he came out, still carrying the hand towel, Sarah was waiting. "Peter is in the car. Cody has told Lobo nothing except that we are ready to leave."

Their Navajo guide waved good-by through the cloud of dust Lobo's Crown Victoria kicked up. The older vehicle fishtailed in the soft roadbed. Unlike the road near Ben's dig, this one had been recently graded.

After five miles, they came to a paved road and turned left.

"Do you know where to drop me?" Ryan asked, checking to see if their security had held.

"Shiprock?" Lobo responded, jaw clinched.

"Do you know where?"

"No."

"At the Taco Bell."

A moment of hesitation then, "OK."

Ryan smelled liquor, but Lobo appeared to be steady enough to drive. With the INS right behind them, Ryan decided not to argue about it — as long as the Navajo got them where they wanted to go. Every few minutes, Lobo wiped his hands on his pants, adjusted his hat, or looked in the rear view mirror. There were no other vehicles on the road as the first gray of dawn lightened the sky.

"How long will it take?" Ryan asked.

"Two hours." The Navajo belched and a foul smell filled the front of the car.

The Navajo drove at 45 MPH, staying well towards the right shoulder. They gradually climbed out of the valley — desert on both sides of the road. In place of trees, power lines and telephone poles. Along the highway, fence poles had been embedded in the soft rock and strands of barbed wire ran between them.

At the foot of a downgrade, there was an unexpected lush meadow with several houses. A huge chunk of ruddy sandstone with vertical sides seemed to have lifted by some giant hand and dropped on the flat plain next to one farmhouse.

Half asleep, Ryan's mind began to contemplate a vision of his world as part of the organized cosmos. He began to see the possibilities as people's priorities changed. If they adopted the cosmic paradigm, they'd reject truth as dictated by Madison Avenue and Hollywood, shopping would probably diminish and people would construct a completely new set of priorities. As if on automatic, his mind began to seek out the commercial possibilities in this new makeup.

A worldwide economic restructuring.

Reorientation of the stock market.

New approaches to the environment.

Marketing based on truth.

Unable to keep his eyes open, Ryan dozed off. He did not see the two light green sedans that passed them going the other way.

Ryan awoke as Lobo slowed to turn onto US 64. Bright sun against the windshield, 7:42 AM, elevation 5310. TEEC NOS POS TRADING POST, ESTABLISHED 1905. Cornfields, cottonwoods, and a collection of small houses. With some difficulty, Lobo's car climbed the steep hill to the southeast. Puffy cumulus clouds obscured sunrise. From the south side of the highway, the steep slopes of the Carrizo Mountains, dark elevations contrasted with the tan desert. On the left, another mesa and, on the northeast horizon tall mountains. If everything worked according to plan, he'd be home by this evening. Tomorrow he'd be back in the office preparing for his meeting with Nick and his father.

When they crested a hill, the tip of Shiprock emerged in the east. The core of an extinct volcano, the mountain thrust itself 1,700 feet above the flat surrounding plains. Settlers used it as a distinctive landmark. Fifteen miles north lay the town with the same name. TseBit'A'I' was sacred to the Navajos; climbing was forbidden.

Near the road, junipers dotted the landscape — twisted and stunted, blue-gray berries. Sparse sagebrush, grass, and rocks. An occasional doublewide. Hulks of autos, discarded wood, and abandoned appliances surrounded each home.

WELCOME TO NEW MEXICO. SHIPROCK 19. The full height of Shiprock became visible. Lobo became more agitated. He glanced in the mirror, studying the faces of the Phantians. He looked sideways at Ryan, but did not speak.

In the distance, the Four Corners Power Plant spewed out a dirty cloud — it hung in the air, obscuring the eastern horizon. The mammoth coal-fired plant supplied electricity to several states. A consortium had built it on the reservation to take advantage of loose environmental standards. Sanitas's monitoring system regularly rated it as a top air pollution source.

They emerged on top of a mesa. Cows grazing. A bright blue house, no clutter. Ryan checked the mirror on his side. No vehicles in sight.

Mile marker 18. Shiprock, the town, lay in the valley before them. The San Juan River, its headwaters in the high mountains, made a gradual turn here, on its way to join the Colorado in Utah. Further north it was a famous trout stream.

They rolled into the outskirts of Shiprock. OPERATION DWI CHECKPOINT. Lobo's breath smelled of alcohol. DINE'H COLLEGE, SHIPROCK CAMPUS. SPEED LIMIT 35. TSEBIT'A'I' SHOPPING CENTER.

TACO BELL, the sign was on the right. Lobo drove past it and took a left at the intersection with US 666.

"Where're you going?" Ryan asked. Pointing behind the car, he said, "There's the Taco Bell. I get out here." From the back seat

Sarah placed a tense hand on his shoulder.

Lobo drove on, heading across the bridge over the San Juan River. They were on the newer eastbound side, two lanes between concrete barriers. The westbound was older, steel trestle construction.

"I fear we are headed for trouble," Sarah said clutching his shoulder.

"Turn around," Ryan shouted. "Go back to that shopping center."

The Navajo turned his head and muttered something.

Ryan grabbed the steering wheel and yanked it his direction. The car headed for the bridge's right side. Lobo hit Ryan's bandaged hand and wrestled the wheel the other direction. The vehicle careened across the left eastbound lane, scraping the concrete center divider.

Ryan grabbed the wheel again and yanked harder, bracing his foot against the center console. From his position in the passenger seat, Ryan wrenched control of the wheel from Lobo and, hand over hand, twisted it his way as far as it would go. The pain in his hand was excruciating, but he held on.

They exited the bridge, the car spun to the right, and with tires squealing bounced over the curb. It missed a pedestrian by a few feet. Shocked by the near casualty, Ryan almost released his hold on the wheel. They careened down the embankment, toward the river.

WELCOME TO NIZHONI PARK. The car missed the sign by inches. Lobo worked the brake, but could not halt their skid. At one point the car threatened to tip over, but a large rock on the left banged it upright. Ryan still gripped the wheel when the car smashed into a tree, 20 feet down the slope. His seat belt dug into his chest, but saved him from crashing through the windshield. A stunned Lobo, blood on his mouth, opened his door and stumbled away. Ryan did not try to stop him.

An unoccupied picnic table stood ten feet to their right. The New Mexico weigh station was a hundred yards east — big rigs, facing the other direction. The stunned pedestrian, on the sidewalk twenty feet above, stood staring at the wreck. After he caught his breath, Ryan released his grip on the wheel and turned to the rear,

"Everybody okay?"

Breathless and pale, the two Phantians signaled they had been thrown against the front seat, but were all right except for bruises.

"Let's get the hell out of here," Ryan's heart pounded. "Lobo's gone for help — it won't be the kind we want."

The key hung in the ignition. Ryan climbed into the driver's seat and twisted it. No response. He jimmied the shift lever and tried again. Nothing. Damn.

"Leave the stuff in the trunk. We'll get it later," he said. Lugging backpacks would slow them down and attract attention.

"No," Peter insisted.

"We must have our things," Sarah cried.

Momentarily uncertain, Ryan hesitated and then said, "I'll get my Jeep. Be right back."

Ryan ran up the hill. He passed the pedestrian they had nearly hit and muttered, "Sorry." He took off across the bridge and, not waiting for a break in traffic, hoofed it across the busy highway to the Taco Bell. In the parking lot, he began searching for his Jeep. Ryan flashed back to the desperate struggle with the steering wheel. Lobo had planned to hand them over to the authorities for the reward.

With adrenaline pumping, Ryan slowed himself to a walk and scanned the parking lot. White Jeep. Why were there so damn many vehicles in this lot? Sunday was a day of rest, a day to go to church.

LITTLE CAESAR PIZZA. CITY MARKET. GENERAL STORE. He headed left, trying to act nonchalant while his heart pounded. His shirt soaked through with sweat. Where was that damn Jeep? He scrutinized the rows of dusty metal and faded colors. Tall trucks and vans blocked his view. White Jeep.

He trotted down an aisle toward the storefronts. That guy three cars down, was he watching? There, two rows over, next to a white Dodge Ram, stood a dusty white Jeep. He scooted between two cars and bumped his hand on a side mirror while fumbling for his spare key.

He walked around it to make sure it was his and banged his right hand on a fender. Damn, that hurt. The last thing he wanted was somebody's car alarm going off. With miles of open space to work with, why did they make these parking slots so close together? There, a Sanitas parking decal was in the rear window.

His spare key opened the door. The interior was as dusty as he had left it. Ben had re-packed the rear with his camping equipment and espresso machine. He hurriedly read a note on the front seat:

INS gave me a hard time, but I didn't tell them anything.

Your keys are in the glove box.

Taking artifacts for analysis.

Good Luck,
Ben

The Jeep started on command. He eased out of the space, turned right at the storefronts, and caught the light as it turned red. A sign on the right read, FARMINGTON 29. GALLUP 93. No indication of the road to Colorado. UNLEADED 135.9. He glanced at the dash; the tank was full. He raced the Jeep across the bridge and turned into the picnic area.

In a minute or two they had their things stuffed into the Jeep's rear compartment. Ryan took an extra moment to wipe fingerprints off the dash, steering wheel, ignition key, door handles, and truck lid of Lobo's car. No use making it too easy for them to trace him.

"Where's your car?" Ryan asked.

Sarah pointed east, the direction Lobo had fled.

"Too dangerous. Need to get away. We'll come back."

She looked at Peter and said, "All right."

They exited the picnic area. NO LEFT TURN. A center divider blocked them from going west. Heavy traffic. He looked east. US 666 NORTH. CORTEZ. The signs were at the intersection, a half block away. Colorado! Ryan darted out into oncoming traffic and into the left lane.

Turning at the corner, they headed up the hill, away from the center of Shiprock. On the right, NAVAJO POLICE DEPARTMENT. DIVISION OF LAW ENFORCEMENT. Was Lobo headed there? He slowed for a dog dodging traffic. SHIPROCK POST OFFICE. Cars pulled out in front of them. FOUR CORNERS ADOLESCENT TREATMENT CENTER. The edge of town. SPEED LIMIT 55. Along with other traffic, he was already doing 65.

Mark Kimmel

"We need the supplies in our car," Sarah said.

"Our clothes," Peter said.

"And we need to get out of here, right now. We'll get them. I promise."

My concern is not whether God is on our side; my great concern is to be on God's side, for God is always right.

— ABRAHAM LINCOLN

EIGHT

They had ridden in silence for ten miles when Sarah asked in a low voice, "Can we ride the rest of the way with you?" She sat in the passenger seat, checking on Ryan then glancing at the rear side mirror. North of Shiprock traffic was light and no vehicle was behind them.

"What about your car?"

"Peter has his supply of lotion," Sarah replied. "It is enough for the two of us for two or three weeks. After that we will need our supplies in the car to make more." They had already discussed how Sarah could replace the clothing she had lost when her backpack fell into the gorge.

A straight road as far as he could see. Mount Elmo to the northwest. "What's your destination?" It was hard to believe this had not come up before. Too many other things — the flight across Fortress Mesa, his trip to Phantia. Until the fight with Lobo, he had assumed they would separate and that he would go his own way.

"Denver." The word hung in the air.

Ryan ran onto the shoulder. "Denver!" This couldn't be a co-

105

incidence. He corrected and brought the Jeep back onto the pavement. Good thing the shoulder was wide and smooth. "That's real close to where I live. So, this was all planned? The INS raid? Lobo?"

He had volunteered to help them across Fortress Mesa, but the fight with Lobo was more than he'd counted on. And that INS reward was still out there. After all, the INS was a legitimate authority and they had agents around the country. Now, they wanted him to ferry them to Denver, to risk god knows what? He had a life of his own to return to. Yes, they had made a big impression, but how far was he prepared to carry things.

"Everything we have told you is true," Sarah said. "The INS did raid Harmony. Lobo's actions were his own doing. We had planned to get our car and drive it to Denver."

ROAD WORK AHEAD. A bright orange sign on the side of the road.

Another sign, a few yards beyond the first one. PREPARE TO STOP.

Traffic slowed; a woman in a hard hat and an orange vest. Men standing around. One waved at Sarah, flirting. They detoured onto the shoulder.

Sarah remained silent as rocks pinged against the Jeep's undercarriage. On the southbound side, a work crew mended the steel guardrail.

"So, I was your insurance policy." The angry words flooded out of him.

No response.

Damn! He hated the feeling of being used. This had sure turned out to be more than a simple hiking adventure.

When the detour ended, Ryan resumed speed. Out of the corner of his eye, he could see Sarah's profile; a tear ran down her left cheek. When she regained her composure she said, "I am sorry, you are right. I should have foreseen Lobo's actions and warned you. However, right now, all of us need to leave this Reservation."

"If he hadn't pulled that stunt of his, I'd throw you out, extraterrestrials or not." Ryan said.

"We thought we'd be getting our own car in Shiprock," she said. She could not go on.

"What have you gotten me into?" He tilted his head left.

Silence.

"What do you want from me?"

"Ryan, we now entrust you with the success of our mission." She said it like a statement, but he knew it was a desperate plea.

Things had become complicated. He knew the truth about extraterrestrials, had seen the civilization of another planet. He sensed this would change his life, his values, everything in time. But, damn it, that was the future, this was now. He had not agreed to become a chaperone for people from a distant world. Where would it end? "What other surprises do you have for me?"

"Oh, I'm sure we can come up with some." The slim Phantian laughed through tears that spilled down her cheeks. "Why not stick around and see?"

That smile, that beautiful face. He concentrated on the road and his anger subsided.

"OK," he said, rising to her challenge. He cocked his head right. "I'll get you to Denver. Pull the Colorado map out of that side pocket."

Sarah complied.

"Find Cortez." He felt trapped by circumstances, and a carload of extraterrestrials. He knew he couldn't dump them, but how far was he prepared to go?

"I have it," she said and smiled.

"See how US 160 heads east to Durango. That's the way we're going."

They were about to enter Colorado at its southwest corner. The San Juan Mountains, the most rugged in Colorado, stood as a formidable barrier between them and the rest of the state. A limited number of roads ran through the San Juans, some paved, all slow and winding. Since their pursuers had no idea where they were headed, Ryan reasoned that they were less likely to monitor these roads than the easier routes in Utah or New Mexico. Besides, going around the San Juans would add hours to their trip.

An hour and a half later they descended into Durango. The highway widened to three lanes in each direction, new concrete. SPEED LIMIT 40 MPH. BEST WESTERN. WAPITI LODGE. For much of the trip from Cortez, Sarah had kept her eyes shut. Ryan assumed she was communicating with one of her celestial allies or remotely viewing the INS.

"Let's think this through," Sarah opened her eyes and faced him. "Lobo doesn't know what your vehicle looks like or where we are headed, the authorities can only guess how we escaped the wreck of his car."

"Makes sense. If we're lucky, other law enforcement agencies won't get involved," Ryan said.

The United States' illegal Mexican problem of itself overwhelmed the INS. Ryan had heard estimates that there were over two hundred thousand illegals in Colorado alone, five percent of the population. But Mexican illegals were now a secondary issue to suspected terrorists. The way things stood, the INS got the attention of other law enforcement agencies only when they could show a felony had been committed, or there was some connection to international terrorism. Still, he suspected that the INS had an office in Cortez or Durango and that they had been alerted. He was surprised they had not seen any INS vehicles on the road.

At a busy intersection near the heart of Durango, Ryan turned left onto US 550. This road would take them through the heart of the San Juan Mountains to Silverton and Ouray and eventually to Montrose, the next town comparable in size to Durango. After that there were several routes to Denver.

"I need food," Peter stuttered. "Can we stop there?" He pointed to a Denny's restaurant.

"I think we'd better keep going," Ryan said and drove past the Denny's.

"You said it was a long drive." It had been four hours since they had eaten at Lobo's.

"I too would like to eat," Sarah said in support of her companion. Their last meal had been a snack under the camouflage.

"All right, but we need to be quick." Ryan grabbed a quick left off Camino del Rio and maneuvered into the Burger King drive-through.

They were waiting for their food when Sarah opened her eyes and said, "When the BIA and Navajo Police did not apprehend us in Shiprock, they alerted the INS throughout Arizona, Utah, Colorado, and New Mexico. Based on Lobo's description, word has gone out to find three people: a light-haired women and two men, one bald and one bearded."

Ryan noticed that Sarah was adapting her speech pattern to his. He had observed himself do the same thing whenever he traveled to England or the South. After a few days he spoke like a native.

"We need to get going," Ryan said as he tapped his fingers on the steering wheel. The van ahead of them was full of kids who kept chatting with the attendant at the window who apparently was their friend. Another vehicle had pulled in behind them — they were trapped in the narrow drive.

A small aircraft buzzed overhead. Sarah touched Ryan's arm. "It's OK. They don't know what kind of a vehicle we're in."

As they waited for the attendant to pass out their food, three light green vehicles drove by on the street in front of them. They were headed north on US 550. Ryan pointed them out to Sarah and Peter.

"I think we've just had a change of plans," Ryan said. The presence of the INS vehicles indicated they were probably staking out the major roads. They might not know what kind of a car they were in, but they did have their descriptions.

When they exited the Burger King, Ryan took a right and then an immediate left onto 14th Street east. After two blocks, he turned right onto 3rd Avenue, a tree-lined parkway. In a block he made a U turn and came around north. In three blocks, the street became Florida and they wound their northeast way out of town.

From a small container that Peter produced, both Phantians added caraway seeds to their hamburgers. "If that's what you're so anxious to get from your car," Ryan said and pointed to the black seeds, "I'll buy you some at a grocery store."

Ryan turned north on LaPlata 240. He knew from visits to a friend in Durango that it paralleled the busier US 550 where he suspected the INS was waiting. This road hugged the east side of the Animas River valley. A narrow two lane road, it was used primarily by locals.

In about a mile they passed the sign for Morningstar Arabians. White fences outlined green pasture. As they continued north, other expensive homes with large irrigated pastures dotted the luxuriant valley. It would have be nice to have one of those — retired from Sanitas, a gentleman farmer, fishing nearby. No more hassles with venture capitalists. But Ryan already suspected he would never realize that dream. Everything had changed when he'd met the two extraterrestrials.

"Why's this celestial stuff so important?" Ryan asked. "Most people just live their lives whoever is running the universe."

"Your frame of reference shifts once you acknowledge the reality of extraterrestrials, the connection of this planet to the cosmos, and the participation of celestial beings in your life. You comprehend, in a very profound way, that you are part of the Grand Plan of an organized universe, rather than an anonymous inhabitant of some isolated planet tucked away in a remote corner of the galaxy, a planet resulting from random coincidences that produced life.

"Once you absorb the plan of the universe and your importance in it, you will appreciate the larger purpose to life, see things differently, and change your actions accordingly. We believe you will want to do something more than hang around accumulating stuff, achieving status, and consuming everything you can get your hands on. It will change the way in which you spend your brief time on this planet." She whispered the last words to indicate their importance.

Traffic halted. Ryan glanced at the dash, 2:37 PM.

After a few minutes, they progressed far enough to see a flagman with his stop sign, hardhat, and orange vest. He had a walkie-talkie in one hand. A second man, dressed in an INS jacket, wandered along the line-up, checking each vehicle.

"Do you see him?" Peter pointed to the INS man.

"Yes," Ryan said. "Everybody put your hats on. Peter, lay down on the seat and shut your eyes."

At a signal from the INS man, the flagman allowed about a dozen vehicles to proceed. Ryan had already noticed that traffic from the opposite direction came in small clusters.

Ryan looked around to see if they could go another way. It was impossible without calling attention to themselves. An INS sedan was parked alongside the road, another man sat in it.

They crept forward until four cars separated them from the

flagman. In front of them was a newer Toyota Camry, Utah license plate. In the front seat, a man and a woman screamed at each other. A red pickup followed them, lone driver, rifle across the back window. Ryan could not see its license. Orange cones blocked the northbound lane.

After noting their license number on his clipboard, the INS jacketed man came to the passenger's side of the Jeep. Sarah rolled down the window and the man asked, "Where're you from?" He smiled at Sarah.

"Albuquerque," Ryan responded from the driver's side. Thank God, he'd remembered the New Mexico plates on his Jeep. "Is there another way around this?"

Ignoring Ryan's question, the man asked, "Going where?"

"Silverton."

The man studied them through Sarah's open window. Peter lay across the rear seat, eyes closed, hat covering his head.

Something about them perturbed the man. He was lowering his hand to his two-way radio when Sarah touched him on the arm. The man froze. Then straightened up. A startled look crossed his face. He turned from the window. As if he were a robot, he raised his hand and signaled the flagman.

The orange-vested man motioned a half-dozen vehicles forward. Ryan followed the Camry into the left lane.

"What was that all about?" Ryan asked.

"I stimulated his brain function, causing many synapses to fire at once," Sarah said. "It blocked his ability to reason and impeded his memory."

"He looked like he was completely overwhelmed."

"He was, for a few seconds. There is no permanent damage."

"Is that what you did to Viejo when he grabbed you in front of Harmony?"

"Yes."

After ten miles on LaPlata 240, they had no choice but to join US 550 north. They crossed the Animas River and the Durango to Silverton Railroad tracks. During the early years of this century, trains had hauled precious ore from the mines around Silverton to the smelters in Durango. Now it was a tourist attraction. The narrow-gauge roadbed followed the river through the spectacular scenery of the Animas River Canyon. The train took two hours to reach Silverton. Their route paralleled the railroad but would take an hour. After Silverton they planned to continue north through Ouray and Ridgway to Montrose and then to Denver.

The broad highway climbed through a forest of Douglas fir and blue spruce. TAMARRON RESORT. PURGATORY SKI AREA. Spacious trophy homes nestled in the pines — part-time residences for the wealthy from California and Texas.

They crested Coal Bank Pass. Ryan pushed the Jeep as fast as the road would allow, passing slower cars.

Trillions of inhabited planets — a thousand times more planets than there are people on Earth! All orchestrated and friendly -- utterly different from the way most people viewed anything alien. He'd been to one of those friendly planets and seen friendly people. Now he knew for certain that extraterrestrials existed — that they were here, on his planet, next to him.

Driving through this beautiful part of Colorado always lifted Ryan's spirits. He didn't mind the winding mountain passes; easier driving lay on the far side. Peter dozed in the back seat. Sarah watched the landscape. If he hadn't been so damn tired, he would have enjoyed it more.

"Beautiful, huh," Ryan said. He flexed a right hand that had stiffened.

"Yes," the slim Phantian said. "The celestial assistants did an awe-inspiring job here."

"I thought God created this."

"Although He could do it Himself, He allows his celestial assistants to create and maintain His trillions of worlds. The celestials assigned to Earth have been here since the beginning of this planet, establishing and nurturing the evolutionary process."

Ryan tried to view the forces of nature in the hands of celestials, clay in the hands of expert potters. He fantasized them nudging forces deep within the earth to sculpt tall peaks and deep valleys. He imagined them assisting the long erosion process that formed something as wondrous as these mountains.

A beautiful extraterrestrial occupied the seat next to him. Her ardor for her mission was never far below the surface. Dedicated to what she saw as a larger purpose, she had pursued it from

Phantia to Earth. Ryan respected zealous people, their commitment.

He had been mulling it over since Shiprock and knew he would go along with Sarah's plea for help. He wasn't sure where the INS was coming from, but there was no way he could turn his back on the reality of these extraterrestrials and their extraordinary information. No way he could abandon those who had given him such an incredible experience.

He heard the voices again. "—INS—" silence "—Denver" silence "—we are—" silence This time he knew the source — both Phantians had their eyes closed. He listened for more fragments while concentrating on the road.

The beautiful terrain was at its most glorious: jagged igneous spires rose from velvet-forested mounds, on the lower slopes yellow-gold leaves played against pine-green. Next to the road, dark red cliffs contrasted with green Douglas fir and yellow aspen. Sunlight burst through the cloud cover and bathed Twilight Peak to the east with a brilliant glow.

The only note of sadness within this splendid panorama was the occasional hillside of dead fir trees. Mild winters had allowed pine beetles to flourish and infest the forest. This was another impact of global warming and one that Sanitas had not, as yet, found a way to monitor with Global Watch.

Ryan kept returning to the Phantians and their cosmic message. Bridging the gap between their frame of reference and Earth's current situation was going to require some real doing. What was the impending disaster, the new world order? What were they not telling him? He had so many questions. He chose one at random.

"Your names," Ryan said. "They're obviously not Phantian."

"We chose common names to fit in, but ones with some historical significance," Sarah said. "I adopted the name Sarah, the wife of Abraham in your Bible, and because it resembles the Phantian word for love."

"All I remember about Sarah is that she was old when she had a son."

"The truth is that Sarah was brilliant and much younger than Abraham."

"And Peter?"

"Peter was a great preacher."

"Why names out of the Bible?"

"You'd prefer Caesar, Cleopatra, Napoleon, or Venus?" Sarah chuckled. "Perhaps Susie or Brenda? How about Candy?"

"OK. OK. What about Dr. Adamson?"

She hesitated and said, "Dr. Adamson is not Phantian. He is an intraterrestrial."

"An intraterrestrial?"

"Yes. Peter and I are extraterrestrials. Dr. Adamson is an intraterrestrial — he was born on this planet and has lived here for thousands of years. He is neither purely human nor purely celestial, but stands midway between the two. He is the one who requested that we come to Earth."

"Are there others like him?"

"Yes, but not nearly as many as the mortals of this planet."

"He looks like —" Ryan was about to say that the white-haired man looked like someone he had seen before, but stopped.

Sarah smiled and said, "Dr. Adamson is one of the sons of Adam and Eve."

"You had 'em at the road block." Raul Viejo blasted an INS agent from the Durango office.

"You're right, Raul. I'm sorry," the man replied into his radio. "My recollection is real fuzzy. It was the flag-man that let them through."

"What about the license plate?"

"Got that. It's for a Ford pickup. Registered to a James Tsotsie in Gallup. Reported stolen last week."

"But you can't remember what kind of a car it was?"

"Sorry, I just wrote down licenses."

"It was them. I knowed it was," Viejo continued to rant. He had to make this look good. Raul Viejo was glad he was alone in his vehicle. He had a hard time suppressing a smile at the fugitives' escape. If they were captured, they could blow his story about thirty people at Harmony — he might have to disappear before getting paid. His greatest leverage on his Iowa client was his continued presence.

When they disconnected, Viejo turned on a Spanish radio station and listened to traditional Mexican ballads. He stopped at Cortez for pie and coffee.

An hour later, he called Oscar Hoehn to report on the continuing saga. Hoehn said he was leaving Morgan and his men at Harmony Center to round up any of the people who might return. He again asked Viejo to confirm that there were thirty people on site when he had visited Harmony a day prior to the raid. The INS agent did so with convincing detail. Hoehn ordered Viejo to pursue the fugitives and to coordinate with local INS agents.

As she rode through the splendor of the San Juan Mountains, Sarah Smith scrutinized Ryan Drake. She liked his voice, the way his mouth formed the English words, the way they flowed so effortlessly. It was a welcome change from the Navajo men who struggled with the language. She recalled the many hours she had spent at Harmony reviewing videos, trying to learn the nuances of English and the customs of the people of her adopted planet.

Her celestial allies had told her that Ryan Drake was a well-regarded, successful businessman. He was powerful and connected to important people. What she saw was a human who had agreed to lend a hand, to help two strangers. When he helped them escape from Lobo, he had gone beyond his commitment to help Peter and her traverse the desert.

His steady blue eyes indicated integrity, the set of his jaw determination. But, what did she really know about the man to whom she had trusted her fate, the fate of her mission? Yes, he had saved her from sliding off the cliff, but she was sure that was an instinctive reaction on his part, testimony to his physical fitness. Still, she had felt his reactions when she pictioned her voyage from Phantia. Although he hid them, he was capable of deep feelings.

One thing she was sure she liked about Ryan was his smile. Whenever he was diverted from focusing on the task at hand, his face relaxed and a broad smile popped out. It reminded her of men she had know on Phantia, reminded her of Peter before his problem with rematerializing.

Did he always wear that beard? On Phantia, most men shaved the hair from their heads as well as their faces. Navajo men had no facial hair, little on their bodies. Ryan's beard was a mixture of gray and brown. She knew he was tired; they had not slept last night. The beard made him look as weary as she was sure he felt.

Now that he was driving them to Denver, what was their relationship to be? He had said that his home was not far from where they intended to locate. She could tell that he had been deeply affected by his trip to Phantia, by the realization that Peter and she were extraterrestrials. She hoped that he would continue to be involved in their mission and that he would come to overlook their different origins. She knew that she did not want him to disappear from her life.

After her children were raised, every woman on Phantia pursued a second career. She had chosen teaching. Her research into the effects of celestial oversight landed her a lectureship at the prestigious Central Academy in Ur'Geay, the town where she had grown up. After seven years, she was inducted into D'Ct-Elds, the high order of teachers.

When the Mother Superior of the D'Ct-Elds first approached her about the mission to Earth, she had refused — it was too soon after the death of her husband, she had family, they asked too much. Mother Superior described the deplorable conditions in which some humans lived, while others resided in luxury.

A representative from Michael, the celestial sovereign of the local universe, talked with her. He told her that Earth was like a lost sheep, was essential to Michael's plan because of its hearty graduates. Someone from Phantia had to go: Unlike those on other planets, her people had a similar physical appearance and the capacity to speak Earth's principal language. Phantia was at a similar stage of evolution and its people could accommodate to Earth's air, water, and nutrients. He emphasized her ability to relate with learners, her ability to remote view, and her unique ability to piction. He reminded her that each living human was her brother or sister. At last, she decided that the unprecedented relocation was the right thing to do. Then she set out to make good use of her remaining weeks on Phantia.

'*How are we going to get our vehicle?*' Peter interrupted her memories with a communication. '*What about our lotion?*'

116

'Ryan said he would get it for us.'
'Do you trust him?'
'Yes.'

Ryan too was lost in thought as they wended their way through the mountains. He thought about Ben Tsotsie and how well they knew each other. He was sure that Ben knew about the origins of the people at Harmony Center and had been a part of the plan to get him together with them. He thought back to when he had first become acquainted with the Navajo.

"Where are you from?" Ryan asked.

"I am Navajo. My family lives on the Reservation." Ben replied.

"Is it far?" The two sophomores relaxed on the lawn beside the geology and archeology building.

Ryan explained that archeology was an elective for him. His major was political science with an economics minor. He planned to go to law school, become an attorney like his father, and enter politics. He had chosen Arizona State University to get away from the Midwest.

"Three or four hours." Ben talked to him about growing up as the oldest in his family. He was the first among his many cousins to attend ASU. He intended to become an archeologist and help the white man understand the rich history of his people.

"I love the desert around here, but I need a break," Ryan said. "I want snow, green trees. Think I'll head to the mountains." Thanksgiving holidays were looming in the week ahead. Ryan had told his father he would not be home.

"Where?" Ben asked.

"Sierra Nevadas. I like the area around Bishop."

"You don't go home for the holidays?"

"Naw. It's too far."

"The San Juans in Colorado are an easier drive," Ben said. "You could have Thanksgiving dinner at my family's hogan."

Ben Tsotsie took Ryan to his home that next week and showed him life on the Navajo Reservation, taught him the way in which his people viewed the land. They visited the San Juan Mountains of Colorado driving along the Dolores River until they reached the area around Lizard Head Peak. They camped one night and returned to ASU.

The city boy from St. Louis, Missouri had already fallen in love with the desert. Now, the forested slopes of the Rockies became a second home. He spent weekends and vacations exploring them, often alone, off and on with friends from ASU. In the wilderness he found a strength that his remote domineering father and the social structure of St. Louis had never allowed.

In the spring of his junior year, events propelled him further away from a father he saw infrequently. As it was, they talked only when he needed money.

"Are you going to the protest?" Ryan asked.

"No," Ben said. "I have to study."

"We could use your help. If we don't stop them, they'll clear-cut everything in sight." Ryan was incensed because a lumber company was preparing to harvest large tracts of original growth forest in northeast Arizona. For him, it was an act of war.

"I know, but I have a test tomorrow."

"Come on. I'll have you back by six."

A hundred people showed up outside the offices of Southwest Forest Corporation. They chanted and milled around with placards held high. There was beer and pot and the crowd became noisier. Soon they were throwing rocks at the front of the building.

Squads of police forced them back and took their names. After warning them to stay away from the facility, they released those that seemed sober enough to drive and took the rest into custody. Ryan staggered back to his room at about 9:00 PM. He was drunk; Ben had driven back to the campus.

The next day he received a phone call. "Hey, Drake. It's for you." The message was relayed down the hallway.

Ryan ran to the pay phone in the dorm. He was expecting a call from a girl, a blonde.

"Ryan, it's your father."

"Hi."

"I understand you've gotten yourself into a little trouble." Ryan recognized the stern voice. He visualized his father's thick glasses and pipe as he sat in the corner office of Drake, Beam, and McKinley.

"What are you talking about?"

"The demonstration in front of Southwest Forest, yesterday."

"How did —"

"Listen to me." The elder Drake used his best lawyer voice. "Those people are friends of mine. I don't want you over there again."

"But they're cutting —"

"You heard me. No more. Get back to your school work, and watch your drinking."

The line went dead and Ryan was left holding the receiver. His father, a prominent lawyer in St. Louis, treated his wealthy clients better than his son.

"She blew you off, huh?" One of his friends was behind him, waiting for the phone.

"Yeah. She blew me off."

Ryan passed on the next demonstration. He studied for the mid-term in a class where he needed to pull up his grade.

The following weekend, someone organized a trip to the site of Southwest's cutting operation. Ryan drove a carload of demonstrators two hours into the forested hills of northwest Arizona. When they arrived, they formed a human chain in front of the logging equipment. When the loggers tried to advance their equipment, the protestors held strong and the equipment was halted, but not before one protestor's leg was broken. When the loggers attacked them with clubs and the blood began to flow, the kids held together and did not run.

The Sheriff of the remote mountain town responded to the plea of its largest employer and started making arrests. Cut, bruised, and drunk Ryan, Ben, and some of others were hauled to the next county and arraigned on charges of disturbing the peace. With no attorney to defend them, a Justice of the Peace sentenced them to a week in the county jail. By the time they got out, Southwest had cleared acres of ancient growth.

Ryan's father called again. "When is this going to stop?" he asked.

"I can't stand by and let them rape the land. We are —"

"I want you to come home."

"No." His father had always been autocratic, demanded that

Ryan center his head and stand up straight. It had taken Ryan years after his mother died to feel at all comfortable around him.

"There are fine schools here in Missouri."

"I like it here. I want to finish."

"I said, come home."

"No."

"I will pay nothing more to that school."

"Fine. I'll do it by myself."

And he had. Moreover the city boy from St. Louis, Missouri had matured and achieved success not only in college but also in business. Sanitas was his fourth significant position. The last two had also been as company CEO. They had proven financially rewarding. He wondered about Sanitas.

The avaricious man is like the barren sandy ground of the desert which sucks in all the rain and dew with greediness, but yields no fruitful herbs or plants for the benefit of others.

— ZENO

NINE

Sarah Smith studied the spectacular rugged terrain. The road over Red Mountain Pass was full of switchbacks and it had snowed for the last hour. She had tried to sleep, but the icy road kept her awake.

In Tibnap, on the far side of Phantia, the mountains rose this high and appeared as formidable. She had visited there once, part of an extended vacation with M'Adan and their two teenage daughters. M'Adan and she had enjoyed the trip, however their two girls couldn't wait to get home to their friends.

"I think this is one of the most beautiful places in Colorado," Ryan motioned to the surrounding vista. "Maybe we should stay awhile."

She knew he was joking and said, "Another time."

Ryan pulled off into a parking area and said, "I want to take care of something."

"I can drive," Sarah volunteered.

"You have a license?"

She reached into the pocket of her jeans and extracted an Arizona driver's license.

Ryan smiled and said, "Maybe a little later. Let me get us off this pass."

Sarah followed him out of the vehicle and watched as he wandered off into the woods. It felt good to move about and she used the opportunity to stretch.

When he returned, Ryan retrieved his Colorado license plates from the rear of the Jeep. After he had substituted them for the ones from New Mexico, they continued down the winding road.

She studied the man who had rescued her a second time in the last twenty-four hours. In the gathering darkness, as he squinted to see the road, deep wrinkles formed at the edges of his weary eyes.

She thought back to Phantia and another man there. After M'Adan died, she had become friends with a man at the Academy, Ja'Ne. They both taught in the section for celestial studies. He was older than she by ten years and had been at the Academy for fifteen years. Before that he was at a school in E'Yt, in the eastern hemisphere where he had grown up.

At first they were just friends, an occasional lunch. Then Ja'Ne asked her to accompany him to a special performance of the Academy's music section. They sat in the first row, seats of honor, and a display of a relationship. She had not anticipated the significance of his invitation to this event. From that point forward, others considered her his special female. Other males, whose company she had previously enjoyed, treated her differently, hesitated to lunch with her, to be seen alone with her. Nonetheless, she enjoyed Ja'Ne's company and continued to see him. Their occasional lunches turned into frequent dinners.

As a little girl J'Li had been told she was pretty. Her parents had reinforced that by encouraging her to participate in various public performances. But it was J'Li's nature to be shy and she did not see herself as particularly pretty. She had also learned in school that Phantians measured success not by how beautiful one appeared, rather success was how one lived one's life, what one did with one's tools. As soon as she had a say, she refused to participate in public displays.

From the beginning of their relationship, Ja'Ne had insisted that she was beautiful. "You are the most beautiful woman in all of

Phantia," he had said, "and I want you to be mine." It did not matter that she was a mature woman with two grown daughters. While she was pleased with his adoration, she resented that he would consider her his own. "Phantians from the western hemisphere do not 'own' each other," she had told him.

Their relationship waned and dinners became less frequent. But Ja'Ne did not go away. He invited her to his home; after several delays she accepted. Ja'Ne fixed a luscious dinner with many drinks of gilg. He pushed himself on her and they engaged in sex. It was rough and repulsive, nothing like the loving experiences with her beloved M'Adan.

The next day she told him that she would see him no more. But he would not relent, hounded her relentlessly, and loudly proclaimed that they were a couple. Out of desperation, she reported him to the head of the Academy. Finally, after he was transferred to another location, she began to feel safe. She reapplied herself to her research and teaching and in two years was admitted to the D'Ct-Elds. It had happened years ago, before she relocated to Earth. Now as she studied Ryan she wondered if she could ever again be intimate with a male.

After Red Mountain Pass they passed through the town of Ouray and the road straightened. Ryan pushed the Jeep at 70 MPH, braking only for blind corners. In an hour they arrived at Montrose, a commercial hub for western Colorado. They had seen no official vehicles, INS or otherwise.

On the east side of Montrose, on US 50, Ryan stopped the Jeep, walked to Sarah's side, and opened the door. "I have to have sleep. Wake me when you get to Gunnison. If anyone tries to stop you, just keep going." He pointed down the road. When she vacated the passenger seat, he slumped into it.

As she walked around to the driver's side, he added, "And watch out for deer on the road." Before she was seated Ryan had closed his eyes.

She put the Jeep in drive and started east. In the rear seat, Peter paid close attention. He told her that he would use his viewing powers to warn her if any INS vehicles were preparing to intercept them.

It took a few miles for her to become accustomed to the vehicle. From the back seat, Peter made comments as she centered herself between the yellow and white lines.

In an hour the town of Gunnison appeared, and she slowed to gaze at the automobile sellers and other retail establishments. Vehicles raced past her as she slowed to look. She found it hard to concentrate on the road and could not figure out why cars honked at her when she failed to yield. One pickup with kids in the rear swerved around her; they screamed, "Get off the road." If she had not been worried about their pursuers, she would have stopped and wandered around Gunnison's interesting streets. She pulled into a service station on the east side of the town.

When Peter and she returned to the Jeep, Ryan was already in the driver's seat. He rolled down the window and held out his hand. She gave him the Jeep's keys and a bottle of Coca Cola and went around to the passenger seat. Peter slipped into the rear and lay down.

"How are you feeling," she asked.

"I'm better."

On the four-hour drive from Gunnison to Boulder, Sarah relaxed and looked around. While she had been driving, she had been so intent on the road that she had noticed little of her surroundings.

Ryan drove fast enough that no other vehicles passed them. She checked each oncoming car to make sure it continued and did not turn around. They saw no police vehicles.

When they descended through the foothills, she had her first glimpse, from the ground, of an American city. From orbit the collections of urban lights had looked smudged. Through the windows of the Jeep, the lights of Denver seemed to spread to the eastern horizon like an earthly blanket of stars. She could make out major streets and concentrations of high buildings, their lights burning at 4:00 AM.

"We have no cities like this on Phantia. The tall buildings, whose are they? What do all the people do? How can they possibly relate to one another?"

Ryan explained that Denver was a pleasant city, over two million people, diversified economy, crazy about sports. Overall it was a typical American city.

There were so many people in one place. What was the purpose? How did they supply this many with food and water?

They rode in silence through the town of Morrison, past the entrance to Red Rocks Amphitheater, and under Interstate 70. "A short cut to Boulder," Ryan said.

As they rounded the outskirts of Golden a sign attracted her attention, COLORADO SCHOOL OF MINES.

Sarah pointed to it and said, "A school for minds? I had no idea."

"Mines, not minds," Ryan corrected her. "That's one of the premier schools in the world for educating hardrock miners, you know, digging for gold."

As they moved up the hill out of Golden on CO 93, Sarah tried to communicate with him. Without words, she asked him to help her rewrite her explanation of the cosmic paradigm, to improve the English and make it more understandable. He did not respond. Such mind-to-mind communication required the minds of both parties to engage. Perhaps Ryan was tired. Perhaps his mind was simply not evolved enough to drive and receive a communication. After several tries and no reply, she concluded he needed more training.

One of the first skills children on Phantia were taught was mind-to-mind communication. Parents used it to perceive a child's needs before they were verbal. After children learned to speak aloud, it was a useful tool to check the truth of the spoken words. Children were encouraged to use this innate ability to communicate with others in addition to their five senses. She suspected that children on this planet also had this ability and wondered why it had not been recognized and developed.

Adults on Phantia used a combination of verbal and mind-to-mind communications. Verbal was more precise, good to express emotions. Mind-to-mind was more useful for concepts and to convey feelings, and of course it was always truthful.

"What is an Environmental Site?" Sarah pointed to the lighted sign at the entrance to a large complex: ROCKY FLATS ENVIRONMENTAL SITE.

"Until a few years ago," Ryan said, "the government made plutonium triggers there. Now they're trying to clean up the radioactive contamination."

She shivered at the destructive force of such weapons. She had seen videos of their explosions at Harmony. "On Phantia we never made a nuclear bomb."

From her limited experience she concluded that the main difference between this planet and hers was their approach to problem solving. Here the most common response was anger, born out of fear. Often this anger led to violence. Trained from childhood to see the larger picture and to rise above her animal nature, she seldom resorted to anger, let alone violence. Would the cosmic paradigm really help earth dwellers to overcome their basic instincts, their desire to build weapons of mass destruction? Their desire to dominate each other?

At Harmony she had read what she could find on atomic and hydrogen bombs. It was a strange topic, clouded in secrecy yet available. It just required ordering the right books. Like all extraterrestrials she was concerned that this planet might blow itself up. The resulting problems for the universe would be many, not the least of which was the release of radiation. Even dematerialized beings were affected by radiation.

"How did you manage to avoid bombs?"

"About a hundred years ago, before the age of technology, the people of Phantia came to understand that the celestial rulers were wiser than their collective human wisdom, and that war did not solve anything. After a twenty-five year process and the acquiescence of everyone on the planet, we submitted to celestial planetary government. By doing this before we had the chance to develop modern weapons, we happily avoided many of the conflicts that have characterized your planet."

"If you don't have nuclear power, how do you generate your electricity?"

"We use zero-point energy to create electricity. In turn, we use the electricity from it to produce hydrogen to power vehicles."

"I've read about the use of hydrogen for automobiles. It sounds pretty interesting," Ryan said. "That other was zero what?"

"Zero-point energy is a vast source," Peter said. He had awakened and was leaning on the back of the front seats. "It is time to make it available to your world."

"So, how's that supposed to happen?"

"The reverse engineering of technologies from crashed UFOs has already shown its feasibility."

"You're kidding. Who's done that?" The prospect of a new source of energy was exciting news. From his association with Sanitas, Ryan had become painfully aware that the burning of petroleum was causing severe environmental problems. As the economies of the underdeveloped countries modernized, their demand for petroleum increased. It was painfully obvious that, sooner or later, there would be insufficient reserves to meet a growing world demand. From what he'd read, Islamic terrorism had its roots in America's demand for Middle East oil.

"It's being worked on by aerospace companies."

"I haven't read anything."

"It appears to be buried in covert projects. That is a part of our mission that we will discuss later."

Ryan did not pursue that thread of conversation further. Instead he asked, "What about the loss of freedom, you know, when you submitted to planetary government?"

"Only the freedom from misplaced nationalism and unnecessary wars was relinquished. In truth, Phantians are freer than your people — violence is rare and they are not constrained by consumptionism and the manipulations of the powerful. They live knowing the truth about everything and treat each other with total integrity."

Inside the city limits of Boulder, Ryan stopped for the light at Greenbriar. He turned to her and said, "I'll be happy to help you rewrite those pages of yours — based on what I saw at Ben's dig, they do need a little help."

She laughed and poked him in the shoulder — he had received her communication.

Ryan explained that Boulder was the home of the University of Colorado with its twenty-five thousand students. It was a source for many of his talented employees.

To get to Ryan's home, they turned left at Linden Avenue and drove up a canyon west of Boulder. After a few minutes on a twisting road, they emerged overlooking the town just as the last sunlight disappeared. They turned from the paved road onto gravel; light snow covered everything. There were no other tracks on this side road. When they stopped to allow a metal gate to swing open, Sarah asked, "This is yours?"

"My ex-wife designed it. I'm a little nervous showing it to you," he said and pulled the Jeep forward.

She watched as Ryan glanced back to make sure the gate shut behind them. Then they drove up a road that showed no signs of recent use. They popped over a rise and approached a large home with a green metal roof and a four-car garage. To Sarah the structure seemed far more than required for a house. It rested upon a level area that had been carved from the crest of a hill. Beyond it she could see the lights of Boulder. Ryan pulled the Jeep to the green front door.

"I think you'll be safe here," Ryan said as he slumped over the steering wheel.

Sarah extracted herself from the seat and stretched. The cool air felt refreshing after the long drive. Peter Jones opened the rear door and stumbled out.

"This reminds me of Phantia." She stooped and reached a bare hand out to scoop up a bit of white. Snow was a familiar sight during the cold times that extended for many months.

Ryan held the tall door while Peter and she stepped into the foyer of his grand house. They each lugged a bag or pack.

She gasped. Three steps below an expansive room spread before her. A rock fireplace dominated one wall, its chimney rising for over two stories to meet the vaulted ceiling. An elaborate blue, tan, and white Navajo rug covered the floor under a huge glass table. Chocolate brown, leather sofas surrounded the table on three sides. This single room was larger than several of Harmony's rooms combined.

Straight ahead, two indoor trees framed a wall of glass that looked east to the city and farms beyond. The tops of ponderosa pines, further down the hill, were visible through the bottom of the window.

Ryan said, "Make yourselves at home." He wandered off to punch keys below a computer display. Lights flicked on throughout the house.

Peter and she followed him up the stairs to the left of the great room and discovered five bedrooms. Peter placed his backpack in the one at the end. Ryan suggested another room for her and pointed out an attached bathroom.

Returning to the great room, she saw an ultra-modern kitchen to the right. An iron rack with pots and pans dangled from its ceiling. It was separated from the main room by a white oak counter with cushioned stools. The dining area, with a long wooden table and chairs, was situated to the left of the kitchen. Ryan pointed out the master bedroom suite beyond.

She stepped down three steps into the living room, past Southwestern paintings. As she strolled, she used both hands to push strands of her hair behind her ears. Pieces of Native American pottery filled several pot shelves, each was labeled: HOPI, ACOMA, ZUNI, or ANASAZI. She was aware that Ryan stood watching her.

She walked to the floor-to-ceiling window. "There are no private houses such as this on Phantia." She stood with her back to him.

"This is a palace," Peter stammered.

Without acknowledging their comments, Ryan asked, "Would either of you like hot tea? A bite to eat?"

Sarah followed him into the kitchen, white oak with a blue countertop and an elaborate indoor grill. Scattered about the spacious counters were appliances and tools she had seen advertised on television and in magazines. Cookbooks filled two shelves. The room was spotless. She suspected that Ryan had not cleaned it himself.

"You have no TV," she observed.

"It's in the entertainment center, on the floor below."

She wandered about the kitchen as Ryan busied himself putting water in a teapot.

Leaning against the island, she said, "Peter and I appreciate what you did back there in Shiprock, but we fear that you are in trouble with the authorities." Ryan had brought them to his own house. He had not mentioned dropping them in Denver.

"Hey, I didn't want your mission to end before it began."

She liked the way he had taken charge after Shiprock. For the last few hours, she had enjoyed stepping back. It had been a long trip from Harmony, and she was exhausted.

"Unless I am very mistaken, it will take them a long time to track us here," Ryan said. "Maybe never."

She smiled and touched his arm. "I sense how overwhelming this must be for you." She motioned to his elegant home. "Changing your point-of-view will not be easy. If it takes you a while, it's okay."

"I never really liked this huge house. We raised our kids here; it worked out fine for that, but I don't need it now. On the other hand, I have acquired some things that I'll have trouble getting rid of. I really do enjoy my espresso. Just where do I have to draw the line?"

"We will work on that together," Sarah said. She was looking forward to further interaction with this most interesting man.

While the water heated, Ryan removed food from his well-stocked pantry and freezer and pointed out the location of the washing machine and other bathrooms. He showed her the master bedroom and a home office that he said he did not often use. He took them to the floor below and pointed out the satellite TV, the billiards table, the indoor swimming pool, and the steam room. Back upstairs, Ryan gave her a blue terrycloth bathrobe and promised a shopping trip to find new clothes.

He said that he planned to rest tomorrow and would go to his office on Monday. He would leave from there to go to Chicago for an investor meeting. He said he would return late Tuesday evening. He assured Peter that he would work on retrieving their car from Shiprock as soon as he returned.

Then he excused himself and went to drive the Jeep into one of the garages. "We'll empty it after we get some sleep," he said. She headed for the bedroom; Peter followed her up the stairs.

"Any reaction from Williams or the others?" Ernest Steiger looked up from the rifle he was holding and studied John deBeque. The young man, a trim six footer, wore a charcoal gray suit, white shirt with red and yellow striped tie. He had dark hair, dark eyes, and a determined set to his jaw. In his right hand, he held a thin black leather briefcase.

"Just requests for funds from their campaign finance managers," deBeque replied with a smile.

The young man traveled several days every week, but returned home each weekend to his townhouse in Georgetown, just outside Washington DC. To his neighbors he was another lobbyist — the capital had many of those. None of his friends knew he was associated with the most influential institution in the world. If they had called his office, the receptionist would have answered, "International League" and acted as if it were some minor organization.

His employees had been carefully screened. Each had signed a secrecy agreement, and each understood that extreme measures would be forthcoming should they reveal any of the highly confidential information that came across their desks. Most of deBeque's twenty-five employees were on the floor below. There was a different name on the door to that suite and a security guard immediately inside.

The study at Steiger's estate in Winnetka was a spacious room, teak wood bookcases, fourteen foot ceiling, teak desk, dark leather furniture. One wall looked east upon Lake Michigan. Learned and legal texts covered the other three. From this vantage point, high atop a bluff, the old man regularly enjoyed sunrise across the water.

"I'm worried about some of Williams's proposals," deBeque said. "They conflict with our program."

"Too bad the incumbent's going to lose. Things were easier with him." The wheel-chaired man looked to the east. The election would be determined in a few weeks. The media affiliates' had used their web of connections and influence to amass enough dirt on targeted candidates to supply their opponents with enough mud-slinging television commercials to fill every remaining hour. No politician was clean, even one as idealistic as Williams. Despite these, Steiger was resigned to several victories that might work against the interests of the media affiliates.

John deBeque had come to Winnetka to argue for more drastic measures in the case of Williams and one other: accusations of illegal dealings, fabricating a mistress. In the end, Steiger had voted with the other media affiliates to release the information they had, but not to fabricate more. He cautioned deBeque to be sure there was no connection between the leaked information and the media affiliates.

Steiger fondled the smooth stock of the Lazzeroni. Through

thick glasses, he checked its firing mechanism. Then he raised it to his shoulder. "We will see to Mr. Williams — after the election." His eyes were failing as the result of his diabetes, but he was not about to let anyone, including his adopted son, know of his increasing infirmity. Aiming at a small target in the corner of his study, the wheel-chaired man squeezed the trigger. Bang! The bullet was absorbed in the foam behind the center of the target.

At the resounding crack of the rifle, John deBeque jumped. "Do you have to do that?"

Steiger smiled and handed the rifle to deBeque. He set it by a display cabinet. Later, when other matters were attended to, the head of Steiger Enterprises would clean it and return it to its place in the cabinet, between a Weatherby and a Remington.

"What's new from the agencies?" Steiger asked.

"Some anti-American literature the FBI picked up in an INS raid on Mexican smugglers — caused a stir until they determined it was harmless. They were advocating that we dismantle our country in the name of a cosmic grand plan. It wasn't a group we've seen before — that's why it caught my eye."

"Not a terrorist cell?"

"FBI doesn't think so. In fact, after seeing the facility, the FBI is questioning the rationale behind the raid."

"Send me a copy." Steiger's nose for a possible story went back to his days as a reporter in Cincinnati, the first job he'd had after returning from his stint in the Army Air Corps.

"Found some strange gear at the site — FBI thinks they had an unregistered satellite communications set-up, maybe coordinated things with the Mexican end of the smuggling conduit. A technical team has gone to transport it to Washington for analysis."

"So, what did they say when the INS interrogated them?

"They didn't. The whole bunch fled into the desert."

"The desert?"

"INS is tracking them."

"Something about this interests me. Keep me appraised," Steiger said. "And I'd like to see that gear." He had developed a passion for anything connected with electronic communications, particularly anything unusual. Part of Steiger Enterprises' latest strategy was to acquire small companies in the electronic communications arena. He could foresee the day when printed newspapers would become obsolete.

"I'll see if I can arrange it."

"Anything from our friends in covert operations?"

"You know that I am not allowed to talk about other affiliate groups."

"Listen, I made you who you are."

"I know. And believe me I appreciate it — more than you will ever know. But, I still cannot talk about them."

Steiger knew that the people from covert operations and other affiliate groups used deBeque to funnel information to the media affiliates. It was usually packaged as a leak from some unnamed government source or cleverly disguised as a juicy tidbit about some corporation. After fifty years of analyzing such packages, he had learned to spot the fabricated from the real. But not all recipients of the information were as astute and much of it was published without further investigation. It was the major way in which the public was kept off balance and the activities of the covert community and other institutions were hidden.

A bang on the door interrupted them.

"Come in," Steiger said.

James "Rebar" Brown lumbered into the room.

"We'll talk later." The old man said to deBeque. "Right now, I've got something I need to attend to." He leaned back into his wheelchair.

When deBeque had closed the door, Steiger asked Rebar, "How'd it go?"

"Like you planned, boss," the former prizefighter answered. "He's in a hospital."

"You attracted no attention?"

"Mr. Charles White." Rebar pulled in his gut, straightened his back, and feigned tightening a tie. For the last two months, he had impersonated another man to gain access to a certain athletic club in Denver. He had patiently waited until one night when the club was virtually empty. "I told him it was for the man. Don't think he knowed what I was talking about."

The old man nodded and smiled. He had recruited Rebar from

Chicago's gutter. The large man had landed too many low blows, failed to heed the referees' calls too many times — he had been tossed out of boxing before he was able to advance into the ranks of professionals. With angry words, even his lifelong friend and trainer had abandoned him.

One night, drunk, he had staggered into Steiger's limousine in downtown Chicago. The old man's chauffeur, a big man himself, had tried to move Brown out of the way, but the larger man decked him with a single blow. Impressed, Steiger tracked him down and put him to work in his private security force. When the chauffeur was injured, Rebar took his place.

"Wish you'd a let me kill him," the hulk said.

"This is better. This way he has time to think about who did it, and why." In addition to guarding his media empire and acting as a conduit for information, the old man used his security force in a variety of assignments.

In recent months, he had noticed with concern that this particular overgrown child increasingly relished violence. Ernest Steiger knew that physical force had to be tempered, used with care, controlled. He could ill afford to have anyone associated with him found guilty of some impropriety.

"Are the girls ready?"

"Yeah."

"Good, I'm about ready for bed."

Rebar opened the door. Two Mexican teenagers sat outside. The hulk grabbed an arm with each of his large hands and pulled them into the room. The girls looked at the old man in the wheelchair and seemed relieved.

"Leave us." Steiger motioned Rebar away. Later he would investigate to see what his chauffeur had been up to with his playmates.

"Come," the old man beckoned the two closer. Both wore expensive skirts and sweaters. Both were pretty and barefoot. Both had the dazed looks of drug addicts.

He grabbed the hand of the newest one and pulled her to him. When he reached under her sweater, she flinched, but did not back away. Nor did she recoil as he fondled her firm breasts.

"Take it off," he commanded.

She removed her clothes to reveal a nubile body, marred only by bruises on her arms and shoulders.

The men who transported illegal Mexicans to his various operations kept an eye out for pretty girls. They supplied Steiger with a new playmate every few months.

On the final switchback, just as US 550 came off Red Mountain Pass and entered the town of Ouray, two light green sedans checked license plates.

"Nothing?" Raul Viejo asked as he pulled up next to the vehicle on the shoulder.

"Nope. Been checking every New Mexico plate," the INS agent said.

"Any other way out of there?" Viejo motioned to the snow capped peaks to the south.

"They could have doubled back and gone over Wolf Creek, but we've got that covered too."

"Hoehn's keen on finding them," Viejo said.

. "Yeah, he talked to my boss. Everybody in Colorado is looking for that license. Two people dead, wow."

"Well, I say stay with it for a while longer. I can't believe they slipped past you."

As Viejo turned his car back toward Arizona, his satellite phone rang twice and stopped. He did not attempt to answer. The caller rang again. Again he did not answer, and the ringing stopped after three. The first of his busses had crossed into Nebraska.

At about 9:00 AM Sarah Smith put on the blue bathrobe and wandered barefoot through Ryan's quiet house. She saw that the door to the master suite was open, knocked, and peeked in. Ryan was not there.

She went to the kitchen to find something to eat and discovered a note on the refrigerator:

> Gone to doctor.
> Be back soon.

She went downstairs to the swimming pool, laid the robe on a chair, and plunged into the refreshing water. On Phantia, swimming in the Academy pool had been one of her regular routines. As a girl she had been on the swimming team.

She paused at the far end to look out upon the forested land-scape. The water and the pine trees reminded her of her home planet. From this angle she could see a gully that descended from Ryan's home down the side of the mountain.

She turned, saw Ryan at the other side of the water, and waved. She felt the urge to swim to him, to be close. It did not matter that she was Phantian and he an earth dweller. He had saved her from a fall; escaped with her from the INS. She felt a bond with him. Then she remembered that she was naked.

She swam to his side of the pool and said, "Can you hand me that robe."

When Ryan realized that she was not clothed, he blushed and turned away. He grabbed the bathrobe and, with head turned, handed it to her. Before she fastened its belt, she saw his glance.

"You noted that I have no navel?" she said as she climbed out of the pool.

"Among other things."

She put her arm around his waist. Together they walked up the stairs to the floor above.

"On Phantia we carry our babies without an umbilical cord. When the fetus is developing, he or she is bathed in fluid like a child of your world. However in our case the fluid is the source of nutrients and oxygen. It is re-circulated by the mother's body.

"That's the reason my skin is so sensitive to environmental pollutants. In the womb it acted as a permeable membrane through which I received my nourishment."

"The lotion, huh?"

Few people are capable of expressing with equanimity opinions which differ from the prejudices of their social environment.

— ALBERT EINSTEIN

TEN

Tired from his trek and long drive, Ryan Drake struggled into his office. On most days, he was at work by 7:00 AM. Today he arrived at 8:03 AM. Sarah, Peter, and he had slept most of yesterday.

"Morning. What's going on?"

"What happened to you?" Karen Borden-Banes glanced up from a desk covered with papers. Her workstation was positioned outside the door to his office. No one saw Sanitas's CEO without passing in front of her. She stared at his sport shirt and blue jeans, and the bandage on his hand.

Ryan recognized her look. It said something was different. After he had showered this morning, he wandered into his closet to find clothes. He glanced at the row of dark suits and white shirts, but opted for a sport coat with blue jeans and a blue and red plaid shirt with a button down collar. Wing tips would not do. His hiking boots seemed to attach themselves to him like magnets. When he looked in the mirror he saw a different person staring back. He could not quite put his finger on it, but it was more than the clothes, more than the bandage on his hand. Everything seemed different.

"Let me get some coffee," he said to his administrative assistant.

Karen smiled. That hadn't changed. She had never volunteered to get the CEO's morning beverage. Ryan did not mind. It gave him a chance to interact with his subordinates, gave him an excuse to get up and move around.

In the executive services room, he filled a clean mug with fresh espresso from the machine, added skim milk from the container in the refrigerator, and steamed it to the proper temperature. He had to direct himself through this familiar routine — as if he was doing it for the first time. No one else was in the area so he returned to his office.

Seated behind an impressive oak slab, Ryan surveyed his domain. His custom-made desk was at the north end of his office. From here he could glance west at the rugged features of the Flatirons, rock formations that dominated the landscape to the west. With his left hand, he clasped his right elbow and pulled that arm over his head, stretching the tight muscle next to his armpit.

Various awards and business mementos, the trophies of a distinguished career, covered the wall to his left. The ceiling in his office was eighteen inches higher than other offices in the building. Before, he had been comfortable in the room. Now, he felt encased by it. He thought back to his dream of the transparent jail.

The sun glinted off a plaque on the wall, an international award, recognition of his company's position at the leading edge of pollution monitoring technology. Many in the industry regarded Ryan Drake as a visionary, a futurist, someone able to see commercial possibilities while repairing the environment. His speeches, or his presence on a panel, insured a large turnout. Further along the wall was a framed certificate, signed by the Governor of Colorado, appointing him to the Colorado Conservation Commission. He tried to attend their quarterly Board meetings.

A Nepalese tapestry hung on the far wall, a memorial of one of his hiking adventures. At the time Nepal had seemed exotic. That was before he had visited another planet.

Ryan stood, placed his hands on the edge of the desk, and moved his feet backward until he felt the dull pain. The resulting leg stretch felt wonderful. His massage therapist called his cramped muscles, executive calves — but this time they were the result of trekking in the desert and the long drive from Shiprock. He promised himself a workout that evening at the hotel in Chicago.

He felt imprisoned — what a contrast to the desert's wide-open spaces, to the vastness of the universe. Here, he was a businessman, constrained by piles of spreadsheets and reports, a multiline telephone, and a computer with dangling accessories.

In the past he had been divided on issues, seeing different perspectives, but always content with who he was. Today the opposite was true. Today he was solid about the issue, the cosmic paradigm, but uncertain as to whom he was. This was no simple Irish versus English or Democrat versus Republican argument about race or politics. This was a completely new way to view his world. Sarah had been right. The cosmic paradigm changed everything.

He glanced down at his Vasque hiking boots — never before had he dressed like this to come to the office. Even on Saturdays, he had insisted on preserving the picture of a successful CEO: coat and tie.

What would he do if he were not Sanitas's CEO? What would life be like without a full schedule, an office, and a company? Over the last three years he had been one with Sanitas. Now, his company felt like an ill-fitting shoe.

His friends were other high-powered business types — men and women dedicated to building their companies, blind to the larger picture, committed to an ego-driven lifestyle. Would any of them be open to the knowledge of a friendly, orchestrated universe? He thought of Aza O'Sullivan and scratched a note to call him.

Ryan stared at a picture on his desk: his son, at about age twelve, holding a trout, and his daughter, a year younger, with a larger fish dangling from her line. In the same frame were pictures of them now: Darren, twenty-five, enjoying life in California, and Danielle with her husband and two-year-old boy at their home in Scottsdale. Neither child liked the idea of their parent's divorce; he had not talked to either of them since the court proceedings had concluded. He reached for the phone and left messages on their answering machines telling them he was back from the desert.

"Are you ready?" Karen Borden-Banes stood in his doorway.

Ryan left his door open, but everyone hesitated before invading the CEO's space. He tried to relate to each of his employees as an important individual. Still, he was the one with the power, and they deferred to him. Even Karen, with whom he had constant contact, hung back before she barged into his office.

He snapped to attention, not ready to display his unfamiliar state of mind. "Sure, come in."

Karen had been his support since Sanitas's early years. She had followed him from his prior company. By the way she took care of the little things, he knew she cared about him. They shared problems and confidences, but he was careful to never cross that line between boss and subordinate.

Karen settled into her usual seat, across the oak expanse. She flashed a stack of papers and laid them on the front edge of the desk. "Are you OK?"

At forty-two, Karen retained a certain schoolgirl charm. She wore her brown hair in a wedge. It complemented her efficient but attractive image as the boss' right-hand. She had two girls, five and six, the result of a marriage that had ended four years ago. Ryan had yet to figure out how she managed to be the head of the household, a mother, and an excellent administrative assistant.

He thought of Sarah as she swam to greet him yesterday, her delightful slender body. But she had no navel, had come from an extraterrestrial womb, was an extraterrestrial. Yet, she had looked damn fine as she tied his robe around herself.

When she received no reply to her earlier question, she asked, "What happened?"

Ryan startled back to Karen and chuckled. He had trekked across the desert with two extraterrestrials, visited another world — who would believe? "I'll... I'll tell you about it — after we deal with the urgencies."

"Do you want your schedule, fax's, or phone calls?" Karen asked. She held up a leather-bound calendar, along with letter-size sheets, and telephone slips. She balanced a notepad and pen on her lap and waited. "I went through your email and responded to most of it. You'll probably want to reply to the few I left."

"What's urgent?" Ryan kicked into operating mode. He knew that a long list awaited him. However, even before he heard the details, he suspected they were less important than the larger, cosmic picture. Ryan Drake had moved beyond the busyness of business, yet he had an obligation to Sanitas's investors, employees, and customers.

Karen reviewed a short list of items that, in his absence, she had already handled. He nodded as she rattled off each — after many years of working together, he allowed her wide latitude in handling routine matters.

"Brauk wants to talk with you as soon as possible," she said. "Nick called. Wants to chat about tomorrow's meeting with his father. Your flight to Chicago leaves at 6:00. And." She lit up in a huge grin. "The arrangements with Carlton Boyle are all set. Your friend, Sam Wellborn, is really organized."

Before he had left for the desert, Sam and he had made plans for Boyle's visit to Sanitas, part of the presidential candidate's campaign swing through Colorado. The publicity would be good for Sanitas. In his absence, he had asked Karen to tend to the details. She had jumped at the opportunity; they had discussed Presidential candidates, and Boyle was her choice. She went on to give him the specifics of the candidate's visit.

"What else?" The CEO indicated the papers she had placed on the desk.

"You'll probably want to glance at these before you meet with anyone." Karen scooted the stack of papers toward him. "Comments from TTT Instrumentation about our agreement, and a dozen other things."

Ryan groaned, "I was hoping it was a done deal."

Karen shook her head. "Not yet. Who do you want to see first?"

"Brauk, then the team. Give me a chance to look at this." He grabbed the TTT document from the pile. He would read the rest of the papers on the airplane to Chicago.

"By the way, I need you to help some folks — a little shopping."

Karen looked surprised by the unusual request.

"I brought back some friends from Arizona." He needed to handle this right.

"OK," she readied her pen over her pad.

"A man and a woman." The CEO placed his elbows on his

desk, fingers intertwined. "Take time tomorrow. Show them around Flatirons Mall and Target." Sarah and Peter were still sleeping when he left this morning.

"Tomorrow?"

"Yes."

"Who are these people?"

"Well, uh… Their names are Sarah Smith and Peter Jones." Later he would explain. First, he needed to learn how to talk about extraterrestrials and celestials without seeming like a fool. "They're some special friends. Part of my adventure. Staying at my house."

"You're sure you're all right?"

Ryan recognized Karen's motherly tone. "I'm fine," he replied and motioned to dismiss her question.

With a broad smile, Karen rose and went toward the door. "I'm looking forward to hearing the story," she said over her shoulder. "I'll have Brauk here at nine."

"No. Tell him I'll stop by his office. The team here at ten."

He settled back in his big leather chair and took a deep breath. He was back in the groove. It didn't feel too bad. So what if he had a busy day, a busy week ahead. It was all part of the game, and he enjoyed it. He experienced an adrenaline rush as he geared to the hectic routine.

He paused. Something was decidedly different, something had changed. For many years he had believed that his planet wasn't the only occupied one in the universe. Yes he had believed in aliens, believed for years. But now he knew for sure there were extraterrestrials. He had traveled to their planet. And there was a big difference between believing something and knowing it was true. Believing versus knowing. Gray versus stark white. Today, he knew.

"What did you learn in the desert?"

Startled, Ryan looked up. No one was there. Yet the words had been precise, authoritative — not like the quiet voice of his conscience or memory. Nor were they the mind-to-mind communications he had heard from Sarah, overheard between Peter and Sarah. No, these words had been spoken, these words he had heard, these words demanded a response.

"I'm trying to sort it out," he said.

The reality of extraterrestrials and their celestial perspective had engraved itself on every cell of his body, on every synapse of his brain, on his soul. He had seen a larger vision of his world, and he wanted to pursue it. But, damn it, he had an obligation to Sanitas. For the first time in many years, Ryan Drake felt a tinge of insecurity at the bifurcation of everything in his life.

He looked again for the source of the words. Seeing nothing, he turned back and tried to concentrate on the document from TTT Instrumentation.

In addition to seeing both sides of almost every argument, every situation, Ryan possessed another ability that he kept mostly to himself. Scientists collected data, on all types of things, and statisticians used it to project what the past must have been like. It was a powerful technique and had produced some amazing conclusions about the geology of the Earth, how people had lived long ago.

Ryan's ability was different. He seldom looked into the past. However, he was very good at seeing where things were headed. Given enough data, he was able to virtually predict the future. In the past, getting others to believe these predictions had caused problems and he now went to great lengths to gather proof in all his business dealings. But his urge to predict broad implications was always just below the surface.

He glanced up from reading and wondered where he was being led. The Phantians had supplied a new paradigm. He was beginning to see the implications of it for himself and, his world.

Chad "Brauk" Braukington's whole life revolved around Sanitas. The Company paid a premium for the janitorial service that cleaned the leftover pizza and pop cans from his office. Once a week, they changed the sheets on the folding bed he kept there. Those that did not know him worried that he had no home, no family, but Sanitas's resident genius was content.

Brauk had started as a talented young engineer with grand ideas for new products. His parents had financed his move out of the basement of their home to a small rented office. For the first few years, he existed as a consultant to various governmental organizations, helping them maintain their antiquated pollution monitoring equipment. In his spare time, he constructed several innovative prototypes.

Ryan had visited with him at the request of a local venture

capitalist. After one day with a technical consultant, Ryan was sold. Impressed with the potential of Brauk's work, he offered to put some of his own money into developing it further.

Although he was broke, Brauk resisted the idea of allowing outsiders to invest in his company. He was convinced that he would be moved out as soon as professionals moved in and was not about to relinquish control. Ryan saw in him a technical genius that complemented his own ability to size up opportunities. He assured the young man that he would be indispensable to the future of the company. After all, who originated all the ideas? Besides, Ryan reminded Brauk, he had no technical degree. After several weeks of conversation, and unambiguous assurances from his family that they would supply no more money, Chad Braukington capitulated.

After the financing was arranged, Ryan's first official act was to change the Company's name. The CEO insisted that Sanitas was not proper for a thriving high technology company. Brauk resisted. As a techie, he did not care that Sanitas meant sanitarium; he liked the name, thought it related well to healthy air. Sensing there would be more important issues, Ryan yielded.

"Hey, Ry. What happened?" Brauk's desk was a collection of papers and ashtrays piled with half-smoked cigarettes. His office had a large window that looked out on the development area. He directed a staff of engineers and technicians dedicated to furthering his ideas. Not handsome, Chad's short black hair contrasted unpleasantly with his pale face. His head seemed small on his bulky frame. Overweight, he refused to exercise.

"Had a good time."

"Why the clothes?" Brauk pointed to Ryan's blue jeans and open-necked shirt.

"First day back." He needed to tell someone what had happened in the desert and about the extraterrestrials. Although he and Sanitas's resident genius had watched Star Trek together on Brauk's office television, Ryan was not prepared to tell him that he had traveled to another world, that extraterrestrials were living in his home.

"Figured out the remote sensor." The inventor tapped the cover of a tomato stained notebook. "The data indicates we'll finally be able to do it by satellite." Brauk spent little time on pleasantries.

Today that suited Ryan fine. "It's all here."

"Great." For a moment, the CEO forgot about the cosmic paradigm and warmed to the prospect of a technological breakthrough.

Sanitas had pioneered Global Watch, a sophisticated system for monitoring pollution levels worldwide. By installing instruments at key sites around the globe and transmitting their readings back to Sanitas's data collection system in Boulder, the company was able to provide government agencies and watchdog groups with accurate, up-to-date information. The major problem was getting data from polluters who wished to hide their fouling of air, water or land, and would not allow sensors installed in their plants. Brauk had been working on the problem for two years.

"Work up a project plan," Ryan said. "I'll get the Board to approve a budget." He began to think about potential funding from various agencies domestic and international. It was in almost everyone's interest that accurate data be available. The temperature of the earth had risen by a full degree within the past ten years.

"Yeah, yeah, budgets. You and I also need to talk about our proposal to TTT," Brauk said. The technical man's mind seldom stayed on one topic long.

TTT Instrumentation was a critical link in their monitoring and data collection system. The system that collected and recorded the massive amounts of data was at Sanitas' facility in Boulder. Communications channels, leased from existing satellite and terrestrial providers, were used to gather that information from the remote sensors. Storage systems at Sanitas recorded everything. In off-hours, computers at the National Center for Atmospheric Research and the National Oceanic and Atmospheric Administration analyzed the data. Both had their super computer facilities in Boulder and were happy to rent computer time to Sanitas for something that aided their missions. This effort was being assisted with grants from an agency of the United Nations that had been set up to respond to the continued rise in worldwide temperature.

Through TTT Instrumentation's global network of sales and technical representatives, Sanitas had been able to place instruments at the right locations in one hundred and forty countries. These instruments, mostly manufactured by Sanitas, were slaved to the communications channels that transmitted their readings throughout the day. Other manufacturers were allowed to tie their instruments into the system but only by meeting Sanitas's rigid specifications.

Under the present arrangement, TTT Instrumentation distributed and serviced only Sanitas equipment for certain measurements. Ryan was aware that other manufacturers had approached his international distributor with various proposals. To date Sanitas had been able to fend them off by incorporating innovations that made their equipment superior. However, as the technology became more and more standardized, Sanitas' ability to prevail through innovation waned.

"I'm meeting with the team in a few minutes," Ryan said. "Join us."

Ryan strolled back to the executive wing. Sanitas's facility was not yet a year old. The plants along the corridor were real; a service kept them at their peak. He had selected the paintings, nice Southwesterns, not expensive. Sanitas was a success by almost any standard: It provided jobs for over three hundred people and was recognized in the industry as one of the up-and-coming businesses.

But the day before yesterday, he had helped two visitors from another planet escape from government agents, his government's agents. The day before he'd visited the extraterrestrials' home on another planet. Sanitas's familiar facility suddenly felt foreign, felt unnecessary to the larger picture. Recognizing his mental and emotional bifurcation, Ryan headed for his second latte.

Later, as Ryan hurried through Denver International Airport, he called Karen from his cell phone. "Be sure everybody knows when Carlton Boyle will be there. It's a great opportunity to show off the company. We need everything clean and working — even Brauk's office."

"Already taken care of," she replied.

"Be sure to alert NCAR and NOAA. We'll want to show Boyle and the press how we process data."

"Will do."

He ran to catch his flight to Chicago.

"The FBI can't figure out that gear from the smugglers hideout." Using a private circuit, John deBeque spoke to Ernest Steiger from his office in Washington. "It's not like ours, or anything the Russians stole from us. I made arrangements for you to get a look."

"So, where are they?"

"Who?"

"The people from that facility."

"The INS chased three of them into the Colorado mountains, but lost them. The others must be out in the desert somewhere. They're tracking them."

Steiger picked up a printed sheet. "I read their papers — dangerous. They're a threat to America, to our program."

The folder, stamped with an FBI date and reference number, had arrived by courier last evening. He had stayed up late reading about friendly aliens, the over control of the universe by powerful spirits, and the true age of the universe. With a reporter's instincts, he suspected this might be the work of an intelligence from beyond this planet. He did not relay these suspicions to deBeque.

For years, the media affiliates' neatly constructed consumption paradigm had not admitted to the existence of aliens, had relegated those concepts to the realm of science fiction, had ridiculed the very notion. The media affiliates' program did not allow for thinking outside the Box and, most certainly, did not include admitting the existence of other inhabited worlds. If people had to imagine such stuff, better that they think the universe was hostile — fear helped win the Big War, and after that the Cold War. Fear kept people focused on the present.

"I glanced at it. A friendly universe, really," deBeque snorted. "It's a good thing the public don't know about the surveillance we've been under from aliens, the way they've interfered with our ICBMs. I think it would cause mass hysteria."

"Hysteria may be useful, when the time is right," Steiger said. "Who's seen this?"

"The FBI. Probably the INS. Maybe some Indians. Copies of it were all around that desert facility."

"Any reactions?"

"The FBI dismissed it," deBeque said. "They're focused on terrorists."

"Good, as unimaginative as ever," Steiger said. "I don't want them involved."

"Why?"

"I have my suspicions, and want to pursue them a while."

"Without the others?"

"Yes." Steiger eyed the young man, taking his measure. Although his vision was not what once was, he was still a keen judge of people.

"That's dangerous. I'm not sure I want to be part of it."

"You owe me."

"All right, all right. But, if something gets out of hand, we have to alert the others. Just what do you think is here?"

"I'll let you know."

"What about the INS?" deBeque asked.

"Keep pressure on them. Get them to track down anybody who ever visited that place."

For a long time things had gone well. Hollywood had done a great job of portraying aliens as adversaries — he'd made good money as a limited partner in several sci-fi films. But, the media affiliates had been excluded from the biggest profit potential. Aerospace and electronics companies had reverse-engineered the alien's technology; some of it had resulted in the wave of electronic communications that threatened his media empire.

The written material from the desert was garbled, but if it was from aliens, it showed an amazing ability to understand the issues of a strange culture, a foreign planet. If it was turned into more-readable English, it might turn heads, lead people to think. Such skills interested Steiger, a long-time student of psychology and communications. Moreover, aliens who possessed the ability to write in English probably had other superior communications technologies. He hoped they had not uncovered the goal of the media affiliates and its network of associated organizations.

Later that evening Steiger noted these observations in his diary. He added his misgivings about Leonard Williams and the problems he anticipated with him. Williams reminded him of another Senator with whom the media affiliates had differed. That man, also an idealist, had contracted an incurable malady as the result of a trip he had taken to Africa during his second year in office. He made a little chart and noted the similarities between the two men. On the chart's last line, he left a space for the final disposition of Leonard Williams.

Chicago's airport was closed because of a bomb threat; Ryan's flight was diverted to St Louis. As they waited for ground transportation to Chicago, he thought back thirty-six years to events in a suburb not far away.

"Ry, you're going to be the death of me," Catherine Drake said as she wiped blood from his head. It was football season. He had just taken a hit from two defensive players who together weighed three times what he did. "By Saint Patrick, all you do is bang yourself up." He recognized the tune of the Irish ditty she hummed under her breath. She had sung him to sleep with it when he was a child.

Dazed, he lay on the sideline where the team's trainer had dragged him. The football game was going on without Florescent Junior High's star running back. Much to Ryan's embarrassment, his mother had climbed out of the stands and rushed to her son's side. He knew she meant well, but the team's trainer was already mopping him up when she grabbed the cotton swab. The next day at school, he'd hear all about his mother's pampering.

After a minute or two, he got up and paced the sidelines. He looked to where his mother had been seated, not far behind the team's bench. He hoped to see his father there, but did not. His grandparents, Gramps on the left and Dada on the right, held his mother's seat and looked back at him with smiles. Ryan watched as his mother returned to her seat.

After his head cleared, he signaled the coach he was ready to play. He went back in on their next possession. His team won by the touchdown he scored in the closing minute.

His mother's ovarian cancer was detected that January and proceeded mercifully fast. Ryan Drake curtailed all activities except school to visit her daily in the hospital. She died in early spring.

The church filled with mourners. Catherine Drake had touched the lives of many. The Catholic service was traditional with the priest and her friends saying how they would remember her. As he sat between his grandparents, tears rolling down his face, he remembered her hugs and the way she'd smelled like lilacs. He was going to miss her very much.

At the graveside, he stood between his grandparents. When he stepped forward and placed a white rose on her coffin, he vowed to be good and to join her in heaven. Her close friends and neighbors stood silently as the priest said the final words. Ryan barely noticed the white-haired stranger who stood close to the grave.

In the weeks following, he came home directly after school and refused to study or participate in sports. His baseball coach called and begged him to help the team. He told him he was sick. Friends called. He told them he did not want to go to the soda shop or a movie. His grandparents brought dinner and tried to cheer him. He picked at his food, but barely talked to them.

One evening his father asked him to come to his study. "The principal called me today," Albert Drake said. "What do you think you're doing? You've turned in no homework for the past three weeks. Ryan, you've mourned enough. It's time to get back to work."

His father, a prominent St. Louis lawyer who claimed to be a direct descendant of Sir Francis Drake, the English explorer, peered at him through thick glasses. That look had always meant trouble. The dark wood of his father's study whirled in clouds of pipe smoke. Ryan had become nauseous and had run to his room.

The next day at school he got into a fight with another boy. Each managed to bloody the face of the other. Both were hauled into the counselor's office and asked to explain. Neither spoke up. The counselor prescribed detention and no after-school sports for a week. He also called the parents of both boys.

Two weeks later his father hustled Ryan off to a boarding school in Omaha. After that, he saw his father only on school holidays and then only for a few hours.

Now as he thought back to those distant events, Ryan Drake realized that it had been Dr. Adamson whom he had seen at the side of his mother's grave. He wondered how his father was doing, but dismissed calling him — some conversations were best left alone.

Collecting is the only socially acceptable form of greed.

— Henry L. Stimson

ELEVEN

Ryan Drake arrived at the front entrance to the Steiger estate promptly at 10:45 AM. This was his first trip to the fabled mansion of Nick's father. The uniformed guard asked to see his driver's license and went into the small building to the left of the tall wrought-iron front gate.

Last evening, after a four-hour bus ride from St. Louis, he had arrived at Chicago's O'Hare Airport. It was very late by the time he rented a car and got to his hotel. The morning paper reported that the airport was back to operating normally.

The investment from the Steiger Family Trust was Sanitas's largest in terms of dollars. He owed them a decent review of the company's operations and future prospects. Besides, Ryan was proud of his company's achievements, and one never knew where connections with people in high places might lead.

Thus far, all of Ryan's dealings had been through Nick. Today he was going to meet with Ernest Steiger. The family's patriarch had a reputation as a collector of original art and member of big money circles. He was known for his support of conservative candidates who made the status quo their top priority. Nick had in-

151

formed Ryan that the Steiger family's media empire, controlled an array of magazines and newspapers, radio and television stations, printing operations scattered around the world, and a few "miscellaneous" businesses. The Steiger Family Trust, that Nick ran, invested in interesting, but unrelated new enterprises.

"You may proceed." The guard handed his license back to him and the gate opened. He drove to the front of the house on the broad circular drive. The imposing three-story building was situated on a bluff overlooking Lake Michigan. The mansion towered above its nearest neighbors to the north and south; they did not sit on such high ground. Oak and maple trees, ablaze in autumn color, shaded the inlaid driveway. Its surface was spotless, no sign that another car had ever parked in front of the brass-adorned double doors. The dark stone of the house contrasted with the manicured lawn and trimmed bushes. There were no flowers.

The five-acre site, by far the largest in Winnetka, had been the summer home of a Chicago grain dealer. Ernest Steiger's father had acquired it in 1953. He had replaced the aging wooden structures with a stone castle and several smaller buildings.

Ryan climbed out of his rental car, grabbed his briefcase, and marched up the stairs. His right hand, bandaged but feeling better, went to the open collar of his shirt. He felt naked without a tie.

He was about to knock when the door opened and a large man said, "Come with me." The man was dressed in black: turtleneck, trousers, belt, socks, and shoes. His shirt was stretched to its limit by a torso bulging from constant workouts. He filled the hallway as he led Ryan forward.

They passed what looked like museum quality original paintings. He paused at one labeled Gauguin. Further on a blank space with a note, ON LOAN TO ART INSTITUTE OF CHICAGO, beneath it a label, Monet.

The man opened the right side of two massive doors and Ryan stepped into an elegant room with tall windows overlooking the waters of Lake Michigan. He glimpsed walls lined with more paintings — a veritable museum of impressionist painters. A lighted crystal chandelier accented the teak wood of the long table.

Nick Steiger rose to greet him as if angry words had never

passed between them. "Hey Ryan, nice to see you. Thanks for coming. What happened?" Nick pointed to the bandage on Ryan's hand.

"A small accident."

"Where were you anyway?"

"I think I'll keep that to myself — in case I want to go back some other time." Ryan gave Nick a wink and a smile.

The CEO laid his briefcase on the teak conference table and they chatted about the young man's other investments. For Ryan, it seemed like a repeat of past conversations with Nick.

After twenty minutes, they were interrupted by the opening of a small door at the other side of the room. The same large man pushed a heavyset man in a wheelchair into the room and closed the door behind them.

Extending his hand, Ryan turned and walked toward the wheelchair. "Hello Mr. Steiger. It's nice to see you again. You may remember that we met at my father's birthday party."

"Mr. Drake." The old man's handshake was brief. His steel eyes observed Ryan's bandaged hand and open collar. His face was expressionless. The wheelchair-bound head of Steiger Enterprises was dressed in a dark suit, white shirt, and red striped tie.

"I've told father how well our investment in Sanitas is doing," Nick said obsequiously. He motioned for Ryan to pick up from there.

"Yes, I believe you'll be pleased." Ryan reached into his briefcase and extracted three neat packages. He presented one to each of them. Out of the corner of his eye, he noted that the large man, arms folded, remained in front of the door through which Ernest Steiger had entered.

For the next thirty minutes, Ryan reviewed Sanitas's financials. Nick asked a few questions. His father did not comment. Ryan was preparing to launch into a discussion on Sanitas's new products when the elder Steiger interrupted, "This is all well and good, but what about next year? I want to hear about the situation with TTT Instrumentation."

Ryan was dumbfounded. He had not mentioned TTT Instrumentation. He glanced at Nick. The young man stared at his father. "What are you talking about, father?"

The old man caught his son in his gaze. "I happen to know

that TTT Instrumentation has not finalized their new distribution and service agreement with Sanitas."

Recovering from his surprise, Ryan said, "We haven't pinned-down the final details, but I'm optimistic that we will."

Ernest Steiger did not react.

"What's your connection to TTT Instrumentation?"

The old man in the wheelchair stared at him. Ryan's question hung in the air.

"Why are you messing with my investment?" Nick asked.

Ernest Steiger shot a glance at his son and said, "If you had asked for this information, our operations people would have made it available to you." Nick's shoulders slumped. He looked down at the table.

The old man turned to Ryan, "There is a risk that TTT Instrumentation will decide against renewing your distribution agreement. If that happens Sanitas's revenues will drop by thirty percent. Correct?"

"If we don't take other actions."

"So, what are you going to do about it, Ryan?" Nick leaned across the table toward him, but he looked at his father not Ryan Drake.

"There is a risk. However, we've had the arrangement with TTT for two years. As far as I know, they're happy."

"Another company, ah... I believe they're German, is offering the same unit to them," the elder Steiger said. "At a lower price."

"Our unit's patented," the CEO said. "They'd be in violation. We have advanced features, no one else —"

"Is your company willing to fight a multi-national corporation?"

"Damn right."

"I think you would lose."

"As an investor in Sanitas, are you offering to help?" Ryan asked.

"Perhaps. Perhaps." A thin smile crossed the elder Steiger's face.

The meeting went on for an additional fifteen minutes. Then the old man asked, "Have you considered what use your talents might be in a larger arena? There are always interesting opportunities within Steiger for a man such as yourself."

"Are you offering me a job?"

"Father," Nick said. "How could you?"

Ernest Steiger did not respond to his son's objection.

"Thank you, Mr. Steiger," Ryan addressed the old man. "I am honored, but I'm quite happy with my current situation."

"Very well Mr. Drake. Thank you for coming. It was interesting." He motioned to the large man who came to the back of his wheelchair and pushed it towards the door through which they had entered.

They were about to exit when Ernest Steiger held up his hand. The wheelchair stopped and Steiger turned his head toward Ryan. "You know about technology — follow me."

Ryan shoved his charts and spreadsheets into his briefcase and followed the wheelchair through the door into a small room. Nick did not follow.

A large carton sat upended in the middle of a table. When they entered, a man in a gray suit stood.

"This is Special Agent Swift from the FBI," Steiger said.

Ryan reached to clasp the agent's hand. Was this a trap? Had the FBI already connected him to the extraterrestrials?

"Show it to him," Steiger growled.

The FBI man hesitated.

"Show it to him. I want another opinion."

Swift removed the carton from a gleaming metal cube, three hexagonal knobs, rounded corners, and sides. The knot in the pit of Ryan's stomach tightened — it was the piece of equipment he had noticed next to the television at Harmony.

"Do you have any idea what this is?" Steiger asked.

"Without knowing what it's supposed to do —" Ryan did not finish his sentence. He shook his head, but forced himself to step forward and examine it. No lettering, nothing to indicate the functions of the three knobs. He looked at its rear. There were no connectors, no power cord. As he looked more closely, Ryan saw no cracks or fasteners to indicate how someone might open the gleaming metal cube.

"If Brauk, my technology guy, were here, he might know," Ryan said. "I don't know as much about technology as he does. What was it connected to?"

Swift said, "Not —" He broke off his sentence.

"Where'd it come from?"

No one responded.

"So, what do you think?" Ryan addressed Swift.

The FBI man looked at Steiger, shrugged, and then said, "We're not sure." It was obvious to Ryan that the man did not like the idea of being here, of showing this piece of gear to just anyone.

Ryan stared at the cube. He was aware of Steiger's focus on him. How did an old man in Winnetka wind up with this piece of extraterrestrial equipment from Harmony?

"Any ideas, Mr. Drake?" Ernest Steiger's eyes bored into him.

"No." He was starting to sweat.

"You're sure? There for a moment I thought you were going to say something."

"Sorry. I can't help you," Ryan said. He picked up his briefcase and headed for the door.

The hulk moved to intercept him, but Ernest Steiger grunted and the man moved out of Ryan's way.

"Mr. Drake."

Ryan halted and turned to the man in the wheelchair.

"As I said earlier, there are interesting opportunities in my organization, a broader horizon than where you are."

"Thank you again, but no thanks."

Ryan said good-bye to Nick as he exited through the room with the million dollar paintings.

As he drove west on Lake Street, the shadows of overhanging branches played on his windshield. Oak, elm, and maple in the final stages of their fall array arched over the road. Manicured hedges bordered the green lawns of well-maintained houses. Fallen leaves strewn everywhere. A man with a leaf blower edged a fluffy brown pile into the street. Pumpkins for sale in a church yard; their bright orange contrasted with the dwindling colors of fall. He paused for the light at Green Bay and then again at Ridge Rd. and continued west to Interstate 294 and O'Hare airport.

Ryan popped several antacid tablets into his mouth and chewed them. The old man he had just visited was a study in power and manipulation. That employment offer had to be phony. The way he had toyed with his son reminded Ryan of his own father. The FBI guy and that cube. Could it possibly have been a coincidence? How long before Steiger or the FBI connected him to the fugitives from Harmony?

After Ryan Drake left and he had dismissed Nick, Ernest Steiger had Rebar drive him to his downtown Chicago office. He had several meetings and one minor matter to attend to. He asked his secretary to connect him to Steiger Enterprises' attorney.

After the usual pleasantries, he asked, "Have you reviewed Ballard's employment agreement?"

"Yes. And you are correct; you can fire him at your discretion. The terms of continued employment, as specified in the purchase agreement for his company, have expired. All you owe him is a nominal severance."

"Good."

"Anything else?"

"Your son came to visit me today," Steiger said.

"My son?"

"Ryan's company is doing quite well — the best in Nick's pitiful portfolio. I offered him a job, which he turned down. Do you happen to know where he spent his most recent vacation?"

"You know I have little contact with him," Arnold Drake said.

"See if you can find out."

"I will try."

"When can we get together?" Steiger asked. "We have other things to discuss."

"You can always come to St. Louis," Arnold said.

"I am not traveling much since they confined me to this damn wheelchair."

"That's fine. I'll come to Chicago. We'll find some cute girls," Arnold joked. His long-time friend and attorney always used the same farewell.

When Steiger hung up, he thought back to when he and Arnold Drake had first become friends. The year was 1947.

"That was so amazing. What did you think?" Arnold Drake asked. He took a last nervous puff on his Chesterfield and ground it into the ashtray.

"I think I'm not supposed to think," Ernest replied. His voice was low.

The two men, both in their early twenties, huddled over beers in a bar in downtown Roswell, New Mexico. Both wore the uniforms of United States Army Officers. Neither was handsome enough to attract unwarranted attention.

"But you can't deny what we saw." Earlier that day they had stripped loose objects out of the disk-shaped craft. Ernest Steiger and Arnold Drake had been part of a small contingent allowed inside the heavily guarded hanger; the other men had been readying the craft for transport. Their mission was to retrieve any unattached objects before the craft left, before any other intelligence service got their hands on it. They had found several: Gray metallic disks with hair-thin lines scratched on their surfaces. A foot-long metal tube with transparent fibers protruding from one end. It was attached to a helmet that appeared to have been worn by one of the aliens. Pieces of metal and material that had been dislodged in the crash were added to the box of debris recovered from the site.

"Look, what if some of these people are Commies?" Ernest motioned to the men and women in the smoke filled bar. Some wore uniforms, others were dressed as civilians. "What if they overhear you and report to Moscow? Do you want to be responsible for leaking classified information?"

"But this means there's things, beings, from other planets." Arnold lowered his voice and joined Ernest in surveying the nearby tables and booths.

Ernest took a sip of his beer and studied his companion. Arnold was a year older; he had thick glasses and a thin mustache. They had met in Officer's Training School and because both came from wealthy families had gravitated to each other's company.

Without ever voicing his own attitude, Ernest knew that Arnold also considered their fellow officers beneath them. His own father had insisted that he join the military — it was time to learn what made ordinary people tick. Until Ernest had enrolled at Harvard University, at age sixteen, he had never attended a regular school. His tutors had been selected from the courts of Europe. They taught him to read and write, to think, and to behave like royalty.

"Listen, we aren't supposed to talk about this stuff, even to each other," Ernest said.

During World War II, Ernest's father had been one of the highest-ranking intelligence officers in the United States Military. While the scientists of the Manhattan Project were busy inventing weapons of mass destruction, his team was equally busy covering up their activities. When experiments with radiation went haywire, his team shielded them from public exposure.

Arnold said, "Yeah, I know. But I also know what I saw. It was some sort of flying disk, all shiny and sleek. Not like any airplane I ever saw." He drew a rough sketch on his paper napkin. It was saucer shaped with a fin on its back, a manta ray without its tail.

"Don't do that." Ernest reached over and grabbed the napkin. He waded it up, plunked it in the ashtray, and struck a match to it. "Do you understand what extreme prejudice means?"

"Yeah, somebody might wind up dead."

"Isn't that what General Thorp said?"

"Yeah."

"Well I can't afford to be on the receiving end. This stuff is top secret. The only reason I even got to see it was because —" Ernest did not finish the sentence. No need to tell Arnold more.

He had been working at an assignment in the Pentagon when the order had arrived for him to report to General Thorp. Over the past eighteen months, Ernest had come to expect mysterious postings. Although his father was retired from the intelligence service, his influence extended well into the military.

"But you do understand what we saw?" Arnold said.

"Yes, I understand and I also understand we need to keep it secret. Remember the panic when they broadcast War of the Worlds? I think the General's right. This information has to be managed. Ordinary people just aren't ready to find out that we're not the only —" He cut off his sentence and followed Arnold's stare toward the end of the table.

"So what are you boys up to?" She was young and pretty. Her friend hung back, waiting for one of the soldiers to respond.

"Just having a beer," Arnold said. "Would you like to join us?"

"Sure," the brunette replied.

Ernest scooted further into the booth; she slid in beside him. The other girl, a blonde, moved to Arnold's side. When the waitress came over, they ordered drinks for the girls and more beer for themselves.

"So where are you from?" she asked Ernest.

"Chicago."

"You going back there?"

"Sure. It's a great town."

"What's so great about it?" The brunette leaned close and put her hand on his leg.

"Good music. Good food."

"So what do you like to do there?" She whispered into his ear and rubbed the inside of his thigh. Her perfume, an expensive brand, filled his nostrils.

Ernest glanced across the table and saw that Arnold was similarly engaged.

Before long Ernest's hand was on the inside of the brunette's leg. When he felt the heat of her silk panties he said, "It's kind of warm in here. Want to go for a walk."

She had taken him to her motel room and treated him to wild sex. The next day he reported her to base security. They arrested her as a Soviet spy.

Those had been good times, those years before responsibility had been thrust upon him. When he returned home from the Army, his father had shoved him into the family's publishing business. In ten years, he was running a newspaper in Cincinnati, the youngest publisher in America. Three years later, when his father died of cancer, he had inherited a media empire.

His intercom buzzed. "Mr. Ballard is holding," his secretary said. The words interrupted Steiger's reminiscing.

"I'll talk to him."

"What's this I hear about a strike at your operation?" Steiger asked. Chris Ballard ran a specialty printing plant in Wichita, Kansas. It printed and packaged high quality stationary that was distributed through card shops. Steiger Enterprises had acquired it from Ballard's family when it was near bankruptcy. Chris Ballard, son of the owner, had been kept on as a hired hand. While not a major piece of Steiger's empire, it had been extremely profitable.

"They walked out yesterday, damn union."

"So what are you doing about it?"

"Been negotiating, all night. I think I can reach an equitable compromise."

"I'm replacing you. Clean out your office."

"You can't do that."

"I'm not throwing away my investment to make you feel good. Get out."

"What do I tell everybody?"

"Tell them you got fired." Steiger hung up before the man on the line could say more.

He called his son Richard and told him to send a man from one of the printing facilities that Richard managed to replace Ballard. He also instructed Richard to replace the striking workers with Mexicans from his Iowa operations.

It is to the commonwealth of mankind that there should be some one who is unconquered, some one against whom fortune has no power.

— SENECA

TWELVE

"Well, hi, Dr. Adamson." Upon returning to his house in Boulder, Ryan found Dr. Victor Adamson, Sarah Smith, and Peter Jones sitting around one end of his dining room table. "You surprised me. I didn't see a car outside."

Dr. Adamson rose and gave him the kind of hug reserved for close friends. This time Ryan noticed a distinct lack of pressure. But the hug produced the sensational experience of warm contact.

"It is nice to see you again, Ryan." The Harmony leader stepped back and examined him "I understand you've had a few adventures since we last saw each other."

Ryan smiled and said, "I had another one today."

"We were just discussing your encounter with Ernest Steiger," Sarah said.

"How? You didn't know who I was going to visit."

"My remote viewing powers are quite effective," Sarah said and motioned him to take a seat.

"There was that FBI guy." Ryan pulled out the chair next to her. "And that cube from Harmony."

"Yes," Sarah said.

"What is that thing anyway?"

"It is equipment to monitor air quality, to detect certain pollutants."

"But there's no display."

"In the event of a problem at Harmony, it transmitted an alarm directly to our minds."

Ryan fumbled for an antacid tablet and slipped it into his mouth. He looked at Sarah, then Peter, then Dr. Adamson. "OK, lay it out for me." He was becoming immune to startling news.

"Let me start," Sarah said. "First of all, Dr. Adamson does not need a car. He has his own means of transportation."

"Other than walking?"

"Yes."

Ryan turned to scrutinize the white-haired man. What he saw was a middle-aged man dressed in hiking clothes, nothing unusual. He recalled that Victor Adamson had never shaken his hand, so, on an impulse, he reached for it.

Rather than accept Ryan's touch, Dr. Adamson raised his hand as if to smack the table. However, as he brought it down, it passed through the surface leaving it untouched.

"Huh," Ryan said. "Do that again."

The white-haired apparition complied, again his hand passed through the mass of the table and disappeared below.

Ryan shook his head. A week ago, before he'd discovered extraterrestrials, before he'd visited another world, he would have been shocked. Now, his reaction was mild surprise, "Wow."

Sarah laughed and placed her hand on his arm. "Dr. Adamson can control his degree of materialization."

"Can you do that?" he asked her.

"No." She offered the same hand he had previously examined.

Dr. Adamson smiled. "After Teddy Leupp and I left you in the desert, I went to California to care for another situation. I arrived here just in time to review Sarah's information about your meeting in Winnetka."

"I saw your hand pass through this table." Ryan was still amazed at what he had just seen. He pounded the table to reassure himself it was still solid. "Why don't you just take control of everything and make it right?"

"That is not my task."

"What is?"

"I am helping to prepare this world for the next step in its evolution: Indisputable proof of extraterrestrials and the truth of the celestially organized universe," Dr Adamson said. "We believe this new paradigm will shock the people of this planet into taking charge of their lives. We want to inform as many as possible in advance of the appearance of extraterrestrials so that their presence will be interpreted as benevolent, not hostile.

"By celestial edict, I can reveal my true nature only to those who show a desire to cooperate. Only in moments of extreme crisis, may I show myself to those who have not invited me, who would not welcome my intrusion. That is why I requested the revealators. They are mortals like you. Their mere presence here indicates the truth of the orchestrated and friendly universe.

"For years, other extraterrestrials have attempted to effect change by making contact with the humans of this planet. But they have been hampered by their cautious appearances and their inability to speak your language. Their activities have been interpreted as adversarial and mysterious, and have been hidden and ridiculed. Sarah and Peter are able to converse with you and others directly. Hopefully, their presence will convince people of our good intentions."

"Many of your legends about fairies and elves stem from the age-old activities of intraterrestrials such as Dr. Adamson," Sarah said.

Ryan nodded. Many had been trying to help this planet, but it was still up to people to evolve this world. It was a heavy burden and he wondered who would understand, who would act for the best. Thinking about Dr. Adamson's age, he wondered if anyone in the past had listened.

As if he had read Ryan's mind, Dr. Adamson smiled and said, "Yes, I was there as they wrote the Declaration of Independence and formed this citadel of hope and the rule of law. And before that when King John signed the Magna Carta. And as Galileo was persecuted for his observations of the night sky. And for many, many years before that."

Ryan leaned into his chair and studied the white-haired apparition. He was definitely the man who had stood at the side of his mother's grave.

"Ernest Steiger suspects that you know more than you let on," Sarah said interrupting his thoughts. "Your bandaged hand and casual dress made him suspicious."

Ryan was not surprised. The elder Steiger had been most curious about his reactions to the electronics gear from Harmony, had risked showing him a piece of FBI evidence, had persisted in recruiting him, and had excluded his son from the conversation. "Nick has an interesting relationship with his father. I feel sorry for him."

"Although he is Ernest Steiger's son, his father only trusts him with minor matters like investments from their family trust," Dr. Adamson said. "Nick's older brother, Richard, runs various printing and publishing operations, but under his father's watchful eye. His sister, an artist, is probably closest to him. She lives in Paris. Although they are all aware of it, Steiger has not allowed any of his children into the secret group to which he belongs."

"Secret group?"

"It is a very complex subject," Dr Adamson said. He stood and paced for a few moments and then addressed Ryan. "They call themselves the media affiliates. They are a group of elitists connected with movies, newspapers, and television. Most operate out of public view, influencing Hollywood and the media by manipulating information. These gatekeepers coordinate the core messages presented in almost all media and motion pictures.

"The media affiliates have helped to move American capitalism beyond satisfying people's basic needs. They have created the desirability of larger houses, second cars and multiple television sets — wants that go way beyond the basics needed for your true purpose on this planet. These wants are based on people's images of what it takes to be loved, accepted, and happy. These contrived needs are a way to pacify the general populace. But possessions always fall short of satisfying anyone, so economic growth is required to give everyone more and more."

"Go on," Ryan said.

"I do not have a complete picture, but here is what I do know," Dr Adamson said. "Ernest Steiger's father was part of the intelligence service, the OSS. They were one of the keys to the allies' success during W.W.II. With the onset of the Cold War, the 'Top Secret' and 'need to know' labels were applied to many activities, ostensibly to hide them from Communist sympathizers. Secrecy oaths were administered and closed mouths measured loyalty. The world was at war, but the vast majority of America's people were not involved.

"With the UFO crash at Roswell in 1947, the intelligence services saw the need to hide yet another thing: unidentified flying objects. Thus began the current dark chapter in American history. In addition to their ingrained reflex of hiding everything from the Soviets, they believed 'the public' could not handle the truth about Roswell and subsequent UFO sightings and crashes. They embarked on a calculated program to bury or ridicule all such contacts. Simultaneously, they initiated widely disbursed development programs to reverse engineer the technology obtained from UFO crashes. Pieces of UFO technology form the basis for much of modern electronics and communications."

"Like what?"

"Integrated circuits, fiber optics, lasers."

Ryan was initially repelled by the idea that Americans had not originated these breakthroughs. Then he thought back to the speed with which these backbones of modern communications had been developed and commercialized. Could their progress have received a boost from technology extracted from a crashed UFO? He had read somewhere that captured German technology had helped the development of magnetic sound recording in this country.

Dr. Adamson waited and then said, "Getting back to the media affiliates, once the men in military intelligence saw how easy it was to manipulate the military, Steiger's father conceived a brilliant plan: Take the principles of information control into the private sector. With financing from the intelligence community, he bought control of newspapers and radio stations. As a fellow media owner, he then sought out people who could be enticed into his scheme. Through advertising and Hollywood, they began to push the belief that a fantasy-like self-image could satisfy people's innate desire for love and security. It was easy to convince manufacturers to develop products based on these new self-images. Thus evolved a marvelous way to focus people on themselves and away from secret agendas and the larger picture. They were, of course, helped along by people's basic animal nature and their willingness to accept duplicity."

"When I told you that you were an economic slave, that is what the media affiliates believe you to be," Sarah said. "Through their efforts, people have become virtual slaves within a 'Box' based on consumption and possessions. The lack of truth about extraterrestrials and the friendly orchestrated universe is one more thing that has contributed to the success of the Box — people are complacent and assume that what they already know is all they need to know. Few look beyond their immediate circumstances."

"That old man in Winnetka?" What Dr. Adamson and Sarah were describing went beyond all reason. "He's been manipulating American culture?"

"One of the very best."

As if someone had lifted a veil, Ryan suddenly saw it all. Information control, on an unprecedented scale, was used to manipulate people so that they had no reason to fight the status quo. They were getting the life of comfort and ease they had always desired. Even if they perceived what was going on, most people wouldn't care about the price as long as they got what they wanted.

"So how do they do it?"

"This is where it becomes a little fuzzier," Dr Adamson said. "I have been unable to monitor all the twists and turns of this nefarious activity. However, I believe that the media affiliates influence comes from supplying carefully packaged information. Inside information, leaked information, secret information, all carefully manipulated to give the appearance that it is genuine. Give a screenwriter a tidbit, and he produces a script for a science fiction movie. Give a reporter a half-truth, and he investigates enough to write a story. Based on combinations of facts and lies they weave interesting new twists to the prevailing paradigm, but do not challenge it."

"But how can just a few people manage to do it all?"

"The media affiliates are packaging experts. They are the front organization for other loosely associated groups. These groups need to manipulate truth for their own interests; the media affiliates disseminate it. If I am an oil company and want to denounce alternative fuels and energy saving approaches, the media affiliates package alternative fuels and energy savings as unrealistic."

"If I am part of the covert affiliates and I foresee a war coming, I get my friends in the media affiliates to suggest to Hollywood that its time for a new crop of war movies," Sarah added.

"Amazing. How have they kept all this secret?" Ryan asked.

"Information is power. People in democratic societies largely regulate themselves," Sarah said. "The elitists have added the elements of accumulated wealth, far-reaching corporate structures, media control, and covert operations."

Ryan thought back to his powerful dream of the transparent jail. He knew that he felt pressures to behave as a proper CEO should. In many situations that became more important than the truth, more important than doing what was right.

"The greatest threat to any power structure, overt or covert, is the infusion of outside, unmanaged knowledge," Dr. Adamson said. "The discovery of the New World and disproving geocentric cosmogony opened people's minds, aided the renaissance, and led to the reformation. The result was the downfall of the traditional power structures in Europe. When the revolutionary truth about the cosmic paradigm is understood, existing structures everywhere will begin to crumble. The world of fifty years from now will be an amazingly different place."

"Why do you think those in power continue to deny the existence of extraterrestrials?" Sarah asked. "And paint them as hostile aliens? And ridicule any serious investigation?"

"So the intelligence people have known the truth all along?" Ryan asked.

"Some of them, yes," Dr. Adamson said, "but in the interests of national security, they abide by their secret oaths and do not discuss it with others in their own organizations. Those who know the whole truth are very few."

"Can you prove any of this?" The two extraterrestrials and the white-haired apparition were challenging the basis of his life, his society, his world. Had he really spent a lifetime living according to the dictates of a secret cabal? Did his society really live according to lies perpetuated by secrecy oaths, insider knowledge, and webs of interlocking self-interests? Was some of Sanitas's success dependent on technology derived from a crashed UFO?

Dr. Adamson motioned to Sarah. She opened a folder and passed a few sheets of paper to Ryan. He scanned the neatly written entries.

"With sadness, I watched as Ernest Steiger recorded in his diary," Dr. Adamson said. "These are copies of a few pages from it."

"Why has it gotten this far," Ryan asked. His predicting ability kicked in; he saw myriad future possibilities, some of them very frightening.

"I have observed the various affiliate groups since their formation and agonized as they manipulated people away from the truth. I am but one; they are many. The possibility of unlimited wealth and power drives some men to do the unthinkable. I have been unable to monitor everyone and every event. Few people have the courage to stand against men such as these, to act against the majority view, to act against an apparently benign paradigm."

"Why?" Ryan asked. "Why would they do this?"

"For power," Sarah said.

"Initially because covert operations wanted to distract people from its nefarious activities," Dr Adamson said. "Ernest Steiger's father saw it as a challenge."

"How did you get these?" Ryan held up the sheets.

"Steiger is old," Dr. Adamson said. "His illness consumes him. He sees his end is near and wishes to preserve his legacy." The white-haired apparition pointed to the pages. "He turned over copies of his diaries to his daughter, Lucia, with instructions to publish them when certain conditions are met and his role could be announced to the world. You see he does not trust the media affiliates of twenty years hence to remember who initiated and led this phenomenal conspiracy. His daughter's secretary, a Parisian, read them and was horrified. She secretly made a copy for me."

"Steiger is beginning to understand that we could undermine all that the media affiliates have built," Sarah said.

"The media affiliates have incredible influence and power," Dr. Adamson said. "You just saw it — Steiger was able to exert pressure on the FBI to bring him the cube from Harmony prior to taking it to Washington for analysis."

"How can we fight something like that?" Ryan asked. The

finger of insecurity had grown into a fist. The burning in his stomach was extreme. He popped two antacids.

"With the truth," Sarah said.

"I think it's going to take more than truth," Ryan muttered.

"The celestial concept of truth means operating with complete integrity towards others, with openness, and with the truth of the organized and peaceful universe."

"And exactly what does that mean, in Steiger's case?"

"That is what we are going to determine."

After another hour of wrestling with the issues, Ryan said, "I suggest we find some dinner."

"I am ready." Peter struggled up.

"Is this OK?" Sarah rose to show Ryan the blue jeans she wore below her bright yellow blouse; both were new. "Your assistant Karen was most helpful."

"We have other clothes in our car," Peter reminded Ryan. "And we need our supply of lotion."

"We also need to discuss where we are going to live," Sarah said.

"We'll talk as we eat." Ryan motioned them to the door. Between his confrontation with Ernest Steiger and this latest information about a massive cover-up, he needed a break.

"I will remain here," Dr. Adamson said.

"Do you always miss the fun?" Ryan asked him.

This time, the white-haired apparition dissipated before his eyes.

As they walked to his car, Ryan said, "I still don't understand why Dr. Adamson hasn't been able to stop the media affiliates."

"He cannot force humans to do anything. Can you imagine, living here for thousands of years, watching the civilization you are nurturing take many wrong turns, waiting for humans to ask for help?"

As they rode down from his mountain house to the city, Ryan thought back to his time in the Army. As a soldier, he had been expected to follow orders. Even then he had known much was concealed — the military enjoyed their secret games. But he did not understand how something so radical and overwhelming as extraterrestrials could have been covered up all these years. He was also not sure he bought into the extent or power of the media affiliates and their allies. He had heard the Phantians speak of a new world order based on cosmic truth. Could it be that there was another world order in the making? One based on power and manipulation?

Seeking a suitable restaurant, Ryan, Sarah, and Peter wandered onto the Pearl Street Mall at its west end on 11th Street. Ryan felt confident that their INS pursuers were far behind and quite possibly would never track them to Boulder. He was less confident about Ernest Steiger.

Chrysanthemums in full bloom filled the red brick planters. Yellow and orange trees shaded the four-block walkway. Street musicians entertained small crowds on the warm, Indian summer evening. They passed by several restaurants but continued to walk east.

When they crossed Broadway, Ryan asked, "Any information about our INS pursuers?"

Peter responded in his usual stutter. "Raul Viejo of the INS wished to divert attention from his smuggling. Luis Litchfield from the BIA was helping him."

"It was Viejo who threw the Mexican woman into the desert — to make us look guilty and insure the raid would go forward," Sarah added. "He planted her jacket in one of the bedrooms at Harmony. The FBI matched it to her through DNA analysis. They now believe she was at Harmony before wandering off into the desert."

"Damn, I was hoping they'd lose interest," Ryan said. It wasn't as if the INS didn't have other problems. He decided to go forward with meeting his friend, Boulder County Sheriff Tom Ertl. Worried, but recognizing their need to meet people, he agreed that it would be okay for the Phantians to roam around Boulder as long as they were discreet.

Their conversation was interrupted. "Hello Ryan."

He turned and recognized his friend with the unique single name. "Hi, Fuchsia." A little more than five feet tall, she wore a long, deep violet dress with several strings of beads about her neck. On her tiny feet were sandals. Her flowing dark hair framed a pretty face. He walked to her and they chatted for a moment. Then making a spur-of-moment decision he said, "I want you to meet some new friends of mine."

They stepped over to the two Phantians, and Ryan said, "This is Peter and Sarah. I met them on my vacation in Arizona."

Fuchsia's brown eyes lit up. "I'm pleased to meet you."

"They're moving to Boulder," Ryan said.

"We would like to talk with you," Sarah said. Without consulting Peter or Ryan, she added, "We are going to eat, will you join us?"

"Yes, I would like that," Fuchsia replied.

The four of them strolled east on the mall. Ryan related the story of meeting Sarah and Peter at Ben's dig and their night trek across the desert. He did not hint at Peter or Sarah's origins.

Boulder people knew Fuchsia as a holistic practitioner. Ryan had first met her when he appeared at her office for a massage appointment. In addition to coming away with relaxed muscles, her comments gave him much needed insights into a people management problem at work. Thereafter, he had sought her out for massage and conversation. Over the past two years, she had stopped giving massages and had turned to writing. Her pieces on the need for a holistic lifestyle appeared in many newspapers and magazines. Most of her time was now devoted to her weekly column and answering letters from her many fans. She never drove an automobile and was a vegetarian.

When Ryan finished his story, Fuchsia said to Sarah, "The universe works in wonderful ways. Now I see why, at the last minute, I decided on an evening stroll."

Sarah smiled. "I too am happy we met this evening, but I would rather call it a well-conceived meeting. Your concept of vague spirituality, 'the universe,' is only the first step toward truth. The wonderful thing is that celestial-reality is *not* vague. Celestial beings are everywhere, assisting you in your daily life, making connections like this evening."

Walking beside Fuchsia, Sarah described the celestial hierarchy supervising the universe. Fuchsia laid out her beliefs about forces in the universe and the power of ancient goddesses.

As they walked east, Peter commented to Ryan on the various stores. BOULDER BOOK STORE. RUNNERS ROOST. PEPPER-

CORN. SMITH SHOE COMPANY. WELLS FARGO BANK. Modern retail establishments on the first floors of historic buildings contributed to the Pearl Street Mall's reputation as one of America's most successful.

"Where does it all stop?" Ryan pointed to the shops.

"When people rise above their animal natures," Peter stuttered.

Fuchsia said, "It is sad to see so much energy expended on shopping."

"And on consuming," Sarah said.

They crossed 13th Street. "Your spirituality is very different," Fuchsia mused. "For years, I have focused on the ancient legends and myths of many cultures. There is great truth in them, you know."

"Those stories do contain wisdom," Sarah said. "However, the ancestral ways of seeing and behaving need to be updated. I honor the old ones for their insights, but we are advocating that mysticism be replaced with a definitive understanding of celestial-reality."

"Yes, but the ancient truths are still with us," Fuchsia persisted.

"Your myths," Sarah said, "and I too have studied them, are the attempts of the people of that time to explain how life appeared to them. Science has uncovered much since then. It is time to integrate modern scientific understandings, ancient wisdom, and celestial truth."

Despite the crowded mall, they were able to find a table at the 14th Street Grill. While they waited for food, Sarah and Fuchsia continued their conversation.

"If we could throw out technology," Fuchsia said. "We could protect the planet from man's destruction."

"Examine the way your ancestors lived," Sarah gave Fuchsia a sharp look. "Do you want to go back to a time before electric lighting and toilets? The challenge is to make your environment more loving, not retreat from sanitation and labor saving advancements. We want to show you how to evolve so that technological man lives in harmony with his natural environment.

"When this happens, your frame of reference will shift and

you will behave differently. You will see that you are part of the grand scheme of a caring and rational universe. You will appreciate your larger purpose in that redefined paradigm. Your behavior, if you are rational, will become future oriented."

Their food arrived; Ryan watched as the Phantians sampled it. When she was not eating or talking, Sarah touched her three concentric circle medallion. She smiled at Ryan when she found him staring at her. Talking about her passionate interests made her look rested, young, and happy. Peter made notes between bites, but said little.

"The cosmic paradigm provides a great context," Ryan said as he leaned forward. "It doesn't throw away what is good, just the spiritual hocus-pocus." He felt uneasy as the others stared at him, but continued. "People long for something better, something more than hanging around for a few years enjoying whatever life has to offer."

They kept talking throughout their meal, lingering over coffee until after 8:00 PM.

"Thank you for listening," Sarah said as they pushed out of the restaurant's door and back onto the Mall.

"I think I see what you are trying to say." Fuchsia stared at Ryan and the Phantians. Her eyes came to rest on Sarah. "Maybe this knowledge will help people change their lifestyles. I'm always looking for ways to help people find a reason to live healthy."

"You're right, but it is much more than that. A cosmic paradigm provides the motivation for people to change their entire reason for living," Sarah said. "Walk over here with me." Sarah took Fuchsia's hand and walked her across the mall and onto the grass in front of the Boulder County building. They sat down.

Ryan and Peter hung back and watched from across the street. The bald Phantian nodded when Ryan looked his direction. Sarah and Fuchsia appeared to be two women sitting on the lawn and holding hands, but Ryan knew that his friend was taking the trip of her life. The two did not stir for twenty minutes.

When Fuchsia opened her eyes, Peter motioned for Ryan to approach the seated women.

Fuchsia looked up at Ryan and said, "Did you take this trip?"

He sat down next to her. "Yes," he replied.

"It was so peaceful there. The people seemed so happy."

After a few moments Fuchsia began to ask questions. From the disjointed way she stumbled from question to question, Ryan could tell that the impact of interacting with an extraterrestrial was similar to his own. The indisputable knowledge that there were humans on other planets was a jolt to anyone's system.

Sarah patiently answered every question. Every so often Fuchsia looked over at Ryan. All he could do was smile.

Ryan noted that Sarah appeared exhausted. He guessed that the pictioning process was a strain, dredging up old memories and painful emotions, reliving those moments again.

After an hour Sarah said, "I know it is difficult to absorb so much at once. I would have waited until I knew you better, but I felt you were open to our message, and we need your help. Peter was injured during our trip from Phantia. He has improved much, but needs physical therapy for his smaller muscles and speech. Can you suggest someone trustworthy?"

Fuchsia thought for a moment and then replied, "I have just the person. Also coaches voice. When?"

"As soon as possible."

"I will arrange it for tomorrow."

It is only through labor and prayerful effort, by grim energy and resolute courage, that we move on to better things.

— THEODORE ROOSEVELT

THIRTEEN

At his office the next morning, Ryan Drake called Aza O'Sullivan. His friend's secretary informed Ryan that her boss had been in Porter Hospital for a week, the victim of an unprovoked assault at Colorado Health Club. Shocked, Ryan called the hospital.

"Hi, Ry," Aza said. "Back from the desert, eh? Find any old bones?"

"Can't leave town without you getting into trouble."

"Just a wee problem. Doc says I'll be ready for a Guinness in a day or two."

"When can I come visit?"

"Anytime. I ain't goin nowhere."

"How about this afternoon?"

Ryan then placed a call to Truman Thompson at TTT Instrumentation. His secretary patched him through to Thompson's flat in London. After a brief discussion, they agreed on modifications to their agreement. Ryan was pleased that Thompson seemed to be acting rationally. They set the closing for their distribution and serving agreement, a week hence, at TTT Instrumentation's offices in Boston.

That afternoon, Ryan Drake's Porsche 911 zipped up the hill out of Boulder, a four-lane, divided highway, green belt on either side. Locals referred to US36 as "the Turnpike," although tolls had been eliminated years ago. There was little traffic; his speedometer read seventy-four. Cattle were grazing in the open fields to the south. On most trips, he talked business on his cell phone and ignored the landscape. Today he contemplated the puffy white clouds against the Colorado blue sky.

Knowing he was part of a larger whole changed his view of everything, his values, his motivations. He looked around his sleek automobile and was almost repelled. Man, oh man, he was changing.

He drove past the MARRIOTT COURTYARD, sandwiched between the HAMPTON INN and the OUTBACK STEAK HOUSE. Housing development on the right, ROCK CREEK, big houses. The highway passed under an old bridge supporting water mains. The original abutments were close to the highway, 15'6" clearance. It was a dangerous spot, an accident waiting to happen.

STORAGE TECHNOLOGY CORPORATION. FLATIRON SHOPPING CENTER. OMNI RESORT HOTEL. The large structures zipped past. INTERLOCKEN BUSINESS PARK. Multi-storied corporate facilities stretched for two miles. The company where he had been CEO prior to Sanitas was headquartered there.

The Phantians would point to these buildings as America's edifices to the gods of economy. In earlier times, people erected churches. Europe was packed with relics from the Middle Ages.

HUNTER DOUGLAS, on the north side. BALL CORPORATION, to the south. Traffic slowed. He moved into the left lane and checked his speed. Red sports cars attracted attention.

Where would it stop? Could the cosmic paradigm counteract the momentum of consumptionism? Ryan found himself hoping so, before it was too late. Before his trip to Phantia, he wouldn't have given the subject a second thought.

Ryan's thoughts moved to more immediate issues. His meeting with Ernest Steiger. His morning's conversation with Truman Thompson seemed to indicate that Sanitas's agreement with TTT Instrumentation was as good as done. What was Steiger referring to? Was it a veiled threat? What was Steiger's purpose in showing him that cube from Harmony? In offering him a job? How much influence did the media affiliates really have?

He still found it difficult to believe that his life was in the hands of greedy puppeteers, that he was living a lie to hide the activities of the intelligence community and others who were intent on grabbing power.

Almost out of habit, Ryan checked for light green vehicles. He spotted a van a few cars back. Suddenly it accelerated and moved up on him. He was about to push the accelerator, but decided against it. He pulled over into the right lane, and allowed it to pass — it turned out to be a mother and a child in a car seat. He relaxed. Who would recognize him, a successful businessman in a sports car, as the battered fugitive who had befriended two extraterrestrials?

He went back to concentrating on the road and recalled Sarah's words, "The cosmic paradigm gives people a reason to change their lives." The people of this world had to want the truth, had to want to control their own destiny. Was it possible to modify America's comfortable lifestyle enough to make it compatible with the larger cosmic picture? Could the cosmic paradigm overcome the momentum of Ernest Steiger and his cabal?

"You can be part of the solution."

Ryan recognized the same voice as at his office. This time he did not need to look around. The interior of his Porsche was visible in his peripheral vision. He cocked his head right and analyzed the words.

Yes, he could be part of the Phantians' mission. He already knew he could not go back to simply being the CEO of Sanitas. But what would a life based on the cosmic paradigm require?

"I'm trying to make sense out of all this," he said.

He heard nothing in response. This voice thing was beginning to trouble him. Never before had he spoken back to a voice.

As he merged into Interstate 25, traffic became congested. When he drove a crowded freeway, he concentrated on other vehicles; there was little time for anything else. In contrast, a country road presented the opportunity to look around, think. Most of America lived at freeway speed. How could he help Sarah and

Peter get the attention of people buzzing along at seventy miles per hour? How was he going to explain his incredibly complex situation to his friend, Aza?

"Hey, Ry. Good to see you." Aza O'Sullivan said effusively. He extended a bandaged hand as Ryan approached his bed. Ryan clasped the outstretched hand but did not squeeze. They laughed as their bandaged hands touched.

Aza's fire-engine-red face matched his disheveled hair. Blotched skin shown through his normally well-manicured beard. But he gazed at Ryan with clear green eyes. In college he had played defensive back — now, his former muscle had turned soft. Ryan had chided him about starting to go to a health club.

"What happened?" Ryan asked.

"Your damned climbin wall." Ryan saw a smile creep across Aza's face. "Been tryin to master it, you know. Going to the club every evening after work." Aza motioned to a bedside chair.

"Doesn't look to me like you fell from any climbing wall. So, tell me."

Aza's eyes stopped smiling and he said, "OK. Last Monday, a week ago, you know, I was at the health club exercising like you told me to. It was late. Place was empty. I was taking a shower. Out of the blue somebody hit me in the kidney. I tried to turn, but he dazed me with a chop to my neck. Before I could come out of it, he knocked me to the ground. Tossed acid on me."

"Did he say anything?" Ryan sat in the chair.

"Just the words, 'This is for the man.' Other than that, I'd never recognize the bastard again — he was wearing rubber gloves and a Halloween mask. I think he was aiming at my dick. I got up and tried to rinse it off with water, but it was too late." He pulled back the sheet to expose bandaged legs and abdomen. Ryan assumed that splashed acid had also caused the burns on Aza's hands and face.

"Any idea?"

"Nope, he was big is all I know. I've been playing around a bit, you know, since my divorce. But I never screwed no married women, at least as far as I remember. Anyway, the paramedics brought me here. They had to do a skin graft for some of the damage." He scrunched his face and added, "I'm itching to get out of here, but it hurts something awful to pee and all my pubic hair's gone."

"That's probably more than I needed to know," Ryan said with a smile.

Ryan had done business with Aza's company, Western Enclosures, at both Sanitas and his prior companies. Founded by Aza fifteen years earlier, Western was the largest supplier of metal and plastic electronics enclosures in the Rocky Mountain States.

But it was not until a crisis at Sanitas that they had become friends. The cabinets for a delivery to TTT Instrumentation had been incorrectly specified by one of Sanitas's engineers. Even though it was not their error, Aza worked his people over a weekend to produce enough of the proper ones. During that stressful episode, the two company presidents had found how much they had in common.

"No ideas?"

"The police haven't been much help. Six members were signed in at the club that night. They've narrowed it down to one suspect, a Charles White. Turns out the address on his application is phony, doesn't exist. Paid his dues in cash, so there's no way to trace him."

"Who hates you enough?"

"Don't know. I told you about my problems at Western, but this is way beyond that. Say, I get out of here in a day or two, do you, you know, want to have a few drinks, chase a few chicks?"

Ryan shook his head. One time he'd visited one of Denver's "meat markets" with Aza. He'd watched as his friend, using his best Irish brogue, chatted up several women. After an hour, he found a willing participant. The entire scene had repulsed Ryan. Henceforth he and Aza had gone their separate ways with regard to women. "I've stopped drinking."

"You've what?"

"Stopped drinking." Ryan wasn't quite sure when or how he'd made the decision, but he had not taken a drink since returning from the desert. Although he had been in first class to and from Chicago, he had stuck to coffee and coke.

"Wow." Aza studied him with the look of someone who knew him well but was seeing a totally new emergence. "Something big happened out there in that desert, huh?" Aza pointed to Ryan's bandaged hand, hiking boots and lack of tie. "Tell me what happened."

"Lots of digging, a few artifacts."

"Yeah, you told me you were looking for something different."

A month ago, Ryan had shared his growing disenchantment with his life, his yearning for a situation where he could be himself rather than playing the role of CEO. Aza, the consummate entrepreneur, had tried to be sympathetic, but dismissed his friend's remarks as boredom. He recommended diversifying Sanitas to keep things challenging.

"So, what aren't you telling me?"

Ryan chuckled and tossed up his hands in a sign of resignation. He described his trek through the desert, his escape in Shiprock, and again at the roadblock.

"That's not the law-abiding Ry Drake I know. I'm thinking there's a whole lot more to this story."

Ryan leaned toward the bed and said, "Let me ask you something. What do you think about extraterrestrials?"

"Well I believe there's more out there than just us, you know. Mind you, Holy Mother Church wouldn't like me saying so."

"Why do you think the government is hiding them from us?"

"Don't rightly know. Probably think we little people can't handle it."

"Right, the most important event since man stood upright, and it's okay for the government to cover it up?"

"National security." Aza said it, and then chuckled. "Can't let those terrorists get hold of it. Hey, if there was anything to all this cover-up stuff, it would have been on Sixty Minutes by now."

Ryan fixed on Aza and said, "All right, I need your solemn promise that what I'm about to say will be kept between the two of us."

"Agreed." The two men had shared their recent divorce experiences, the loneliness of running companies, and their perpetual struggles with debts and cash flow. Aza was better off financially than Ryan, as he was able to withdraw cash from a company he owned outright, but Ryan was handling the emotional aftermath of his divorce better. The company chiefs had managed an occasional workday afternoon for fishing, beer, and sorting things out.

Ryan walked over and shut the door. "The Harmony people are from another planet. That's why they fled to the desert."

"No way. You're giving me a bit of the old blarney." Aza studied his friend.

"It's true. When we were in the desert, they sprung it on me."

"You said this Sarah was cute."

"She is."

"Big head, big eyes?" Aza chuckled and fashioned a large head with his bandaged hands.

"No. Cute as in human. Cute as in Nordic."

"Can't be."

"It's true."

"How about her friend?"

"Short and darker, but very human-like."

"How about the way they acted?" Aza scrunched his face. "Maybe the real aliens are hiding inside." As he raised himself up in the bed, his voice rose an octave.

"They're as human as you or me," Ryan said.

"So, you believe them?"

"They're living at my house." Ryan watched his friend digest that announcement.

"Aliens living at your house, eh. Now, if anyone else was telling me this." Aza lay back and shook his head. Peering at Ryan through squinted eyes, he said, "So, describe them."

"First of all they are extraterrestrials, not aliens," Ryan said. "There's nothing hostile about them. They look like you or me. A little longer hands and feet, larger pupils." He made a circle with his forefinger and thumb to show the size of the Phantians' eyes.

"Not like the pictures? Or Star Wars?"

"Not even close, they're normal looking." Ryan motioned to Aza and himself. "This woman, Sarah, is beautiful — delicate features, flawless skin." He was not about to tell Aza that he had seen her nude, seen that she had no navel.

"I find it hard to believe that aliens, uh excuse me extraterrestrials, would look anything like us. I mean, the pictures of them — big ugly insects."

"You can see for yourself."

Aza paused, as if he was expecting Ryan to break down at any moment and say that it was a great joke. When Ryan did not make that expected announcement, Aza chuckled, "Ry, looks like you're into something real big."

"There are people in the government who know about UFO's and extraterrestrials, been covering it up for years," Ryan said. "It's like they want to keep us back in the days of Columbus — sea monsters and ships falling off the edge of the world."

"I think it's too big to cover up all these years. Besides I'm not sure I'm ready to shed my comfortable view of a flat world."

"They've used secrecy oaths, ridicule, and threats to hide the truth."

"It's not possible. Too many people are involved."

"The truth about extraterrestrials will challenge people's thinking about a lot of things, challenge the existing power structures. The ones who have visited Earth over the years aren't hostile, they care about us, and they come from highly advanced civilizations. Let's face it, if they were really hostile, they'd have eaten us long ago — besides, we probably would have tasted better about nineteen-o-one."

"So your extraterrestrial friends have been here all along? Flying around in UFO's?"

"No, my friends from Phantia just arrived a year ago. Anyway, they're from a different planet than the other extraterrestrials. You can carry on a real conversation with them. They came here specifically to live among us, to try and help us."

"Not everybody's going to like this." Aza held up his hands. "UFO's. Aliens living among us. Why just the other night, I saw an episode of the X-files — scary. It'll take some doing to change my mind."

"It took me a while, and a trek across the desert. But now that I understand, I can never go back to seeing things the old way." Ryan's passion was reasserting itself. He remembered shouting at the timber company executives and his days in jail during college. He was passionate then. Now, he felt that old fire flicker anew.

"Remember how we hiked up Mt. Wilson?" Ryan asked. "And how we talked about viewing our situations from the vantage point of fourteen thousand feet? Or forty thousand feet like from an airplane? Or hundreds of miles like from a satellite?"

"Yeah," Aza said. "It's been helpful once in a while to step back and take that broader view."

"Well, the Phantians have given me a cosmic perspective, from a trillion miles away, a way to see our society in a celestial context — as an integral part of an inhabited universe, guided by celestial beings. And I've found out about covert intelligence operations and reverse engineering programs. If they've covered up something as important as UFOs and aliens, no telling what they're capable of. The Phantians believe that the truth about extraterrestrials and the knowledge that the universe is both orchestrated and friendly will shock us back onto the right track."

"You lost me with all that."

"Hey, I'll let them explain it — when do you want to meet them?"

"I'll think about it."

"Come on. Give you something new to think about, instead of women."

"I'm not sure I want to get mixed up in this. Aren't you worried about the INS? What if some intelligence type finds out about you and your alien friends? With terrorists running around, you won't find much tolerance for anything unusual."

"Aza, I'm convinced they didn't do anything wrong and all I did was help them avoid a dangerous confrontation — one of their Navajo workers got killed that day. All they want to do is advance the maturity of this planet." Ryan did not want to scare his friend off, so he did not tell him about his meeting with Ernest Steiger even though he knew Aza knew the man.

"Maturity? Do you realize how complicated this stuff is? People have their own lives, children, careers. You're suggesting they uproot everything and change. They won't like it, won't even start. Why should they?"

"If we don't start, it will never happen. If we're going to move this planet along, the most important thing is to begin."

"You're wasting your time, you know — mixed up with stuff like this, trying to save the world. Nobody's going to thank you."

"You're sure you're not involved in some sort of a scheme?" Sheriff Tom Ertl concentrated on Ryan's reply. It was the following afternoon. Both men had carved time from their busy schedules for this meeting. At his own request, Ryan had come to see Ertl in his Boulder office to discuss what he had described over the phone as a "miscarriage of injustice." When Ryan described the desert trek, they both laughed. He was more solemn when Ryan recounted the escape in Shiprock. From earlier conversations on the banks of high mountain streams, Ryan knew the Sheriff of Boulder County would enjoy the story — as long as no crime had been committed.

Ryan did not tell Ertl of the origins of his friends or that they were staying at his house. He looked around Ertl's office and was reminded that he had decided to buck the authority that this man had been elected to preserve. The finger of doubt poked his gut. He had taken a calculated risk in coming here.

A husky man, with curly black hair and gold-rimmed glasses, Tom Ertl carried himself like a prizefighter, prepared to battle at the least provocation. He wore a rumpled white shirt with the cuffs rolled up, tie loosened, top button undone. He had a reputation as a tough and honest law enforcement official.

"They went out of their way to comply with every law." Ryan returned his friend's inquisitive stare. "They haven't harmed any-one. Hey, I believed them enough to risk a trek in the desert."

"OK. I'll accept your word on it, for now," Ertl rose and paced behind his desk.

Ryan nodded and said, "What doesn't make sense is why the INS targeted Harmony in the first place. I saw it myself and there is no way an honest agent could ever imagine they were harboring illegals."

"I know a few people in Arizona."

"How about turning the tables?" Ryan reasoned that his best defense was to attack. "If my friends are innocent, and I think they are, then somebody had another agenda with that raid."

"What makes you say that?"

"It's the only thing that makes sense. I want to prove it." Ryan knew if he started throwing accusations about Raul Viejo around, he would probably do more harm than good. His best course of action was to let the honest guys figure out that they had a rotten apple.

"Going to take some doing." Ertl peered over his reading glasses. "We'll see what my contacts say."

He began to think that coming here was a mistake. But it was too late, he had already told Ertl the story. Now when the lawman made his inquiries, if he made them, the INS would be alerted that someone in Boulder was connected to the people who had fled Harmony. Just how far was Ertl willing to stretch their friendship?

"I think there's real danger," Ryan said. "If someone's willing to throw an innocent woman out of a car just to throw suspicion on my friends, who knows what they might do. She died as the result of exposure and bruises."

"Who said anything about throwing her out?"

"Well she didn't wander out there by herself — she wasn't an Indian, no vehicle anywhere close, all bruised and scratched. I think somebody threw her out."

"I'll let you know what I find out." Ertl's words were guarded.

Ryan could tell that his friend was not convinced. Just how far could he push before Ertl's sense of duty forced the Sheriff to cooperate with the INS? If that happened, if Ertl's contacts in Arizona didn't see things the way Ryan did, he was in trouble. He hoped there was an honest man or two on the other end of Ertl's inquiries.

When Ryan exited the Boulder Justice Center, a police car pulled to the curb. He flinched and walked on. He respected legitimate authority, but hated anyone who misused it. Somehow, he wasn't sure exactly how, he intended to nail Raul Viejo, and clear his friends. Then he would go to work on Ernest Steiger — hopefully before Steiger or his gang found the Phantians.

In the world to come I shall not be asked, "Why were you not Moses?" I shall be asked, "Why were you not Zusya?"

— RABBI ZUSYA

FOURTEEN

"I agree that you need to meet people." Ryan Drake had said last evening. "But, keep in mind, you don't know who you can trust. Don't tell people where you live." Sarah recalled his words perfectly and had communicated them to Peter and Dr. Adamson.

'You must honor his request.' Dr. Victor Adamson communicated. *'You are not yet ready for events that would lead to a public disclosure of your origins.'* Sarah had proposed that people come to Ryan's home to meet with her. In a heated outburst, Ryan had refused to allow it. She now saw that he had been angry because he was genuinely fearful for her and for Peter. She also understood his insecurity about openly identifying with extraterrestrials.

'Ryan faces obligations to his company,' Dr. Adamson communicated. *'Let us give him time to work through them. Then he will be more willing to expose himself.'*

Her departed mate, M'Adan, and she had disagreed about things. He wanted their two daughters to wait before enrolling in the parenthood course, wanted them to pursue a career before embarking on the road to children. But the girls had been adamant and Sarah had backed their choice, after all, it had worked out well for her. After she had become a respected teacher at the Academy, she used her experiences with family to enrich her lectures. She hoped her daughters would likewise achieve satisfaction in their postponed careers. She felt an ache in her heart — she missed interacting with them, missed watching her grandchildren grow up.

"I'll… I'll never see you again," her elder daughter's tears had choked her words. J'Li recalled the scene when her eldest daughter had uttered these words. She had gone to visit her at her home. It was about an hour from Ur'Geay.

"You don't even know if that spaceship's safe. Nobody from Ph'Nta has ever been transported in one and nobody has ever relocated to some faraway planet."

With tears in her eyes, J'Li had acknowledged the realization that in a few days she would indeed never see her daughter or family again. "Wait for me, on the fifth Between world," Sarah had said to her eldest.

Sarah's conflict between leaving her two daughters and her commitment to teach others about the Grand Plan of the cosmos grated on her. If she could convince others like Ryan and Fuchsia to listen, then the sacrifice would have been worth it. But if she died, as had almost happened in the desert, or Peter and she were captured and their message suppressed, then leaving Phantia would have been a terrible mistake. As she gazed out on the city, she wondered if she could possibly convince enough people to make a difference.

The day J'Li moved from her home she had harvested a single flower from her beloved garden, a yellow romm. Of all the many flowers she had lovingly cultivated, the romms were her favorite and yellow was her favorite color. The garden had been her quiet place where she could work in the rich soil or contemplate the wonder of co-creation. In their wisdom, the celestials had left a role for humans to improve upon the results of their evolutionary efforts. Yesterday she had seen what looked like yellow romms in a flower shop in Boulder. It had reminded her how far she was from her home on Phantia.

'*I am sure he will support us.*' Over the past few days, Sarah had found herself defending Ryan more and more. The strength of her feelings puzzled her. Why was she behaving this way, arguing with Peter, someone she had known for so many years? '*As Dr. Adamson*

188

keeps telling you, Ryan fits the celestial-allies' criteria.'

Yet here she was defending Ryan again. Since Peter and she had come to Boulder, she had watched Ryan and his struggle to fit his new awareness into his old lifestyle. She was quite sure that the new was winning. She was also sure that Peter was prejudiced against earth dwellers, that he saw them as inferior to Phantians. Although Peter and Ryan had become friendly, there was awkwardness about their relationship.

In support of her, Dr. Adamson communicated, '*There are few on this planet who possess Ryan's ability to predict future trends combined with his success in leading organizations. Also he is attracted to blonde women.'*

Sarah blushed.

'*Too set in his ways,'* Peter clasped his fingers together to indicate rigidity.

'*You need to understand that the emotions of earth dwellers influence their ability to shift to a cosmic paradigm,'* Dr. Adamson communicated. '*I think you will see Ryan and Fuchsia and others embrace everything, after we disclose the celestial Journey.'*

'*But I have talked with him, explained everything to him,'* Peter communicated.

'*I have learned from watching him that a stronger understanding can be reached through his heart than through his head,'* Sarah communicated.

For a while, they sat together on this rocky ridge about a quarter mile from Ryan's house. Each was lost in his or her private thoughts. Sarah took the opportunity to remote view Ryan. He was in a meeting at Sanitas with others whom she had not met. From what she could gather, they were discussing some sort of a new product that had been proposed by Brauk — she figured out which one he was from Ryan's description. She watched as Ryan patiently listened to everyone's opinion — whether based on facts or guesses — and then brought the group to a decision. There was little doubt in her mind that he was a special man, the special man they needed to further their mission, the man she felt close to. She was tempted to send him a communication, but decided not to bother him right then.

For her part, Sarah was determined to persist and was taking steps wherein people would talk with her. Today she had volunteered at the Boulder homeless shelter and tomorrow she would attend two lectures at the University. She had discussed her plans with Peter, but he had insisted it was too slow, that they did not have the luxury of time. Since his expertise was in speaking to large groups, he was anxious to arrange an opportunity to do that.

'*Karen seems nice.*' Sarah communicated. As she and Ryan's Assistant had searched for clothing, Karen had told her about her own two children. '*She took great care with us. She doesn't understand that we are Phantians, thinks we are friends of Ryan, new to this country.*' Sarah had met with Karen again yesterday. They talked for an hour. Tomorrow she had scheduled time with Fuchsia.

'*To live in accordance with the cosmic paradigm requires maturity,*' Peter communicated. '*Can Ryan do that?*'

'*I have lived with my people for thousands of years,*' Dr. Adamson admonished the bald Phantian. '*You cannot expect them to react to the cosmic paradigm the way people on Phantia respond to it. Earth dwellers have not grown up knowing about the inhabited universe, nor do they have a peaceful world ruled by celestials. You must learn these differences. After that you will be better able to unveil cosmic truth.*'

She took out a small vial and rubbed lotion on her arms. The tea tree aroma soothed her. In addition to stopping pollutants, the lotion supplied critical ingredients to nourish her body, not unlike high potency vitamins. Peter was right; they needed to retrieve their supply of lotion and the ingredients to make more.

She looked at Peter and marveled at his progress — soon he would be ready to find a forum from which he could unveil the cosmos, from which they would acclaim their celestial perspective to all. But before that could happen, she needed to engage more people, build a base of support to carry on. Once Peter went public, there would be only a limited time before Ernest Steiger, some covert operative, or the authorities intervened.

This was all happening too fast. The original plan was to engage people for a year or two before they made any kind of a public appearance. That plan had assumed that they would gradually transition into this society, that they would contact people and have time to convince them. But time was running out.

In her weekly column, HOLISTIC HAPPENINGS, Fuchsia posed the following question to her readers. "If you knew that this planet was an important cog in the grand scheme of the universe, rather than the lone outpost of sentient life, how would it change you?" She went on to describe what a cosmic viewpoint might look like and how it was enlarging her perception of holistic living. She solicited written and email comments.

It was Sunday when Aza O'Sullivan limped to the table at Turley's and sat cautiously on the wood chair. He was dressed in a sport coat with a blue button down shirt. Beneath the shirt Ryan could see white bandages.

Seated between Sarah Smith and Peter Jones, the entrepreneur glanced at each of them as he pretended to study his menu. The Phantians wore comfortable hiking clothes that they had purchased from one of the local mountaineering stores.

"Are you OK?" Ryan Drake leaned across the table and asked his friend.

"I hurt a little." Aza said.

The two Phantians inspected the unfamiliar menus. Ryan suspected they were also discussing Aza, but he was unable to intercept any of their unspoken communication.

After everyone placed orders and coffee was served, Aza leaned across the corner of the table and whispered to Peter, "You look too human to be from another planet. Prove it to me."

The bald Phantian did not respond, but picked up his place setting and began to play with it. Ryan concluded that Peter was totally unprepared for such a direct challenge.

Sarah said, "May I?"

Aza turned to his left and shyly looked at her. It was obvious that he found her attractive.

"I may disappoint you," she said. "We have no super powers."

"Convince me anyway."

Sarah paused for a moment and said, "Your company, Western Enclosures, has been experiencing certain hardships. There were a series of accidents. People were hurt. You lost customers to a competitor that is under-bidding you and dumping low-quality products into your market."

Ryan watched the lithe Phantian as she spoke these words. Her command of English had markedly improved since coming to Boulder, since interacting with highly educated people at the University. He found himself enjoying the opportunity to sit back and observe.

"Ry did a good job of telling you all about me," Aza said.

"We did not discuss any of this," Ryan said.

"So, how do you know?" the entrepreneur asked Sarah.

"I received the information from my celestial allies." Sarah smiled.

"So, you're saying that you received this information from some sort of spirit? How do I know that you didn't read my mind, or some magic trick like that?"

Without responding to his challenge, Sarah said, "Two years ago you divorced your wife. That is when your troubles began. The accidents at your facility can be traced to one source. The competitor is a company that sells fabricated parts to the aerospace industry. At the time of your divorce, it was acquired by a certain conglomerate and directed to enter your business. The recent incident at your health club was carried out at the command of the same man who directed this company to undermine yours."

"Ernest Steiger." Aza's hand slapped the table and spilled his water. "That old bastard never did like me. Fought like hell when his daughter married me. Cursed me when I divorced her."

"Is that company part of Steiger Enterprises?" Ryan asked. He offered his napkin to Aza to dam the water spilling into his lap.

"It is an obscure subsidiary of his book publishing arm," Sarah replied.

"She's right," Aza said. "It all fits. I just never put it together. That bastard." He hailed a waitress to clean up the spilled water.

Ryan remembered their recent conversation about Ernest Steiger's empire and glanced at Sarah. She nodded once. Did Aza know that Steiger was involved with the media affiliates?

Aza said to Ryan, "Exemplar's another one of his companies."

"Oh."

"Yeah. They came to us while you were on vacation. Wanted to order the same enclosures we make for Sanitas, same color, everything."

"I just got a report about them selling a big order to one of our customers," Ryan said. Why would Exemplar want to start to compete with Sanitas? Historically the company had been a minor producer of electronics that had more to do with communications than instrumentation.

"Did you sell to them?"

"No. They weren't willing to pay for quality."

"When you were married to Steiger's daughter, did the subject of the media affiliates ever come up?" Ryan drained his latte and motioned for the waitress.

"No. Who's that?"

"Some of Steiger's crowd." Ryan let the subject drop.

The waitress brought their orders. Ryan's was a California omelet with home fries. He attacked his eggs, avocado, tomato, and cheese and watched Aza study Sarah's eating.

"Let me see your hand," Aza said.

"Of course," Sarah offered her hand for inspection.

"Let me," Peter presented his. Aza stared at the two proffered hands, human-like but with longer fingers. All three laughed.

"Take your pick." Ryan joined in and offered his own.

Aza chose Sarah's hand, examined it, and said, "OK, your hand's different. What else?"

Sarah used one of the fingers on her other hand to point to her large gray eyes. Aza turned his head to study her larger-than-normal irises. At last he said, "OK, because Ry says so, I *might* accept that you're from someplace else."

Sarah said, "When Ryan told you of our origins, he asked you for confidentiality. We would ask again that you abide by that."

"That's easy," Aza said, his voice relaxed. "My friends'd think I was crazy if I told them I'd had a meal with a couple of aliens. Everybody knows they eat humans for lunch."

They all chuckled as the waitress returned with Ryan's latte.

Ryan enjoyed Aza. His humor and occasional slip into brogue made him think of his Irish mother. His skepticism resembled his father's but was less intense. Talking with Aza helped Ryan see both sides of issues.

"Their lives may be at stake," Ryan said becoming serious again.

"And our mission," Sarah added.

"Tell me about that," Aza said.

Ryan watched as the entrepreneur relaxed a bit, took a sip of his coffee, and prepared to listen. He was most interested in Aza's reaction to the Phantians' message. He was trying to figure out how to talk about extraterrestrials and the organized universe without coming off like some kind of a nut case.

After about thirty minutes, interrupted only by re-orders of coffee and tea and the clearing of the dishes, Aza said, "This sounds nice, but it's way too idealistic. Nobody will ever buy it. What about UFOs? Abductions?"

"Mortals from other planets do visit Earth," Sarah said, "and have for thousands of years. However, some of the so called 'alien encounters' are connections with celestials or intraterrestrials. People have a hard time explaining anything so startling. In an earlier age, they might have been called visits from angels or gods.

"Did you say intra something or other?"

"Yes, intraterrestrials. They are beings who have lived on this planet for thousands of years. They are neither human nor celestial. They are the caretakers of this world."

"Like leprechauns?"

"Something like that, only a lot more helpful. Other encounters are with extraterrestrials, humanoids from other planets. People have a hard time explaining such meetings. At the same time, extraterrestrials have difficulty understanding the emotional impact of such an encounter."

Aza leaned back in his chair and stared at Sarah and then Peter. For a long time he did not speak. Finally he said to Ryan, "I'm just not sure. But I do know it's way too complicated, all those different kinds of critters, intraterrestrials, extraterrestrials. People want simple ideas. You know, catchy slogans, sound bites. This'll never sell."

"Your country is waging a war to preserve its lifestyle," Sarah said. "It is a lifestyle that may not be compatible with sustaining this planet."

"So you're siding with the terrorists?"

"No. Violence solves nothing; it is another disappointing element of your civilization. What I am saying is that America's lifestyle of consumptionism is higher than it needs to be and, as things stand now, is not sustainable vis-à-vis the rest of the world."

When they exited Turley's, Sarah asked Aza to walk a ways with her. The two of them headed south toward Boulder Creek, about two blocks away. Ryan and Peter followed along behind but kept their distance.

When Aza and Sarah reached the bank of the stream, she had him sit. She took his hand and repeated the now familiar procedure. Ryan watched as the expression on his friend's face changed from suspicion to wonder to awe.

After about a half hour, Aza's eyes blinked open. He looked around. Spotting Ryan he motioned him over and said, "You were holding out on me."

"Would you have believed?"

"Probably not." Aza sat back with a dazed look on his face.

Aza began to blurt out all kinds of questions. Ryan once again observed that a human's initial thoughts were disoriented. Peter and he sat down and helped Sarah answer the barrage.

Finally Aza turned to Ryan and asked, "Now what the hell am I supposed to do?"

The next day, Aza called Ryan and said, "I can't stop thinking about that trip to Phantia. Nothing else seems to matter.

"Your friends really are extraterrestrials and I met them.

"That place was so beautiful.

"Reminded me of Ireland.

"That Sarah is really something.

"Those houses on that planet.

"Everything seemed so neat.

"And Peter. Man, he was really something before his accident.

"How did they get here?

"Where's their spaceship?"

He babbled on until Ryan said, "I'll set it up for Peter to come visit you. There's a lot more."

"Great, but I was hoping for Sarah."

Ryan laughed. "Not a chance."

If you're strong enough, there are no precedents.

— FRANCIS SCOTT KEY FITZGERALD

FIFTEEN

"Magdalena wants to talk with you," Karen said through Ryan Drake's intercom. Ryan was preparing his remarks about Sanitas for the visit by presidential candidate Carlton Boyle the following day. Since he had returned from his vacation last Tuesday, he could not seem to wade through the work that had piled up.

"Send her in."

"Two people from the Immigration and Naturalization Service are in my office." Magdalena Quintana, Sanitas's personnel director came into his office.

"Oh." He added, shit, under his breath.

The heavy set woman had been with Sanitas since its beginning. She had started as a secretary to Brauk. Through evening classes at the local junior college she had educated herself in the nuances of personnel management. Ryan had come to count on her as one of the solid pillars of Sanitas.

"Something came up. I wanted you to know."

"Shoot." He'd had the black coating removed from his Jeep, but it was parked in the company lot near the front entrance.

196

"They've found two people without proper documentation."

"Who?"

"Theresa Alvarez is one. That's why I thought you'd like to know. The other is Angel Gomez."

Ryan groaned, recalling Theresa's battered face. He did not connect with the other name.

"Who's Angel?"

"You've met him. Works in shipping."

Ryan made it a habit to wander through his operations. He prided himself on having met and talked to all the over two hundred people. "Oh, yeah. How'd this happen?" he asked.

"I don't know. We were busy staffing up. I must have overlooked it somehow."

"What now?" he asked.

"There'll be a fine. And, of course, they'll be deported."

He looked at Magdalena and said, "I want a written report."

"Yes, sir."

When Magdalena left, he shut the door and slumped into his chair. It had been a routine visit. Sanitas employed unskilled laborers in their warehouse and electronics assembly. The INS visited his company periodically to check for illegals.

He and the Phantians were safe — for a while longer. He made a mental note to talk to Sarah once again about being discrete. He picked up the phone and called Sanitas's attorney. They discussed how he could prevent Theresa Alvarez and her children from being deported to Mexico.

The Tuesday afternoon publicity event for Carlton Boyle at Sanitas came off with one hitch — the company shut down for the day. The trucks from the major networks showed up mid-morning. Camera crews and reporters arrived by noon. After lunch, the candidate's entourage wheeled up to Sanitas's front entrance. It had taken Karen Borden-Banes and people from Sam Wellborn's staff two weeks to arrange the myriad details of the candidate's stop.

Despite the sensitive nature of Sanitas's development projects, media people were allowed to accompany the candidate on an excursion that included the data collection center. Brauk demonstrated how Sanitas's Global Watch system was able to retrieve timely data by polling instruments at a semiconductor facility in Kuala Lumpur.

Ryan had arranged for several off-duty Sheriff's deputies to assist with the crowd and had announced that all non-critical employees could attend the various proceedings. Karen busied herself with Tiffany Wheeler, Sam Wellborn's assistant, as they attended to last minute details.

The main event was held at the front entrance to Sanitas. There a crowd of media people, employees, and pre-arranged party loyalists gathered to hear the candidate speak. Carlton Boyle, dressed in a dark suit and blue tie, appeared tired when he first approached the lectern. But two minutes into his speech he was ablaze with fervor and cited examples where he, as the Governor of the State of Washington, had made impressive strides. He promised to extend the shining example of his governorship to the entire country.

The candidate pointed out how the data collected by Sanitas was vital to state, federal and international agencies. CNN carried the event live: the other networks aired it on their evening news. As Ryan talked about Sanitas, he hoped that no one recognized him as the fugitive from Harmony. It turned out to be a wonderful piece of publicity and reinforced Ryan's stature as the CEO of a successful enterprise.

That evening, Sarah stood next to Ryan in the grand ballroom of the Brown Palace Hotel in downtown Denver. Karen had helped her find a suitable outfit for the occasion, a simple powder blue, knit dress that clung to her slim figure. Her light hair was woven into a French braid. Ryan noticed men staring at his stunning companion. Only a close examination of her attractive eyes and long fingers would have provided clues that she was from a world light years away.

"That facility of yours is most impressive," Carlton Boyle said to Ryan. "Also your communications network. It's wonderful that you can monitor pollution from the other side of the world. I learned a lot about state-of-the-art instrumentation and communications. Thank you."

"Thank you, it was my privilege," Ryan said.

"I am told the Environmental Protection Agency regards your company highly," Boyle said and turned to say hello to a large do-nor. In a moment he was embroiled in a discussion with a local dignitary. The thousand-dollar-per-plate fundraiser was about to begin.

Ryan and Sarah chatted with Sam Wellborn who was ready to direct the candidate toward his seat.

Ryan thought they were going to lose Boyle's attention, but he turned back and Sarah quickly asked, "Mr. Boyle, are you aware that this planet is part of a friendly, organized universe?"

"Well of course, I know we are part of the universe," he replied with a chuckle.

"What I am addressing is Earth's role as a member of the organized worlds of this galaxy," the lithe Phantian said.

"If you're asking if I believe in life on other planets, the answer is yes." The candidate leaned toward her and whispered so that the gathering crowd could not hear him. "However, I don't want that to get around, you know. Might be bad for my ratings in the South."

"May I give you something to think about?" Sarah handed him a bound sheaf of papers. The cover read, COSMIC PARADIGM. Ryan had insisted that it needed a title page.

Boyle accepted the pages from her and passed them to Sam Wellborn. Without glancing at the binder, Sam gave it to Tiffany Wheeler who was standing behind him. The young woman put it into her briefcase.

"Why are you unwilling to consider a broader view of your world?" Sarah asked Boyle.

"I believe you asked me that earlier. My answer is still the same. We are the greatest country in the world. My job, if I am elected, is to make sure we continue to be the greatest country in the world."

When the announcement to be seated was made, the crowd began to drift to the adjacent room. Carlton Boyle turned smoothly to his right to walk in with the Governor of Colorado. Earlier Ryan had introduced Sarah to Colorado's chief executive.

As Ryan and Sarah moved into the grand ballroom, Ryan bumped into several prominent local businessmen. They all congratulated him on the day's publicity event.

Ryan and Sarah found their seats at one end of the head table. He had told Sam Wellborn that although he was coming to like

Carlton Boyle, for financial reasons he was unable to contribute to the candidate's campaign. Sam had insisted that Ryan be present at the reception and the dinner.

"Perhaps, you now understand how strong the dominant paradigm is in this society," Ryan said as he helped Sarah to her seat overlooking the packed room. "You see all those people. Each of them has paid thousands of dollars to get their candidate elected, to prolong their lifestyle. And these are the supposed liberal, open-minded people."

"How do I make them listen? What can I say?"

"Maybe these are not the ones," Ryan said. "People who have succeeded within the dominant paradigm will fight against discarding it. Your best course may be to go to those who have been disenfranchised — revolutions do not start with the people in power."

"But you are successful."

"Yeah, but you had a few days to work on me — a trek in the desert, that drive from Shiprock, a little trip to Phantia." He smiled and placed his hand on hers. It was cool to his touch.

She turned from observing the crowd and said, "Tell me if you think our mission can succeed."

"I don't know. Other revolutions have succeeded when people felt oppressed, had lost their freedom. Most people in this country feel they are free. They don't realize how much better their lives could be if they knew the whole truth."

"How do you suppose they'd react if they knew they had extraterrestrials in their midst?"

Ryan listened to Boyle's speech and found that he appreciated the positions the candidate espoused more than he had before. Although Boyle did not have a cosmic perspective, here was a man who earnestly believed there was a better way. What would he do when he learned that he had spoken with an extraterrestrial?

As they left the reception, Ryan said, "I know you're anxious to retrieve your car and the supply of lotion. How about this? I'll get Ben Tsotsie to pick it up in Shiprock and drive it to Alamosa. We can drive it back from there — it's a straight shot from Alamosa to Boulder, three or four hours. I'll get a friend to fly us down.

That way you and I avoid the Four Corners area where we might be recognized."

She nodded her concurrence.

"I have to fly to Boston on Sunday for the closing with TTT Instrumentation. We'll go as soon as I get back."

"You are still worried about the INS."

"Yes, but I'm more worried about Steiger. Be careful who you piction." Earlier they had bumped into a couple of Ryan's business friends and their wives. Ryan and Sarah had made dates with them to have lunch, "to solve the world's problems." He reflected on the fact that in helping to spread the Phantian's message he was also helping Steiger find them.

At Lobo's suggestion, the INS had searched for Cody Tsotsie. When they tracked him down, he told them he had been off hunting. When queried, he refused to discuss his trek across the mesa. They brought him to Tuba City.

He had been sitting in the stark room at the Navajo Police building since dawn. His two INS interrogators sat across from him drinking coffee and eating donuts. Cody had neither.

"All right old man, talk to us."

"I do not speak of them."

"Look, we're gonna sit here til you talk." This INS agent was a burley giant of a man. "Would ya like something to eat? Breakfast, lunch, dinner — then speak up!" He made a loud slurping sound as he sipped from his cup.

Cody asked to use the restroom. The big man said, "After you tell us what we wanna know."

The second man, smaller and thin, looked at the Navajo and said, "Jimmy Lobo told us you delivered three of them to him. Where did the rest of them go?"

"All we want a do is question them." The big man leaned across the table and grabbed Cody's shirt. One of his front teeth had been broken off. It gave his smile a cruel slant. He was one of Raul Viejo's men, here to report to his boss. The smaller man worked for Oscar Hoehn. He was here to determine what had gone wrong with the raid.

The final rays of sunset leaked through the window. Cody

Tsotsie slumped on the table. He had remained calm for most of the day as the two agents peppered him with questions. He even remained calm when the smaller agent left the room and the big man punched him in the back. "To nudge you," the INS agent snickered. Cody's bladder, that he had held since morning, let loose.

They had finally supplied food and water after a Navajo officer intervened. "He is an old man. Do not harm him."

The big man repeated his physical attacks each time the smaller man left. After Cody ate, the man hit him in the stomach. When he retched, the big man pushed him to the floor and shoved his face into it.

As he gradually gave them bits and pieces of what they wanted, they allowed Cody to go the restroom and clean himself up. By the end of the day they had pieced it together.

"Let's go over it one more time." The smaller agent said. "I want to see if I understand. You picked up three people from Harmony and a fourth from your nephew Ben's dig. They split up and one of the Harmony people went another direction with your friend Teddy Leupp. You took three people over the mesa — two from Harmony and this other guy — and handed them over to Jimmy Lobo. Is that correct?"

"Yeah."

"Then what happened?"

"Go hunting."

"You guided three people over the mesa?"

"Yeah."

"Not thirty"

"Yeah."

"Did you see thirty people at Harmony?"

"No."

"The man you picked up at the dig, who was he?"

"Don't know."

"Was he from Harmony?"

"Don't know."

"Where were they headed?"

"Don't know."

"Where is your cousin Ben?"

"Don't know."

"Do you know where the men headed south went to?"

"No."

At his downtown Chicago office, on the thirty-third floor of the Hancock Building, Ernest Steiger gazed out over the bustling city. He had to stop the humanoids. They were a menace to the affiliates' carefully fabricated American dream, to his empire.

Beyond that he wanted their technology. If he could capture it for his conglomerate, it could give him a giant leap forward. Until now Steiger Enterprises had been excluded from the cabal exploiting the technology from downed alien craft. These aliens from Harmony were keen observers of his society. They had learned to speak and write English — a fantastic accomplishment. What other communication technology did they possess?

He had studied the written material and was convinced that it was of alien origin. How could anyone but an alien know such details about millions of other inhabited planets and how they were organized? What human could fabricate spirits designed to create galaxies and direct evolution? The concepts were indeed vast. The document was expressed in words radically different from traditional thinking, and it was detailed beyond the capacity of any human imagination.

Yes, there had been other contacts with aliens. He had seen the remains of their spaceship at Roswell. Ever since then he'd tracked developments. UFO's and aliens had remained mysterious; it had been easy to portray them as hostile. But these Harmony aliens were something else — they were human-like enough to convince people to cooperate with them. That in itself was dangerous.

John deBeque had sent him material that an aide to Carlton Boyle had acquired somewhere. She found it interesting, was suggesting that Boyle pay attention to it. She had summarized it for Boyle and shown how it might influence the candidate's agenda for the environment and energy policies as well as international relations. The woman didn't remember where she'd obtained the package, just knew that Sam Wellborn had passed it to her somewhere at one of their many campaign stops. Steiger had read and reread this later version. The English was stronger, clearer — was someone helping them?

He picked up the phone and called deBeque at his Washington office. "What's the latest on our friends from Arizona?"

"The INS caught the Navajo that guided them in the desert," deBeque said. "He says three of them left the facility with him. They picked up a fourth from an archeological excavation nearby."

"What were they digging for?"

"Artifacts, supposedly. It was run by some Navajo archeologist."

"I'll have one of my people go there," Steiger said. "Maybe there's more there than buried artifacts." He hated using his own people. It wasn't just the money, but the risk of someone connecting him to clandestine activities, to aliens and UFOs. But this time it was worth the risk. "What do we know about the archeologist?"

"He took off the morning of the raid. They've been trying to find him ever since."

"The INS report said there were thirty of them. What do you think?"

"Their Navajo guide says differently," deBeque said. "Say, you're really focused on this, aren't you? Why?"

"I believe the Harmony fugitives are the most human-like aliens to have visited our planet."

"Did you say aliens?" deBeque chuckled.

"Very human-like aliens. They wrote the material you forwarded to me. I'm sure of it."

"Was it that gear the FBI showed you?"

"That's part of it."

"We know about alien technology. You think this is something else? If it's true, I need to inform the other groups —"

"No. Do not tell anyone. I will handle this."

"If you've read your memos from intelligence, you know what a threat aliens are."

"Don't patronize me," Steiger said. "We are not discussing ordinary aliens. Read that document from Boyle's office. Look at that electronics gear, that facility in the desert. I'm telling you, these are not your usual aliens."

"Look, I've got lots to take care of. The other members all want something handled personally too. There are hearings at the Capital I need to attend. Your requests aren't the only ones, you know."

"You owe me."

"Yes, I know."

"What else?" Steiger asked.

"About them or something else?"

"About them, damn it."

"Hold on. My assistants have been handling this, so I have to rely on their assessment." Steiger could hear the rustling of papers. "OK. It appears that the Navajos really liked the people from that facility. The INS isn't getting any cooperation from the locals." From the way he referred to the whole subject, Steiger concluded that John deBeque was humoring him.

"John, I want you to take this seriously."

"Why do you want to talk to them?"

"I want to ask them where they got the information for those papers, how they wrote them, and about their communications technology."

"OK." The young man's words held no conviction.

"Keep me posted. Make sure the other groups don't get wind of it — this is my operation."

"It'll make it harder," deBeque said.

"I don't care." He slammed the handset onto its base. He could not rely on deBeque — deBeque did not believe.

Steiger contacted an employee at his Chicago newspaper, Frank Simon. "I want you to add something to your usual screen."

"Yes, sir."

Steiger then went on to explain what he wanted the man to do and asked him to report immediately when any of the items showed up, as he was sure they would.

He next called an old contact at the Federal Bureau of Investigation, Mack Jorgensen. On previous occasions this man had provided inside information that he had found to be amazingly accurate. This time he received a briefing on the status of the FBI's investigations into purported aliens.

"Basically Ernest, we've got our hands full with this terrorist thing. It's curious, but aliens haven't shown up much in the last few months. I'd say they were about a fifth priority, right after underground biological manufacturing operations and unaccounted for nuclear devices."

He received a similar briefing from Warren Ophir at DIA. When Steiger tried to pin him down, he found the man evasive.

"Have your people examined that gear from the desert?" Steiger asked.

"The damn FBI's hanging onto it," Ophir replied.

"So what is your organization doing about this matter?"

"Nothing. If the INS ever finds those people, we'll reopen the file."

Steiger hung up and shouted to the empty room, "Damn, I knew I was right." He opened the second drawer of his desk and checked the recoding device that monitored all telephone conversations. A year ago it had failed; this was not the time to take a chance on a repeat. It was time to take charge of the situation.

He rang for Gregor Hauptman, the head of his security force. "I want you to send a man, one of your most discrete, to snoop around in northern Arizona." He went on to explain what he wanted the man to do and that this was an immediate priority.

Later that day Steiger returned to his home in Winnetka and rang for his playmates. When the two girls stumbled into the room, he directed them to wheel him to his ultra-modern theater. There they wrestled him out of his wheelchair and onto a reclining couch. After shedding their clothes, they undressed him. He relaxed and closed his eyes.

This room… When he was a youngster he had come here with his parents to watch Ginger Rogers and Bing Crosby. The films were happy, and they had been happy. He liked the dramas with Humphrey Bogart. Some days, when he could convince his nanny to bring him here, they would watch the same film over and over. It was here, after a war movie, that his father had talked to him about his clandestine work and his success at managing the government's top secrets. For an impressionable boy it was exciting, the stuff of movie thrillers.

After his mother died, his father changed. He resigned his government job and began acquiring newspapers and radio stations. Ernest and his father remained close. The elder Steiger trained his son to disdain the common people with their base appetites and introduced him to the families of those few who were destined to rule. Later he learned that his father's money to acquire the newspapers and radio station had come from covert sources.

"This is so beautiful," Sarah Smith gasped, her breathing labored. "I'm glad you suggested this hike." She touched the rough red rock. "It's larger than it appears from town, and more rugged. I think the Creator's assistants left some excellent reminders of their abilities."

Ryan Drake and she had walked from the Chautauqua parking lot and stood at the foot of the First Flatiron, an upright monolith leaning against the foothills west of Boulder. Ryan had told her it was a favorite climb of his. He pointed out the route he had used on his last ascent.

On the way up the trail she had made it a point to say "hi" or "hello" to every hiker coming the other way. She liked the way her congenial greeting caused others to respond. Out of the corner of her eye, she watched as Ryan rambled along behind her. He seemed to enjoy watching her interact with people.

"Let's sit for a minute," she motioned to a flat spot.

Ryan removed his backpack. Judging from the size of it, she guessed he was prepared to hike for several more miles. She could only hope that it did not contain climbing rope.

She was not feeling well and the landscape whirled before her as she sat. She put out an arm to steady herself. "I guess I'm having trouble adjusting to city life," she said, sighing. "I've had to cut back on my use of lotion."

Ryan nodded at the urgency of retrieving her supplies in the car at Shiprock. Earlier he had told her that he'd contacted Ben and that everything was moving forward.

Sarah remembered her days in orbit about this sphere. Sensitive instruments had monitored the planet's atmosphere. The gases within their quarters aboard the spaceship had been adjusted to match. They had detected various pollutants and begun to compensate for them. It was months before she and the others were sufficiently conditioned to set foot on the planet's surface. They had formulated the basics of the lotion from supplies aboard the ship and then added tea tree and other ingredients after they arrived at Harmony.

The Phantians had chosen to come to the Denver-Boulder area because it was close to Harmony and much cooler than Phoenix. They desired a major city to provide anonymity and a large number of potential contacts. Thus far, Boulder had proven ideal.

"Oh look, there's a bofrey." She pointed to a hawk that circled overhead.

"That's a hawk," he said. "Not whatever you called it. Remember where you are."

She smiled reassuringly at him. In the last few days she had noticed the edge in his voice, his impatience. The strain of running Sanitas plus caring for Peter and her was showing. They had discussed the increasing likelihood of discovery as they contacted more and more people. But Ryan had gone along with her. In the past two days he had introduced her to more of his friends.

After they had rested for a while, Sarah said, "I think that's all I'm good for today."

He put his arm around her and she leaned against his warmth. It felt right to be next to him. It had been a long time since she'd felt close to a man. She looked into his eyes and saw that he cared for her.

They lingered in that position for what seemed like a long time. Neither attempted to speak or communicate. For the moment they were lost in each other's presence.

When he bent his head to kiss her, she slipped away and struggled to another rock. She was not ready. The memory of Ja'Ne was too fresh. She longed to be close, but reminded herself that she was not of this planet. On Phantia a simple kiss meant people were committed to each other. If it went beyond kissing, no telling what biological reaction either one of them could have. The cultural differences were enormous. Besides, she had her mission. "I need time," was all she could say.

"Time for what?"

"Time to decide. Ryan, I like you very much. And I am… I am very grateful for all that you've done. But we just can't risk getting further involved until we see what happens with the INS and Ernest Steiger. I don't want to jeopardize you further."

His face registered disappointment. He turned and strapped on his backpack. "I think we'd better get you home." Ryan offered his hand

Neither spoke as they descended to his Porsche. When they were in the car, she said, "Ryan, please try to understand."

Prepare yourself for a wondrous adventure. Your brief sojourn on this planet is but the first step of your celestial Journey.

— SARAH SMITH

SIXTEEN

The following day, they gathered at Turley's. At Ryan's request, the popular restaurant's proprietor had saved them a table in the rear. Sarah Smith asked that her guests, Bernadette Andrews and Mitch Young, take seats on either side of her. Peter, Aza, Fuchsia, and Ryan occupied the remaining places.

The waitress, a student from the University, took their orders. The aroma of coffee, spiced tea, omelets, pancakes, bacon, and Turley's home fries permeated the air. From the pocket of her jacket Sarah took a spice container and set it in front of her.

As they drove down the hill this morning, Sarah had told Ryan that she had selected the two newcomers from the many with whom she had talked. Since first arriving in Boulder, she had attended a dozen lectures and volunteered her time at several organizations. She had managed to talk her way into auditing three classes at the University. From conversations with people she met in these various arenas, plus those Ryan had introduced her to, she had recruited twenty interested individuals and was continuing to talk to others. Sarah had assured Ryan that her guests understood the cosmic paradigm.

Bernadette was a local activist in women's affairs. Fuchsia chatted with her about courses they had taken together at Naropa, the local Buddhist University.

Mitch ran a shelter for the homeless. Ryan had bumped into him when he came to Sanitas looking for a donation.

Peter sat next to Aza. They had spent several hours together since the last time they were at Turley's. Although Ryan could not overhear their conversation, they seemed to be getting on. The bald Phantian's plaid shirt was tucked into freshly laundered jeans. His new windbreaker hung on a nearby hook.

Sarah wore a Boulder outfit: blue jeans and a wool cape over a scooped-neck blouse. Her hair was in a loose ponytail with a bright red ribbon. She chatted amiably with Mitch.

After they received their orders and everyone began to eat, the lithe Phantian fixed Mitch with her gray eyes. "I would like to begin with a question for you."

He had just taken a bite of scrambled tofu with mushrooms, green onions, and tomatoes.

"Do you think that you understand what life on this planet is all about?" Conversations from adjacent tables provided background noise so that everyone at the Phantians' table struggled to hear Sarah's soft-spoken words.

"Don't know." Mitch mumbled. When he had cleared his mouth, he said, "I've got parts of it figured out — helping people, raising money, everyday living. I haven't had the opportunity to see much of the rest of the world."

She asked the same question of the others. Each told of experiences, interesting places they had been, unique acquaintances. Each was different.

Sarah said, "This is indeed a big world, many people, lots of places. In a short lifetime, it is impossible to understand your world of origin, and your billions of brothers and sisters. The next part of our celestial perspective is how, in time, you will come to interact with the peoples from other worlds."

"Reincarnation?" Ryan tried to anticipate her remarks. His right hand, no longer bandaged, played with the collar of his blue open-necked shirt. A camel's hair sport coat hung over the back of his chair.

"No, not reincarnation." Sarah gave Ryan a glance and inclined her head toward Peter, "Will you start off?"

"All first level beings, like you and me," Peter motioned to Aza and himself, "are born with animal bodies." Over the two weeks, Ryan had seen a remarkable improvement in the bald Phantian. He still spoke in formal English, but no longer stuttered. "After physical death, mortals congregate on 'Between spheres,' worlds dedicated to graduates from the physical planets. These are not planets, such as Earth or Phantia that have developed through the processes of evolution, rather they are spheres that have been constructed by the celestials for specific purposes."

"What do you mean, 'Between?'" Ryan spoke the words and then shoved a bite of omelet into his mouth. This morning the mixture of egg, cheese, and vegetables tasted particularly good.

"We call them Between spheres because they are not the home of physical beings nor that of celestials, they are intermediary. They are our homes as we grow to become celestials."

"With aliens from other planets?" Aza wrinkled his nose.

Peter had told Ryan that he thought the entrepreneur seemed preoccupied. Ryan had reminded Peter that Aza was still recovering from his exposure to extraterrestrials and the cosmic paradigm.

Sarah said, "The celestial Journey is the most wonderful adventure I can imagine. After I die, I will be transported to one of the Between spheres. When I awake, surrounded by now-visible celestial beings, I will know that I have survived the test of animal existence.

"The promise of the celestial Journey is a more wonderful, more beautiful, more challenging life at each level of advancement. This enlightenment procedure will repeat itself many times, each at a higher, more expanded level, each with additional brothers and sisters from other worlds, each on a new Between sphere. I will discover things that cannot be imagined by humans and meet celestial beings far beyond anything I can conceive. I will evolve, based on the accumulated wisdom of many levels and many relationships, into an accomplished celestial-being."

"Sounds complicated. How long does it take?" Ryan asked and cocked his head right.

"You will experience more than a billion other spheres on your way to Paradise." Everyone stopped eating.

"A billion different spheres?" Fuchsia gasped.

Sarah nodded and waited for everyone to grapple with the idea of visits to a billion worlds.

Ryan's mind whirled. Just how different could each of those worlds be? How long would they spend on each sphere? What were the criteria for going to the next one?

Sarah continued, "On each new Between sphere, I will take up the same problems and unfinished work that I left behind. But I will be provided with greater resources to resolve them. It's like advancing to higher grades throughout the schooling process."

"Sounds pretty complicated," Ryan said.

Sarah stared at him and asked, "Why does everything have to be complicated? Every time we try to talk about something celestial, any reference to something beyond what is here and now, you brand it as complicated. Why?"

"To me it sounds complicated," Ryan responded.

"I think that you are afraid to accept new ideas and that you brand things 'complicated' in order to avoid dealing with them. It's a technique you have to dismiss honest inquiry.

"We are giving you truth about a higher level of functioning and an incredible Journey and you get everyone off track by calling it complicated." Sarah's face had taken on a look that Ryan had not seen before. He could tell she was hurt by this trivial exchange, hurt by the fact that he had initiated it.

She caught him in her gray eyes and shook her head. He knew from the look that something more was behind her reaction to his fooling around. He suspected that if anyone else at the table had commented, they would not have elicited such an emotional response.

After a few minutes, while everyone concentrated on eating and politely ignored Sarah and Ryan's squabble, Fuchsia spoke up. "So, after death we wake up on some other world? When do we get to return to this planet?" Today she wore a forest-green dress under her ever-present beads.

Ryan glanced about the room and spotted several people he knew. Two of them nodded. Turley's was "the establishment" in Boulder, the place where local businessmen and women came to eat and chat. Ryan wondered how many of them would appreciate the conversation being carried on at his table, a conversation involving two humans who were born on another planet. It seemed so long ago that he had eaten here with those occupied with business and the talk it engendered.

"We are trying to describe a wonderful process." Sarah addressed the person with whom, next to Ryan Drake, she had spent the most time since coming to Boulder. "Yes, you will continue to exist after you die, but you will never again occupy an animal body. If you will allow it, you will experience the full extent of the cosmos, from your humble beginnings on this planet, through many wondrous adventures, to eventual evolution into a celestial being."

"Just like that?" Ryan snapped his fingers and directed his question at Peter rather than Sarah. "I get to go on this celestial Journey, just like that?" His head was cocked right. He regretted his earlier exchange with Sarah and suspected he knew what was troubling her. He would discuss it when they were alone.

"Everyone is invited to partake of the celestial Journey," Peter replied. "But it is long and difficult. To go forward, you must choose. No one will force you."

"So, the celestial Journey begins when I die?" Ryan asked. He noticed that Peter had a bit of food clinging to his chin and motioned the Phantian to use his napkin.

"That is an important question," Peter replied. His gray eyes were now as clear as Sarah's. "The celestial Journey starts here, in this life — this is the initial level. As you live your life on this planet, you take the first steps of your Journey to Paradise."

"Do I start over on each new sphere?"

"You do not leave your relationships and activities behind — you build on your successes, and failures. You carry your memories with you. You will recognize those with whom you had Earthly relationships."

"What's Paradise?" Fuchsia asked.

"Paradise is the Cosmic Nucleus," Peter said, "the center of all, the home of the Universe Father."

"He's in charge of the Journey?" Bernadette spit out the pronoun.

Sarah reached across to grasp her hand. "Bernadette, there is a God. He is the creator, controller, and upholder of the cosmos. And yes, He is in charge of the Journey. He created it for his children of time and space.

"Try to understand His intimate involvement with each of us. If for one moment, the Universe Father were to withdraw his support of that which he created, or caused to be created, the entire cosmos of time and space, all the galaxies, all the trillions of planets, every atom, would be no more. All of His vast creation would disappear in that instant."

Ryan was completely absorbed by this incredibly powerful image. No one said anything.

At long last, Bernadette asked, "But does this whole thing have to be patriarchal?"

"The creator and upholder of galaxies, of trillions of solar systems, is beyond anything so petty," Sarah said. "Male and female characteristics are most pronounced in mortals where they are necessary biological and psychological attributes. Male and female is less apparent in celestial beings; it is encompassed within the nature of God." Sarah squeezed Bernadette's hand. "I understand that many Earth males have abused their positions of power, but don't allow that to color your concept of the Father of the cosmos as anything other than a loving parent."

"I was taught that heaven was a place where I'd go and have everything I ever wanted." Aza was attacking his ham and eggs. "This sounds like work."

"Heaven is a mistaken perception," Peter said. "Yes, you will go to a heavenly place, but it is the beginning, not the ultimate destination. You will soar to wondrous places, enjoy incredible experiences. What you may think you want at this stage will change as you advance to new heights. Your idea of joy and wonderment will evolve."

"So, this is like a never-ending school?" Aza reached up with his napkin and brushed biscuit crumbs off his red beard. One afternoon, during one of their long discussions, he had confessed to Ryan that he had not finished college. He had left to help support his family. By the time he met Lucia, Ernest Steiger's daughter, he had become a successful businessman.

"Yes." The bald Phantian took a sip of water, his fingers encircling the glass. "Think of your Earthly existence as preschool; death as a commencement and entrance into a new school."

"The way the good nuns taught me, I was an unworthy sinner. Anything I got was a gift." Aza polished off a biscuit, dripping with butter and jam, and wiped his lips.

"This planet is the initial school," Sarah said. "Here the Creator has provided you with what you need: a marvelous physical body, free choice, myriad brothers and sisters, a splendid natural environment, and an evolving mind and soul. Rather than seeing these as gifts for someone undeserving, see them as tools that He has provided for your use."

"I don't get the difference."

"In one case the emphasis is on gratitude for gifts, without feeling accountable for their proper use. They are just *gifts*. In the other, the focus is on maturing yourself by learning how to use the tools, of learning to take responsibility for who and what you are. You see, you do not own anything of this planet, you are only a tenant, a craftsman."

"Do I get to have some fun? I was looking forward to relaxing in heaven."

"Yes, you get to have fun," Sarah smiled at Aza. She had come to like the human who questioned her every statement. Sarah and Ryan had spent hours coaching Peter on how to handle the entrepreneur, how to reply to his queries without being upset at his seeming irreverence.

"Tell me again." Aza said. "Why can't I just leave all my problems behind?"

"The goal is to perfect you, not to shelter you," Sarah replied.

"No running away, Aza." Ryan teased his friend. His head was cocked left, scrutinizing the give and take between Aza and the Phantians.

"What about UFO's and abductions?" Mitch asked.

Ryan had wondered when the man from the shelter would join the conversation. Since answering Sarah's first question, he had sat back and observed the others, nibbling his food.

"As we discussed the other day, extraterrestrials function in ways they believe will benefit the people of this world," Sarah responded. "What people may have experienced as an abduction, could have been merely an encounter with a highly evolved human from another planet, or an out of body experience, or a near death experience, or an encounter with an intraterrestrial."

Had she pictioned Mitch? What about Bernadette? What exactly had Sarah told her two newcomers? How much did she understand about reading humans of this world, about openness versus discretion?

Mitch returned to picking at his food.

Ryan knew there were risks, but he saw that Sarah had no choice but to reach out to people, to spread the message of the cosmic paradigm. For himself, he was learning how to speak of celestial things, learning how to tell people wondrous things existed beyond the Box of consumption and self-involvement.

"This all makes sense, but what proof do you have?" Aza asked.

"One piece of evidence is that nature doesn't waste anything," Sarah said. "If that holds true for creations as lowly as a mushroom, why not us? Why would God waste the accumulated experience of your lifetime? He doesn't; it's to be put to a higher use."

As they left the restaurant, a cold breeze blew scattered snowflakes against Ryan's cheek. He turned up his collar and thrust his hands deep into the pockets of his sport coat. Everyone but Sarah and Peter was shivering.

Peter said to those gathered, "Will you all join me? I have something special I want to share."

Aza led the parade, striding beside the bald Phantian. He had taken this same walk when Sarah had pictioned for him. They walked south to the banks of Boulder Creek. There they turned west and crossed the footbridge leading to the University. When they had all gathered, Peter smiled at them, took two steps off the trail, and disappeared.

Ryan peered at where he had gone. He saw trees and bushes, but no Peter. It was as though he had stepped through some sort of door into another dimension. Sarah came up next to him and said, "Please follow Peter."

Ryan hesitated, and then stepped forward. He passed into a dome-like bubble, warm, no breeze. Glancing back he saw that a kind of transparent wall shielded him from both the weather and outside observation. He could see the others standing outside; they could not see him.

Turning forward, he saw Peter standing next to Dr. Adamson. The white-haired apparition, dressed in a white robe, greeted him with a smile. Ryan watched as Aza, Fuchsia, and Bernadette stepped into the space.

Outside he saw Sarah and Mitch discussing something. He watched as Mitch gestured fearfully and ran off.

After a moment, Sarah appeared inside the dome. "Mitch found something urgent he had to attend to."

Before spending time with the Phantians, Ryan too might have run from something as strange as this. He glanced at Aza and Fuchsia. Arms linked, they stood staring at Dr. Adamson.

"For those of you who have not met him, this is Dr. Victor Adamson," Peter said. "He will be our guide for the next few minutes. Please form a small circle."

When everyone crowded together, arms entwined, Ryan positioned himself between Fuchsia and Aza. Sarah and Peter stood on either side of Bernadette. With Aza and Peter on either side of him, the white-haired apparition reached around to touch as many as possible.

'*Hold tightly to Fuchsia.*' Ryan recognized a different tone to the communication. It was from Peter. '*Prepare to be amazed.*'

"Please close your eyes," Dr. Adamson said. "I think you will enjoy this." His voice retained that same hollowness that Ryan had observed the first day at Harmony.

Fuchsia tightened her arm around Ryan. He smiled to reassure her and closed his eyes. When he did, he felt a surprising warmth enfold him, as if he were a child again cuddled in a soft, warm blanket.

He accelerated straight up, as if gravity had been suspended. He heard a gasp and tightened his grip on Fuchsia.

He saw the ground beneath him fall away, saw the Earth as a sphere, saw it recede to a dot against the starry backdrop. Despite the cold of space, he felt warm and protected in his blanket.

He was passing through some sort of a tunnel, traveling fast, a sensation of speed, but no sound. With the others, he was moving head first up the tunnel. The tunnel's sides sparkled with stars. They looked close enough to touch, but when he reached for them, they were far beyond his grasp. Then everything switched and their feet led down toward the end of the tunnel, toward a soft purple light.

Soon, a glowing violet sphere filled his vision. It's light radiated from within. As they descended to its surface, a subtle fragrance filled him with memories of high mountain meadows.

Floating across a landscape filled with purple trees, bushes, and grass, Dr. Adamson led them to a large white building. It was filled with rooms occupied by all manner of creatures, most resembled humans, others were somewhat different, all were exquisitely beautiful. The room's occupants appeared to be studying.

In another room, a magnificent being stood at the front of a classroom. He or she was clothed from neck to feet in a shimmering white garment. Ryan understood that this was a celestial being lecturing to graduates of material worlds. They passed by other rooms where learners were engaged in conversation, another served as a place for eating and drinking. There were no signs for rest rooms.

They visited buildings and outdoor amphitheaters where artists abounded and musicians played. A sense of joy and lightness permeated everything.

Dr. Adamson led them past villages and farms attended by strange creatures resembling teddy bears. Purple rather than green dominated the landscape. They arrived at the edge of a vast lake, its surface a mirror of the cloudless sky.

They lifted from this Between sphere, alighted on a second one, and wandered through one of the buildings. Here the people were more radiant, their forms less physical, and the building's interior more magnificent.

Then Ryan saw her. She was seated at a table with three companions, disagreeing with the person across from her. She retained her gentle way of making her point, but seemed more at peace, more sure of herself. The survival of death had strengthened her. Ryan wanted to run to her and tell her all the things that had happened to him. She turned in his direction and smiled. Somehow he sensed that his mother felt his presence, that she knew much of what had happened to her son, and that she was proud of the man he had become. The little boy in him melted with joy.

They lifted from this Between sphere and went to a third, and on through a total of seven. On each sphere the graduates of animal-life planets attended classes, wandered about campuses, engaged in activities, but their forms became less animalistic, more brilliant, more ethereal. On each successive Between sphere the buildings became less rectangular, more ethereal.

They hurtled upward. The starry heart of the Milky Way beckoned, and they threaded their way past innumerable stars and planets to its center. A huge sphere, a thousand times larger than any they had visited, anchored the galaxy. He could see irregular lines etched on its surface. A rainbow of colors emanated from certain locations. The rest of the sphere glowed with a soft blue light. Its surface reflected the countless suns surrounding the core of the Galaxy. They circled it once. Then they retreated from this inspiring presence to the far reaches of one of the spiral arms of the Galaxy, to the third planet from a familiar star.

Ryan felt his warm blanket dissipate and opened his eyes. The others too looked around. Everyone seemed reluctant to disengage from the circle, from the incredible experience, from a preview of his or her future.

"Now, you know," Dr. Adamson smiled and faded from view.

Fuchsia tightened her grip on Ryan. He hugged her back.

The group had undergone something extraordinary, something they would not forget, something that transformed mere belief into knowing. Ryan recalled stories of people who'd had near-death experiences and the changes it wrought in them. It would be interesting to watch the further transformation in his friends, in himself.

Peter released his arms and walked toward the entrance of the bubble. The others stumbled along behind him.

"Why didn't we land on that gigantic sphere?" Ryan asked Sarah.

"That was a celestial sphere. We would not have been able to see its residents. They are far advanced from those of the Between spheres."

"Are mortals on other spheres more advanced than on Phantia?"

"Some are, some are not. On some planets the people are advanced enough that they resemble the graduates we saw on the Between worlds. The mortals who visit Earth are quite advanced."

We may risk a generalization and say that at any given moment of history it is the function of associations of devoted individuals to undertake tasks which clear-sighted people perceive to be necessary, but which nobody else is willing to perform.

— ALDOUS HUXLEY

SEVENTEEN

The following morning, Sunday, Ryan Drake received a call at his home from Andy Milliken, one of Tom Ertl's deputies. Ryan was up early, trying to get in a short hike before the four-hour plane ride to Boston.

Milliken said that Mitch Young had reported an attempted abduction and they were following up to make sure Ryan was okay. Ryan assured him he was fine and that some sort of a mistake must have been made.

As soon as he put the phone down, he walked to the other side of the house and awakened Sarah. He told her about the call and urged her to be careful. All she would promise was to avoid meeting with Mitch until things cooled down. She was adamant about continuing to meet with others.

Ernest Steiger wheeled himself to the long dining table and waited for his food. The room was bright and cheery. Martha had insisted that it be decorated this way. She had brought high-priced consultants from Spain, people who recommended bright colors and many plants. He had complained that it did not mesh with the rest of the house. It did not matter; Martha had prevailed. This was

Martha's room as she had left it. His wife had died ten years ago.

The twenty-two years she had ruled this household had been merrier times. They had entertained the wealthy and influential from around the world, here as well as at their homes in Palm Beach and Washington, DC. In those days, he had schemed with presidents of companies and countries. He had coached them on the benefits of a present-time focus, of an ever-expanding economy, of information manipulation and its power.

Then Martha died, and his illness set in. His doctor diagnosed diabetes. For a while the treatments had seemed to help, then complications forced him to retreat more and more from an active life. He began to mistrust his personal physician and sought the advice of others. The diabetes was affecting his legs and eyes. He had existed in his wheelchair for the last two years. If she had been here, none of it would have happened.

He remembered how, long before his illness, Martha had brought home an acquaintance, a Dr. Victor Adamson. The white-haired man claimed he was a doctor of history, philosophy, and cosmology. He tried to convince Steiger that there was a link between the manipulation of truth and disease. They had discussed it for an hour before Steiger told his wife to usher the man out. "I don't want you wasting your time with the likes of him." Now as he thought back to that conversation, he decided that the man might have planted ideas in his mind that had led to his infirmity — a man's mind was a powerful thing. He recalled seeing Adamson again at Martha's funeral. Despite his wishes, she obviously had maintained contact with the so-called doctor.

A pain shot through his chest. He gently rubbed it. The pains were becoming more frequent, but he refused medication that might dim his mental acuity.

The chef arrived with lunch, poached salmon with a delicate cucumber-dill sauce. Since Martha had died, he had continued with the monthly menu she had set. Lunch on the first Sunday of the month was always salmon with new potatoes and green beans.

The prospect of talking to an alien had always excited him. He had studied the pictures and autopsies of extraterrestrial biological entities. None of them had vocal chords. Those that had been captured alive had communicated without speaking, had used some kind of mind talk. Until now he had been sure aliens had nothing resembling human thought or speech.

This time was different. The aliens from the Arizona desert had constructed their secret base with the help of the Indians and used contractors and conventional materials. This time they wrote in English and their words painted a precise picture of their view of the universe. At a deep level he knew that some of their concepts were undoubtedly true, but he could not accept that they were benign. He was convinced they were cleverly manipulating ordinary people while they were plotting the subjugation of the planet. Although he feared them, he admired the fact that they had learned the language of the world they planned to enslave. What other communication technologies did they possess?

After lunch he returned to his study and called his son Richard at his home in Des Moines, Iowa. His older son reported that the last of the last shipment of Mexican illegals had arrived on Friday. Steiger directed him to pay off Raul Viejo. Richard said that he had settled the strike in Wichita, within the guidelines his father had laid down.

They went on to discuss their newest opportunity. At Richard's insistence they had moved into electronic publishing and dabbled in other forms of paperless communications. While they had spent a considerable sum, there were no profits. They both agreed it was too early to expect results.

He then tracked down his daughter, Lucia, at her Paris apartment. It was evening there and she was preparing for bed. They laughed as he told her of the revenge he had exacted on her former husband, Aza O'Sullivan.

He paged Gregor Hauptman. After his security chief promptly returned his page, he inquired about what their man had found in northern Arizona. Hauptman said that he had sent a man with experience in archeology. The dig appeared to be quite conventional, although they did appear to have uncovered some interesting artifacts. The resident archeologist was not around; no one would tell his man where to find Ben Tsotsie.

He called John deBeque. The INS was reportedly investigating a large shipment of illegals. No news on the fugitives from Harmony, but the INS was still working on it. On the basis of Cody

Tsotsie's interrogation, they had abandoned searching for any more than the four they were still pursuing.

Steiger called Richard back and told him to disburse the Mexicans as quickly as feasible. Richard said it had already begun, but that many of them were sick. Steiger directed him to refuse to pay Viejo for any sick Mexicans.

Steiger reread the material that he believed had been written by the aliens. He concluded that they were very clever. There was no hint of their ultimate intent with regard to Earth. The document kept talking about people taking responsibility for their actions. He laughed at their naiveté; he was quite sure the Box had taken care of that old adage, at least among most Americans.

He checked the clock. Sundays were frustrating because people were not in their offices. He rang for Rebar who hustled up his playmates.

The Charles River reflected the morning skyline of Boston. Ice, covered with a fresh blanket of white, clung to the rocks on the bank of the slow moving river. No crews manned the sculls this dreary Sunday morning. Except for light traffic on Memorial Drive, few sounds disturbed Ryan Drake's peaceful view.

He had come to the East Coast to personally meet Truman Thompson and sign the critical agreement with TTT Instrumentation. Ryan had stayed the night at a hotel in Cambridge, across the river from the city.

Last evening he had arrived after dark. This morning he arose early and concentrated on a mountain of paperwork. Everything was piling up.

The room was standard hotel, a king size bed and a bathroom. Its windows were frosted from the outside cold. He rose from the desk in the hotel room and stretched his legs by bracing against the wall. He faced a framed print of a sailboat, red and white sails, keeled over in a brisk wind. He reached over and touched his stocking feet. Rising, he linked hands behind his back and reached as high as he could. Next he grabbed each elbow with the opposite hand and pulled them over his head.

He recalled Sarah swimming to greet him the afternoon of the day they had returned to his home outside Boulder. Her bronze body, no swimsuit lines, had seemed at home in his pool. Her strokes determined and smooth as she crossed the pool, a seasoned athlete. He had turned away as she climbed out, but he'd glimpsed her shapely front. She was slender with attractive breasts. But no navel and no pubic hair. It had startled him at first. Now, he wondered if people on Phantia made love the way they did on Earth.

He knew he cared for her and suspected she cared for him. She was from another planet, but she was a human. Yes, she had a slightly different biology, but the rest of her seemed remarkably similar. He suspected her mind and soul were very much like his.

He went for a workout in the hotel's spa and then wandered among the nearby buildings of Harvard and MIT. These older structures stood in vivid contrast to the newness of the West. Students and professors, tightly wrapped against the weather, hurried to early classes. Yet it was out of the western desert that a new paradigm had emerged — driven, not by the intelligence of erudite men, but by celestial wisdom. The cosmic paradigm, when accepted — and it would eventually be accepted, regardless of the intervening course of events — would reorganize many traditions, many institutions.

He shivered. To him East Coast cold penetrated more than even the crispest mornings in Colorado. As he walked up the driveway to the hotel lobby, snow began to fall from the overcast sky.

All of his earlier attempts to find truth and to live it had been modified by the revelations of the Phantians. Theirs was a profound truth that exceeded anything constructed by man. He was sure he did not understand every detail, but his heart grasped its significance. Startled, he realized he was no longer bifurcating — a single perspective existed for cosmic truth.

It was just over two weeks since the Phantians and their celestial perspective had been thrust on him. His head was just now clearing from the shocking realization that he had encountered extraterrestrials, that humans lived on other planets. What a transformation. Two time lines: After and before. In addition to the picture of Phantia, hazy words were beginning to emerge on the white slate of his future.

There was more to him than his physical body, more than life on this planet.

Spirit was no longer mysterious. Celestial was just a higher dimension, as real as this one.

The cosmic paradigm affirmed the specialness of all on the celestial Journey — whether they recognized it or not.

Something powerful, deep inside him, rallied to reinforce his new insights, pulled him along.

Ryan laid out his clothes for the meeting with Truman Thompson and stepped into the shower. He relaxed as the warm water flowed over his body.

"Are you ready to proclaim what you know to be true?"

The voice was loud and close. He opened the shower door, expecting to see someone standing in the bathroom. He looked around, but there was nothing. He closed the shower door. As before, the words had left him with a sense of wonder, awe.

"Are you ready to help reorder this world?" the assertive voice asked. This was not the whisper of some quiet inner voice. Forceful and penetrating — it was not a voice one ignored. Ryan tried to move, but his legs and arms were immobilized.

"I am not sure," he said. He shuddered at the implications of what was being asked of him and the source of the query. The Phantians were real. He understood the cosmic paradigm. He wished to partake of the celestial Journey. "Who are you?"

"I am sent from Michael, the ruler of this local universe." A glowing figure appeared through the mist.

Ryan stepped back and banged into the wall. "Oh," was all he could say. He felt powerless in the presence of a messenger from the one in charge of millions of planets.

"Will you lead?" The commanding voice blasted through the steam.

The shimmering figure was the same size as he, but did not intrude on the confines of the shower stall. The magnificent white-robed being seemed to exist regardless of material boundaries. The tile wall did not interfere with Ryan's perception of the celestial emissary. Warm water from the showerhead continued to splash over Ryan. His nakedness seemed appropriate.

"Why me?" Rather than the gut-wrenching insecurity Ryan had experienced at other moments of decision, he felt humility and a sense of awe. His inner essence seemed to pulsate with the ethereal visitor.

When he did not receive an immediate answer, he asked again, "Why me?" The weight of his resistance pushed him against the cold tile of the stall.

"Because you can."

He tried to take a step, but could not move.

Could not run away.

Could not resist.

There was no way to avoid the query of this preeminent celestial presence.

Finally he blurted out, "If that is what you want." As he said the words, Ryan felt incredible relief. His body slumped to the floor. The warm spray caressed his limp form, soothed him as he imagined his mother had done when he was a helpless infant.

The glistening figure disappeared.

While the water cascaded over him, he found peace. Implications flooded him. He was no longer alone, no longer uncertain. He had embraced his role in the Grand Plan of the universe and had, in turn, been welcomed to the next step of his celestial Journey.

He cried, as he had not done since a child — tears of release, joy, and realization. Ryan, the man, sobbed as he reconnected to the Father who had never abandoned him, who wanted what was best for him, who loved him. Ryan, the CEO, volunteered his expertise for use by wiser, celestial powers. Ryan, the human, grasped the steadfastness of knowing. The fire of the passionate young idealist re-ignited.

In addition to a clear picture of Phantia from space, Ryan's blank sheet now contained one word in crisp bold letters: REORDER. Other words were present, but they were too hazy to discern.

His imagination soared with possibilities of an unlimited future — not suppressed, not qualified, not controlled. For himself, for all people of the universe.

True freedom, knowing that he was cosmically important.

His life integrated with new possibilities, new adventures.

Personal purpose aligned with a celestial cornucopia.

No longer controlled by mixed messages from other humans.

A long term ordering, instead of merely wandering through life.

Meaning and motivation.

Ryan Drake was humbled.

"Our customers are demanding a second source for your product," Truman T. Thompson said. "If I don't give it to them, someone else will." The President of TTT Instrumentation gazed at Ryan Drake through tinted glasses. Years ago Thompson had played offensive tackle for the Pittsburgh Steelers. His bulk spilled over the sides of his substantial chair. Massive hairy arms bulged from the rolled-up sleeves of his white shirt. Folded hands displayed a Super-Bowl ring. He was the key to TTT Instrumen-tation's worldwide distribution juggernaut. Today he was playing tough guy.

"Second source? I thought we'd concluded our deal." When Ryan arrived at TTT Instrumentation, he had been escorted to the showy executive office by the President's attractive secretary, offered a drink, and asked to wait. Thompson appeared ten minutes later and issued his ultimatum. Ryan looked beyond the president's huge head; sunshine reflected the red TTT logo off the glass and aluminum building next door. "What do you have in mind?"

"We have found someone acceptable. You license them and receive a royalty. We'll guarantee to take eighty percent of the product from you and twenty percent from them — then everybody's happy." Thompson leaned forward and locked Ryan in his gaze.

"Who is it?" He returned the president's stare.

"Exemplar."

"Exemplar! You have to be kidding. All they've ever done is copy our products and underbid us in the market. They aren't anywhere near our quality or expertise." Since he had learned that TTT Instrumentation was talking with competitors, Ryan and his team had been preparing for some unexpected possibility.

"It's our customers in Europe. They want a larger company."

"Why Exemplar?" Ryan realized now that Ernest Steiger had deliberately misled him by suggesting a German company. Exemplar, one of Steiger Enterprises family of companies, had been the adversary all along. Steiger wasn't content to just invest in Sanitas; he was using Nick's inside knowledge of Sanitas's business to benefit a company he controlled. What other surprises did the wheelchaired man have in store for him?

"Hey, with a ten percent royalty from them, you'll make money on every unit that gets sold. Ryan, I know this looks like a last minute deal." Thompson stood. His body seemed to fill the glass panel behind him. "But the market is talking."

This whole scene was implausible. This morning he had committed himself to lead a movement that could revolutionize his country, and in turn his world. Yet, here he was arguing with this man over the details of a straightforward business agreement. Ryan resolved to extract himself from Sanitas as soon as possible. But first he had to close this deal. He owed his shareholders and employees that much.

"We'll need guaranteed minimums," Ryan said.

"Your products are hot, but I still can't guarantee the same volume as last year."

Ryan shoved his papers into his briefcase and stood. "It won't work."

"Hold on." Thompson motioned him down.

"We need a minimum fifty percent increase in sales," Ryan said. His instincts screamed that he'd been set up. Thompson had strung the negotiations along until this moment, hoping Ryan would cave in, grasp any deal. The outcome of this battle would determine the future of Sanitas.

"Twenty-five percent." The big man's eyes bore into him.

"Not good enough." Ryan stood again. Despite his inner turmoil, Ryan could not let the other man rattle him. Sanitas had superior technology and had made a name for itself. Yes, he needed TTT Instrumentation's marketing and service, but Sanitas had value to offer the giant company. Two could play this game. If the deal became too onerous, Ryan was prepared to walk out of the negotiations — as a last resort.

The CEO and the President went on for an hour, hurling demands back and forth, finally settling on middle ground. At the end of the negotiations, they had agreed to a new three-year deal at an increase of forty percent and a second source arrangement with Exemplar for fifteen percent of the unit volume.

"Ask the attorneys to step in," Thompson barked into his intercom. Two men, in dark suits appeared. "So, here's the deal." The president of TTT Instrumentation recited the final terms of the negotiations as he and Ryan had agreed. "We want to sign it tomorrow morning."

As he walked from TTT Instrumentation's headquarters, Ryan knew that he had done his best. Sanitas would survive and prosper. But he had a nagging worry that the fingerprints of Ernest Steiger were somehow all over the contract to which he had just agreed.

BOYLE WINS! The front page of the Boston Globe showed a picture of the president-elect and his wife at their victory celebration. He had captured fifty-six percent of the popular vote and all but seventy-nine electoral delegates. As was Ryan's custom, he had voted by absentee ballot.

After he signed the agreement with TTT Instrumentation, Ryan called Karen with the good news and asked her to inform the management team. He also asked her to send out a fax to each member of Sanitas's Board. He further asked her to send a congratulatory note to Sam Wellborn.

Ryan sat in first class on the Boston to Denver flight. He turned down the complimentary champagne.

Looking at the results for Senatorial races he noted that Leonard Williams had won by a narrow margin. The Globe speculated that his victory would tip the scales in the Senate.

In HOLISTIC HAPPENINGS, buried in section five of the newspaper, Fuchsia reported on the many letters she had received in response to her recent column. Almost uniformly, her readers said that if they could really be sure they were part of a larger whole, it would change their current lifestyle. But most of them went on to question the entire proposition.

Fuchsia reported that she had had what some people might call a near death experience, had seen what comes next. She said she now understood that death was a transition along a continuum and viewed her life here as the first step in an ascending Journey. She asked her readers for letters about similar experiences.

After he landed in Denver, Ryan called and asked her if she had received any unusual replies or inquiries about her recent columns. She replied that someone from a newspaper in Chicago had called her and wanted to know the source of her information. It seems they had been asked to track any references to a cosmic point

of view. Ryan told her to be cautious and to tell Sarah to be prepared to take evasive action.

"You really stepped in it this time." Tom Ertl was not smiling.
Ryan Drake and the Sheriff of Boulder County sat at Turley's, steaming coffee at hand. It was the day after the election.

Ertl had left a message for Ryan that he had talked to his contacts in Arizona. When Ryan returned from signing the agreement
with TTT Instrumentation, he had rushed to meet with his friend.

"Oh?"

"Yeah, the INS is more determined than ever to talk to the
people who escaped from Harmony Center," Ertl said. "The whole
agency is getting hellacious pressure from Washington to track
down anybody connected to it. Two people died, you know."

"This whole thing doesn't make sense. I'm telling you I saw
Harmony, I know these people. They didn't do anything wrong."

"You might be right. Although he can't prove it, my contact
believes this guy, Raul Viejo, was masterminding the illegal conduit through the Navajo Reservation.

"Viejo was under suspicion, but the Harmony incident tem-
porarily derailed it. Now, the internal investigation is back on. He
must have gotten help from someone at BIA — that would explain
how they were able to pull off the raid. What my contact can't figure is the interest from Washington. In normal circumstances, they
let him run his own operation and moan about Mexican Border
problems."

"What about clearing the Harmony people?" Ryan asked.

"Your friends shouldn't have fled. Makes them look guilty."

"What would you have done if your home, out in the middle
of nowhere, was about to be invaded?" Ryan asked.

"I'd rather not answer that," the law enforcement officer replied with a smile. "If you'll produce your friends, I think we can
meet with the INS and clear up this whole matter."

"I wish it were that easy."

"If the Mexican woman's death turns out to be homicide, you
could be involved as an accomplice. And a Navajo was killed."

"The only murder was the Navajo. We were a long ways away
by then. I don't know anything about the Mexican woman except

that workers at Ben's dig found her. She was still alive when they took her to the clinic."

The Sheriff studied him for a few minutes. "Look, Ryan, there are some people who think your friends might be mixed up with Viejo in this thing. They think maybe Viejo killed the Navajo to keep him from talking and let your friends sneak away from the INS pursuit. The only way to sort this out is to interrogate your friends, see what they know. At the very least, you could be implicated as a material witness."

"What about Viejo?"

"He's disappeared."

Ryan sat back. At length he said, "Tom, I'm counting on the fact that you know me pretty well and you know I wouldn't be doing this without a damn good reason. Did you tell your Arizona contacts that you knew where to find one of the fugitives?"

"No." Ertl shook his head and looked down at his coffee cup.

Ryan could tell that his friend was not happy about the situation. "Thanks, I owe you one."

Ertl looked up and studied him again. At last he said, "Got some stuff on your buddy Ernest Steiger."

Ryan had called Ertl and asked him for information on Steiger. A member of the Denver Police Department before becoming Sheriff of Boulder County, Ertl had contacts all over the country. When Sanitas had suspected someone was attempting to shut down Global Watch, Ertl had recommended a firm in Minneapolis who had installed Sanitas's sophisticated security system. His department had also helped flush out a Sanitas employee who was offering to sell company secrets.

When Ryan was suffering through the first months of his separation from Vicki, Tom Ertl had come to his rescue. They had gone fishing, but Ryan cut it short insisting that he needed to get back to the office. Ertl cajoled him, and he finally took an evening off from Sanitas. After consuming the luscious baked ham dinner that Nancy Ertl had prepared, they sat around for hours talking about favorite vacation spots. After that Ryan became a frequent guest at their home and even consented to meet one of Nancy's lady friends.

"A friend of mine with the Chicago Police Department knows a lot about this guy. Tried to investigate him, got nowhere — he's untouchable. Wealthy, runs a lot of businesses, newspapers, radio and television stations — everything's under the umbrella of Steiger Enterprises. Probably worth a billion or two. Officially, no one's ever had a complaint against him."

"Go on."

"Has his own private security force. Keeps everything hush-hush. Rumors, and so far they're just that, rumors are that he buys and sells politicians, not just local ones either. My friend would really appreciate knowing anything about this guy."

"Maybe I can return the favor."

Ertl paused and then said, "Ryan, it's time you leveled with me. What are you mixed up in? Smuggling? Steiger? It's not like you. My office got a call from a guy named Mitch Young, said some real strange stuff about you and some aliens. I thought I knew you pretty well."

"You do."

"Well?"

"Can we just leave it at that?"

"No. I want answers."

"All right, let's go to my house," Ryan said. "There's someone there who can help explain."

One must be able to strip oneself of all self-deception, to see oneself naked to one's own eyes before one can come to terms with the elements of oneself and know who one really is.

— FRANCES G. WICKES

EIGHTEEN

On the way to the airport at Alamosa, Sarah requested that they divert the plane to pass near a tall frosted mountain to the east of the town. "This valley was very sacred to Native Americans," she said as she gazed out the window of the small airplane. "It was never permanently settled and no battles were ever fought here. That mountain," she pointed to the tall rugged peak, "is special for many reasons."

"How so?" Ryan asked. One of Colorado's fourteeners, he had climbed Blanca Peak six years ago. Although it was a long hike, it was rated intermediate. He'd bagged Ellingwood Peak, an adjacent fourteener, on the same trip. He'd experienced nothing special on the climb.

"Not only was it sacred to the indigenous peoples, but it is the home to both intraterrestrials and extraterrestrials."

"You mean they live on the side of a mountain?"

"No, in it."

The remnants of yesterday's storm had moved to the east, but fresh snow blanketed the area. The pilot, Ryan's friend, Evan Bromley, dropped them off on the tarmac and was already taxiing his twin-engine Beechcraft for the return flight as they trudged toward the terminal.

Both Ryan and Sarah wore heavy coats and hiking boots. Ruts from recent snow remained on the icy asphalt. He sported a baseball cap reading, DAN'S FLY SHOP. His hiking pack was slung over his left shoulder. The lithe Phantian carried her new daypack by its strap. She used her right hand to hold blowing hair out of her eyes.

Ryan knew it was dangerous to reconnect with Ben Tsotsie. However Peter and Sarah had insisted — their supply of lotion was gone. They had been able to find all but two of the ingredients for it in Boulder. Those critical substances were part of a supply they had brought from Phantia. They were the only ones they had not been able to replicate in Harmony's lab. Their car in Shiprock contained a quantity sufficient for several months.

They walked through the terminal and out to the parking lot. Ben Tsotsie was leaning against the fender of a maroon Buick sedan. It was one of about twenty cars in the parking lot.

None of them took particular notice of a gray sedan with Federal Government license plates parked outside the gate. It carried no other markings on its exterior.

The Navajo walked towards Ryan and gave him a bear hug. "You two look pretty good, considering."

A week ago, after Ryan had tracked down Ben at his family's hogan, he had given him a capsule account of the night trek across Fortress Mesa, the escape in Shiprock, and the roadblock near Durango.

"Next time, I'll listen to you." Ryan grinned. "Then again, maybe not." He had his arm on Sarah's shoulder.

Ben looked at Sarah and said, "I guess my intuition was correct. Things seem to be working out."

She patted Ryan's arm and said, "This is a very special man."

Ben smiled and said, "Sorry to rush off, but my flight to Shiprock leaves soon. It's the only one today." The Navajo handed the car's keys to Sarah. Ryan and Sarah threw their packs on the car's rear seat and walked Ben to his flight.

"Why now? Why not some underdeveloped country or Europe?" Ryan asked Sarah. They had turned north onto US 285 and were proceeding through the broad San Louis Valley. Ryan wanted to use the drive to address several issues that still puzzled him. With so much happening, Sarah and he had few moments to themselves.

Sarah thought for a few moments and then replied. "When extraterrestrial visitors make themselves clearly known, it will be sensational. By painting any such appearance as adversarial, the affiliates are hoping to use people's fear to totally solidify their control over the population. In contrast, we want to provide a context in which people can absorb the truth about extraterrestrials, not a scripted media version. We want them to see past their fears to a friendly, organized universe, a universe bent on helping Earth become the beautiful place of which it is capable. We were selected because we resemble you so closely, to allow people to get comfortable with the idea of friendly extraterrestrials, of humans residing on other planets.

"If we had arrived sooner, say fifty years ago, the mood in this country would have been even more fearful and hostile than it is today. Your country was recovering from World War II, when it was plunged into the Cold War. Now, America has become the lone super power in the world and feels less threatened, terrorist attacks not withstanding. Your astronomers are just discovering planets that circle distant suns. Plus extraterrestrials are accepted as possibilities — even if they are fictional and hostile.

"Dr. Adamson and the other guardians of this planet saw that you had developed technology capable of destroying this planet, capable of detecting and downing extraterrestrial spacecraft. On your current track, your country will export its violent attitude and these weapons into space. They requested humans like us to convince you of the friendliness of the cosmos.

"As for the United States. You are quite correct. In many ways it is the greatest country of this planet, or at least it was until the affiliates began to mislead people. Yours is an open society, with a history of living by the rule of law. Religion and government are separated. English is as close to a universal language as exists on this planet. Your country has risen to heights of power and wealth never experienced before. If we are to make an impact, to set this world back on its proper course, it must begin here, and it must begin with a recognition by your people of who you really are, in relation to the rest of the world, in relation to the rest of the cosmos."

"Peter's new world order?"

"It is a unique moment in the history of this planet, an opportunity for worldwide change. There are those who want to ignore the larger picture, to control the process so that they wind up in charge. We do not want this planet's reordering to result from the forces of power, wealth, deceit, and self-interest. We want you and others like you to transform your world into the beautiful place that is its rightful destiny."

The sun broke through and Ryan reached for his sunglasses. Lost in his thoughts and fascinated with the woman who sat beside him, he did not pay attention to the gray sedan that followed them at a distance. He felt Sarah's eyes on him and turned. She immediately glanced away, but a brief smile crossed her lips.

"That mountain is spectacular," Sarah said pointing. Mt. Shavano, 14,229 feet tall, its bulk covered with a fresh blanket of glistening white, rose to the northwest of their route.

"Climbed it, a few years ago. Is it a home for intraterrestrials?"

"Not that I know of."

They crossed US 50 and continued north on US 285, retracing the route they had taken three weeks ago.

Ryan struggled with the Buick. It wanted to veer left; he had to concentrate to keep it from wandering over the yellow line. An occasional patch of ice added excitement to the drive.

"I am pleased with all the people I have met since arriving in Boulder," Sarah said. "They have helped me understand the grip your culture has on everyone."

"Three weeks ago, I'd have taken offense at that statement." Ryan smiled at the changes that had overtaken his comfortable life. "Now, I have to agree. You've opened my eyes. The amount of disinformation and manipulation is appalling."

"Your society reminds me of a school of fish," she said. "People arc pushed and pulled by the currents of change, reacting to the latest fad or threat to their security and comfort. America is drifting, marking time. That must change before it is too late."

Sarah turned and laid her hand on Ryan's shoulder. "We are developing a cadre of people who see the truth. They will need a leader."

Ryan shuddered and recalled his Boston commitment. This was the first time he and Sarah had been alone since he had returned. So much was happening so quickly. He told her of the celestial.

She smiled and gently patted his shoulder.

Sarah was quiet as the miles crept by. Ryan rambled on about his problems with Sanitas and how he would like to extract himself.

"What are your hopes for a resolution?" Sarah asked. When they had stopped for gas near Buena Vista, Ryan had instructed the attendant to replace the car's worn, left front tire with the spare.

"In order to do what you want me to, I have to find a way to extract myself from Sanitas." Despite a cold wind, they had walked into the field next to the service station. Brown stubble from last summer's growth protruded through a layer of dirty snow.

"When will that happen?" The lithe Phantian pulled up the hood of her parka and zipped the front to her chin. She slipped her bare hands back into the coat's warm pocket. Despite the bright sunshine, the winter wind was bitter even for her Phantian physiology.

"I don't know." Ryan kicked a rock and sent it flying. His hiking boot probed for a second one beneath the skiff of white. "It's not that easy."

Sarah walked across the snow-covered ground, head bowed, thoughtful. "From what you have said, there are several agendas in your company. You would like to extract yourself from it, with your investment and a profit. Your venture investors would like to continue running it and will hold out for large financial rewards. What about Nick Steiger? Why did he invest in your Company?"

"That's an interesting question. I thought it was to make money, but now I'm not sure. Truman Thompson manipulated me into the license with Exemplar — that troubles me. Steiger must have engineered it."

Sarah captured him with her large gray eyes and asked, "Can you sell your company?"

"I'm thinking on it," he said. He found another rock and kicked it. "The key to any of this is my financial status. I need to come out of it with enough money to live on."

Seeming to ignore his last remark, Sarah said, "Maybe it would be best to complete the transaction before Nick Steiger finds out you are helping us." She turned her back to the cold wind and peered at Mt. Princeton to the west, another fourteener.

Ryan reached down and touched the toes of his boots. He felt his back muscles stretch and remained in that position for a few moments. Next he placed one foot forward, the other behind, and stretched each leg.

The ramifications of such a dramatic change of course spilled into his mind, he felt as if he were gripped in the jaws of a gigantic vice. "I think I've done a good job at Sanitas," he said. "My investors have said they're happy. But a major distraction, such as taking time to shield Peter and you, will not be well received. They expect my total devotion to the enterprise they funded." His divorce had left him with no liquid assets, a huge mortgage, and expenses of almost a thousand a month just for the utilities on his mountain home. Without the income from Sanitas, how would he meet those obligations?

While the idea of selling Sanitas was not entirely new, the company wasn't ready for sale, hadn't reached its full potential. The two prior companies he had sold, both with some of the same venture capitalists involved, had been more mature. It was like shoving an adolescent from a comfortable home. Any buyer would want a functioning company, a company without problems, a company with management team and market position intact. They would probably want him to remain on.

"At the same time I want to devote my energy to what I see as a process of worldwide transformation, the time is ripe," he said, as much to himself as to Sarah. "The problems of Sanitas are miniscule compared to what's unfolding around me. I've been asked to play a part in the creation of a new world order."

Ryan was sure complications would occur when the Steigers found out about his involvement with the Phantians. As a Board member, Nick would give him trouble. The old man might step up competitive pressures from Exemplar. If Steiger Enterprises was willing to live with losses from this subsidiary, Exemplar could sell products at such a low price they would erode Sanitas's profits and might force his company out of business. He felt the vice around him constrict another notch.

They turned and walked back to the Buick. Ryan said, "Peter seems to be well, but I see that he is struggling with something."

Sarah said, "Peter's main contribution to this mission is his ability to present to audiences. When the time is right, you will see. He does not have the easy access to universe mind that I do and he struggles with accepting earth dwellers. For instance, he cannot understand why you did not embrace the larger picture long ago."

"What do you mean long ago?"

"Peter is quick to point out that the truth about life after death has been known for thousands of years."

"But not like you've told it, not in the cosmic context, not like the celestial Journey you've painted for me."

"Peter sees how few have embraced the truth and tried to live it. The majority continues to be caught up in their own self-centered lives. In the advanced countries it centers on consumption. In the underdeveloped it is a matter of survival."

"But I know lots of good people, people trying to make this a better place, people like teachers, firemen, public servants."

"Yes, but what are they willing to give up to make it so? Injustice pervades your society, your world. The rich and powerful manipulate good people for their benefit. Secrets and lies are commonplace. As the richest and most powerful nation, you have become a comfortable people and are willing to go to war to preserve the status quo. Are you willing to make some sacrifices so that everyone else on this planet can live as well as Americans? Are you willing to reorder the world in accordance with cosmic truth? We will see."

"So we should give in to all the underdeveloped countries with their two-bit dictators?" Ryan asked. "Let them make us feel bad about who we are."

"Your world could be so beautiful, and peaceful. But it will not be so until you begin to treat all people on this planet as your brothers and sisters. That is what troubles Peter. He does not understand why Americans are resigned to allowing things to continue the way they are, allowing other countries to enslave their people."

"So you want America to reduce its lifestyle to the level of Bangladesh?"

"No. In addition to a sustainable lifestyle, America must set a high moral standard for itself. Then the emphasis should be uplifting the people of Bangladesh and other poor countries to America's level."

"You can't be serious. There's not enough of anything to go around. There's barely enough oil for the industrialized countries. If the rest of the world rose to our level, we'd consume it in a few years."

"Do you remember talking about zero-point energy?"

"Yes. On the way from Harmony, when you first saw Rocky Flats."

"Zero-point energy and other undeveloped forms of energy are virtually unlimited. If these were made available, in a few years the poorer nations could approach the lifestyle of America. With an improving lifestyle come other advances."

"So why hasn't it already happened?"

"That is something Peter and I are trying to find out."

The government sedan idled behind the service station across the road. The driver had slipped around the side of the building and was taking pictures as he waited.

An hour later, Ryan brought the Buick to an abrupt halt as the light changed at the intersection of US 6 and CO 93. They were just to the west of Golden. Traffic was heavy on this fall afternoon in early November. There was no snow on the ground; the temperature was in the sixties. Sarah and he were on the last leg of their return to Boulder. The gray sedan was three cars behind them.

She removed her parka and tossed it into the rear seat. Ryan noticed her lithe form and shapely breasts as she re-buckled her seat belt. He wondered if there was any hope of a relationship with this enticing woman.

When the light changed, he accelerated the Buick to 45 MPH.

Without speaking, she communicated, ' *Thank you for doing this.*'

It took him a moment to digest the message, and then he said, "You're welcome. Hey, I understood what you said." And he had, despite concentrating on the road.

They rode across the high ground to the south of Boulder. Bathed in sunlight, the Denver metropolitan area spread to the eastern horizon.

As they passed a small lake Sarah said, "Look swose."

"What did you call them?" A flock of Canada Geese wandered about the water.

"On Phantia we call them swose."

Ryan chuckled. "Sounds complicated."

Sarah closed her eyes and shook her head.

'What's wrong? Can't stand a little teasing?' Ryan was beginning to get the hang of this mind-to-mind stuff. He could see all kinds of possibilities.

'You do know how to get to me, don't you?' she communicated.

'Do you know what that means?' he communicated back. He felt a longing to be close to her. She had rejected him when he'd tried to kiss her near the Flatirons. However, something seemed to have changed.

'That I care for you.'

When they approached the Rocky Flats Environmental Site, she asked him to speed by it. The fear in her voice jarred him. He accelerated to 70 MPH.

'Zero-point energy, huh.'

'Yes.'

'I'll look into it. Maybe get Brauk to do a little research.'

As they drove into Boulder, Ryan glanced at Sarah. For an instant their eyes met. His chest tightened. *'I care about you — very much. It is extremely difficult seeing you in my home every day and not being able to express how I feel.'*

'It is the same for me.'

The gray sedan, two cars behind, was forced to stop for a red light at Baseline Road. It lost the Buick in Boulder's afternoon traffic. The driver had radioed for assistance, but no one from the Denver office of the INS had responded.

"What's the latest?" Ernest Steiger asked. The telephone crackled so he knew the call had been forwarded to John deBeque's cell phone.

John deBeque did not reply to the question. Instead he asked, "What did your man find at the archeological site?"

"Nothing. Navajo crew, but no archeologist. Nobody was

willing to talk."

"The INS had it staked out," deBeque said. "Seems the anthropologist came around once in a while to check on things. One of them tracked him to Shiprock, New Mexico where he picked up a Buick sedan in the parking lot of the post office. He drove it to Alamosa, Colorado where he met two people, a man and a woman, and turned it over to them. They drove it to Boulder. The New Mexico license on it was from a car reported stolen."

"So?" Steiger tapped his fingers on his desk. He was losing patience with this drawn out discussion. He wanted the bottom line.

"The INS lost them again."

"Damn!" He could not believe what he was hearing. No wonder the country was full of foreigners and terrorists.

"However he did get photos of the man and woman."

"Good. When can I get copies?"

"I sent them, but I already know where to find one of your 'aliens,'" John deBeque chuckled.

"Don't play games with me."

"Hold on, it gets better. I recognized the man in the picture. He's no alien. In fact, I met him in St. Louis, about two years ago, at his father's birthday party. Do you remember attending Albert Drake's eightieth?"

"We would like your help in locating this woman," John deBeque said. He learned forward and passed a picture across the table to Ryan Drake. It was grainy, shot from a distance, cropped from a larger photo. A sharp pain intruded in Ryan's stomach.

"What makes you think I can help you?" Ryan asked. He had known this day would come. He had not imagined it would happen so soon. He guessed Steiger's interest, but where did deBeque fit in? The man's approach was slick, too slick.

Ernest Steiger, the large man from Steiger's house, and the Harvard type had shown up at Sanitas's reception area at 10:00 AM. When Ryan discovered who was in the lobby he directed Karen to escort them to the large conference room reserved for Board meetings. He called Brauk and told him to turn on the surveillance camera and to watch the proceedings as well as record them.

As he walked to the room, he received a communication from Sarah. *'They do not know as much as they might portray.'*

When he was introduced to Rebar Brown, the hulk had squeezed his hand with a powerful paw. Ryan knew the man was trying to make a point. Ryan recognized John deBeque from his father's birthday party.

All three were dressed in dark business suits, white shirts, and red ties. The large man looked very uncomfortable. Now, like a formal Japanese meeting, Ryan faced Steiger and deBeque across the cherry wood table. Unlike a Japanese meeting, he wore a sport coat and open-collar shirt. Rebar stood guard behind Steiger's wheelchair.

John deBeque passed a second picture across the table. This one showed Ryan Drake, his hand on the shoulder of Sarah Smith, along with Ben Tsotsie, framed against the front of the Alamosa Airport.

"Where is she?" Steiger asked.

Ryan did not respond.

The old man's face froze. Ryan was sure that this furious gaze from one of the most powerful men in America had melted many an adversary. He too would have been uncomfortable once, but now with his commitment to the larger celestial purpose he looked back calmly. The power with which Ryan Drake was aligned was a million times greater than that of the misguided media affiliates or this supposedly powerful and wealthy man.

"You obviously know her." deBeque said.

"What do you want with her?"

"I want to ask her about that gear you saw at my home," Steiger said.

"You should bring that box here," Ryan said. "Let my engineers have a look at it. They'll be able to tell you a lot more about it than she ever could. She knows nothing about technology."

"I don't believe you." The old man leaned forward in his wheelchair. The other two took their cues from him.

"So you admit you know her," deBeque said.

Ryan returned their stares.

"The INS has issued a reward for her and others from Harmony," deBeque said. "We are prepared to increase that reward to say, five hundred thousand."

"Not interested." Ryan felt compassion for the three men across from him. They had no idea who or what they were dealing with. Or did they? Dr. Adamson had told him that Steiger was aware of extraterrestrials, but how much did the old man really know. Did he know about celestials and the organized universe? John deBeque might know a little, Rebar Brown probably nothing.

"I can make things difficult for you," Steiger said. "On the other hand, if you cooperate, I will make sure that Sanitas is a success."

"What else can I do for you today? A plant tour?"

"I read their material," Steiger said. "Impressive. Must be very smart to come up with that kind of stuff. Could be construed to be very anti-American."

Ryan did not comment. So Steiger did know, or at least suspect Sarah's origins. Painting Sarah as anti-American would probably garner him support from certain corners.

"Your Company does a lot of business with government agencies," deBeque said.

"Are you threatening me?"

"There are issues of national security here," deBeque said. "Mr. Drake, I suggest that you think about that before you agree to aid this woman further. This is not child's play."

Ryan said nothing.

"Listen, Mr. Ryan Drake," Steiger said. "I don't like the idea of aliens trying to tell us how to run our country, our lives."

For a moment Ryan was taken back by the old man's comment. Somehow he knew that Sarah was an extraterrestrial. Then he recalled that he was sitting across the table from one of the media affiliates — the same gang that had shielded the American public from the truth about extraterrestrials for more than fifty years. But if he was as powerful as Dr. Adamson had said, why was he here? Why not the FBI or military intelligence? Ryan noticed an annoyed look on deBeque's face, a flicker of the eyes when the word *aliens* was mentioned. Something told him that the young man was not aligned with Steiger.

Ignoring Steiger's words, Ryan said, "And here I thought this was a free country."

"That's right and I intend to keep it that way," Steiger said.

"What do you want from me?"

"Her location."

Ryan returned the old man's powerful gaze.

"We can ruin you, and your precious company," deBeque said.

"I doubt that."

Frustrated, Steiger said, "My advice is stay away from her. She's trouble."

"And, if I don't?"

"Mr. Drake," deBeque said. "Back off."

Ryan stood up, an indication that the meeting was ended.

At Steiger's signal, Rebar wheeled the old man from the room. Without further exchange, Ryan escorted the threesome to Sanitas's lobby.

"Hey, Ry." Brauk hailed Ryan from the far end of the hallway. It was obvious from his agitated gestures that Sanitas's genius wanted to talk.

"Get it on tape?"

"Yeah. Who are those people? What's that gear they were talking about?"

Ryan smiled. He should have known Brauk would fix on that. He hesitated a moment and answered, "Brauk, remember that meeting. If something happens to me, give the tape to Sheriff Tom Ertl."

"OK, but what's going on?"

"Nothing to do with Sanitas." Beyond witnessing the meeting, Ryan did not want to involve Brauk in problems he considered his own. "I happen to have something of great value. They want it."

I will not follow where the path may lead, but I will go where there is no path, and I will leave a trail.

— MURIEL STRODE

NINETEEN

Ryan Drake waited until dark to return home. He pressed the button for the front gate and was pleased when it responded normally. He made sure it closed behind him. As he crested the hill, no lights were visible from the house. He entered through the front door and heard the buzzing of the security system. He disengaged it — no other sounds or movement. He had called as soon as Steiger left and told Sarah and Peter not to leave under any circumstances. Had they ignored his warning?

"Hello," he called out.

Nothing. He turned on only a few lights. Ryan was quite sure the house was being watched. Unless someone had penetrated his perimeter security, they could not get closer than about a hundred yards. He looked into the dark rooms; everything seemed in place.

Again he called out.

No reply.

He eventually found them downstairs in his entertainment room. They were engrossed in an old John Wayne movie.

"We have a decision to make," Ryan said. "You can stay inside and wait until this blows over — I think you'll be safe. For some

247

reason, Steiger wants to go it alone — he's not bringing in the heavy artillery."

"Artillery?" Peter asked. "He would bombard this house?"

"I mean he hasn't involved the military or FBI. At this point he only suspects that you are extraterrestrials."

"I can't just stay locked up in here," Sarah said. "I have people I must continue to meet with."

"My physical therapy," Peter said. "I too must speak out. I now have my voice."

"Steiger doesn't know about you, Peter. You're safe, as long as you're not connected to Sarah or me."

Ryan turned to Sarah and said, "I thought you'd react that way. Steiger has a picture of you. I'd bet his men are already out searching. I'm sure they're tailing me and have this house under surveillance. I contacted Fuchsia, you can stay with her — let people come to you there, stay off the streets. Peter, you'll stay with Aza in Denver. Sanitas's phone system processes a huge volume of calls. We've installed the best security available. We can all stay in touch that way."

"And by using universe mind," Sarah reminded him.

"Can we take our car?" Peter asked.

"No." Their vehicle still had its New Mexico plates and they had not transferred its Arizona registration to Colorado.

In dark rooms, the Phantians stuffed their clothing and personal items into luggage and hanging bags. At midnight, they exited out the lower door of Ryan's house and moved into the surrounding trees. Dense pines blocked the view. Ryan carried a large suitcase in each hand and led the way down the hill.

When they arrived at the perimeter fence, he used his code to disengage the security system controlling a gate. They passed through, re-engaged the security system, and continued down the hill.

The gully led into the side yard of another home. When they approached, the house the lights flashed on and a dog began to howl. "Stay here," Ryan said. "Let me see how we can get past this house. Fuchsia's waiting with her car." He dropped the suitcases and moved forward.

"Yes, sir. My men followed the duck to his house." Steiger listened to Gregor Hauptman. This man had been with him for twenty years and was one of the few employees he trusted. "But they didn't see anybody else, and he didn't make any phone calls — we got that part covered as soon as you gave us the word. All the lights are out now; looks like he's gone to sleep."

"Can you get inside the house?"

"Not tonight. The perimeter security system here is almost as good as at the duck's facility." Earlier Steiger's men had reported that Sanitas's security was the best available — closely related to the technology the military used for its own facilities. "We'll work on getting into the house as soon as he leaves in the morning."

"How many with you?"

"Four, two watching the house, two searching the town."

Sarah Smith watched as Fuchsia set the suitcase on her sofa. Her townhouse was modest compared to Ryan's palace, comparable to the house M'Adan and she had on Phantia. As Fuchsia turned on lights, she saw that in addition to the large living room the townhouse contained a dining area and sizable kitchen on the main floor. On Phantia this much space would suffice for several people.

Fuchsia was dressed in blue jeans and a sweater. Her long hair was held in place with a large barrette. She told Sarah that Ryan had tracked her down at an evening meeting and set the late night plan in motion.

Peter had gone off with Aza O'Sullivan for the one-hour drive back to his house. The two Phantians promised to stay in close touch. Sarah looked at the unfamiliar setting and felt abandoned.

"Can I get you something to drink? A tea?" Fuchsia asked.

"No thanks," Sarah smiled.

"Well then, let's get to it. My guest bedroom is a mess."

"I could find somewhere —"

"Forget it."

"But this seems like —"

"You're staying right here — until Ryan figures out what to do about Steiger."

"It may not end quickly."

"I know."

Sarah had come to like Fuchsia and to trust her. The writer and holistic advocate had shown her where to shop, how to select food that was organic and contained few chemicals. During their frequent contacts, Fuchsia had absorbed the details of the cosmic paradigm like an eager child. At their last meeting, with Fuchsia and three of her friends, they had laid plans for a weekly gathering that would include others.

They climbed to the upper level and set to work carting books, papers, and boxes of herbs into the basement. Fuchsia used her guest room as her writing studio.

When they rested for a moment Fuchsia said, "I want to thank you."

"For what? I should be the one thanking you."

"For helping me see the limits of the old ways. After our conversations, I see how my old beliefs were doomed to provide a limited perspective."

Sarah smiled.

"The holistic health movement has long searched for ways to motivate people to care for themselves *before* they become sick. I now see that the cosmic paradigm can provide the motivation for that, and more."

They went back to work and uncovered Fuchsia's spare bed and a dresser.

"We are all one," Fuchsia said. As she spoke, her words took on a dream-like quality.

"There is truth in that statement," Sarah said. "We are all connected through universe mind, but each of us — mortal and celestial — have unique personalities."

"So what's the difference between mind and celestial?"

"Celestials are unique beings who function in a higher realm. Universe mind is not unique; it links all, celestials and mortals. Our individual minds, when connected to universe mind, can communicate with celestials. Mind is diffuse. Material and celestial beings are specific and individualized.

"All mortals utilize functions of universe mind, such as the desire to acknowledge something greater than themselves, the ability to accumulate wisdom, the development of higher ideals."

They continued and soon the room was cleaned and ready for occupancy.

"We always touch base with the people we've helped get elected," John deBeque responded to Leonard Williams's question as to why he had insisted on this meeting. They were standing in the Senator-elect's temporary office.

"So what is this really about?"

John deBeque straightened his tie, re-settled his coat on his shoulders, and said, "This coming year you will undoubtedly be appointed to one of the important sub-committees. That sub-committee will be reviewing key issues: the military budget, strategic petroleum reserves, covert operations."

"Possibly," Leonard Williams said.

"You will hold your vote on any proposed legislation, until after we have seen the language."

"You can't tell me how to vote. I have to be free to probe, to negotiate. I intend to vote my conscience."

"Remember our agreement."

"You and your damned agreement."

"Hey, you got elected didn't you?"

"Yeah, and I did all the work."

"It would never have happened without our money. Remember that, and remember we want to see the wording of all proposed legislation."

"So you admit you were in the desert with her?" the INS man addressed Ryan Drake. "And that you transported her to Colorado?"

Three days after Steiger had visited Sanitas, the INS had called Ryan and demanded a meeting.

A.J. Winston, senior agent from Denver, and he were seated at a conference table in a small room at the INS's Denver office. The room's lone decoration was a picture of the outgoing President.

Winston was in his early forties. The slim black man wore his wavy hair long and displayed a large mustache. A charcoal gray suit, blue shirt, and navy blue patterned tie completed the picture of an intense immigration officer.

251

Winston continued, "It seems unusual for a respectable busi-nessman to be mixed up with someone like her." Earlier in the con-versation, Winston had established that since Ryan had not been a resident of Harmony Center, the $25,000 reward did not apply to him.

Ryan stared at the INS agent but did not reply. It was hard to concentrate on the situation at hand when he knew about extrater-restrials, when he saw everything from a celestial perspective. Did A.J. Winston have even the slightest appreciation of those facts?

That morning, a litigater from Sanitas's law firm had coached him on answering questions. During his business career, Ryan had sued others and had been sued several times. His messy divorce had kept him in court for two weeks, and that was after six months of discovery and depositions. But this was his first involvement in a criminal matter since his college days — in those days he'd had no money with which to hire an expensive attorney. As it was, Ryan had imposed on Sanitas's law firm for advice.

"The report from Arizona lists her name as Sarah Smith. Is that correct?"

"Yes." He had been cautious about his responses; restricting his answers to what he knew the INS had already discovered. Thus far, Winston's query had been directed solely toward Sarah.

"Where is Ms. Smith?" the INS man pointed to a copy of the same grainy picture John deBeque had shown him.

"I can't answer that question," Ryan replied.

"Can't or won't?"

"Whichever." Ryan heaved a sigh and reached into his pocket for his antacid. They had been at it for over an hour. Winston's questions were becoming repetitive. He knew the other man was taking his measure, calculating how much to believe, how hard to push.

"The charges against the people from Harmony Center are quite serious, and you are an accessory."

"What crime was committed?"

"Harboring illegal immigrants."

"None were found at Harmony."

"One was found nearby. She died before she could talk to any-one."

"I was sorry to hear about that. She could have cleared every-thing up."

"You seem awfully sure that your lady friend is innocent."

"I am."

"A man was killed during the raid."

"She was with me when it happened. We were a long way off."

"How long have you known her?"

"I met her at Harmony Center. It was a short distance from where I was camped."

"That would have been Ben Tsotsie's dig?"

"Yes."

"Where is she now?"

"As I said before, I won't answer that." After consulting with his attorney that morning, Ryan had decided his best strategy was to draw the INS's attention to himself and away from the Phantians.

Ryan stood and walked behind his chair. While Winston re-ferred to his notes, the subject of the inquisition stretched his back and lower legs. He noted with a smile that he had not tilted his head since entering the room with the INS agent. In fact he had not done so since his conversation with the celestial messenger.

"She's wanted for questioning. By harboring her, you may be committing a crime."

"She's not at my house." According to Ryan's attorney, this was one of three key issues to test for illegal activities.

"You helped transport her."

"I didn't help her enter the United States." The second key.

"She needs a work permit."

"She doesn't work for money." The third.

This man insisted he wanted to question Sarah about illegal Mexicans and a dead Navajo. What questions would an INS agent ask if he knew she was from a planet seventy-eight light-years away?

"An Amelia Lighter, a Peter Jones, and a Dr. Victor Adamson were also listed as residing at Harmony. Do you know their where-abouts?"

"I won't say."

The INS man made a note and the questioning went on.

When it appeared Winston was nearing the end, Ryan said,

"You should know that I have undertaken an investigation into certain questionable operations of the INS's Arizona office."

"You're investigating us?" Winston sat back in his chair and stared at Ryan.

For the next twenty minutes, Ryan talked and the INS agent took notes on a yellow tablet. "While this is not complete, I believe it warrants further investigation."

"Do you know Oscar Hoehn?"

"Yes."

"I have already submitted it to him. Through a mutual friend, I have asked Mr. Hoehn to revoke the $25,000 reward. And I want the INS to return Harmony to its owners, with a full apology and compensation for any damage done to their facility."

When Ryan departed from the INS's offices, he did not recoil at the uniformed officers that abounded in the hallways or the light green vehicles parked in front of their offices.

'You must listen to Ryan,' Dr. Adamson communicated to Sarah Smith. He was seated at the kitchen table in Fuchsia's townhouse. *'Ernest Steiger wants to capture you. He is interested in your communication skills.'*

'But I could never teach them to someone as devious as him.' Sarah and Dr. Adamson chose to communicate rather than speak aloud because Sarah awaited a learner. She did not want to be overheard, nor did she want the learner to imagine that anyone might be listening to their private session.

'Steiger does not know that. He sees your knowledge of the cosmic paradigm as a threat to the foundation of the media affiliates. He thinks your communications skills come from some sort of technology.'

'What can I do? Did I travel for eighty years to hide?'

'The only other option is a public announcement of your origins, and those of Peter. I don't believe we are yet ready for that — we don't have a critical mass of people who understand the cosmic paradigm. The naysayers who believe only in the paradigm of the Box would swamp our small cadre.'

'What do we do?'

'I recommend that you continue to meet with your learners. Try to get them grounded so that the ensuing struggle will not shake their com-

mitment.'

'*What about Ryan?*'

'*I believe he is influential enough that Steiger will be circumspect about challenging him.*'

There was a knock on the door. Dr. Adamson vanished. Sarah opened it to greet Karen Borden-Banes.

Almost every seat was occupied. Ryan had found an open night in the theatre's schedule as they transitioned from one play to the next.

He had convinced Peter to convene a targeted audience for his first presentation. Fuchsia managed to get a carefully worded article into the Boulder Daily Camera announcing a gathering at 7:30 PM for those interested in "A larger purpose to life."

Aza and Peter were late coming from Denver — probably evening traffic on the Turnpike.

Ryan had spent an hour speeding around Boulder's busiest streets in one of Sanitas's company cars. He had parked it near the Boulderado Hotel. He went in the hotel's front door on 13th Street, walked up a curved staircase to the second floor, crossed to the new wing, hurried down a long hall, ran down exit stairs to the ground level, slipped out the back door on Pine, and walked to the space. It was dark. He hoped that no one had been able to follow him.

Until Steiger had confronted him at Sanitas, Ryan had been introducing Sarah and Peter to his friends and business acquaintances. He had used his credibility as a successful businessman to entice people to take time. They had coffeed, lunched, and dined at restaurants and people's homes. Sarah or Peter presented the cosmic paradigm. Some had expressed interest. Those the Phantians followed up with on their own. Now, as Ryan glanced around the theatre, he saw many of those he had introduced to them. He also recognized people from the University and from local establishments. A cluster of students.

Karen sat a little behind him. Brauk was on the far side. Fuchsia and several of her friends sat in the second row, Bernadette behind her. Several people stood at the rear. Among them was a white-haired man in western clothing. Not far from him, Tom Ertl stood wearing a sweater and slacks. The rest of the crowd was a mixture of typical Boulder folks, jeans and sweaters, and a few not so typical in formal business attire. Ryan hoped there was no one from the INS among the crowd, and none of Steiger's people.

Aza and Peter arrived and climbed onto the stage. In an effort to avert any connection between Ryan and the bald Phantian, Aza, who was not particularly known in Boulder, had agreed to make the introduction. Peter wore a long white robe. From where he sat, Ryan could detect nothing extraterrestrial about the Phantian, but he suspected someone in the first row might wonder about his longer fingers or the larger irises of his eyes.

At the last minute, a tall woman in a navy blue coat and slacks came and sat in the seat next to him. She wore a paisley turban that covered her hair and tinted glasses with black frames. When the lights dimmed, she reached across and laid her long-fingered hand on his. Ryan squeezed her hand, but made no other motion toward her.

Tonight, Peter Jones was getting his wish: his chance to deliver the cosmic paradigm to a crowd. For the past week, Aza had worked with him to make sure the talk would be easy to understand. On two occasions a bald man in a business suit had walked into Sanitas's lobby and asked for Ryan Drake.

Peter's accent intensified as the presentation went on. It lent an air of authority — the visiting scholar. His passion rising, the bald Phantian stepped from behind the lectern, voice resounding, reaching out to the audience with masterful enthusiasm. Ryan nodded to Sarah. Peter was an impressive speaker. He was as compelling with large groups as Sarah was with individuals, or with her pictioning. Now Ryan understood why the two of them had been paired.

The audience sat spellbound as Peter explained Earth's current evolutionary stage and the friendly, organized cosmos. The bald Phantian explained that celestial beings seemed mystical and mysterious only because humans possessed limited sight. He contrasted the cosmic paradigm with traditional earth-bound points-of-view.

When Peter ended, no one stirred, no one clapped. People were completely immersed in the wondrous vision his words had evoked. Most importantly, Peter had pulled it off without revealing his origins. Ryan didn't know where the time had gone. It was as if he was hearing about the cosmic paradigm for the first time.

Peter opened the floor for questions. Twenty hands shot up. "Before I take your questions," Peter said, "let me say that I will restrict my answers to the cosmic paradigm. If you have other questions, leave your phone number or email address. There is material at the back of the room that may help you to remember some of what I presented."

Then the questions began: Visits by extraterrestrials, abductions. Creation versus evolution. Life after death, judgment and damnation. Mixing the cosmic paradigm with the old. Peter fielded these, playing the audience like the conductor of a well-rehearsed orchestra always bringing comments back to the main ideas of the cosmic paradigm. People were asking the questions that the Phantian had hoped for, and for which he had prepared.

After an hour of this, Peter called a halt. He again asked everyone to take copies of the material and promised to be in touch with anyone who cared to leave their information.

"One of our publishers passed this along," John deBeque said. He dug into his briefcase and handed five double-spaced pages to Ernest Steiger. It was copy for a proposed article. It summarized the points of a recent presentation by someone named Peter Jones. Through his network, deBeque had informed all of the major newspaper and magazine publishers to be on the lookout for any articles containing certain key words. They were to refuse to publish anything with those words and to send a copy to him immediately.

"When did it take place?"

"A few days ago, in Boulder, Colorado," deBeque said. "Looks like he was quite a sensation. The gathering was estimated at two hundred."

"He could be one of the aliens," Steiger mused.

John deBeque had spent the night at the Steiger mansion. They had talked until late. Steiger could recall only bits of their wide ranging conversation about Russia's former satellite nations, their desperate need for cash, and offers to buy their stockpiles of nuclear weapons, about a group of terrorists who claimed to be ready to use biological weapons, about the transition of administrations in

Mark Kimmel

Washington, and about the rising sea level that was inundating land along the Gulf Coast.

They discussed how deBeque and his people would package these and other developments for the media: Feed people's worries about biological and nuclear threats. Play up the new President as committed to a return to the good times. Debunk the rise in sea level as anything permanent.

Steiger noted that throughout their long discussion deBeque had not raised the topic of aliens — until he pulled out the proposed newspaper article.

"Does anybody know anything about this Peter Jones?"

"No listing in the Boulder phone book, if that's what you mean."

"Other sources?"

"I talked to the FBI, they're searching — don't worry, I didn't connect this Jones to 'aliens' or to Harmony. I also have Immigration, Social Security, and Defense checking. They'll find him. Everybody needs identification of some sort."

"What about the author of this article?"

"An obscure writer, sticks to the medical area, herbs and that kind of stuff. I talked to her. She says she thinks he's from Arizona."

Steiger glanced at the pages. What he did not tell deBeque was that Frank Simpson had already forwarded a copy of the same article to him. It had arrived yesterday.

The article relayed similar explanations of the universe to the pages from Boyle's office that Steiger had read and reread. But new things had been added. It showed the evolution of their thinking and ability to communicate. Someone was helping them — probably that damn Ryan Drake.

In his speech, Jones insisted that the government had covered up contacts with extraterrestrials for years, that many of the reports of UFO's and extraterrestrials were true. He suggested that some stories about abductions might be people trying to make sense out of contacts with celestials.

Steiger liked that last one. If the commoners penetrated their alien cover-up, the media affiliates could fabricate a new story: "It's just people talking to spirits, nothing to worry about." It had a certain ring to it.

Of greater concern was the estimate of the crowd at the gathering: two hundred. Two hundred marginals. How did the bovines find out about these things? Probably one of those rags from the underground. He knew they should have closed them down, but the other media affiliates felt it was too much trouble for a few fringe types.

Steiger looked at deBeque and said, "I'm sending more of my men to Colorado. Who knows, maybe they'll be invited to the next performance."

"Maybe I should go along."

"My people know how to handle it."

"Like Rebar?"

"He'll stay here." Steiger picked up the telephone and dialed the number for Sanitas. "I think its time to call our friend Mr. Drake."

After the receptionist forwarded his call, he heard more than the usual number of clicks as the call was routed through Sanitas's security system. A female voice said, "Mr. Drake's office."

"Is he in?"

"May I tell him who's calling?"

"Ernest Steiger."

"One moment please. I'll locate him."

The line went to a steady buzz. The Chairman drummed his fingers as he waited. A faint beeping preceded the voice.

"Ryan Drake here."

"Good day Mr. Drake. Are you ready to tell me where I can contact your lady friend?"

"No." The dial tone came on the line.

Steiger looked at deBeque and said, "I do believe we are making progress."

John deBeque's manner troubled Ernest Steiger. It was probably just as well that the young man was not interested. He did not tell deBeque that Gregor Hauptman was already in Colorado and was planning to talk to this woman, Fuchsia, and to Drake's secretary.

After deBeque departed the old man turned to face Lake Michigan. A winter storm was in process. Snowflakes tumbled in the stiff breeze. Secure in his warm study, he watched a motorboat battle the white-capped waves. He thought back to that time so long ago when he'd had a young, healthy body. That brunette in Roswell had taught him a few things — before he'd had her arrested as a Russian spy.

He and Albert Drake had remained congenial, as congenial as he could be with an employee. Albert had served him well. He was a fine attorney and an even better manipulator of the truth. Could Albert coerce his son to cooperate? He called and left a message.

He opened the leather-bound book and made notes for his posthumous memoir. After detailing current events, he explained how his father had trained him for his current role. The new world was not to be a physical empire; it was an empire of information management, of control over people's minds. The elite were to rule by subverting their subjects' values, by replacing traditional beliefs with those of a present-time focus on consumption. Some might believe it was about money, but it was really about power, the power of information control. Money would follow the power.

He also made note of deBeque's behavior. It was clear to him that his adopted son was shrugging off his assertion that the fugitives from Harmony were aliens. Just as well. It would keep the other affiliates out of the picture.

That finished, he locked his diary in the safe in the corner of his study and rang for his playmates.

For those to whom much is given, much is required... We will be measured by the answers to four questions: First, were we truly men of courage... Second, were we truly men of judgment... Third, were we truly men of integrity... Fourth, were we truly men of dedication?

— JOHN FITZGERALD KENNEDY

TWENTY

"I have something I want to propose," Nick Steiger said. He puffed himself up preparing to deliver his speech. Ordinarily he sat back and observed the more seasoned Board members.

It was 2:00 PM and the Board of Directors of Sanitas had spent the past three hours reviewing operations and forecasts for the next year. The four investor Board members had shed the coats to their pin-stripped suits and loosened their ties. To their surprise Ryan Drake had showed up in a sport coat, slacks, and open-neck shirt. To no one's surprise, Brauk wore jeans and a sweatshirt.

The three venture capital investors along with the Steiger Family Trust held sixty-seven percent of the common stock of Sanitas. Ryan owned eleven percent. The founders, including Brauk and his family, owned the remainder of the outstanding shares. The management team's options, including Ryan's significant piece, amounted to an additional twenty percent. When exercised, these would dilute the current shareholders. They would only be exercised if the company was successful enough to give the option holders a profit.

Neil Murphy, the Board's chairman, was a distinguished man

in his late fifties, impeccably groomed, gray hair, white shirt with initials on its cuff, diamond studded watch, and MIT ring. Murphy's venture capital firm owned the largest single piece of Sanitas, twenty-six percent. This was the third company in which he and Ryan Drake had been involved.

Although Sanitas was privately held, its shareholders believed that it was worth over one hundred million dollars. That was based on the current year's revenues of thirty-four million dollars, up from twenty-three million the prior year. Sanitas had managed this rapid growth while remaining profitable. Similar high growth companies were trading at astronomical prices on NASDAQ.

The remains of sandwiches and drinks littered the cherry wood table of the Boardroom. Each Director had piles of operating statements and reports scattered before him. Nick took notes on his portable computer.

After Murphy motioned to him, Nick cleared his throat and said, "The Steiger Family Trust would like to purchase your stock." He pointed to the three venture capitalists at the table. He did not point to Ryan or Brauk who sat together at one end of the table. "We are willing to pay fair market value, as determined by an independent appraiser."

"Why?" Neal Murphy asked.

"My father sees a fit with some of our interests."

"Not interested," Murphy replied. "We should be able to take this puppy public in a year."

"We'd be talking big dollars," John Dunlop, another board member, said. "More than a hundred million."

"Not when you factor in the problems for next year."

"What problems?" Ryan asked sharply. "We signed TTT Instrumentation. Our Global Watch revenues should be up thirty percent. And we have the AT&T project." The Board had earlier ratified the agreement he had finalized with TTT and given a green light to a development project with AT&T.

"There's a new competitor in the market, Exemplar," Nick said. "They're selling the same instruments, at two-thirds the price." He passed out glossy brochures. "You just helped them acquire your latest technology." He snickered.

"These products are copies of ours from two years ago," Ryan

262

said. "Our agreement prohibits Exemplar from using our technology in units they don't sell to TTT."

"Yeah, but how long will it take them to design around us?" Brauk asked. He had complained bitterly when he had heard about the TTT Instrumentation deal because it gave Exemplar access to their latest equipment. Ryan had argued that Global Watch's rigid system specifications limited any harm that Exemplar could do to them.

"Do any of you know who owns Exemplar?" Ryan clenched his fists.

"Who?" Murphy asked.

"Steiger Enterprises owns controlling interest," Ryan addressed the senior VC, but did not turn from Nick.

Everyone at the table knew Steiger Enterprises was the corporate giant behind the Steiger Family Trust. "OK Nick, what's your proposal?" Murphy asked.

"Are you open to selling?"

"Anything's for sale," Murphy said, "for the right price." When Ryan's prior company was being sold, he had watched Murphy offer to throw in his wife and kids to cement the deal.

"If you do this," Ryan addressed the senior VC. "You'll destroy everything we've worked for."

He smiled and said, "Relax, Ryan. I said, at the right price."

Murphy turned to Nick and said, "Give us your best offer."

"I'll have it ready in a week," Nick said.

Ryan Drake turned to check on the noise. It was late and the underground parking structure was dimly lit. He had remained after his Colorado Conservation Commission meeting to talk with other Board members about a pending proposal that he believed gave away too much to mining interests.

As he approached his car, a door slammed on his left and Ryan turned to see a man in a blue-gray parka walking to intercept him. He stood his ground and asked, "What do you want?"

"I wanna talk to you," the unshaven man said. A scar bisected his lips, dark menacing eyes, and stale cigarette breath.

Ryan tensed and wondered what was coming. An anti-environmentalist? Robbery?

The man reached out to grab Ryan's sport coat.

"Not today, thanks." Ryan swung and landed a solid punch in the man's gut. He followed it with a smash to his face. The man stumbled and fell against the hood of a pickup.

Examining his options, Ryan went for his car. The man staggered after him. When he leaned to unlock his Porsche's low door a second man grabbed his shoulder, yanked him around, and landed a glancing punch to Ryan's jaw.

"Not so fast," the second man said.

Ryan planted his feet and landed a punch on the face of the second man, but as he prepared another, the large man came from behind and encircled him in powerful arms. The second one smashed Ryan in the mouth, in the nose, in the mouth again. Ryan tasted blood.

"Where is she?" the second man sneered and punched Ryan in the stomach. He brought his unshaven face close and said, "I didn't hear ya."

For a moment they stared at each other. Ryan glared at the scruffy face. The man moved closer and punched Ryan in the stomach and again in the face.

Ryan brought up his knee into the man's groin. He screamed, doubled over in pain, and backed away. The big man squeezed harder but an elbow into his mid-section and a stomp on his foot released the grip. Ryan turned and struck out. His fist connected and the first man staggered back into a support column. He straightened and came for Ryan. Ryan stepped to one side and swung. The blow caught the man in the front of his neck. He heard cartilage crunch. The man slumped to the ground.

The second man straightened up and yelled, "Let's get out of here." He stumbled toward a dirty yellow van, parked three slots away.

The man at Ryan's feet made a gagging sound. His hands were on his throat as he rose and stumbled toward the van. It sped away, tires squealing around the corners of the parking ramp until it exited two floors above.

Ryan lifted his hand to his face. It came away red. He opened the door of his red sports car and reached for his cell phone. A few spaces away a dark blue sedan started up and drove toward the exit. Ryan glimpsed two men in the front seat. Both wore dark glasses.

Later that night when Ryan Drake drove to the entrance of his mountain home, he almost ran into a yellow backhoe parked on the edge of the road. A four-foot deep trench ran from his front gate to the electrical junction box at the entrance to his property. It was in the same spot the contractor had dug to bury his power and telephone cables.

When he tried his gate opener, it did not respond. He got out of his Porsche, unlocked it, and swung it open. Remembering his encounter in the underground garage, he proceeded with caution, senses alert.

He parked his car at his front door and unlocked it. None of the lights worked. The phone was dead. He went back to his car, pulled out his cell phone, and called the telephone and electric companies.

Back inside the dark house, he felt his way to the master bedroom. He retrieved his .357 revolver from the nightstand and tucked it into his belt. Alert to any noise, he gathered clothes for the next day and left the dark house to find a hotel room.

At the office the next morning, the electric utility returned Ryan's call. They reported they had accidentally severed his cable. They promised to have it fixed by noon.

That evening, Ryan went home to find several lights in his home burning. Gun in hand, he scoured the house for anything out of place. Finding nothing he initiated the alarm system and went to bed.

As he sought sleep he wondered what Nick would propose to the Board and whether Murphy would find it appealing. He wondered what Sarah was doing. He had called that afternoon from Sanitas. She assured him she was well and that people were fine with coming to meet her at Fuchsia's townhouse. His house seemed empty without her. Finally he practiced connecting to universe mind and said good night to Sarah. The peacefulness of this relaxed him, and he slept.

The light of the oncoming train flashed on and off. Startled out of a dream, Ryan sat upright. A light playing over the walls of his bedroom had awakened him. Someone was shining a high-powered light in the undraped window. By the time he struggled out of bed and looked outside it was extinguished. He saw no one. Exhausted, he returned to bed. The clock showed 1:17 AM.

His mind buzzed. Ertl had called today and said someone from the INS's Denver office had contacted him about Sarah Smith. The Sheriff had told them he had no information. Ertl had also said that the FBI was still investigating the death of the Navajo at Harmony. The forensic evidence was in conflict with Viejo's story.

Ryan remembered the expression on Ertl's face after Sarah had pictioned for him — a week ago. Like Fuchsia and Aza he had opened his eyes and looked around in a daze, babbled a few incoherent questions. At that moment Tom Ertl was no more the hard-nosed lawman, no more the fighter. He had a peace about him that Ryan had not seen before, even on the banks of a high mountain stream.

When Ertl had met with Ryan a few days ago, they had talked about Ernest Steiger and the media affiliates. Ertl asked if it would be all right to turn the additional information over to his friends in the Chicago Police Department. Ryan said sure. Ertl told him that he had met with Sarah a second time at Fuchsia's.

He had just fallen back asleep when loud knocking awakened him. Someone was pounding on the front door. Ryan grabbed his gun and bathrobe and struggled to the foyer. The peephole revealed no one. Gun in hand, he yanked open the door. Large footprints in a light dusting of snow.

He returned to bed. It was 4:33 AM. After an hour of tossing, he decided to shower and go to the office. He had plenty of paperwork to occupy him until his staff arrived. On the way out he set his house and property alarm systems.

The following morning, he wandered out to look for the paper. It had not been there when he took the trash out a half-hour earlier. He had spent a restless night, but there were no further disturbances. It was 6:30 AM; he needed to get moving, but a second cup of coffee and a glance at the paper sounded better.

As he hiked down the drive to the gate, an unfamiliar noise disturbed the morning quiet.

He crested the rise in his driveway just in time to see a young, well-built man pulling bags of trash from his container and tossing them in the trunk of a blue sedan. "Hey, what do you think you're doing?" Ryan shouted.

The man looked up, slammed the trunk lid, and jumped into the driver's seat. Before Ryan could make out a license number, the vehicle sped away in a cloud of dust.

"That can't be right." Ryan looked at the woman. The gift for Sarah, already wrapped, lay on the counter. "Here try this one." He pulled another credit card from his wallet, a Platinum American Express.

"Same thing Mr. Drake, denied." The shop's proprietor glanced at the display on the credit transaction device. She had known him for several years. He had bought other gifts from her exclusive boutique.

"Please, dial one of these credit card companies for me. I'd like to talk to them."

The woman on the phone informed Ryan, that because of the size of his outstanding balance, his credit had been suspended. Ryan called two other credit card issuers and received the same story. While he completed his phone calls, the proprietor waited on a man in a blue sweat suit.

Leaving the wrapped package at the boutique, Ryan walked across the parking lot to a branch of his bank. He planned to withdraw enough cash to pay for the gift. A worse story. His balance was under fifty dollars. When he exited the teller window, he bumped into the same blue sweat-suited man.

Two men were waiting for him when he came out of the bank. At least he thought he saw two — there could have been more. As he walked to his Porsche, one followed him, keeping well back, the other in a blue sedan crept along parallel to his path. The guy in the car was the one he wasn't sure of for several moments; Ryan thought he was looking for an open space to park.

Although he had suspected he was being followed before, this was the first time his surveillance had been so obvious.

The one on foot was medium height, wore sunglasses and a heavy parka. His stride proclaimed fitness. The one in the car was balding and wore dark glasses. He recognized the blue sedan from the other night in the parking garage.

If he had spotted two, were there others that he hadn't? Were they from the INS, or were they a contingent of Steiger's goon squad? Or the FBI? Or military intelligence?

He glanced around. Neither tail was closing. Undecided as to how to handle this, he continued to walk toward his Porsche.

No one moved to intercept him. When he was seated he locked all the doors and checked to be sure his gun was in the car's side pocket. When he pulled out of the lot, they tagged along. The blue sweat-suited man jumped into a car that followed his.

They had been waiting for him. These men either knew his schedule or had followed him from his breakfast appointment — he had not been to the office as yet. They probably had tailed him in the past, but he hadn't seen them. Now they wanted him to see them.

Ryan thought back to Junior High, to the years he had played football, the years before his mother died and his father hustled him off to boarding school. His team had played well, had beaten teams from larger schools. He was now engaged in a game. It was like a contest against a much larger school, like a football game, but football had rules. This game had none, at least as far as anyone had told him.

"Glad you're here," Karen Borden-Banes hailed him as soon as Ryan entered Sanitas's building. "We've got problems. Someone at the bank called; we can't cover tomorrow's payroll."

"That's great," Ryan said. "I'm having money problems of my own. Get McCain on the phone."

Edmund McCain had been a vice-president when Ryan had opened the original Sanitas account. He had made the first loan to the Company. In those early days, he had been careful to obtain Ryan's personal guarantee on everything. Two years later, McCain was elevated to president of the Bank of the Rockies. Sanitas Technologies was now one of his major customers, and Ryan no longer needed to guarantee loans. McCain and he saw each other regularly at the health club.

After waiting a few moments, the bank president came on the phone. "Hello Ryan. My secretary tells me you have a problem. I'm pulling up Sanitas's account. Wow! What's going on? Why did you clean it out?"

"That's the problem," Ryan said. "We didn't."

"You're quite sure?"

"Yes."

Ryan could hear the banker typing on his computer's keyboard, querying his system. Who had the resources to drain both his personal credit and Sanitas's accounts? He recalled Dr. Adamson's story of the power the media affiliates commanded — the men shadowing him, the guy taking his trash, the two toughs from the underground garage, now his bank accounts. He now understood that this game of cat and mouse was designed to break his resistance, or to make him so tired and angry that he slipped up and revealed her whereabouts.

"Our computer shows that a wire transfer hit this morning."

"But we didn't authorize it."

"This is going to take some time," the bank president sighed.

"Time, hell," the CEO shouted at the speakerphone. "We have a payroll to make. Ed, I want you to check my personal account. It's empty too and I did not write checks to clean it out."

More typing and the banker said, "One large check for almost everything."

"But I didn't write it."

"OK. I'll make arrangements to get you some cash — until we can clear this up," the banker said trying to calm a good customer. "Be back to you in an hour. You're quite sure you didn't withdraw those funds?"

"Positive."

Ryan reflected on the fact that his conversations with McCain were always couched in implications that the banker did not quite believe what Ryan was telling him. Many business conversations held such implications. Few people really spoke with each other in total integrity — there was always the jockeying for advantage, the hidden innuendos, the humor that belied the truth.

Our duty to God is to make of ourselves the most perfect product of divine incarnation that we can become. This is possible only through the pursuit of worthy ideals.

— EDGAR WHITE BURRILL

TWENTY-ONE

"We've traced the source of the wire transfers against Sanitas's account to a Swiss bank," Edmund McCain was on the phone to Ryan Drake. He had taken two hours to call back. "They're closed until tomorrow. I'll call them when they open, Swiss time. I'm sure it was a mistake in wire transfer instructions; probably can be cleared up in no time.

"The check against your private account appears to be a forgery. I examined the signature — close to yours, but not quite. It was presented to one of our branches yesterday with a driver's license. Strange how your personal account and Sanitas's account got messed up at the same time. I've reinstated the amount of the forged check into your checking account."

Ryan Drake was propped up on pillows thinking about the guys in the sedan who followed him everywhere, his recent assault, and his credit card problems.

Yesterday had been a waste. It had taken the entire day to straighten out Sanitas's account. If he hadn't had such a strong personal relationship with McCain, the situation would have been much worse. After several lengthy conversations, the Swiss bank finally admitted that the withdrawals were a mistake and agreed to reverse the transaction. He had called his credit card companies and begun the long process of contesting bogus charges that amounted to over $50,000.

He glanced up at the smoke detector on the ceiling of his bedroom. Its cover was closed at an odd angle.

He jumped up and tried to straighten it. Something was in the way. He popped it open. In addition to the simple circuitry of a household smoke alarm, this one had a small plastic box with a wire trailing from it crammed into the detector. It was taped to the inside of the lid. The extra bulk of the black box had prevented the smoke detector from completely closing.

He found a screwdriver, unscrewed the base of the unit from the ceiling, and sat down with the two halves in his hands. His home had been invaded. He checked the house for anything else out of the ordinary, but spotted nothing.

The dark blue sedan followed him from his gate to the office, two men in the front seat, both wearing dark glasses. Feeling as if the police were following him, Ryan observed every speed limit and regulation. It was such an obvious tail. Another quarter in the football game without rules.

Ryan's grandfather on his mother's side was a tough old Irishman. He had immigrated to the U.S. as a child and had fought against the discrimination of his day. Ryan remembered that he had attended each of his football games. He also remembered gramps telling him, over and over, "Never give up."

"You were right, it's a transmitter," Brauk said to Ryan. "No identification. The package is sealed. See, here is the microphone. If I open it, I'll destroy its functionality."

"Open it. Let's see if we can tell who it belongs to."

Sanitas's technical genius pried apart the welded shell to expose three small microcircuits and a battery. Using a loupe he studied the unit. "This," he pointed to a small chip with the tip of a pen, "is the amplifier. This unit was made for government spooks."

"Why do you think that?"

"Part of my checkered history," Brauk grinned. Before Ryan

had joined Sanitas, Brauk had supported himself by consulting for various government agencies. Brauk's ideas for instrumentation products had grown out of that earlier work.

"They could track you by satellite, you know," Brauk said, "and put your home under remote surveillance by using listening devices." Ryan's house was situated in the middle of thirty-five acres. The high fence with its motion detectors surrounded the house at a distance of a hundred yards.

"If they're doing that, why tail me? Why bug my house?"

"Satellites aren't much good after dark or inside buildings. Listening devices have their limitations."

"How can I find out if there's more of these?" Ryan pointed to the small transmitter.

"Let me get my equipment. We'd better check your cars too."

The sedan followed them throughout the day. Brauk's search revealed a beacon in each of Ryan's four vehicles and more bugs in his home. Brauk also discovered that the communications link from Ryan's home security system to the Sheriff's office had been severed. Someone had rewired the circuitry inside Ryan's house to make it appear to function normally. As it stood, an alarm might sound in the house, but no one beyond his property would be aware of it. Brauk rewired it correctly.

Late that afternoon, while they were checking Ryan's office, Karen said that Ernest Steiger was on the line. "Tell him I'm busy swatting bugs," Ryan said.

"You're different, you know," Brauk said. They were seated in Ryan's office with the pile of transmitters on the CEO's desk. Brauk had disabled each of them with a piercing blast from an air horn followed by a screwdriver into the microphone. After a careful search, they determined that Ryan's office was clean. Brauk promised to scan the rest of Sanitas's facility.

"What do you mean?"

"You've changed. Ever since you got back from your vacation. You're not hyper about everything."

Ryan smiled.

During the day they'd had a chance to discuss many things. It was like the early days when Sanitas had been a tiny organization and they had spent long hours discussing and solving problems.

Brauk had been the wide-eyed technical genius. Ryan had focused his creative urges into usable products. In the process they had become good friends.

Now as they relaxed in Ryan's office, they talked about extraterrestrials and the organized universe.

"I've believed in aliens for a long time," the electronics genius said. He grinned as he recounted how he had stood in line to see the first showing of Star Wars and had recorded every Star Trek program.

"But this is more than believing there are intelligent beings out there somewhere" Ryan said. "This is about knowing there's a friendly orchestrated universe and about your ultimate destiny."

"What do you mean?"

"I have someone I want you to meet." Ryan picked up his office phone and dialed Sarah. He was relieved that he had not led Steiger's men to her by using a bugged circuit. He told her about the contamination of his home and cars and urged her to be very careful — the people who wanted her were close.

He told Brauk what Sarah looked like and where Fuchsia lived. Brauk promised to use extreme caution and not to go until the following day. Ryan could not tell whether he was more excited about meeting an extraterrestrial or playing sleuth and evading potential pursuers.

The next day Ryan's father called. They had last talked when Ryan called to wish him a Happy Father's Day — six months ago.

"I would advise you to cooperate with Ernest Steiger. He is a very powerful man and can make lots of trouble for you."

"Thanks Dad. Nice to hear from you."

"Please listen to me. I do not want to see you hurt."

"I gather you know Steiger. So tell him to back off or I'll —"

"You will do what? He is more powerful than you understand."

"Oh, I understand all right. I know about the media affiliates."

"I see." His father rang off without further comment.

"Well it's about time somebody took me seriously," Mitch Young said.

"Oh, we take things like this very seriously," Gregor

Hauptman's man said. Another member of Hauptman's security force, a burley six-footer stood next to him. Both men wore dark suits and ties. They had flashed badges at him and said they were from a government agency.

The three stood in the Boulder homeless shelter's main room. A number of people lounged around the periphery. The morning meal had been served an hour earlier.

"I get lots of wild stories from the people who come in here, you know. All kinds of strange things happen to street people. But that abduction thing was the strangest I ever had."

"Can you tell us where to find this Sarah woman?"

"Like I said, she's a friend of Ryan Drake's, you know. I never knew where she lived — and I didn't know she knew Drake, until that day she tried to kidnap me. She came around and wanted to volunteer. Then she started to talk — about wild stuff, the universe. One time she hypnotized me, and I saw all kinds of weird stars and planets. Real strange. Never saw a car. She just appeared."

"What about the other people?"

"Don't know them. Like I said the other alien's name was Peter Jones. There were four others, including Drake. That Freesia person seemed like a local, but I haven't seen her since. Probably a captive in that cloaked saucer of theirs."

"Have you seen Sarah recently?"

"Not since that day she tried to get me into their spaceship."

"We don't want to be difficult, but my colleague has your children," the burley man said. "His instructions are to drive off in one minute, if we have not returned with the information." His hard eyes stared through any pretense she had of resistance. "You do know where Sarah Smith is, don't you."

Karen nodded her head. She stole a look over her shoulder at the second man leaning against her dishwasher. The look on his face reinforced the words of the burly one.

When the two had knocked on her door, the burly man had grabbed her arm and pointed to the children in the rear of the blue sedan. A balding man with sunglasses sat in the driver's seat. Then they had pushed their way into her home.

After the men left and her children came running into the

house, she hugged them, and they cried together. Karen called her mother in Cheyenne, Wyoming, "We're coming for a visit."

"Hi, Truman," Ryan said. "How are things in Boston?" The call from Truman T. Thompson had come through just after lunch.

"Things in Boston are fine, but I'm calling you from Paris," the President of TTT Instrumentation said. "Listen, Ryan, I want to talk about Exemplar. I understand they're trying to buy your company."

"Bad news travels fast," Ryan Drake said and waited for Thompson to make the next move.

"Are you interested in selling to TTT?"

He started to say no, but paused. This could be his ticket out of the squeeze in which he found himself. He said, "I wasn't, but I'd rather it be you than Exemplar."

"Look, we don't want Exemplar either. It wouldn't work for them to be the sole source for your kind of equipment," Thompson said. "I also understand you have a development contract in the works with AT&T. In the event of a sale of your company, is it transferable?"

"I can make sure we include that provision. You'd buy out all current shareholders?"

"Yes."

"My Board meets next week."

"Get me your detailed financial forecasts. I'll also need to know about product development, domestic product sales, and the contracts with your data customer." The list went on and Ryan scribbled reminders to himself. He had already supplied Sanitas's audited financials as a part of the due diligence for their recently signed marketing agreement.

"This is going to cost you a bundle," Ryan said.

"Understood."

"When can I expect something?"

"We'll have it for you in a few days."

Ryan hung up and reflected on Sanitas's situation. Nick Steiger seemed intent on buying out the venture investors and would probably offer them a deal just good enough they couldn't refuse. Ryan was sure Nick would transfer the Steiger Family Trust's ownership to Exemplar. Brauk and he might have little choice but work for

Exemplar.

Ryan stood and placed both hands on his credenza. He walked his feet backwards until he felt that familiar tightness along the back of his knees. He remained in that position for a minute. Then he went on to stretch other tight muscles.

If Thompson followed through and produced a reasonable offer and he could persuade the Board to accept TTT's offer, maybe he'd come out of this okay. No, not okay, superb — this way he'd be bought out too. For the first time since his divorce, he'd have some liquid assets.

With Nick Steiger's offer he was screwed. With the TTT's deal he'd be able to live up to his commitment to the celestial messenger. Reverting to his business persona, he imagined himself a mouse dancing among elephants.

How much of this was Ernest Steiger engineering? Was it possible that he controlled both Nick and Thompson? Would Murphy and the other VCs, the ones who owned two-thirds of Sanitas's stock, reject both offers? After all they had made their investments based on a plan to take the company public and make many times their money. At best Thompson would give the shareholders something less than that potential future value. If the Board rejected both Nick and Thompson's offers, he'd have to look for another way to exit — gracefully and with some cash.

The door chime rang. Sarah Smith set down the container of caraway seed. She had just sprinkled some on her turkey sandwich. She was not expecting a visitor for another hour.

She walked across the room and opened the door.

"I'm looking for Fuchsia." The balding man in a brown leather jacket wore sunglasses.

"She does not live here." Sarah was surprised that anyone would connect her new apartment to Fuchsia. She was reasonably sure Fuchsia did not know this man.

After Fuchsia had received strange phone calls about her HO-LISTIC HAPPENINGS columns, they had rented this apartment in a nearby building for Sarah. She had moved a few days ago. This was before Peter's presentation and Fuchsia's article on it was rejected by all the newspapers, and before Fuchsia had received calls inquiring about the piece.

"You are a friend of Fuchsia aren't you?" Sarah could tell by the way the suited man pronounced her friend's name that he could not possibly know her well.

"Well, yes. Yes I am. Who are you?"

"My name is Gregor."

"I'll… I'll tell her you were looking for her."

When she started to close the door, he shoved his foot in the way. Another man appeared and put his shoulder against it and pushed it open. The force of it threw her back. She almost tripped over the coffee table.

"What is going —"

"Hello Sarah Smith. We'd like you to come with us."

Backing away, Sarah said, "Why?" Men rarely accosted women on Phantia. She had no training for this situation. Her only recourse was to flood his brain as she had done with Viejo and the INS man at the roadblock.

"Ernest Steiger wants to talk with you." She smelled cigarette smoke on his clothing.

"What if I don't want to talk to him?" She took a step backward and tried to calm herself enough to summon her special power. But like the unexpected actions from Lobo, this was all happening so quickly. She backed into the wall.

"I will kill Ryan Drake." The man who called himself Jake suddenly brandished a handgun.

"No," she uttered without thinking. His words distracted her. She relaxed the hand that she readied to touch his arm, to flood his brain and divert him. She could not let that happen. Not Ryan. She recalled the recent beating Ryan had sustained. Was there a way she could overwhelm both of them? If they would only get closer. She tried to concentrate, but could not.

The men stayed just beyond her reach.

Finally, seeing no other way she said, "All right. Let me get my things."

"We'll leave, now." The balding one motioned to the other man. He raised his hand and squirted something into her face. She passed out.

That evening Ryan was working late. It was a habit he had resurrected since the Phantians no longer lived with him. The longer hours helped make up for his difficulty in concentrating on the details of Sanitas. He kept struggling with his commitment to the celestial messenger. How was this going to happen? How was he going to lead anything when he could barely get beyond shielding Sarah and Peter from Steiger? Karen had failed to show up for work and had not called. This added to the confusion.

His after-hours line rang. "Hello."

"Ryan I'm worried. I'm at Sarah's apartment. She isn't here," Fuchsia said. "The door was ajar. All of her things are in her room. The makings for a sandwich were left out on the counter."

"I talked to her just before lunch," Ryan said. "Everything was fine. God, they must have found her right after we talked."

"There's no note or anything."

"Any signs of a struggle?" Sarah had not communicated with him for several hours. This was not all that unusual, afternoons and evenings were when she met with most of her people.

"None. I'm really worried. What do we do?"

"I'll get back to you."

Ryan closed his eyes. If ever he needed a little help from a celestial this was it. He was unable to act until he knew more.

He left, barely remembering to close up what he had been working on — an analysis of buy-out possibilities. He checked out through security. He was tempted to go to Sarah's apartment, but decided to head home first, hoping that she might be waiting for him there.

On the way up the hill, he tried to communicate with Sarah. Nothing.

When he opened the front door, lights were on and his spirits rose. He walked into the great room and spied the white-haired apparition standing near the floor-to-ceiling windows.

"It was Steiger's men." Tonight, Dr. Adamson wore a long white robe. The cloak, gathered at the waist with a gold chain, made him appear more ethereal. "They have taken her to his estate in Winnetka."

"I'll bust her out." But, Ryan did not feel as confident as his bravado indicated. Panic set in. He might be able to rescue Sarah, but then what? Look at the havoc Steiger had already made of his life, his company. He had committed to be a leader, what did a leader do in these circumstances?

The white-haired apparition motioned for him to sit on one of the chocolate leather sofas.

"Let's look at possibilities," Dr. Adamson said.

"Possibilities? What possibilities?" Ryan asked. "We have nothing to bargain with, nothing to stop Steiger and his gang. Even if I do rescue her, there is nothing to stop them from coming after her again, from coming after Peter." He felt utterly helpless in the face of the overwhelming odds.

"Let me suggest a way."

To die will be an awfully big adventure.

— J.M. Barrie

TWENTY-TWO

When Sarah Smith regained consciousness, strong lights glared in her face. She saw vertical bars: she was in a cage. She pulled herself upright in the hard chair.

"You had us worried." Shading her eyes with her hands, she could make out a man in a wheelchair and another man in a white coat standing next to him. "My apologies. That fool did not understand how sensitive your system might be to chemicals. He has been disciplined. Now then, may I have your name?"

She shaded her eyes and struggled to make sense of her situation. "Sarah." Her throat was raspy and her name came out slurred.

Her nose was running and she looked about for something to dab it with. There was nothing in the cage except the chair upon which she sat. She used the sleeve of her garment to wipe the mucus from her chin. She guessed that her runny nose must be the result of the chemical that man had sprayed at her.

"No, I mean your alien name. I know you are an alien."

She considered his question for a moment and said, "My name is Sarah Smith."

Ernest Steiger looked exactly as she had remotely viewed him when Dr. Adamson and she had discussed the media affiliates. From her prior observing she knew a lot about him, knew he suffered from diabetes and heart disease, knew he was a powerful earth dweller, knew he was awed by extraterrestrials, feared them. What did he hope to gain from kidnapping her?

"Oh. We are going to play games are we? You need to know that I have Ryan Drake in the next room. If you do not tell me what I want to know, I will have him killed. Better yet, I will have him tortured." Steiger looked up at the man in the white coat. "Karl here is a doctor. He is also an expert in unpleasant experiences."

When the man who Steiger had called Karl leered at her through rimless glasses, she did not understand. She had seen videos of doctors at Harmony. All of them had helped injured or sick people. Unpleasant experiences did not jibe with her definition of doctors.

"Can you turn off these lights?" She had to squint to see anything. Everywhere she turned the bright lights glared at her.

"No."

"They hurt my eyes." The lights made her eyes water — that made her nose run all the more.

"No."

Sarah closed her eyes and shut out her circumstances. She thought of her pleasant home on Phantia, her garden, and her romms. With great difficulty she accessed her remote viewing powers and confirmed that Ryan Drake was in his office in Boulder. It was daytime there.

Relieved, she opened her eyes and said, "What do you want?" She watched as the two men studied her. Dr. Adamson had said that Steiger wanted her secrets of communication. What good could come from his learning to remotely view? From his learning to access universe mind?

"OK, I'll play your game," he said. "Let's go on. I know that you are an alien. While you were unconscious, Karl examined you."

They had dressed her in a gray sweat suit with no undergarments. She knew that she had indeed been examined. How long had she been unconscious? Her shoes and socks lay next to the chair. She bent over and put them on. Her nose drizzled on the floor.

"I want to know how you were able to learn our language, to see the complexities of our culture, to express yourself so clearly.

No other alien has come close. Tell me about it."

Until she learned more, the best course of action was to play along. Besides, she had not acquired an earth dweller's skills in misinformation. "I am a revelator. I am here to teach your people about the cosmos."

"I too am a revelator," he laughed. "I publish newspapers and magazines. Where is your spaceship?"

Sarah hesitated. "After it deposited me, it returned to its planet of origin."

"It is not one of yours?"

"No, it was provided by people of another planet."

"Why would they do that?"

"The people of the universe cooperate in accordance with celestial rule."

"You must know many things. Tell me everything."

"Why?"

"If you do not, I will kill you."

"I do not fear death. It is as if I died when I left my home world."

"How long have you been here?"

"One of your years."

"Are there others?"

"I will not say."

"By your answer you have already betrayed their existence." The man in the wheelchair moved closer. "If you tell me everything, I will release you from this cell. Then we can cooperate in many ways."

She said nothing. Although she had not acquired an earth dweller's ability to taint words, she could tell that Steiger did not intend to ever release her from his control. He wanted her to cooperate, but to what nefarious end?

She tried to read Steiger's thoughts, but they were tangled and nothing made sense. Her head was dizzy. She closed her eyes.

"I will let you think about your situation." Sarah heard the wheelchair move away and a door close.

She wobbled from the chair and examined her cage. How long had she been here? It was Tuesday when they kidnapped her. As was her routine she had lotioned herself that morning. If it was more than a day, Earth's pollutants had probably already started to invade her body. She desperately needed the nutrients the lotion provided. She reached for her medallion. It was gone.

It was a jail cell like she'd seen in videos, steel bars on three sides. The floor and rear wall were concrete and cold. The only furniture in the cell was the wooden chair. She stood on the chair and touched the seamless ceiling. It was warm; she concluded there were heating ducts above her.

The room outside was larger than the cell, allowing people to view her. Lights glared from three sides. She was sure cameras recorded her every movement, but she could not see them.

The cage was old; she suspected that she was not the first to occupy it. The only door was locked. Due to the bright lights, she could not see the extent of the room beyond.

The temperature was cool, but that did not bother her. The musty smell indicated that she was probably below ground. In one corner of her cell was a six-inch hole. The foul smell from it permeated that area. Without the benefit of lotion, she wondered how long it would take contaminants to kill her. Once the contaminants had taken hold, Amelia had lingered for weeks. She hoped her own demise would be swifter.

After an hour, the white-coated man returned with a pitcher of water and a glass. He approached cautiously and slid it through the bars of the cell. She saw that the brown hair on top of his head was thin and that he had combed it across from the opposite side. His hands were white and appeared delicate. He did not speak to her.

Sarah did not drink for fear the water contained a mind-altering substance.

She sat and closed her eyes. She viewed Ryan at his house. '*I am being held by Ernest Steiger,*' she communicated. Ryan's message back to her was to stay alive and wait for him to come.

'*You are at his mansion near Chicago,*' Dr. Adamson communicated. He materialized in the cell with her. He hugged her and told her to cooperate with Steiger. Since there was no reaction to his appearance, Sarah assumed the cameras were unable to detect the white-haired apparition.

Other than the confrontation with Viejo, this was the first time she had been directly threatened by the dark intentions of an earth dweller. Her pursuers in the desert had always been at a distance, and she had understood that they were carrying out orders. The arguments she'd had with Ryan were mere discussions, differences of opinion. But Viejo had threatened her, had grabbed her arm, and subsequently caused others to invade her sanctuary. Now Ernest Steiger was threatening her. She hurt where Karl had probed her when she was unconscious and wondered if he had extracted blood. From the way he looked at her, she questioned how he would treat her in the event she became ill.

After a long time, Steiger returned, pushed by a large man. Karl was not with them. When he was positioned close to the front of her cage, Steiger directed the other to step away.

"I want to know how you learned my language and how you perceived the conditions of my planet so accurately from your desert retreat."

She could tell that he strained to appear to be gentle. But she had learned from Dr. Adamson that Steiger disdained most of his own people. She also knew that he found talking to an extraterrestrial exciting and decided to use that to her advantage.

"We studied your world from orbit, from your television broadcasts."

"But you have seen beyond the messages in those. How?"

"The people of my planet live according to cosmic truth. The same high standards could become a reality for this planet."

"No, that is a lie. You wish to dominate us. Steal our resources, enslave our people. The universe is not some sort of a utopia."

"Oh, but it is."

The interrogation continued for a long time. He insisted they were at war, that she was a prisoner of that war. She talked about the orchestrated and friendly universe. Sarah was thirsty, but refused to drink. He offered her food, but she refused it.

"May I demonstrate my communications ability for you?" Sarah asked. "Move closer so that I may touch you."

Steiger hesitated.

"I will not harm you. It is beyond my capacity to do so."

Steiger moved his wheelchair close enough that she was able to touch his arm.

284

"I don't want any more of your pious messages," he said. "I want to know your secret of communication, how you are able to perceive with such clarity, how you are able to convince people to help you."

"If you close your eyes, you will experience it."

"No." He tried to retrieve his arm, but she held on.

"Allow me a few moments," she said. "Your bodyguard is right here. Just close your eyes."

Steiger slowly complied, but his eyelids fluttered as he attempted to relax. She waited until he had calmed himself. Then she began the familiar process of pictioning her journey. She felt him startle as she took him above the Earth and into space. She allowed herself a moment of hope — she sensed a long buried part of him responding to her vision of a peaceful universe.

Suddenly he jerked and opened his eyes. "I already know that you are an alien. I have no time for this nonsense. Tell me what I want to know." He yanked his arm away.

"But I have just begun to —"

"I don't want your history or your messages. I've read your material. It is nonsense. There is no friendly organization to the universe." His voice rose to a shout. "You wish to rule us. I will fight you, all of you."

The large man stepped forward and wheeled him out the door.

That night no one came to the room, but she was sure the cameras continued to observe her. She found it impossible to sleep in the hard chair. She tried sleeping on the concrete floor.

When no one else was present, Dr. Adamson came and stayed with her. She and Ryan exchanged messages. He said he was working to free her.

When Steiger entered the room the next morning, he asked why she did not eat or drink. She did not reply. After the incident yesterday he kept well back from the bars of her cell. He began to question her again about her communications technology.

When she again did not give him the answers he searched for, he asked the large man to get the sticks. He returned a moment later carrying two long sticks with metal tips.

The old man thrust one through the bars at her. She moved away. The large man moved to the side of her cage and poked at her. She dodged both sticks until the large man's connected — then she felt the electrical charge. She stumbled and fell.

Steiger pointed his at her. "Now, you will tell us what we want to know. How does your communications technology work?"

"I tried to show you."

He jabbed the stick at her and another shock rocked her. "Don't lie to me. Where are the transmitters?"

"I am not lying."

"You will tell me where I can find the transmitters or whatever they are." He jabbed her again. This time he aimed for her abdomen. She rolled. It caught her in the leg. The large man's stick teased her breast. She screamed when he pressed the trigger. The contact from the old man's stick caught her arm. She screamed again. Three more bolts caught her; she passed out.

When Sarah regained consciousness, she was sprawled on the hard floor, and she was nude. Her nose continued to run and she felt dirty because she could not properly wipe it.

She raised her head and looked around. The white-jacketed doctor stood just outside the door to her cell.

Sarah lay back and tried to focus on the home she had enjoyed on Phantia. One of her great delights was to tend her garden in her bare feet. The feel of dirt under her toes was wonderful. She wondered if she would ever again smell the wondrous odor of romms.

She focused on her mission to this angry planet. If she died, would Peter and Ryan be able to carry on? If she were given more time, what would she desire? She fervently hoped that she would survive to tell other people about the beautiful world this planet could become. If only she could convince them.

The actions of the self-centered men who held her must not impede the proper transformation of this planet. Derailments like this had been going on for too many years.

She had to survive, had to continue to help Ryan Drake and the others. Billions of good people were trapped in a bad system. A new system had to be forged. The future of this world was at stake.

How many more of the electric shocks could she sustain? *'Please hurry,'* she communicated to Ryan. She struggled to her feet and put on the clothes that were tossed on the chair. Then she sat on its hard seat.

She heard the door open and heard the sounds of Steiger's wheelchair. "Where do you hide your transmitter?" Steiger's voice came at her from amidst the blaring lights. "We have examined you again but cannot find it."

"As I have told you, I am a revealator. I traveled from my home planet to show people the celestial vision for this world, for the cosmos. Your world could —"

"You're lying. No one would sacrifice themselves to such a cause." He motioned to the large man who approached the cage with his long stick.

As Sarah felt the sting of electricity, she said, "You have for the media affiliates."

During the two-hour flight from Denver Ryan and Aza changed into black wet suits. They landed at Pal-Waukee Airport, a few miles east of Steiger's estate. It was dusk. Ryan's pilot friend, Evan Bromley, taxied the rented Lear Jet to a remote corner of the field where a truck with a boat and trailer were parked. They unloaded two waterproof duffel bags into the back of the pickup and took off.

Exiting the airport, they headed east on Willow Road. In fifteen minutes, they turned on Sheridan Road and passed Ernest Steiger's mansion. The front gates were shut. Ryan could see guards with weapons standing in the shadows just inside. A frontal approach would be impossible; the risk to Sarah was too high.

At a small marina near Northwestern University, they launched the boat and unloaded the bags into it. Then they headed north along the coast of Lake Michigan. The choppy waters were white-capped from the cold wind. Lights from Steiger's mansion, the highest point along the shore, guided them. Their small powerboat struggled from wave to wave as they maneuvered close to shore in the darkness.

They pulled the boat onto the slippery rocks at the base of the bluff on which Steiger's mansion rested. A light snow made things appear white as they unloaded their supplies. The wet suits offered scant protection from the icy waves crashing onto the rocks. Both men pulled the hoods of the wetsuits over their heads.

Ryan hoped no one was guarding this approach. The face of the cliff was loose conglomerate, bad rock; no one in their right mind would attempt to climb the seventy-five feet to the house. The structure above undoubtedly rested on pilings that went through the compacted sand to bedrock. No stairway or other approach was visible for a quarter mile in either direction.

Ryan hammered his first piton. The soft surface crumbled and dirt hit him in the face. He hammered a second, the same result. Finally they found a boulder lodged in the loose conglomerate and hammered a piton into it. Then they placed another, inching their way up the vertical face. They strung ropes between pitons and crept upward to the foundation of the mansion. With great trepidation, Ryan pounded a final piton into the masonry. They flattened themselves against the wall and waited for a response to the noise.

When none came, they scooted to a window and looked inside the mansion's dark basement. Using a cutter, they removed the glass and squeezed through. Trying to make as little noise as possible, they pulled the bags through the opening. Ryan and Aza found themselves in a storage room.

The mansion was huge and Ryan had no idea where to go. He had expected a reply from Sarah, something to direct them to her, but she did not respond when he tried to communicate. Dr. Adamson had told him that she might be unconscious.

Ryan crept to the door and turned the knob. The door opened into a dimly lighted room. One wall was covered with a bank of closed circuit monitors. They displayed the front gate and the exterior entrances to Steiger's mansion, all were illuminated with landscape lighting. Seeing no one, he cautiously stepped into the room.

"Stop right there," a voice said.

Ryan froze.

The man came up behind him and jabbed something into his back. After checking his wet suit for a weapon, the man said, "That way," and shoved him forward. He heard a similar exchange as a second man captured Aza.

The men marched Ryan and Aza down a narrow hallway and up a flight of stairs. They emerged into the mansion's main hallway with the impressionist paintings. They had walked a only few steps when the man said, "In here."

The man guarding Ryan opened the door into a room with floor to ceiling bookcases. Through its high windows Ryan could just make out Lake Michigan with its low clouds and angry gray waves. Ryan heard the door close behind Aza and the other man. Behind a large mahogany desk sat Ernest Steiger.

"Good evening Mr. Drake. We've been expecting you." He looked at Aza O'Sullivan, frowned, and said, "You travel in bad company."

"Do you think we came here unprepared for this kind of a reception?" Ryan asked. "The police know you have Sarah Smith, and they know we are here."

Steiger laughed. "And just what do you think they are going to do about it? Nothing — just like they always have." He laughed again. "No, Mr. Ryan Drake, no one is coming to rescue you."

"If you release Sarah Smith and promise her no further harm, we will cause no problem," Ryan said.

"Problem? Oh, you will be no problem. That is unless you scream as you fall. Your bodies will be discovered in the morning on the rocks below this very window. Two intruders who lost their footing. 'See, their boat is right there.'" Steiger mocked the supposed police investigation. Then his voice turned hard and he said, "Dispose of them."

As the man grabbed Ryan's shoulder to turn him, he swung an elbow into the man's face. The gun went off and Ryan reeled from the impact of the slug. Ryan regained his balance, spun around, and hit the man with two quick blows to his face and a chop to his neck. The man collapsed on the floor.

Ryan looked to his left. Aza was struggling for the other man's gun. The gun fired and Ryan saw red ooze from the side of Aza's head. His friend slumped and both men fell to the floor. Ryan grabbed the first man's gun, clubbed the other guard with it, and shoved it into the belt of his wetsuit.

Ryan checked Aza. The bullet had made a furrow along the side of his head; Aza was stunned but fully conscious. In a moment he sat up and began to dab at the blood.

"Nicely done, Mr. Drake. I too was prepared for something more from you. I don't think a Kevlar vest will stop the bullet from this." Steiger brought the Lazzeroni from behind the desk and aimed it at Ryan.

Ryan stopped and stared at the old man. Although he was condemned to a wheel chair, it was clear he had lost none of his aggressiveness. The room became quiet as the two men gauged each other.

Steiger was about to lift his phone when a hollow voice said, "Witnesses always complicate matters, don't you think?"

Steiger twisted in his wheelchair. At the closed doors to his study stood a white-haired man in a long white robe.

"Where did you come from?" Steiger swung the long barrel of the rifle in Dr. Adamson's direction, but checked to make sure Ryan did not move.

"It is time." The voice from the white-haired man resounded with the resonance of a foghorn.

"What do you mean, it is time. Who are you?"

"Don't you remember? Martha introduced us."

Steiger grimaced and grabbed his chest. He fought off the pain and re-aimed the gun at the white-robed apparition.

Dr. Adamson stepped forward passing through two chairs and a table with books and papers. He stretched his hand forward in a sign of friendship.

"I remember," Steiger said. But the expression on his face said it was not a pleasant memory.

"We talked of many things that day."

"All nonsense. I threw you out of the house."

"Yes, but you did not forget."

"Why are you here?"

"To help, to offer you friendship." Dr. Adamson moved so that he was partially blocking Aza and Ryan from Steiger's view.

Aza slowly raised himself from the floor.

Steiger caught the motion and said, "Get out of my way." He waved the gun at Dr. Adamson.

"No."

Bang! Steiger fired point blank at the white-robed man. The sound echoed in the close confines of the room. The bullet embedded itself in a book on the far side of the room. The old man quickly levered a new round into place.

Dr. Adamson stood his ground and did not withdraw his hand.

When Steiger saw that the gun did not have the desired effect, he fired again. Bang!

Steiger saw that the second shot did nothing more than the first. He slumped back into his wheelchair and grabbed his chest.

Ryan stepped forward, grabbed the rifle, and moved it beyond Steiger's reach. He also picked up the telephone and scooted it to the far side of the desk.

"You have misled many people," Dr. Adamson said.

"I did what I thought was best for them."

"No, you took advantage of your wealth and influence. You misled an entire society. The Universe Father gave you much. Look how you have twisted it."

"God went away when I learned about other worlds."

"When you learned the truth about extraterrestrials, your concept of God should have enlarged and become more wonderful: the God of the Universe. You could have used the power of your media empire to help people understand."

"God has no meaning for me."

"You are pitiable indeed."

"Are you here to judge me?"

"No. I will let a higher power deal with you when your time comes."

"What do you want?" Steiger asked.

"Your diary," Ryan said. He now stood next to the wheelchaired man.

"No! It's mine." Steiger clenched his chest and reached for the telephone. It was beyond his grasp. "I need help. Please."

"Your diary," Ryan said and pointed to the safe in the corner.

"The combination?" Aza asked as he moved toward it.

Steiger spit out a string of numbers.

"The correct combination," Dr. Adamson said.

"No." Steiger's response was weaker. He tried to reach the rifle, but it too was beyond his reach. Steiger's head slumped onto the back of his wheelchair.

Aza placed his hand on the safe's dial.

Dr. Adamson gave him the proper combination.

"No," Steiger raised his head and protested. "The future of this country, the world."

"History will record how you manipulated people, lied to them, used them for your gain," Ryan said. "You will get your wish. You will become infamous."

Steiger watched as Aza extracted copies of the agreements with various Senators and Representatives in addition to the two most recent volumes of his diary.

Ryan grabbed one of the leather bound volumes and held it up. "We will keep these safe to make sure no further harm comes to Sarah."

Advancing to Steiger, Aza said, "I can see that you're already hurting, you poor old bastard. So, the only revenge I'll be exacting for what you've done to me is to see that these are used in a proper way." He held the agreements with various public officials in front of the old man's nose.

Ryan lifted the handset, dialed 911, and reported a medical emergency. He pulled the wire from the phone and hurled it into the far corner of the room. Then he reached over and picked up Sarah's three concentric circle pendant from the blotter on Steiger's desk.

The three opened the tall doors and exited into the main hallway. Ryan glanced at the magnificent paintings and said, "What a shame more people can't see these."

"She is this way." Dr. Adamson pointed down the stairway they had come. "I will show you how to release her."

When they opened the heavy door to the prison room, Ryan gasped. Dressed in a dirty sweat suit, Sarah lay on the stone floor of a cage. A man in a white coat was bending over her. He held a large syringe in his hand and appeared to be ready to plunge it into her neck.

"Don't," Ryan said. "If you value your life."

The man froze.

Ryan stepped forward and grabbed the needle. "What is this?"

"I have my instructions," Karl said.

Ryan smacked the man with the back of his hand. It sent him reeling against the bars of the cage. Dazed he got up and stumbled from the cell.

"She has refused to eat or drink and is very weak," Dr. Adamson said.

Ryan stepped to the wall and shut off the floodlights. A lone bulb continued to burn in the room beyond the jail cell.

Ryan laid Sarah on a heavy blanket that Aza had retrieved from one of the bags. After he checked for certain vital signs, as Peter had instructed him, he began to rub lotion on her face and arms. She flinched, but then realized who held her and smiled weakly. He gently pulled up the top of the sweat suit and lathered lotion on her back. Her skin felt cool, but it readily soaked up the thick lotion. Peter had improvised a stronger formulation to revitalize her. He kept his touch gentle. In a few moments she responded and said, "Water."

When Ryan offered a flask, she drank. After a few moments she began to rub lotion on the rest of her body. When she was finished, she drank the remainder of the water.

Ryan had helped Sarah to her feet. They were ready to move out when Aza hushed them. A hulk appeared in the doorway. He walked to the switch for the floodlights.

"I wouldn't do that," Aza said. He shone a flashlight into Rebar's eyes.

"Says who?"

"I say so."

Rebar whirled and squinted to see his dimly illuminated opponent. After gathering strength, he charged.

Aza got in a blow with his heavy flashlight that staggered the big man.

He straightened up, thrust out his chest and said, "Now I'll finish what I started. This is for the man." He swung a giant fist at Aza.

Aza ducked. Then with a glimmer of recognition he said, "Hello, Mr. Charles White."

Rebar paused long enough for Aza to land two good punches. Then he struck back with a quick punch to Aza's right jaw.

Aza staggered.

Rebar grabbed Aza and hurled him against the bars of the cage. Dazed, Aza got up and attacked again. Rebar rewarded him with a slam to his head. Aza slumped to the ground.

Ryan grabbed the guard's gun from his belt. He pointed it at Rebar. "Stop."

The big man saw the gun and turned away from Aza, his hands slightly raised.

"Back off." Ryan motioned with the gun.

"Enough," the white-haired apparition said. Ryan eased off the trigger, but continued to point the gun.

As Ryan watched, Dr. Adamson stepped toward the black man and offered upturned hands. Rebar took a swipe at him, but his fist found nothing solid. He swung again and almost lost his balance when he did not connect. On the third swing he stumbled backward.

Rebar's jaw dropped, eyes went wide. He screamed and ran from the room.

Ryan picked up a dazed Sarah and stuffed her into a long heavy coat and a knit hat. In the confusion surrounding the arrival of the paramedics, they lowered her to the boat.

Genuine meekness has no relation to fear. It is rather an attitude of man co-operating with God... It embraces patience and forbearance and is motivated by an unshakable faith in a lawful and friendly universe.

— THE URANTIA PAPERS

TWENTY-THREE

Sarah Smith lay on the rear seat of Ryan Drake's Jeep wrapped in warm blankets and fastened in with seat belts. When they approached the gate to his house, he pushed the control button, the gate swung open, and he proceeded to the front door.

He carried Sarah to the room she had occupied until her hasty departure. She did not stir as he laid her on the bed, wiped her nose, and kissed her forehead. Fuchsia and Peter arrived a moment later and shooed him away. Exhausted, he sought his own bed in the master suite. He glanced at the clock: 2:45 AM.

Late morning Ryan went to check on Sarah. Fuchsia sat by her bedside and shook her head when Ryan inquired. He walked over, took Sarah's hand, and tried to communicate. She did not respond. The lithe Phantian's skin had a gray cast that reminded Ryan of Amelia the time he had glimpsed her at Harmony.

At noon he left for a quick trip to Sanitas. An important document had been delivered.

At one point he thought he saw a sedan following him down the winding road. He pulled over in a blind spot, but it did not appear. He had not seen a tail since Steiger had kidnapped Sarah.

When he returned home, Fuchsia gratefully accepted his help and left the house long enough to collect the information she needed to continue her writing. Peter had formulated more lotion and advised Ryan on other things that might help the lithe Phantian's recovery.

Fuchsia brought back her massage table and provided Ryan with some relief from his stress. She also continued a modified version of Peter's physical therapy.

The next morning Ryan went into Sanitas to meet with his Board of Directors. When he joined them, the other Board members with the exception of Neal Murphy were already seated in their customary places. Murphy was always the last to arrive. Ryan had decided, two companies ago, that Sanitas's lead venture capitalist thought his tardiness added to his prestige.

Coffee, tea, and pastries were on the side table. A few minutes later Murphy arrived, helped himself to black coffee, and settled into his chair at the head of the table.

"So, do you have something for us?" Murphy addressed Nick Steiger.

Nick presented a written proposal wherein the Steiger Family Trust would buy out the venture capital investors, leaving Ryan, Brauk, and the employees with their current holdings of stock and options. He offered Exemplar stock in exchange for shares of Sanitas. Its worth to the venture investors was based on the current price of Exemplar's publicly traded stock and the predictable rise after it was combined with Sanitas. "In a few months everyone will forget about the name Sanitas," Nick said. "You'll easily exceed the valuation you had targeted, and you'll eliminate the expense and risk of a public offering."

Murphy's reaction was predictable. "You're trying to steal this company."

Ryan watched Brauk as he concentrated on straightening paper clips and bending them into new shapes. Earlier they had discussed Ryan's strategy.

When Murphy asked the other board members for their thoughts, Ryan asked to present an alternate proposal. Without further comment, he passed out copies of a firm Letter of Intent from TTT. He had received it yesterday and talked through the details with Sanitas's attorney and Truman Thompson earlier this morning.

"How long have you been negotiating this?" Nick held up the five-page document when he figured out what it was. "Why haven't you talked to the Board members about it?"

"In light of your close association with Exemplar, I felt it was necessary to handle it this way," Ryan said icily. "In situations like this I have always found it easier to get forgiveness than permission."

Nick scowled and returned to examine the offer.

Turning to Murphy and the other two VC's, the CEO said, "I apologize for springing this on you, but I just finalized it this morning."

Murphy smiled.

Ryan said, "I want to make it clear, I will not be staying with the company, regardless of the way this vote turns out."

"You're bluffing," Nick said. "You can't afford to walk away. Your whole net worth's tied up here."

"Why?" Murphy asked.

"The time has come," Ryan said.

"You've discussed it with TTT?"

"Consulting agreement."

Murphy nodded. He now had two offers in front of him. Either one cashed him out with a nice return. Without Ryan, the decision to accept one of the offers was a foregone conclusion.

Brauk told the Board about the side deal that Nick had offered and concluded by saying, "I wouldn't work for Exemplar — under any circumstances. You can stick your side deal."

The investors scrambled for phones to discuss events with associates at their home offices. Ryan and Brauk adjourned to the CEO's office.

The TTT Instrumentation proposal was an all cash deal. Every investor would receive a substantial profit on his or her investment. Ryan and Brauk were obviously in favor of TTT's bid. They were sure that Nick would support his own proposal. The three VC Board members would decide the vote.

"What about your key people?" Murphy asked when they reconvened.

"They'll name Brauk as Chief Technologist for all of TTT Instrumentation's products, a nice promotion," Ryan replied. "The other employees will also be well taken care of."

The final vote was five to one in favor of approving the acquisition of Sanitas Technologies by TTT Instrumentation. When he saw the way the vote was going, Nick said he wanted time to make a counter proposal, but the other Board members refused to delay. They saw TTT's proposal as a good deal and were uncertain about future events.

Ryan called Ben Tsotsie and told him about the sale of Sanitas as well as the rescue of Sarah. He also told Ben he would make a donation to continuing his archeological endeavors. Ryan could well afford to be generous; his $500,000 investment had multiplied ten fold.

He had barely hung up when Fuchsia called. Ryan raced home, stopping only to get flowers.

Sarah smiled and reached out to accept his hug. *'I knew you'd rescue me,'* she communicated and clung to him until he fell on top of her. They laughed as he sprawled across the bed.

"Welcome back," he said as she released him.

He brought his hand around, and she grabbed the yellow roses. "Ouch," she said. The word was strained. Her throat was still swollen from the lack of water.

Examining them closer she saw their thorns and communicated, *'On Phantia, romms do not have thorns. Oh, but they are so beautiful.'* She laughed and hugged him anew. *'Well, I didn't die. Guess you'll have to put up with me for a while longer.'*

ACKNOWLEDGMENTS

This book is a parable. The research for it began fifteen years ago, although at the time I was unaware the extraordinary information I was uncovering would result in a work of fiction. The truths incorporated within these pages have been derived from a number of sources: philosophy, psychology, medicine, science, and cosmology. The characters, all products of my imagination, tell the impact of knowing the larger purpose to their lives.

The creation of this book has been a cooperative effort. In many ways, I feel rather more like its editor than its author. I am humbly grateful to have participated in the incredible adventure that has led to its writing.

We can all produce a list of people who have touched our lives in profound ways, people who have shared their truth, people who have seen in us the best there was to see, people who have challenged us, people who have caused us to grow. These people, in addition to my parents and grandparents, four siblings, and two sons Kristopher and Kenton, include Merle Ackerman, Steve Bennett, Rob Ivker, Will Limon, Larry Mullins, Brian O'Leary, Jack Savidge, Keith Schwayder, Michael White, and Chet Winter. I also want to include my former mates, whose privacy I respect by not naming them, but whose contributions to my life are deeply appreciated.

I would especially like to thank my helpmate and spouse, Heidi, for nurturing our joined lives in so many ways, for believing in my dream, and for allowing me the freedom to pursue what I see as the larger purpose to my own life.

John Boyle helped me understand my potential. The wonderful people of Creative Initiative helped me see what my role in this world could be. The Urantia Papers showed me the friendly organization and infinite love of the universe, and so much more. The Center for the Study of Extraterrestrial Intelligence introduced me to extraterrestrials, and reinforced their peaceful intent toward our planet.

Finally, I would like to recognize several people who have rendered invaluable assistance in editing this manuscript: Caitlin Blasdell, David Morgan, Sara Coulter, and Jill Hull Strunk. Without their help these words would be unintelligible.
Mark Kimmel
June 2002

ABOUT THE AUTHOR

Since 1987, Mark Kimmel has studied the messages provided by extraplanetary beings. His writing and speaking is based on first-hand experiences and interviews with people who have had contact with non-human life forms. By focusing on the implications of UFOs, extraterrestrial contact, and paranormal phenomenon, Mark presents an uplifting vision for the future of this planet.

Mark exited a thirty-year career in business and venture capital to pursue his investigation and reporting of what he calls, "the most important event in human history." He has been listed in Who's Who since 1985. I Ie has degrees in engineering, marketing, finance, and psychology.

After Trillion, comes the sequel…